David Xavier Junkin, Frank Henry Norton

The Life of Winfield Scott Hancock

Personal, military, and political

David Xavier Junkin, Frank Henry Norton

The Life of Winfield Scott Hancock
Personal, military, and political

ISBN/EAN: 9783337079062

Printed in Europe, USA, Canada, Australia, Japan

Cover: Foto ©Raphael Reischuk / pixelio.de

More available books at **www.hansebooks.com**

THE LIFE

OF

WINFIELD SCOTT HANCOCK:

PERSONAL, MILITARY, AND POLITICAL.

BY

Rev. D. X. JUNKIN, D. D.,

LATE CHAPLAIN UNITED STATES NAVY;

AND

FRANK H. NORTON,

FORMERLY ASSISTANT LIBRARIAN ASTOR LIBRARY.

.

ILLUSTRATED ON WOOD WITH BATTLE-SCENES BY A. R. WAUD,
AND STEEL PORTRAIT BY HALL, FROM SARONY.

NEW YORK:

D. APPLETON AND COMPANY,

1, 3, AND 5 BOND STREET.

1880.

PREFATORY.

Tнis memoir of Winfield Scott Hancock is founded on an extended biography, compiled by the late Rev. D. X. Junkin, D. D., an eminent Presbyterian minister. Dr. Junkin was engaged during many years in the preparation of—what was to him a labor of love—the life of his hero, and his standard of excellence; the life of a man who, to his mind, represented all that is noble, wise, and generous in human nature. Esteeming General Hancock above all other men, he confidently believed, up to the day of his death, that the American people would eventually pay just tribute to the statesmanlike qualities, the stanch integrity, the magnanimity, and the patriotism of his hero by elevating him to the highest executive position within their gift. Dr. Junkin died in April, 1880, respected and lamented.

In undertaking the revision, condensation, and completion of Dr. Junkin's voluminous and comprehensive material, the undersigned has been aided by having free access to all the necessary documents, including the official reports of General Hancock. He desires to recognize in this place the value of the information afforded him and the aid rendered by Colonel and Brevet Brigadier-General W. G. Mitchell, of General Hancock's staff, for eighteen years the General's principal aide-de-camp, and at present his close and valued friend.

It has been the conscientious intention and scrupulous effort of the undersigned, in performing his responsible duty in connection with this work, to present to its readers such an account of its distinguished subject as should best convey the means for a just estimate of General Hancock's profound and varied nature, and of the vivid and important attitude which he sustains as a prominent figure in American history.

General Hancock's single-minded patriotism, his deep sense of the duty of man to his brother man, his contempt for the employment of narrow, vicious, and degraded methods to sustain selfishness and illegitimate ambition, his remarkably acute and just perception of the relations of things, his comprehensive accumulation of knowledge, and the natural wisdom which has rendered his ability and his knowledge valuable to his fellow countrymen— these are some of the qualities and characteristics which have been made prominent in the acts and life of General Hancock, and which this biography has sought to render evident.

FRANK H. NORTON.

CONTENTS.

CHAPTER XV.

CHAPTER XVI.

CHAPTER XVII.

CHAPTER XVIII.

CHAPTER XIX.

CHAPTER XXV.

CHAPTER XXVI.

CHAPTER XXVII.

CHAPTER XXVIII.

CHAPTER XXIX.

CHAPTER XXX.

CHAPTER XXXI.

CHAPTER XXXII.

CHAPTER XXXIII.

CHAPTER XXXIV.

CHAPTER XXXV.

CHAPTER XXXVI.

CHAPTER XXXVII.

ILLUSTRATIONS.

PLANS OF BATTLES

LIFE

OF

WINFIELD SCOTT HANCOCK.

CHAPTER I.

Birth of Hancock—His Birthplace—Montgomery County, Pennsylvania; its Scenes and Associations—The Hancock Family—Ancestry and Early History—Benjamin F. Hancock and his Wife—Character and Characteristics of the Norristown Justice—Elements of Family Character—Family Politics.

THE elasticity of the American system of government offers advantages to the sons of America, possessed, perhaps, by those of no other country. To the typical American—versatile and adaptable—all things are possible: for him are the most exalted achievements in action and in fame. Unrestricted and unbounded, the American character would appear capable of grasping success in whatsoever field of effort it enters into; a peculiarity of our people which has long been the admiration and the wonder of foreign nations. How frequently and how peculiarly is this comprehensiveness of capacity exhibited may be seen in the lives of most of our eminent men; but, perhaps, in the history of none has this profound, aspiring, and all-pervading nature been better illustrated than in that of the eminent hero and skilled statesman, an account of whose life is herein to be attempted.

1

Winfield Scott Hancock was born February 14, 1824, in a small village or hamlet in Montgomery County, Pennsylvania, called Montgomery Square, located twelve miles east of Norristown, and midway between that village and Doylstown, the county seat of Bucks. This region of country is one of rare beauty, teeming with natural wealth. Bounded on the north by the Kittatinny or Blue Mountains, on the east by the Delaware River, on the south by the States of Delaware and Maryland, and on the west by the Susquehanna, it embraces the old counties which constituted the original province to which was given the name of the illustrious Penn. Comprising a scenery varying with all the lavish possibilities of nature, it exhibits rolling hills and waving plains, stately mountains and smiling valleys, tall gray cliffs and deep ravines, sparkling brooks and noble rivers—its wooded ridges and fertile plow-lands presenting to the eye of the tourist a succession of landscapes marked with ever-changing beauty and picturesqueness. It is a land of rare loveliness, affording to its industrious and thrifty inhabitants beautiful, healthful, and happy homesteads, and is even to-day visited by thousands of travelers as a portion of the country especially favored in its landscape and scenic resources.

The County of Montgomery, named after the gallant and accomplished Irish General who fell while leading an assault on Quebec in the early period of the Revolutionary struggle, was set off from Philadelphia County in 1784. Within its bounds were located some of the earliest settlements that were effected by Europeans in the Middle States. Indeed, as early as 1640, Swedes, Hollanders, Welsh, Germans, and English had sought the banks of the Delaware, the Schuylkill, and the Neshaminy. During

BIRTHPLACE OF GENERAL HANCOCK.

the Revolutionary War, this section of the country became famous for its historic fields—Brandywine, Paoli, White Horse, Germantown, and Valley Forge—while the forces both of Sir William Howe and General Washington encamped upon the plains of Montgomery County and traversed her roads.

Born amid such surroundings, and within the memory of such associations, Winfield Scott Hancock came of British ancestry, his father, however, Benjamin Franklin Hancock, having been an American, born in the city of Philadelphia, October 19, 1800. He was the son of Richard Hancock by his second wife, Ann Maria Nash, who was born in Edinburgh, Scotland, in 1777. Richard and Ann Maria Hancock were married in Philadelphia. They had two children, Benjamin Franklin, the father of General Hancock, and Sarah, born in 1802, who became the wife of Henry E. Reynolds, Esq., now deceased. Richard Hancock had, by his previous marriage, two daughters, Eliza and Ann, who died at or near Philadelphia. This Richard Hancock, grandfather to the subject of our biography, was a mariner, who, being on a voyage while his son Benjamin, Winfield's father, was quite young, was with others captured by the British, and, under pretext of their owing allegiance to Great Britain, was confined in Dartmoor prison, and did not return to America for several years. This occurred in 1812, when 2,500 impressed American sailors were incarcerated in this huge jail, where most of them were detained, receiving exceptionally harsh treatment, until the end of the war. The Dartmoor prison inclosure occupied an area of thirty acres, encircled by a double line of lofty walls. The moor itself is a desolate tract of land in Devonshire, about 150,000 acres in area, alternately swamp and barrens.

It is possible that this occurrence may account in part for the firm adherence of the Hancock family to that party in politics which always most firmly resisted British aggression, denied the right claimed by Great Britain of searching American vessels for British seamen, and which has always advocated a policy distinctively American. The long and unjust imprisonment of the father caused the breaking up of the family. His son Benjamin was reared by John Roberts, Esq., a member of the Society of Friends, residing near Montgomery Square, with whom he continued to live until his marriage. The daughter, Sarah, was, at a later period, provided with a home in the house of a Mr. Harper, at Providence, in the same county, where she remained until about her sixteenth year, when she rejoined her brother, with whom she lived until she returned to Philadelphia and there married. Richard Hancock, after his release, returned from England, but again embarked for a voyage to that country, and died of ship fever while at sea. His wife, the mother of Benjamin, and grandmother of Winfield, died about 1822, a few years after the death of her husband. Benjamin F. Hancock, named, of course, after the great patriot, statesman, and philosopher, was, when quite a young man, thrown upon his own resources for a livelihood, owing to his having displeased his guardian by not marrying in the Society of Friends. In order to support himself and wife, he resorted to teaching, which he practiced at Montgomery Square, and also for a time in the northern part of Bucks County. While thus employed, however, he prosecuted the study of law, under the direction of the Hon. John Freedley, of Norristown, formerly a member of Congress, and an eminent lawyer. Mr. Freedley died, leaving a large estate, of which he appointed his former

student one of the executors, thus exhibiting the great
confidence he felt in Mr. Hancock. The latter was admitted to the bar in Montgomery County in the year
1828, about which time he removed with his family to
Norristown, the subject of this memoir being at that time
in his fourth year.

In that town, now a city, Benjamin Hancock continued
in the diligent practice of his profession until his death,
which occurred on the 1st of February, 1867, in the 67th
year of his age. His remains lie buried in the Montgomery cemetery at Norristown. He left to survive him
a widow and three children — Major-General Winfield
Scott Hancock and Hilary B. Hancock, twins, and John
Hancock. He was a well-read, judicious, and industrious
lawyer. His opinions were always held in high respect,
and, being patient and careful in his investigations, to
these opinions when formed he always firmly adhered.
Of calm, equable temper, his character was marked by
great decision. He was preëminently a just man, specially qualified for the bench, and often spoken of in that
connection. Nothing but his modesty and the absence of
a self-seeking spirit prevented his reaching high judicial
position. In his early years at the bar he was appointed
District Attorney by the Governor of the State, but,
although he served also in several other official capacities,
it was always without effort on his part in his own
interests.

Both he and his wife were consistent and exemplary
members of the regular Baptist Church, and from 1842
until his death Benjamin Hancock was a deacon of the
church, besides being superintendent of the Sabbath-
school for more than thirty years.

Of Mr. Hancock, a writer in the Philadelphia "North

American " of February 2, 1867, said : " Thus has passed away, without an enemy, one of the oldest residents of Norristown. For more than forty years his deeds of love and charity and his acts of benevolence and enterprise have been conspicuous, and have endeared him to the entire community. During his long practice at the bar, his uniform kindness, his modest and unassuming manners, and his faithful attention to the interests of his clients, won the respect and esteem of his brethren at the bar and the judges on the bench. In almost every work of public benefaction of his town he was an active and prominent participant. He died as he had lived—a firm believer in the Christian faith, and of a certain hope in immortality." Mr. Hancock was considered by all who knew him one of the finest specimens of a gentleman of the old school, a thorough Saxon in his form and fair complexion, six feet in height, and, in his latter years, portly, erect in carriage, dressing with elegance and scrupulous neatness, his entire bearing being that of a gentleman, his kind and dignified manners, radiant with Christian benevolence, causing him to be universally esteemed and admired.

General Hancock's mother, Elizabeth Hoxworth, was born in Montgomery County, and died in 1879. Her ancestry was English and Welsh. Her father, Edward Hoxworth, was born in Hatfield township, Montgomery County, in 1760, and died in 1847. He descended from a long line of Hawkesworths (for thus the name was anciently spelled), one of whom was a soldier in the old French and Indian wars, and captain in the American patriot army, and died in camp in 1777. Edward, General Hancock's grandfather, was a Revolutionary soldier, whose brother was an officer in the War of 1812.

From these brief notices of the ancestry of our subject, it will be seen that, while military experience characterized the family from the beginning, the warlike tendency was chastened by sincere and earnest Christian belief and practice, and by professional labors in the paths of education and law-making. From such roots, struck firmly and deeply into the ground made sacred by the blood of his forefathers, might well spring forth a branch, combining in the elements of its growth the qualities of firmness, patriotism, and respect for law and order for which the family were eminent.

It is related of the Hancock family that its political principles were always, especially after the presidency of John Adams, those of the anti-Federal, or Democratic, party. Benjamin Hancock's convictions of the necessity for a strict construction of the Constitution of the United States were very decided, so that the subject of this memoir was early indoctrinated into the Democratic faith, and strongly impressed with its importance to the perpetuity of the Union and the preservation of American liberty. A regard for personal liberty, freedom of speech, and a marked spirit of adherence to the right of local self-government have always characterized the Hancock connection from the beginning of its history in America.

CHAPTER II.

At the time of the birth of the twin brothers, General Winfield Scott had borne so conspicuous a part in the
then recent war of 1812–'15 as to make him one of the
most admired of American soldiers, and, although he had
not yet reached the zenith of his fame, his name was
upon every tongue. Mr. Hancock did not know him
personally, but, under a patriotic impulse, named one of
his boys after Winfield Scott, and the venerable Lieuten-
ent-General more than once in after years acknowledged
the compliment, and referred in terms of pride and commendation to his rising namesake.

Young Hancock's education began in that best of pri-
mary schools, the Christian family. In regard to this he
was highly favored. His father had been a teacher before Winfield's birth, and had been also a director in the
new public-school system; but now to his experience as
an instructor was added the tender solicitude of a father,
stimulated by the devout piety of the mother of his boys.
In this home-church and home-school our hero received
from the parents whose character we have indicated his
first lessons. There he became imbued with the princi-

ples and sentiments on which was established as on a rock the character of the future leader of men.

It is the testimony of his playmates in these early days that he was at all times a patient, cheerful, courteous, truthful, kind, and manly boy. Meanwhile, he was a boy among boys, taking his share of the hard knocks and precarious usage of the playground, but holding always—in an honorable and manly fashion—a prominent position among his school-mates. Although the brothers had more than ordinary home advantages, Winfield and Hilary were sent in early boyhood to an excellent select school. Norristown Academy, then established, was beautifully situated, with spacious grounds around it, and in its day was esteemed a highly respectable seat of learning. At about this period the public-school system was inaugurated in Pennsylvania, and a high school in that system became so well established, under competent teachers, that it soon superseded the old academy, and became the *alma mater* of its pupils. The teachers in both of these schools have placed on record their warm affection for young Hancock.

Winfield was early recognized as a leader among his young companions in all the manly sports and enterprises of boyhood. Possessed of a vigorous physique, excellent health, and fine muscular development, he seemed chosen by Nature to be a leader. His fondness for military exercises was early remarked. He organized a military company among his school-mates, being chosen their captain by acclamation. Winfield's mother is said to have contributed the uniform for this band of young soldiers, who, with mimic muskets and other equipments, presented quite a respectable display, as they paraded the streets, or were drilled by their boy commander upon the court-house green. A drum and fife stimulated their marching and countermarching, and, as they followed their flag, their soldierly bearing attracted much attention and many compliments. Occasionally their toils and dangers were rewarded by rations of dough-nuts and lemonade, while the orchards and chestnut and walnut groves in the neighborhood of Norristown frequently bore witness to the determined raids of these nascent patriots. It has been, however, conceded by the Norristown farmers that the boy foragers were quite welcome to all they obtained, and seldom violated the rules of justice and propriety.

The peculiar characteristic of young Hancock, which specially rendered him popular among his companions, was a certain disinterested manliness of disposition, upon which they always relied to induce him to sacrifice himself in defending the weak, and in insuring fair play to all. Many anecdotes are related of this period of his life, illustrating his truthful nature and his large-hearted sense of honor. In all those native characteristics which most endear a lad to his comrades, young Hancock displayed clearly that "the boy was father to the man." Not all his spare time, however, was devoted to rough sports or imitation military exercises. It would appear that he had aspirations in other directions, and it is specially related of him, as also of his brother, that the two collected quite an extensive cabinet of mineralogical and geological specimens, and were members of a literary and scientific society organized in the high school. In this society experiments were made in chemistry and natural philosophy—the educational facilities of the school embracing most of the branches generally taught in the better class of academies of that day.

The young students delivered lectures on the scientific subjects named and other topics, which, of course, were not very profound, but were by no means destitute of real merit. Friends of the scholars, and others who chose to be present, were admitted as auditors and spectators, and it is clear that, in all of these more intellectual exercises, the Hancock boys bore their share, Winfield especially being in demand whenever a call was made for special energy or executive tact.

In those days patriotism ran high in Pennsylvania, and the anniversary of the Independence of our country was generally celebrated with great warmth and earnestness by the people of Norristown and vicinity. The ceremonial included the customary firing of cannon, the ringing of all the bells, the display of the national flag in prominent places, the parade of volunteer soldiers, both adult and juvenile, and, in fact, all the usual demonstrations in honor of the day. A public dinner, accompanied by the reading of the Declaration, and an oration and appropriate toasts, further gratified the patriotic proclivities of Norristown. In all of these festivities and ceremonies young Hancock took a deep interest, and not unfrequently bore an active and laborious part. His home guards sometimes had their place in the military pageant, and, when not in command of his company, Winfield generally devoted himself very earnestly to the care of the little cannon whose noisy exhibition contributed to the excitement of the day. But upon one of these occasions, when in his fifteenth year, the boy received a marked expression of esteem in being appointed to read in public the Declaration of Independence. The conclusion of this experiment justified his selection. Both in his understanding and his enunciation of the world-renowned proclamation, young Hancock covered himself with glory. It is by no means designed to intimate that this boy was in any sense precocious or a prodigy, but the whole history of his school days and early life presents him as differing from others of his age, in being less inclined to frivolity than they, and of a sedate and thoughtful nature, indicating depth of character and reflective powers beyond his years. It was doubtless owing to his home training that he developed, at an earlier period than is usual, features of character which caused him to be so much esteemed. He exhibited a tendency to associate rather with his elders than with those younger than himself or of his own age, and among those he was always welcome, his attentive, earnest, and modest demeanor, and his character of being a good listener, rendering him a general favorite. Probably it was while listening to the discussions of the intelligent citizens of his section of the country, that the boy gathered the material upon which were based the opinions which became so marked and emphatic in later years. It is certain that here he became familiar with affairs, with the history of his country, and with political principles. Thus, between sturdy and healthful amusements and thoroughly enjoyable intellectual communion, the boy's school days passed rapidly away, during which he was steadily developing a character of manly firmness and a mind marked by strong good sense and great self-reliance, deliberate judgment, and decided convictions. His attainments in useful learning, meanwhile, if not brilliant, were substantial, thorough, and practical. Naturally kind and generous, there was also manifest in his character a warm sympathy with the neglected and the oppressed. An instance illustrating this phase of his character is related in a little memoir called "Winfield, the Lawyer's Son." When young Hancock was only eleven years of age, there was brought to Norristown a poor orphan boy, whose father had died when the child was three years old, and who was placed in charge of a relative of his family. This boy, two years the junior of Winfield, became his playmate and, before long, his friend. It would appear that the little orphan was much neglected, and was often tyrannized over by his larger associates. But his young friend stood by him and took his part; if need be, employing the most decided measures to protect him from annoyance. His magnanimous firmness on such occasions was generally successful, and even the persecutors themselves respected him all the more for his courage and kindness to the orphan. Such conduct on his part was so evidently based on a strong and clear sense of justice that he gradually became the acknowledged umpire in the disputes which frequently arose among the boys. When all means had been employed by themselves to reach an amicable adjustment of their difficulties, the cry would be raised, "Oh! leave it to Winfield; he'll settle it." This being done, his arbitration was almost always deemed satisfactory, and willingly accepted.

The story of the orphan boy and his champion friend has a sequel which brings it justly within the romance of history. The boy in question left Norristown at an early age and repaired to Philadelphia, where he became a journeyman carpenter. It is related of him that, when he crossed Market Street bridge, but a single penny remained in his pocket; but he was intelligent and industrious, and rose rapidly, and eventually he acquired wealth and social standing, becoming, in the course of time, a member of the City Councils, honored and trusted. Meanwhile the courageous and just friend of his youthful days had become renowned as a great commander, and had obtained high rank in his country's service. It devolved upon the Councils of Philadelphia to offer a series of resolutions commending the patriotism, courage, and skill of Major-General Winfield Scott Hancock. These resolutions—passed unanimously by both branches of the City Councils—were engrossed and sent to Washington (where the General then was), in charge of a committee for the purpose of presentation. The surprising incident in this history exists in the fact that to John William Everman, the abused orphan of his school days, fell the honorable duty of presenting the resolutions to General Hancock.

Returning from this digression, we have to note an episode in the early history of young Hancock, which shows that even at this period the versatility of his character had begun to display itself. It was in 1835, and an election for governor in Pennsylvania was impending. There chanced to be a split in the Democratic party, and two candidates of that party were in the field. The Democratic organ of the county having declared for one of these, a number of prominent citizens, including B. F. Hancock, established a rival paper advocating the election of the other. Young Winfield, although only a boy of eleven years, at once took a lively interest both in the campaign and in the new paper. Printers at that time were hard to obtain, and so it happened that, when school hours permitted, the lad turned into the office, and, *con amore*, helped on the cause by setting type, distributing, or even working the press. By the time the canvass was concluded, he had become quite a printer, besides having acquired considerable interest in the politics of his native State.

CHAPTER III.

In 1840, at the age of sixteen, young Hancock entered the Military Academy at West Point, having obtained his cadetship through the influence of Hon. John
B. Sterigere, a lawyer, and a prominent citizen of Montgomery County, who had represented his district in the
Congress of the United States. Mr. Sterigere was a man
of eccentric temper and habits, strong in his friendships
and resentments, but possessing great adroitness as well
as energy in the management of men and affairs. He
was the personal and political friend of Mr. Benjamin
Hancock, and, having observed the manly bearing as well
as the comprehensive intelligence of his friend's son Winfield, he voluntarily caused his appointment. To West
Point accordingly the young man repaired, entering the
Military Academy as a cadet July 1, 1840. He passed
the examination for admission respectably, not being ex-
traordinarily advanced in scholarship, although he had
studied regularly all his previous life and had read a
great deal; indeed, he once, later in life, expressed to a

friend the opinion that he entered the Academy too early.
"I developed late," was his remark, "and at sixteen was
too much of a boy, too full of life, to feel the importance
of hard study. It would have been better if I had not
entered until I was eighteen." In fact, he has frequently
confessed that he was not a student for the love of it.
His class at West Point at first numbered about one hundred, but, owing to the failures in examinations and other
causes, it became reduced by the end of the first year to
fifty-four, and ultimately graduated only twenty-five.

At the present time General Hancock is himself the
only surviving member of his class in the active service
of his country. Some have fallen in battle, some died,
and others, for other reasons, are out of the service. But
among the names of those who were contemporaries of
Hancock as cadets in the Academy are many who have
since become by their achievements and reputation eminent in the annals of the country. Such are Generals U.
S. Grant, George B. McClellan, Franklin, William F.
Smith, J. F. Reynolds, Rosecrans, Lyon, and others of
the Union army; and Longstreet, Pickett, E. K. Smith,
and Stonewall Jackson, who distinguished themselves in
the Confederate service.

With regard to Hancock, the same qualities and qualifications which had made him popular among his school-
fellows and friends at home won for him a sustained and
similar popularity in the Academy, and which did not
abate during his entire cadetship. During the first two
years of his life in the institution, his habits of study
appear not to have been so close and assiduous as they
became during the last two. Then he steadily advanced
upon his previous standing, and would have graduated
higher than he did, had it not been from the fact of his

having been less atttentive to his work in the beginning.

The code of discipline at West Point is very severe,
and demerits are incurred on the slightest violation of
this, and for acts of neglect or carelessness which would
pass without notice in any ordinary educational institution.

The early age at which young Hancock entered—his
mind not being yet fully formed, or cast in the mold of
earnestness which afterward characterized it—militated
greatly, during his first two years in the Academy, against
that understanding of the value of strict discipline which
is there necessary. It may, however, with justice, be
assumed of him that his rapid advancement during his
last two years was due to his better appreciation of the
situation.

During his academic course young Hancock attended
considerably to general reading, and he relates, himself,
the incident of his father having presented him with a
copy of "Chitty's Blackstone," accompanied with the
expression of a desire that he should read it and re-read
it. He fulfilled his father's injunctions, though perhaps
in a great degree from a sense of duty. To this particular
work were added "Kent's Commentaries," and others,
chosen from the library at West Point, of a similar character, and to this course of reading may be attributed,
doubtless, the skill and readiness which, at an after period
of his life, became of such value to him in the illustration
of important questions of organic law.

Hancock graduated at West Point on June 30, 1844,
being breveted second lieutenant in the Sixth Infantry
July 1, 1844. While young Hancock remained a cadet,
General Scott, whose name he bore, had frequently visited
the Academy, and always exhibited a warm interest in his

namesake. At the time of the latter's graduation, the old general asked him to what regiment he preferred being assigned, to which the young man replied, "The one which is stationed farthest West." He sought such service from a desire to see the distant frontier, to roam over its prairies and through its passes and ravines, and to obtain personal knowledge of the red men. Doubtless, also, there arose before him visions rather of sport with the shot-gun, the rifle, and the rod, than encounters on the field of battle.

The company to which he was assigned was stationed at Fort Towson, in the Indian country, near the Red River, on the border of Texas. Another station of this regiment was at Fort Washita, ninety miles west of Fort Towson, and was then the most remote station on our western frontier—New Mexico and California not having been acquired, and the boundary then being the 100th degree of west longitude. The other companies of the regiment were stationed on the Arkansas River, at Forts Smith and Gibson, and General Zach. Taylor, afterward President of the United States, commanded the whole. Although in the vicinity of the hostile Indians, Hancock's first field of service was chiefly in the region occupied by the half-civilized Chickasaws, Cherokees, and Creeks The country was healthy and fertile, partly prairie and partly wooded, and well watered. It afforded a fine range for the sportsman, and our young soldier and his companions in military duty made frequent excursions into the neighboring country of Texas. Time passed rapidly in the face of this new and exhilarating life, and on June 18, 1846, Hancock received his commission as second lieutenant in a company of his regiment stationed on the frontier of Mexico, where the difficulties, which afterward eventuated in the Mexican War, had already commenced. The commander of Fort Washita, deeming Lieutenant Hancock's services necessary at that post, declined to permit him to join his company; and it was not until General Scott, in passing through New Orleans on his way to Mexico, had heard from some friend of Hancock's that he was thus detained, and sent peremptory orders for him to proceed on other duty, that he was allowed to depart. He was ordered first to report at Newport Barracks, Kentucky, thence to take recruits to Mexico. But before the execution of this order he was sent with troops to the Missouri frontier, and was afterward stationed at Cincinnati for a brief period as an assistant to the officer who conducted the mustering-in of volunteers; and it was not until after repeated applications to his superiors and to the War Department that he was permitted to proceed to Mexico. Lieutenant Hancock's anxiety to join his regiment was expressed in the following letter to his twin-brother:

"NEWPORT BARRACKS, KENTUCKY, *May* 5, 1847.

"MY DEAR HILARY: I was exceedingly glad on my arrival here to find two long and interesting letters from you. The only thing that grieves me is that I can not go to Mexico. I made an application to-day to join the army going to the front. Whether the adjutant-general will favor it or not, I do not know, but I think it doubtful. I am actively engaged as assistant superintendent of recruiting service of the western division, and acting as assistant inspector-general; but, though my services are said to be useful, I still want to go to Mexico.

"Your affectionate brother,

"WINFIELD."

Before the permission he craved was given, the battles of Palo Alto, Resaca de la Palma, Monterey, and Buena Vista had been fought, and northern Mexico was held by our army of occupation. General Scott had effected a landing at Vera Cruz, had bombarded and captured that city with its fortresses, and was on the march to the Mexican capital; he had fought and won the battle of Cerro Gordo, and was still advancing on his conquering progress.

CHAPTER IV.

AT length the impatient young soldier was ordered
forward. The troops landed at Vera Cruz in season
to join General Pierce's column, which was about to
march to reënforce General Scott at Puebla. He was
assigned to duty with a battalion commanded by Colonel
M. L. Bonham, and was appointed its adjutant. On this
march there was no extended or heavy fighting, but frequent and vexatious skirmishes with the Mexican Guer-
rillas brought our troops under fire, and that of a more
dangerous character often than would have been the case
in open field-fighting. The chief encounter of this character was had at the National Bridge, which the Mexicans
had barricaded and held against our forces; the heights

overlooking the bridge, and within musket range, were occupied by the enemy. This bridge—El Puente Nacional—was a fine stone structure, built by the Spaniards on the national road from Vera Cruz to the city of Mexico. It had only a low stone balustrade, on account of which our troops in crossing it had little protection from the enemy's fire. Hancock was in command of one of the companies detailed to charge and capture the bridge, and the barricade near the farther end of it. It was the first action in which he had immediate prospect of being under a severe fire. In fact, so sharp and galling a fire was opened upon the troops from the heights overlooking their position on our own side of the river, that it became necessary to dislodge the firing party before a further advance, and this duty fell to the lot of Lieutenant Hancock's company. The movement was a success, and immediately after the bridge and barricade were carried by two companies under Major Holden.

It soon became known that the enemy had reoccupied Cerro Gordo, a few miles in advance, and a night expedition was sent forward, under Colonel Bonham, to discover a path by which the enemy's rear could be reached. Of this detachment Lieutenant Hancock was adjutant. The night was dark and the rain fell in torrents, the ground was rugged and precipitous, and, to add to the difficulties of the situation, the guide presently lost his way. The night expedition proved a failure, but, as the enemy made no serious stand at Cerro Gordo, the fact was of little consequence.

General Pierce's column reached Puebla in time to join the army of General Scott in its advance upon the Mexican capital. Hancock there joined his regiment, of which he was the junior lieutenant. The army of invasion began its march on the 8th of August. It proceeded in four divisions, marching a day apart. This was a hazardous undertaking, as General Scott's force, counting every man, numbered but 10,738, many of whom were teamsters and non-combatants. The invading column numbered, in fact, less than ten thousand available men. Much time had been spent at Puebla, though this was not lost time, since reënforcements had to be waited for, supplies collected, and, above all, the men, a portion of whom were volunteers and raw recruits, had to be drilled to prepare them for effective service.

Fortunately, the commanding general had the movements of his little army under his entire control. He was too distant from the capital of his country, and from impatient civilians and a clamorous press, to be badgered into a premature advance, such as he reluctantly consented to fifteen years later, and which was so ingloriously checked at Bull Run. General Scott wisely got his gallant force into good condition before pushing into the heart of the enemy's country, with a hostile population of eight millions surrounding him, with fortifications in front, and a force of three times his number opposing his advance.

It was a sublime sight, the advance of that little army amid such surroundings, and with such fearful odds against it. But, as the brave old General Towson once remarked—and he was not a West Point man—" Many of our young West Point lieutenants are fit to command armies."

The march to Mexico, and the battles and the assaults which resulted in its capture, illustrated the advantage of science and discipline over mere force and numbers in the terrible struggles of war.

General Hancock, in referring to this march, once remarked : " To me our march was as good as a picnic, and, although conducted with care, we placed no pickets except on the roads, and they were kept by details of companies or detachments. The regimental guards were kept up, however, and we felt secure."

Hancock marched on foot with his company during this campaign. The army entered the beautiful valley, in which the city of Mexico reposed, on the southeast side, probably along the same route by which the Spaniards under Cortez had marched three centuries before. The city is almost surrounded by beautiful lakes, which add to the picturesqueness and magnificence of the landscape. To all, and especially to the young and enthusiastic officers of the army, that grand panorama must have proved impressive and interesting. The very majesty that hangs over its history previous to the Spanish conquest, its great antiquity, its subjection by the Spaniards, the tragic death of the unhappy and amiable Montezuma and his no less unhappy dynasty, all belong to the romance of history, and would naturally gather around the valley and the beleaguered city an intensity of thrilling associations. But, whatever the first impression the scene may have produced upon the minds of our officers, they were all soon absorbed in the stern and terrible realities of war. Besides the less important collisions connected with the capture of Mexico, there were four principal battles: Contreras, Churubusco, Molino Del Rey, and Chapultepec. The first action of any importance in which Lieutenant Hancock was engaged was that of San Antonio, which preceded the battle of Churubusco, the latter occurring on the 20th of August, 1847, at a locality a few miles nearer to the city of Mexico. In the latter conflict, a charge was made upon a *tête de pont*, in which the commander of Hancock's company, Hendrickson, was severely wounded, and the command of the company devolved upon Lieutenant Hancock, a position which he continued to hold until his wounded commander resumed duty after the army entered the city. The first assault along the main road met with obstructions caused by the blowing up of the enemy's ammunition wagons, which, owing to the rapid advance of our troops, he had not been able to carry inside of the lines. The deranged battalion was again formed, however, and, on a second advance, the enemy's intrenchments were carried by companies of different regiments, the Fifth, Sixth, and Eighth Infantry, and artillery regiments acting as infantry. Simultaneous with this advance, attacks were made upon the Church by the Third Infantry and other troops. Meanwhile Shields's brigade, of South Carolina, New York, and other troops attacked the enemy's rear. Captain William Hoffman was the commander of the battalion of the Sixth Infantry at the culmination of this attack, Major Bonneville, of Astoria reputation, having been disabled in the early part of the engagement. Lieutenant Hancock's company was of this command.

The enemy's position at Churubusco having been forced, our troops promptly advanced upon his reserves, soon driving them from the field. This fight is memorable for the gallant cavalry charge of Generals Harney and Phil Kearney, in which the latter lost his arm.

The capture of Contreras and Churubusco on that day left two other strongly fortified points before the city could be reached from the south side—Molino del Rey, and the seemingly impregnable castle of Chapultepec. Contreras is situated nine or ten miles south by west of the city of

2

Mexico and at the south end of an almost impassable field of lava, while Churubusco lies north of this field on a main approach to the city. Molino del Rey is about three miles west by north of the city; Chapultepec one mile nearer to it, and directly between the two. Prior to the assault on Molino del Rey an effort was made by the Mexicans to obtain terms of capitulation. General Scott, however, having rejected all terms except absolute surrender, a cessation of hostilities was agreed upon, to give Santa Anna time for consideration. Negotiations ensued, which protracted the armistice until the 7th of September, which period Santa Anna treacherously employed, contrary to stipulation, in increasing his strength. Scott finally terminated the armistice, and ordered an assault upon Molino del Rey. At three o'clock on the morning of September 8, 1847, Worth's division, with which was Hancock's company, advanced upon the enemy's batteries and strong defenses at Molino del Rey. Before dawn two twenty-four pounders were placed in position, and opened at short range upon the solid walls of the defenses of that stronghold. At first there was no firing in response, but presently, from an unexpected point, grape and round shot poured upon the assailing column. Met by this unlooked-for attack, the column recoiled, with a loss of eleven officers and a considerable number of men killed and wounded, while an attack in some force was made by the Mexicans from within the walls. Reënforcements being rapidly thrown forward by General Worth, the position temporarily lost was retaken, and an assault was made upon the enemy's defenses, which were scaled or broken through by the infuriated soldiers with their bayonets. While some, lifted by their comrades, clambered to the top of the wall, others battered down the main gate. Door after door was forced by the intrepid Americans, and, the Mexicans being driven back, a white flag was presently raised upon the parapet in token of surrender. When it is considered that the Mexican force greatly outnumbered ours, besides being intrenched within stone walls, and that the fire from the castle of Chapultepec, standing just north of the Molino, raked the field within effective cannon range, it is to be conceded that this was one of the sharpest and most successful hand-to-hand struggles of the war. The days of drums and fifes have passed: France even has abolished them. But when Clarke's brigade and the storming-party under Wright, of Worth's division, advanced to the attack in the foggy morning, on a smooth, descending plain—the drums beat patriotic marches, while not a gun was fired until the line of battle had reached within two hundred yards of the enemy, and received his fire from an intrenched position. Our troops moved at the double-quick, without returning the fire, and drove them out of their intrenchments. This is mentioned as one of the latest instances which have occurred on this continent of troops advancing in line of battle to meet the enemy to the sound of music. In this attack were Longstreet, Pickett, Armistead, E. K. Smith, Edward Johnson, Buckner, Hancock, and many others since known to fame.

Here died Martin Scott, the man to whom the treed coon said, "Don't shoot! If you're Martin Scott, I'll come down." He commanded the Fifth Infantry. The Sixth was commanded by Captain William Hoffman, owing to the absence of Colonel McIntosh, who commanded the brigade, Colonel Clarke being sick.

Taking the advanced position of the enemy—a rifle-pit—our troops found themselves under heavy fire from stone walls twenty or thirty yards away, seemingly an impregnable position. Occupying this spot in a moment of hesitancy, they laid down, and commenced firing on the enemy. The only two persons observed not to lie down were the commanders of the Fifth and Sixth Infantry, who were near to each other, and between the two regiments. It was certain death to stand up, isolated, and Captain Hoffman, representing the honor of the Fifth Infantry, said, "Major, you had better lie down." To which the officer addressed replied, "The ball was never molded to kill Martin Scott." In a second he was shot through the heart, fell, rested his head on his hat, handed his purse to Hoffman, saying, "For my wife," and expired. Then the honor of the Fifth Infantry permitted Major Scott to lie down. It is to be recorded that, in the reports of the officers in command during this engagement, the conduct of Lieutenant Hancock is handsomely mentioned. Hoffman's report says, "Hancock behaved in the handsomest manner."

In this battle the adjutant was killed, and Hancock was appointed in his place. He occupied this position but a brief period, however, and not long afterward was breveted first lieutenant "for gallant and meritorious conduct at Contreras and Churubusco," his brevet dating from the day of the battle of Churubusco, August 20, 1847. Lieutenant Hancock was now placed in command of a company, chiefly composed of old soldiers of the Florida and other Indian wars.

It is a notable fact in the history of this battle, as related by General Hancock, that, when the enemy's lines were taken at Molino del Rey, Lieutenant Ulysses S. Grant, who was regimental quartermaster in General

Garland's brigade, which took part in the final assault, said to the General, "Now, take Chapultepec!" The immediate capture of that stronghold was not in accord with General Scott's plans, though this took place in due course; but the incident illustrates General Grant's prescience, even at this early period in his career.

There still remained much serious work to be accomplished before the city could be gained, and before even the safety of our own little army could be assured. Through sickness and other causes General Scott's army had been reduced to a little over six thousand, and the slightest error or failure on his part might easily have brought the Mexicans upon him with overwhelming force. The strong castle of Chapultepec, with its fortified surroundings, was to be taken, and after that a barricaded causeway and other complicated defenses must be assailed before the city of Mexico could be reached. It was skillful strategy on the part of the commanding general, and an instance of rare heroic conduct on that of his men, which prevented the destruction of the American army and rendered it victorious. Cut off from all hope of reenforcement, removed from its base of supplies, victory or destruction seemed the only alternatives.

The Mexicans were active and alert in the defense. Men, women, and children were constantly engaged in strengthening the fortifications of their beautiful city, and the capture could only be completed by the use of the utmost skill, science, and bravery. But it was accomplished. Chapultepec was stormed in a style rarely equaled in the history of wars for strategy, cool deliberation, and *elan*. Our troops advanced along the causeways, over which extended the stone aqueducts which supplied the city with water, until they reached the *Gari-*

tas of San Cosme and Belen which were carried by assault—San Cosme by Worth's command, and Belen by the troops under Quitman—and by nightfall of that terrible day—the 13th of September—the gates were won, the enemy, driven back, and the city of the Montezumas was in the power of the American invaders. The resistance made by the Mexicans was gallant and desperate. After being driven from their outer works and back into the streets of the suburbs, they fired upon our troops from windows and from the roofs of the houses, and nothing but the indomitable courage of our men could have succeeded in the face of such resistance. During the early part of the night of the 13th of September, Huger opened upon the city with a mortar and some heavy guns, and soon after General Santa Anna and his army quietly evacuated Mexico and escaped. Scott ordered Generals Quitman and Worth to feel their way slowly into the city, which was done at considerable peril, as the inhabitants were exasperated and desperate. But, on the same day, the 14th, a deputation of the city authorities repaired to Worth's headquarters, whence they were sent under escort to General Scott at Tacubaya. This deputation proposed terms of capitulation greatly favoring the city, the church, and the citizens, but were assured by General Scott that the city was in his possession, and no terms would be signed ; and that the magnanimity of a conqueror and the spirit of modern civilization alone would dictate the course he would pursue. Meanwhile, the American flag had been raised upon the palace, and, at eight o'clock in the morning of the day last named, the new conqueror of Mexico, accompanied by his staff and by other officers, rode in from Tacubaya, and entered the Grand Plaza of the city amid the acclamations of the army.

With the exception of a brief interval of service with his regiment at the city of Toluca, under the command of General Cadwalader, Lieutenant Hancock remained with the troops that occupied the city of Mexico until the American army was withdrawn. He was among the last to leave the city, with the brigade of Worth's division to which he belonged, after having transferred the capital to the Mexican authorities, lowered our flag, and seen that of Mexico raised over the National Palace. This was in 1848, in which year the treaty of peace between the two countries was signed at Guadalupe Hidalgo. So soon as this was ratified at Washington, the war was concluded, and our troops withdrawn. During the march from Mexico to the coast, Lieutenant Hancock acted as regimental quartermaster and commissary of his regiment. Embarking on transports, the division proceeded to New Orleans, and thence to Jefferson Barracks, Missouri, where it remained until the autumn of 1848. In the distribution of troops made that fall, Hancock's regiment was assigned to a position on the Upper Mississippi, Hancock himself going to Fort Crawford, Prairie du Chien, where he filled the position of quartermaster. This post was the regimental headquarters, and here he continued until the spring of 1849, when he was ordered to Fort Snelling, Minnesota, which he reached in May. He was then granted a five months' leave of absence, and proceeded to revisit his home and relations in Pennsylvania, whence he had been absent five years.

CHAPTER V.

LIEUTENANT HANCOCK had entered into the Mexican
War with so much spirit and energy, he had so much desired to experience active service in the profession which
he had chosen, that, although his acquaintance with actual
warfare was but a slight one, it probably accomplished
more for him in the way of instruction, as well as of en-
couragement, than usually would have been the case under
such circumstances. His experience in Mexico may be
briefly summed up as follows:

He fought in three general engagements and a number of skirmishes, was slightly wounded, established a
reputation as a brave and reliable young officer, and was
promoted for gallantry on the field of battle. Already
his talent for organization and his administrative abilities
had attracted attention, in so far that, as we have seen,

he had been appointed to act as quartermaster and commissary on the return from Mexico; and, to add to the achievements of the young officer in his brief episode of actual warfare, we have to recount the fact that in the reports of his immediate senior officers, he was specially commended. He was also particularly named in the report of Major Bonneville as to the part borne by the battalion commanded by the latter in the battle of Molino del Rey.

Finally, the Legislature of Pennsylvania passed a series of resolutions complimentary to the courage and general conduct of the officers and men from that State during the Mexican War, and among those mentioned the name of Hancock appears.

It was in the spring of 1849 that Lieutenant Hancock took advantage of his leave of absence to revisit the home of his childhood. Here he was welcomed with all the affection and cordiality which might have been anticipated, not only the tenderness of his family and kindred uniting in this display of regard, but his townsmen receiving him with respect and admiration. They were proud of his rising fame and glory, and gave open expression to their friendship and esteem.

In the following autumn Lieutenant Hancock rejoined his regiment, to which he had been appointed adjutant, being now stationed at St. Louis, Missouri, and acting as aide-de-camp to Brigadier-General N. S. Clark, already named, who commanded the military department embracing that section of the country lying between the "Indian country of the South" and the British Possessions. The duties connected with a service of this nature require chiefly laborious and continuous attention to the business details of military life, and were of rather a routine character, giving little scope for adventure, and supplying less material for glowing account.   In this service, however, Lieutenant Hancock undoubtedly contributed valuable results.   Through the education which he had already received in the different lines of duty involved in his profession, he was being unconsciously trained for the higher and broader field of command for which he was destined.   Particularly was it the case that he now became educated in that very important branch of military labor—the skillful, accurate, concise, yet full and scholarly preparation of reports of military operations, orders, and all that class of writing which pertains to official records, reports, and correspondence.   As a result, it is a fact that the young officer grew to be exceptionally qualified in the art of conveying his impressions and his ideas to paper, gaining that degree of accuracy in the determination of his judgment and of facility in expression, which have ever since stood him in such good stead in the many important emergencies of his life, that have made demands upon precisely that talent and these acquirements.

Hereafter it will be shown in this history that our hero has displayed not less skill, judgment, and sense of the proper relations of things, in his manner of wielding the pen, than he has of bravery and generalship while using his sword.

On the 24th of January, 1850, Lieutenant Hancock was married to Miss Almira Russell, daughter of Samuel Russell, a merchant of St. Louis, in which city the ceremony took place.   It may be here declared that the union thus formed has proved one of the happiest.   Mrs. Hancock, besides being a lady of acknowledged personal charms, has proved the possession of sterling good sense and of many accomplishments, and as a wife and mother has nobly sustained the high and delicate claims which have devolved upon her in the eminent station to which she has been called. It is fully recognized, among those who have been so fortunate as to possess her acquaintance, that she has cheered and adorned her home, while, with her husband, gracefully dispensing its genial and generous hospitalities.

Of this marriage there were born two children : Russell, named after his maternal grandfather, now living at the age of thirty, and Ada Elizabeth, born February 24, 1857, and who died March 18, 1875; the former was born in St. Louis, the latter at Fort Myers, Florida.

On November 7, 1855, Lieutenant Hancock was appointed quartermaster with the rank of captain, and was immediately ordered to Florida. It was at this time that the Florida Indians, the Seminoles, who had been troublesome for some years, had commenced active hostilities, and a force of United States soldiers was now sent to that section to protect the whites. Captain Hancock was stationed at Fort Myers, on the river Calloosahatchee, and became engaged in supplying troops in the field. His duties here were unquestionably arduous, since the frequent changes in the position of the troops, in a country so broken and impracticable for military operations, demanded the most constant vigilance and judgment, and no little fertility of resource in forwarding supplies to the points where they were needed. The brave and efficient General Harney was placed in command of the United States forces, and, shortly after his arrival, Captain Hancock had under his direction some one hundred and fifty boats, varying in size from the canoe to the steamer, and by means of which he conveyed his supplies to the various points where they were required.

Meanwhile, it is to be observed that the military operations in Florida against the Seminoles were exceptionally perplexing and difficult, requiring constant watchfulness, and, of course, involving in frequent danger those who had charge of the important duty connected with the supplies.

Hardly had the troubles in Florida been settled when there commenced that series of agitations which gradually led to the disorders in Kansas. When these troubles began to assume a serious aspect, General Harney was transferred to that department, and, upon his personal application, Captain Hancock was also ordered thither. He joined the troops at Fort Leavenworth, where he remained from August 1 to December 31, 1857, serving in the quartermaster's department with the efficiency which had now become recognized as a part of his character. He continued at the depot from January 1 to March 31, 1858, when, the Kansas troubles being over, he was ordered to accompany General Harney's expedition to Utah, where serious complications had arisen between the Mormons and the Gentiles.

The accession of California as one of the results of the Mexican War, and the stimulus given to emigration by the discovery of gold in that distant region, had attracted a wave of population toward the Pacific, and, as Utah lay in the route, the emigrants were brought in contact with the Mormons, who began to manifest hostility to the Gentiles, and even to assume an attitude of independence of the United States Government. In fact, in the beginning of 1857, Utah Territory was in a state of open rebellion, the Mormons trusting to the mountain fastnesses, which lay between them and the States, as their protection against that national authority which they were disposed to set at defiance. It was so eminently necessary to bring this people into subjection to the Constitution and laws of the whole country, that President Buchanan took summary and sufficient measures to put down the unnatural condition which existed. Brevet Brigadier-General Albert S. Johnston was sent with an advance detachment, and General Harney followed him with a reënforcement. Among the latter, Captain Hancock, still on duty as quartermaster, proceeded, administering his department so effectually as to greatly contribute to the safety and comfort of the troops.

Fortunately the Utah outbreak was not long-lived, and, it having been disposed of, Captain Hancock was ordered to proceed to the headquarters of the Department of Utah, there to join his regiment, the Sixth Infantry, which was expected to move into Oregon. Accordingly he transferred the public property in his charge to his successor in the quartermaster's department, and left General Harney's command at Cottonwood Springs, on the 17th July, 1858, in company with Lieutenant-Colonel G. H. Crossman, Deputy Q. M. General, and Captain J. H. Simpson, of the Topographical Engineers, and an escort of sixteen soldiers of the Seventh Infantry, began their journey. A march of twenty-seven days brought the party to Fort Bridger, Utah, 709 miles distant from the point of departure, the journey having been accomplished in twenty-six days. A train of wagons was taken along in this overland journey, with teamsters, extra horses, etc., yet, such was the care and prudence with which the march was conducted, that they averaged more than twenty-six miles each day. At Fort Bridger all the companies of the Sixth Infantry were united, for the first time in sixteen years. Captain Hancock immediately reported for duty to Colonel Andrews, commanding, and was at once appointed regimental quartermaster.

The destination of the regiment was now changed by General Johnston, who had discretionary power in the premises, to Benicia, California. The task which now devolved upon Captain Hancock, to supply means for the transportation and subsistence for the expedition on its long journey, was a most difficult one. Supplies were limited, the animals were in poor condition, and the wagons out of repair. The train of this expedition, when ready for the start, consisted of 128 wagons, 5 ambulances, 1 traveling forge, and 1,000 mules. Harness, saddles, and other various appliances had to be repaired and inspected; quartermasters' stores selected and packed; teamsters, herdsmen, and other employés hired. The entire business of organization of this part of the expedition and its inspection being the duty of the quartermaster, it will thus be readily seen that the position was no sinecure; added to all of which, the fact of the season being far advanced, rendered it doubtful if the expedition would succeed in crossing the Sierra Nevadas, without encountering the terrible snow-storms which occur in that region. On August 21st the expedition was in motion.

An inspection of the report made by Captain Hancock to the Quartermaster-General, giving all the details of this journey, affords one sufficient subject for amazement in observing the degree of vigilance, energy, and arduous toil which must have been involved in its progress. Day and night it was incumbent on the Quartermaster to exercise constant watchfulness over his charge, and how assiduously this duty was fulfilled, is determined by the fact that, on the arrival of the expedition at Benicia, its entire belongings were delivered, actually in an improved condition, and without any important loss or accident whatsoever.

An examination of the report just alluded to displays also a facility and comprehensive knowledge in the construction of such a document which is certainly highly commendable in its author. Valuable statistics; descriptions of the country through which he marched; a map of the route; a table of distances taken by the odometer, and marking geographical points and dates; the character of the wood, water, and grass found in each locality, with notes affording a vast amount of valuable general information concerning the geography, botany, and the other features of the country—these are some of the elements of this report which display the vast amount of labor and painstaking which must have gone to its making. When one considers that it was prepared amid the cares, dangers, and embarrassments of this protracted and difficult march, it becomes matter of surprise that so scientific and generally excellent a statement could have been made under the circumstances.

From Fort Leavenworth to Fort Bridger the distance is 1,009 miles; from Fort Bridger to the barracks at Benicia it is 1,119, making the entire distance 2,100 miles— a journey which was performed by Captain Hancock entirely on horseback. The road lay through some of the wildest and most magnificent, as well as some of the most beautiful, scenery in America, and the statistics and suggestions which were set forth by him, or under his direction, were a valuable contribution to our knowledge of the country, and have since facilitated the establishment of the great improvements now uniting the oceans by the route across the continent.

Having performed this important service, Captain

Hancock awaited orders in California for some time, but, receiving a leave of absence, he returned to the East *via* the Isthmus of Tehuantepec and rejoined his family. After a short sojourn at home, he received orders to repair again to the Pacific coast and report for duty, and this time, accompanied by his family, he proceeded to California by way of the Isthmus of Panama. Shortly after his arrival on the Pacific coast, he was stationed at the old Spanish town of Los Angeles, in Southern California. Here he had charge of the quartermaster's depot at the station, from which the troops in Southern California and Arizona were supplied with trains and all the necessary aids to their subsistence and efficiency. The duties of this position demanded from the officer in charge wisdom, energy, business tact, and administrative ability—the peculiarities of climate, the diversity of production, the formation of the country, the roads and the modes of transportation, making the task of supplying the troops in that section a vastly different one from a similar duty in more highly improved parts of the country. Unlooked-for exigencies and unexpected obstacles were constantly arising, to meet which with skill and promptness, so as to promote the public service in the most efficient manner, and at the same time with a due regard for economical expenditure, required a mind of no ordinary resources and energy of no common degree. But the natural ability of Captain Hancock had, all this time, been educated by his experience, and, during the two years in which he continued in his responsible position, he succeeded in filling it to the full benefit of those dependent upon him and to the entire satisfaction of his superior officers.

Los Angeles is situated in one of the most beautiful

and picturesque regions of the Pacific coast. For sub-
limity and variety its scenery can scarcely be surpassed.
Flanked on the east by the coast range of mountains,
hills, valleys, and plains of great beauty and fertility extend from these to the sea, presenting every variety of
landscape. The climate is delightful, invigorating, and
healthful; the productions of all latitudes are here present, at different elevations. To this country the discovery of its gold, and the opening of rich mines, had
attracted people from all parts of the world, the greater
number, of course, being Americans, and among them,
as well as among the other classes of inhabitants, Captain
Hancock was soon fortunate in establishing a reputation
which was to be of signal service both to him and to the
country. He was universally liked and respected, and
his personal influence was felt among all those with
whom he came in contact, notwithstanding that many of
the inhabitants, as is always the case in newly settled districts, were rough adventurers, not a few being outlaws
from various parts of the civilized world.

Such was the situation of affairs in Southern California in 1860, and now it was that the first portentous rum-
ble was heard of that discordant and confusing outbreak
which had already begun to perplex the Eastern shore of
our country, and which was presently to burst forth in
all the anomalous and terrible emotion of the rebellion.
At this time, as is well known, there were no railroads
crossing the continent, no telegraph, no direct overland
mails even—for Butterfield's had been suspended—and
so tidings of what was being enacted in the Atlantic
States were slowly transmitted by the dubious and constantly delayed resources of the Post-office Department,
and by way of a circuitous route, *via* the Isthmus of

Panama, which delayed news from the East about two months. The agitations, therefore, which now aroused the populations of the Eastern States, and threw them into a turmoil of political disturbance, were not yet felt upon the Pacific Slope; but the wave soon swept across the continent, and, if later in beginning, the storm was scarcely less violent there than at its source. Adventurers and excitable emigrants and prospectors had flowed into California from every section of the Union, many of them from the Southern country. Every shade of political opinion could be found among the American settlers. Those from the South, as was natural, sympathized with secession, even to the extent of inclining toward action and movement that should display this sympathy. They were reminded that their kindred and homesteads were in the Southern States, to which, indeed, this portion of California, lying far south of Mason and Dixon's line, might be considered almost as belonging. The reckless character and incendiary disposition of many of the population which had rushed to the gold regions favored a popular outbreak, and even with some degree of hopefulness of the success of a possible Disunion movement. For a time there seemed to be imminent danger that such a movement might be successfully undertaken, and thus this entire region, with all its vast wealth and promise, be swept away from the American Union before even the serious struggle for supremacy between the warring sections might fairly be said to have commenced.

That this danger was indeed imminent will be readily appreciated, when it is considered that besides the elements to which we have referred, must be included also the old Spanish population. It was clear that this por-

tion of the inhabitants of Lower California could feel no
sentiment of loyalty to a government which had so recently conquered the country, and this class, being of a
roving and adventurous disposition, might easily be de-
pended upon to unite in any movement which should
offer advantages to them which they did not then possess.
To these add the considerable number of the population
who sympathized with the South, and those others whose
attachment to the Union was more figurative than real, and
it will be seen that such a project as the establishment of
an independent Pacific republic would possess attractions
not readily to be overcome. Such, indeed, was the. case,
and it is an historical fact that, while some were ready to
give their adherence to secession and the South, others
inclined to raise the "Bear" flag and actually engage in
the erection of a Pacific republic; and it required much
prudence, courage, and address on the part of the friends
of the United States Government to prevent one or the
other of these projects becoming an accomplished result.

It was, indeed, a crisis full of danger and difficulty,
but, fortunately, Captain Hancock and his officers, aided
by a few staunch and influential friends of the Government, were equal to the emergency. Indeed, the position of Captain Hancock was sufficiently critical. If the
storm had burst, whose suspicious under-current of in-
trigue was being made manifest, its first fury would have
fallen upon him. The depot of military stores under his
control, and the supplies and munitions of war which he
guarded, were deemed a first necessity by the proposed
insurgents, some of whom actually boasted that their first
step in the direction which they purposed would be to
possess themselves of this material. Captain Hancock
was early made aware of the situation of affairs, and at

once took measures for the protection of the integrity of his command. He personally appealed to the patriotism of his countrymen, curbed the insolence and turbulence of seditious aliens, and exhibited a firm and determined purpose which overawed those who showed a disposition to interfere with the authority of the Government.

The occurrence of the 4th of July, 1861, gave an opportunity to the Union men of Southern California, particularly to those of Los Angeles, to organize a plan, whose successful conduct, it was hoped by Captain Hancock, who devised it, would at once annihilate the incipient seeds of treason, and serve to retain that section prominently under the old flag. Determined to make such a display on this occasion as should effect his purposes, Captain Hancock ordered up from a distance of one hundred miles a squadron of United States cavalry, which, added to his force, and to the number of out-and-out Union men within reach, made a respectable procession; and, certainly, all the customary features of Independence Day that could be undertaken were made a part of the Los Angeles celebration. Not the least effective of these was a public speech made by Captain Hancock, his first attempt at oratory, and which is given here in full from a report published in a Los Angeles paper at the time. It is strongly suggestive of the situation, as well as indicative of the patriotism and the oratorical powers of our hero at this period of his life, and is illustrative of the prudent firmness with which its author bore himself in the difficult circumstances in which he was placed:

"We have here met to commemorate that day, of all among Americans the most hallowed and cherished of the national memories of a lifetime—the Fourth of July, 1776; that day when the reign of tyrants in the colonies of America closed, and the reign of reason, of fraternity, and of equal political rights began.

"Who on this continent does not know of the great events which occurred on that day, the anniversary of which we are met here to celebrate—the event so interesting to all true Americans: the Declaration of our National Independence? And who among us would wish to see the day approach when that occasion should cease to be commemorated? I will not believe that any can be found so destitute of patriotic pride as not to feel in his veins a thrilling current when the deeds of his ancestors in the battles of the Revolution are mentioned.

"Can any one of us hear related the great events of that contest without wishing that his ancestors had been honorably engaged in them?

"Who of us can forget the names of Lexington, of Monmouth, of Brandywine, and Yorktown, and who can regret that they are descendants of those who fought there for the liberties we now enjoy?

"And what flag is that we now look to as the banner that carried us through that great contest and was honored by the gallant deeds of its defenders? The Star Spangled Banner of America, then embracing thirteen pale stars, representing that number of oppressed colonies; now thirty-four bright planets, representing that number of great States. To be sure, clouds intervene between us and eleven of that number; but we will trust that those clouds will soon be dispelled, and that those great stars in the Southern constellation may shine forth again with even greater splendor than before. Let them return to us! We will welcome them as brothers who have been estranged, and love them the more that they were angered and then returned to us.

"We have an interest in the battle-fields of those States not second to their own. Our forefathers fought there side by side with theirs; can they, if they would, throw aside their claims to the memories of the great fields on our soil, on which their ancestry won renown? No, they can not! God forbid that they should desire it.

"To those who, regardless of these sacred memories, insist on sundering this Union of States, let us, who only wish our birthrights preserved to us, and whose desire it is to be still citizens of the great country that gave us birth, and to live under that flag which has gained for us all the glorious histories we boast of, say this day: 'Your rights we will respect; your wrongs we will assist you to redress; but the *Union* is a *precious heritage that we intend to preserve and defend to the last extremity.*'

"Let us believe, at least let us trust, that our brothers, then, do not wish to separate themselves permanently from the common memories which have so long bound us together, but that, when reason returns and resumes her sway, they will prefer the brighter page of history, which our mutual deeds have inscribed upon the tablets of time, to that of the uncertain future of a new confederation, which, alas! to them, may prove illusory and unsatisfactory."

Whatever may have been the real importance of the incendiary opinions which for a time disturbed the political atmosphere of Southern California, it is certain that after this Fourth of July celebration little or nothing was heard of them, and it was generally conceded on the spot that the wisdom, forbearance, and calm determination of Captain Hancock, in the execution of what he recognized to be his duty to his country and his profession, were important elements in quelling the rising spirit of disaffection.

By this time, sufficient information of the serious nature of the outbreak in the Southern States had reached California to make a profound impression. As might be supposed, a soldier, possessing the energy, courage, and devoted patriotism of Hancock, would hardly remain contented in the comparatively quiet and serene position which he occupied at Los Angeles, and, in fact, he made early and earnest application to be relieved from duty on the Pacific coast, and to be transferred to more active service at the seat of war. This request was at length granted, and, as soon as orders arrived, Captain Hancock terminated his official duties at Los Angeles with his customary promptness and dispatch, and hastened to embark for the East, accompanied by his family.

On the 4th of September, 1861, he landed at New York, and, without waiting even to visit his parents, within a few miles of whose home he passed *en route*, he reported himself at Washington for active service.

CHAPTER VI.

At the time Captain Hancock reported for duty at Washington he was thirty-eight years old. That he sought more active service than that in which he had been recently engaged, was not alone for love of his profession and from a natural and proud ambition to seek distinction in the service, but from principle.

He drew his sword in maintenance of those political theories in which he had been raised, and from love for his whole country and for the flag. It was, indeed, at this time that he wrote, in a letter to a friend: "My politics are of a practical kind—the integrity of the country, the supremacy of the Federal Government, an honorable peace or none at all." Fortunately for the cause, the nature of the important services which Captain Hancock had already rendered, and his marked ability and

HANCOCK AT WILLIAMSBURG. "GENTLEMEN, CHARGE!"

full appreciation of a soldier's duty, had been recognized by his former commanders, Worth, Harney, and others, and were well known to the army and to the country.

In the beginning, it was rightly felt that the success of campaigns depends as much upon the efficiency of the quartermaster's department certainly as upon any other; and for this reason, and because of his special experience, and his administrative and organizing qualities, Captain Hancock was at first assigned to the post of chief quartermaster on the staff of General Robert Anderson, who had been placed in command of the Union forces in Kentucky. But he was destined to a far more brilliant career, and, even while preparing to obey this order, General McClellan, who appreciated Hancock's high military talents, proposed his name for the appointment of brigadier-general. The commission was issued by order of President Lincoln on the 23d of September, 1861. It was at once accepted, and Brigadier-General Hancock entered upon active duty.

It is esteemed a remarkable instance in the life of an officer, whose duty had hitherto consisted, chiefly, in the performance of purely official and administrative functions in the position of a quartermaster in the United States army, and with the rank of captain, that he should be transferred at one step to such high rank, and ordered at once on active military service. No greater compliment, perhaps, has ever in the history of the United States army been paid to a record chiefly accomplished in times of peace. To be sure, Hancock was no novice in the art of war; his experience had been varied and arduous in Mexico, in the Seminole War in Florida, and among the hostile Indians of the West. Through all his military life he had been favored by circumstances calcu-

3

lated to inform him in all the elements necessary to a
soldier's career, and to draw upon all the qualities which
he might possess calculated to be available to him thereafter.   General Hancock at once bent all his energies to
aid in the organization of the Army of the Potomac.   It
is more difficult to superinduce thorough discipline in
the Volunteer service than in the Regular army.   With
all the superior intelligence, patriotism, and self-reliance
of such soldiers, it is difficult at first to inaugurate and
sustain in such an army a high degree of efficiency; but
this is essential, and the young organizer and commander
of the Army of the Potomac found in General Hancock,
as also in other West Point graduates, capable coadjutors.
And here it is proper to state that, throughout the war,
General Hancock never commanded any but volunteer
soldiers.

Toward the close of September General McClellan
held the first grand review of the Army of the Potomac,
the President being present, when seventy thousand men,
the largest number assembled up to this time, were ma-
nœuvred.   Meanwhile, additional troops were constantly
arriving and being dispatched to appropriate positions.
General Hancock's brigade, the first of Smith's division,
consisted of the following regiments : the Fifth Wisconsin, Colonel Amasa Cobb ; Sixth Maine, Colonel Hiram
Burnham ; Forty-ninth Pennsylvania, Colonel William
W. Irwin ; Fourth New York, Colonel Francis L. Vin-
ton ; in all, four thousand men.

Soon after the brigade was organized, its camp was removed to a position in front of the Chain Bridge road near
Lewinsville, where it remained until the embarkation for
the Peninsula.   In the following spring, on the advance
of our forces beyond the Potomac, the enemy retired be-

fore them with some slight skirmishing, but without any engagement of importance. The nearness and boldness of the enemy, however, were indicated by these collisions, and they had the effect of familiarizing the men of both sides with danger. Occupying an advanced position, Hancock's troops bore their full share in these skirmishes, and were effective at once in deterring the enemy from foraging raids and in obtaining much that had else been bestowed to their comfort.

On the 21st of October General Hancock took part in a reconnoissance in force from the camp. In this both infantry and artillery were employed, and the movement resulted satisfactorily.

The time until spring was devoted by the entire volunteer army in drilling, and instruction in the art of war, many of both officers and men being, of course, new to the service, and having everything to learn that might render them efficient. It was during this time that General Hancock, through the exercise of the strong self-reliance, firmness, and address, which he always displayed to such an eminent degree, succeeded in establishing such relations with his officers and men as thenceforward characterized his military career. In fact, Hancock excelled in the exact qualities required by his important position at the beginning of the war, and he succeeded in a marvelous degree in inaugurating military authority and discipline, and yet in such a way as to inspire love and respect for his presence to so great an extent that his very name thereafter stirred the enthusiasm of his troops like the tones of a trumpet. Officers and men found him to be exact and unyielding in requiring subordination, in military discipline, and in the prompt and faithful performance of duty. Sometimes, on the march

and on the field of battle, he was impetuous and stern in
the enforcement of his orders; but combined with these
habitudes of command he displayed the most inflexible
justice and impartiality, and a warm and generous appreciation and acknowledgment of service well performed.
He aimed to administrate the affairs of his command
with absolute fairness and justice. Those who were
most intimate with him socially received from him the
same official treatment with those whom he only knew as
belonging to his command. No officer or private ever
preferred a complaint which did not receive thorough
and prompt investigation; and it was a well-recognized
fact that he was as prompt to redress the wrongs of a
private soldier as those of an officer in high position. It
was also a characteristic of General Hancock that he was
as active and exact in obeying the orders of his military
superiors as he was in requiring obedience from his subordinates. This inflexible maintenance of justice, both
to those under his command and to the interest of the
public service, no doubt made for General Hancock some
enemies in his various commands, but it is acknowledged
that in very few instances did he ever give reasonable
grounds for complaint. He treated all impartially, and,
if his requirements were ever severe and strict, or his
reproofs of delinquencies stern and prompt, these were
such as the very nature of the military service demands.

During the winter of 1861–'2 General Hancock and
his subordinate officers were so diligent in the instruction
and drill of his brigade, that when, in the spring of 1862,
the Army of the Potomac landed on the peninsula formed
by the Chesapeake Bay and the James River, which became the theatre of the first grand operations of the war,

his brigade was one of the most complete and effective in the army, and at once came to the front.

Shortly after it landed at Fortress Monroe, Smith's division, to which it was attached, was assigned to the Fourth Army Corps.

Its first serious conflict with the enemy was in the action at Lee's Mills, on Warwick Creek, April 16, 1862, when it took part in the attack on that position by Smith's division. A light skirmish had previously occurred at Young's Mills, in the progress of a reconnoissance made from Newport News by General Hancock, but in this affair there was little that was noteworthy. Subsequently, the brigade was hotly engaged in several severe skirmishes during the operations in front of Yorktown, and in which it lost a considerable number of killed and wounded.

In the march from Lee's Mills to Williamsburg, May 4, 1862, and during the operations at that point, General Hancock was in command of Davidson's brigade of Smith's division, in addition to his own. The connection of General Hancock with the battle of Williamsburg, and his importance in relation to the general action, give good reason for some description of a part of this engagement. With a comparatively small force, numbering less than 2,000 men, he fought and won an important action, which really resulted in the immediate evacuation of Williamsburg and its works by the enemy; while it is a fact that such of our troops as were engaged against the enemy's right met with repeated repulses, and at the close of the day had gained no substantial advantage. The force handled by General Hancock in this engagement consisted of five regiments of infantry, the Fifth Wisconsin, Sixth Maine, Forty-ninth Pennsylvania, of his own brigade, Seventh Maine, a portion of the Thirty-third New York Vol-

unteers, of Davidson's brigade, and Wheeler's and Cowan's
batteries, both from New York, in all, less than 2,000 men.
The enemy sent about 5,000 men to drive Hancock's command from Queen's Run ; but such was his success in repelling them that the attacking force became alarmed lest
their communications up the Peninsula might be cut off,
and this apprehension doubtless caused the retreat of the
night of the 5th of May.   Hancock's loss in the battle of
Williamsburg was 126 in killed and wounded.   The fact
of such a loss from his small number showed that the
fight was close, while the additional fact that the enemy's
loss was from.500 to 700 in killed, wounded, and prisoners
in this engagement, and that he was put to flight, shows
that the fighting was effective.   In regard to General
Hancock's connection with this battle, General McClellan,
in his published Report, page 185, says : " Being satisfied
that the result of Hancock's engagement was to give us
possession of the decisive point of the battle-field, during
the night I countermanded an order for the advance of
the divisions of Sedgwick and Richardson."

This was the first hard fighting of the brigade, and
its conduct was creditable to both the men and their
commander.   In the morning of the battle a portion of
the force received a scathing fire from the enemy, and
retired, in obedience to orders, to gain a crest which General Hancock had chosen for his line of battle.   This
movement, always difficult under the fire of the enemy,
was executed with great steadiness and coolness, and
when the enemy advanced to the foot of the crest, not
fifty paces from our line, and delivered a heavy fire upon
our troops, they were met with such spirit and their fire
returned with such deadly effect that they fled from the
field, routed and dismayed.   On this battle-field was cap-

tured the first color taken by the Army of the Potomac, and it is proper to state that so high an appreciation did General McClellan have of the results of Hancock's action that he personally thanked each regiment, and directed that they should be honored by having the name "Williamsburg" emblazoned on their colors. The report of the commander-in-chief as to this action says: "At 11 A. M. General Smith received orders from General Sumner to send one brigade across a dam on our right, and occupy a redoubt on the left of the enemy's line. Hancock's brigade was selected for this purpose, crossed the dam, took possession of the first redoubt, and, afterward finding a second one, took and occupied that also, and sent for reënforcements, to enable him to advance further and take the next redoubt, which commanded the plain between his position and Fort Magruder, and would have enabled him to take in reverse and cut the communications of the troops engaged against Generals Hooker and Kearney. The enemy soon began to show himself in strength before Hancock, and, as his rear and flank were somewhat exposed, he repeated his request for reënforcements. General Smith gave the order to reënforce, but each time the order was countermanded at the moment of execution, General Sumner not being willing to weaken the center. At length, in reply to General Hancock's repeated messages for more troops, General Sumner sent him an order to fall back to his former position, the execution of which order General Hancock deferred as long as possible, being unwilling to give up the advantage already gained, and fearing to expose his command by such a movement. . . . As heavy firing was heard in the direction of General Hancock's command, I ordered General Smith to proceed with his two remaining brigades to support that part of the line. . . . Before Generals Smith and Naglee could reach the field of General Hancock's operations, although they moved with great rapidity, he had been confronted by a superior force. Feigning to retreat slowly, he waited their onset, and then turned upon them, and, after some terrific musketry firing, he charged them with the bayonet, routing and dispersing their whole force." (Hancock's order was, "Gentlemen, we must give them the bayonet—Charge!") "This," adds McClellan, "was one of the most brilliant engagements of the war; and General Hancock merits the highest approval for the soldierly qualities displayed, and his perfect appreciation of the vital importance of his position in putting an end to all operations here. All the troops who had been engaged slept on the muddy field without shelter and many without food." (See McClellan's Report, pages 181–183.)

After the battle of "Williamsburg," the Army of the Potomac advanced up the Peninsula to the Chickahominy, a river that rises in the hilly grounds northwest of Richmond, and flowing southeast, almost parallel with the Pamunkey, suddenly turns with a short bend to the south about midway between the James and the York, and debouches into the former some dozen miles above Williamsburg. At about this time, General McClellan, with the President's consent, organized two additional army corps—Fifth and Sixth—and Smith's division, to which Hancock's brigade was attached, was included in the Sixth, General William B. Franklin commanding.

The next close encounter of Hancock's brigade with the enemy was in the action of Garnett's Hill, June 27, 1862, on the right bank of the Chickahominy. In this fight his brigade, in conjunction with several other regiments and some batteries of artillery, all under Hancock's command, repelled a strong attack of the enemy in a battle of less than two hours' duration. In this action the brigade lost quite heavily. It occurred on the same day that the main portion of the army was so severely defeated at Gaines's Mill, on the left bank of the Chickahominy. Only one division of the Sixth Corps—Slocum's —took part in the battle of Gaines's Mill; while the other division—Smith's—was held on the right bank of the stream near Garnett's Farm, to prevent the enemy from breaking through our lines at that point, seizing the bridge, and crossing the river, thereby separating our army in two parts. The fight made by Hancock's command at Garnett's Hill derived its chief importance from the fact that it prevented such a disaster as would have resulted from a separation of our army by the enemy.

"Hooker's fight," says Swinton, "was really quite unnecessary, for the difficult obstacles against which he had to contend might have been easily turned by the right. This was actually done by Hancock, who, with slight loss, determined the issue" (Swinton, page 118). It ought also to be remembered that Hooker fought under Sumner's orders, and fought splendidly.

The Chickahominy River, along the valley of which McClellan advanced upon Richmond, is a sinuous stream, flowing through dense forests and bordered by swampy land, very impracticable for military roads; besides this, it overflowed its banks during this march. If bridges had been built across the Chickahominy high enough to avoid the floods existing at that time, the battle of Five Forks never could have ended in disaster. In the terrible state of the roads, produced by the heavy rains and the overflow of the river, it required amazing care and

tact on the part of the officers to effect the advance movement, but both officers and men proved equal to the difficulties that they had to encounter.   Space will not permit
the entering into any description of the direct movements
of McClellan's army in its march on Richmond.   The whole
plan and its later actions are so inextricably mingled with
political questions and the administration at Washington,
features of history with which this work has no concern,
that they demand no consideration here, particularly as
they involve no question concerning General Hancock
necessary to enter into here.

Having determined to change his base of operations
to the James River, General McClellan fixed the 26th of
June, 1862, as the date for his advance; but on this day
the enemy, which had been reënforced by Stonewall
Jackson, attacked him in force.   This fight inaugurated
the famous and terrible movement known as the "Seven
Days," and which began on the 28th of June.   The
enemy on that morning attacked the rear-guard of Hancock's brigade at Golding's Farm, a point held by it.
This attack was handsomely repulsed.

On the 29th the brigade participated in the engagement of Savage Station, where General Hancock commanded his own and Davidson's brigade.   During the
night march from White Oak Swamp to the James River, Hancock commanded the advance of the rear-guard of
the Sixth Corps, at a time when it was supposed that the
enemy had interposed between our troops and the James
River, and when it was momentarily expected that his column would be attacked on the road.   It is but justice to
Hancock's brigade to say that, at the end of the seven days
(when it moved into its position at Harrison's Landing),
during which time it was constantly exposed to the ene-

my by daylight and in its night marches, it presented an unblenching front, and, so far was it from demoralization, that the next morning, when called upon, it was ready to move to the front of our lines and offer battle to the enemy. Hancock's brigade had no further active service on the Peninsula, and accompanied the other troops ordered up the Potomac.

CHAPTER VII

Movement from Harrison's Landing to Acquia Creek and Alexandria, to join General Pope—Hancock's Brigade at Centreville—Defeat and Demoralization of Pope's Army—The Capital in Danger—General McClellan placed in Command of the Defenses around Washington—Battle of Antietam—General Hancock made Commander of the First Division, Second Army Corps, on the Field of Battle—Loss at Antietam—The Army delayed by the Want of Clothing and Supplies.

ON the 23d of August, 1862, General Hancock's brigade embarked with the rest of the Sixth Corps at Fortress Monroe, whence the troops were transferred to Acquia Creek and Alexandria to join the army of General Pope. The Sixth Corps did not, however, participate in the campaign, its operations consisting merely in marching from the vicinity of Alexandria to Centreville, where it met Pope's retreating army. The corps occupied the intrenchments at that position during the night of August 30, 1862, and the following morning; it then moved back to the line of defenses on the south side of the Potomac near Washington, where it remained in camp until the opening of the Maryland campaign, which terminated at Antietam.

This movement was the result of an order issued by General Halleck, newly appointed Commander-in-chief, and which was conveyed by telegraph to General McClellan. It was briefly to withdraw his entire army from the

HANCOCK, AT ANTIETAM, TAKING COMMAND OF RICHARDSON'S DIVISION.

Peninsula to Acquia Creek, and join the army of General Pope.

The situation of the army, and indeed that of the whole country, at this time was appalling. General Pope had been defeated and discomfited, and his broken battalions were all that lay between Lee and Washington. The capital itself was in peril, and the most serious rumors spread through the country and alarmed the nation. The movements of Lee up the Potomac seemed to portend either the invasion of Maryland, or possibly the capture of Washington, and at length, forced to an act of acknowledgment, General Halleck recalled McClellan and put him in command, begging that he would assist in this crisis with his ability and his experience. The news of McClellan's restoration spread rapidly through the army, and restored the *morale* of the demoralized force. The army was immediately put in motion, the process of reorganization being continued during the march. This process was in no slight degree aided and encouraged by the excellent example of the Sixth Corps, to which General Hancock's brigade belonged. The perfect order and magnificent bearing of these troops presented a model which told favorably upon the reorganization of the whole body.

The Sixth Corps was engaged in the battle of South Mountain, or rather in the two actions which made up that engagement, and in which Hancock's brigade actively participated.

After Crampton's Gap and Turner's Gap, the passes through South Mountain, had been carried, three days before Antietam, the Sixth Corps, with Hancock's brigade in the advance, pressed forward and arrived on that now celebrated battle-field at about ten o'clock on the morning of September 17th. Smith's division, to which Hancock's brigade belonged, at once went into action to support the right wing of the army, which, under General Sumner, had been badly shattered, and was now hard pressed by the enemy.* At the moment General Hancock's line of battle was formed, and just before he gave the order to move under fire, he addressed a few words to his brigade, telling them in substance that he knew he could depend upon their steadiness and gallantry in the struggle before them, which would undoubtedly be a fierce one, and calling upon them to fight with their accustomed valor upon this field, which he hoped might prove the one to terminate the war. These few words from the General seemed to put officers and men upon their metal; and, when the order was given to advance, the brigade swept forward in quick time, and struck the enemy just as he was attacking some of our unsupported batteries in the corn-field at our right, near the Dunker church, which stands about a mile northward of the village of Sharpsburg on the Hagerstown road.

It was but the work of a few moments to push the enemy back into the woods from which he had emerged to charge our batteries, and by this movement the latter were undoubtedly saved, for the onset upon them was determined, and there was not a single regiment of in-

---

* General Sumner was, in fact, badly beaten, and his force terribly cut up; but this determined old soldier persisted in retaining the command. Urged by both Generals Hancock and Franklin to attack the enemy, he stubbornly refused; sent Slocum's division to reënforce Burnside; and, by forcing General Sedgwick to take his division into action in solid column, instead of with an interval between his brigades, as that general desired (which would keep them at supporting distance, without endangering the whole, on the repulse of the advance), actually destroyed the value of his reënforcements.

fantry within supporting distance of them when Hancock's brigade came into action. As the force so promptly
driven back from our batteries were Stonewall Jackson's
men, the reader will infer that it was no child's play.

Our line, after this engagement, was so firmly established on that part of the field, that the enemy did not
again assail it with infantry, although it suffered considerably from the artillery fire at grape-shot range.
These operations largely contributed to the victory
gained upon that hard-fought field—a victory which might
have been sooner achieved, and more complete in its
results, but for the unaccountable delay of the officer
having command of the left wing of our army in obeying the repeated orders of the Commanding General to
cross Antietam Creek and assail the enemy's right. The
battle of Antietam arrested General Lee's march of invasion, and compelled him to retire across the Potomac
into Virginia. No military man doubts that, had this
advantage been followed up, very different results from
those that occurred might have crowned the campaign.
The superseding of General McClellan, and the events
which ensued, are well known to history, and have been
frequently and sufficiently criticised.

The operations of the Sixth Corps on the bloody but
victorious field of Antietam closed General Hancock's
official action with the gallant brigade, which he had un-
interruptedly commanded from the time when he had
organized and trained it, in September, 1861. The somewhat abrupt character of that termination occurred in
this wise : About two o'clock P. M. of the day of battle—
the 17th—Hancock had been directed by General Mc-
Clellan in person to proceed to a point some distance to
the left of our line of battle, and assume command of

Richardson's division of the Second Army Corps, that brave general having been mortally wounded on the morning of this terrible day. Although this transfer on the field of battle to a higher command, by selection of the General-in-chief, was highly complimentary to General Hancock, and placed him in a more prominent and important position, yet it was a severe trial to his sensibilities to be separated from "Hancock's Brigade," as it was known throughout the army and the country, and by which name it was familiar during its existence. He had formed, drilled, and disciplined it; had molded it into a perfect condition; had led it to its first "baptism of blood"; had commanded it in many actions, and had never seen it abandoned or demoralized in the darkest hours of the Peninsula campaign. He knew personally every officer and almost every soldier in it, was warmly attached to them all, and he followed its after career with intense solicitude, proud of the glorious part it bore in the splendid storming of the heights of Fredericksburg, its desperate fighting at Marye's Heights a few days afterward, its magnificent assault upon the works at Rappahannock Station, November 7, 1863, its brilliant conduct in the campaigns of 1863–'4 with the Army of the Potomac and in the Valley of the Shenandoah. A military authority writes on this subject as follows: "I shall never forget the first meeting I witnessed of General Hancock and his old brigade after he had been transferred from it at Antietam. It occurred near Falmouth, Virginia, in the spring of 1863. The Sixth Corps was marching past the camp of Hancock's division of the Second Corps, during General Burnside's movement known as the 'Mud March.' The brigade had halted for a rest near General Hancock's headquarters, and sent word to the General that they had come to see him. He mounted his horse and rode over to meet his old comrades. Upon his appearance among them, officers and men broke out into cheer after cheer. Caps were thrown into the air, and every manifestation of pleasure was exhibited at the sight of the commander who had first taught them to be soldiers and first led them into battle."

The First Division, Second Army Corps, to which General Hancock was assigned as commander on the field of Antietam, September 17, 1862, was composed of three brigades, commanded respectively by Brigadier-General Thomas Francis Meagher (the Irish Brigade), Brigadier-General John C. Caldwell, and Colonel John R. Brooke, Fifty-third Pennsylvania Volunteers. It contained many of the best regiments in the service, and numbered among its officers some of the brightest and most gallant spirits in the army. Prominent among these may be mentioned General Francis L. Barlow, then colonel of the Sixth New York Volunteers, afterward major-general of volunteers, commanding the First Division, Second Corps [he was, after the war, in 1872, Attorney-General of the State of New York]; Colonel Henry B. McKeen, Eighty-first Pennsylvania Volunteers, afterward killed at the battle of Cold Harbor, June 5, 1864; Colonel Nelson A. Miles, Sixty-first New York Volunteers: after Colonel Barlow's promotion to be brigadier-general, he was made major-general of volunteers, commanding the First Division of the Second Corps, and, 1872, Colonel of the Fifth United States Infantry; Colonel Edward E. Cross, Fifth New Hampshire Volunteers, who was killed at Gettysburg; Colonel S. K. Zook, afterward promoted to be brigadier-general of volunteers, also killed at Gettysburg; Colonel John R. Brooke, Fifty-third Pennsylvania Volunteers, promoted before the close of the war to be brigadier-general, and, in 1872, Lieutenant-Colonel of the Third United States Infantry. There were many others, whose daring, courage, coolness, intelligence, and promptitude in the execution of orders, imparted great efficiency to the division. When General Hancock assumed the command of this division, it had just distinguished itself by a tremendous assault upon those portions of the enemy's lines known in the descriptions of the battle of Antietam as the "sunken road" and "Piper's house," which points it had carried after a stern and bloody struggle. In the "sunken road," especially, the fighting had been so fierce and obstinate that, when the enemy gave way, their dead lay in such large numbers as to cause them to appear as if their whole line of battle had perished. The division was under a sharp musketry fire when General Hancock joined it. As rapidly as possible, he set himself to making the acquaintance of the brigade and regimental commanders, and then to taking measures for preparing the lines for the attack which, he had been informed, was to be made upon the enemy's position at four o'clock that afternoon. The attack, however, was not ordered, and the enemy retreated the same night from the field and recrossed the Potomac.

The loss of this division at Antietam amounted to five thousand men.

The battle of Antietam, or, as the Confederates called it, Sharpsburg, was fought upon a piece of territory forming a sort of peninsula made by the Potomac River and Antietam Creek, with the village of Sharpsburg near its center. General Lee had chosen the ground and invited the battle. There it was stubbornly contested, and, although the victory was with the Union forces, no immediate results followed, except the withdrawal of the Confederate army from Maryland.

The losses at Antietam were 2,010 killed, and 9,407 wounded, and more than 1,000 missing, aggregating 12,469. Besides this sum, 12,000 of the Union troops were captured at Harper's Ferry, where Halleck had retained them, against the advice of General McClellan, as being in "a position of strategic importance," whereas it was only important as a trap for its occupants. As Lee had retreated to the south side of the Potomac on the night of the 18th of September, our army was so disposed as to be ready to follow him after burying its dead, disposing of its wounded, and obtaining needed supplies of clothing, etc., of most of which the army was exceedingly destitute.

CHAPTER VIII.

ON the 19th of September, the Second Corps, in which General Hancock commanded the first division, marched to Harper's Ferry, where it lay encamped until the movement southward to Warrenton, and thence to Fredericksburg, in October and November. In the mean time, however, General Hancock made an important reconnoissance from Harper's Ferry to Charlestown, Virginia, where he had a sharp skirmish with the enemy, who fell back on Winchester. This reconnoissance was made with a mixed command of cavalry, artillery, and infantry, about six thousand strong, and was accompanied by General McClellan in person. Its object having been accomplished, General McClellan ordered Hancock to return to camp, and this was effected without disturbance on the following morning.

A period of discouraging delay now followed, while the army waited for blankets, shoes, and other articles of clothing, without which it was impossible to march.   The movement began on the 1st of November, when the Army of the Potomac left Harper's Ferry and its vicinity for the Rappahannock.   During the progress of this movement General McClellan was again removed from his command.   Late on the night of November 7th, amidst a heavy snow-storm, a special messenger arrived post haste from Washington, and repaired to the tent of General McClellan at Rectortown.   He was the bearer of the following dispatch, which he handed to the commander of the army:

"WAR DEPARTMENT, ADJUTANT-GENERAL'S OFFICE,
"WASHINGTON, *November* 5, 1862.

"GENERAL ORDER No. 182:

"By direction of the President of the United States, it is ordered that Major-General McClellan be relieved from the command of the Army of the Potomac, and that Major-General Burnside take command of that army.

"By order of the Secretary of War.

"E. D. TOWNSEND, *Assistant-Adjutant-General.*"

It chanced that General Burnside was at that moment with McClellan in his tent.   Opening the dispatch, and reading it without a change of countenance or of voice, McClellan passed the paper to his successor, saying as he did so: "Well, Burnside, you are to command the army."   General McClellan was ordered to proceed to and report by letter from Trenton, New Jersey.   He is now (1880) a resident of that city as Governor of the State of New Jersey.   There is reason to believe that General Burnside himself was strongly opposed to the removal of General McClellan, and that it was with unfeigned reluctance that he assumed the command of the army.* Swinton says: "The moment chosen for his removal was an inopportune and an ungracious one, for never had McClellan acted with such vigor and rapidity, never had he shown so much confidence in himself or the army in him; and it is a notable fact that not only was the whole body of the army, rank and file, as well as the officers, enthusiastic in their affection for his person, but that the very gentleman who was appointed his successor was the strongest opponent of his removal." In his testimony before "the Committee on the Conduct of the War" General Burnside said, with honorable frankness: "After getting over my surprise and shock, etc., I told General Buckingham that it was a matter that required very serious thought; that I did not want the command; that it had been offered me twice before; and that I did not feel that I could take it. I told them (his staff) what my views were with reference to my ability to exercise such a command, which views I had always unreservedly expressed, that I was not competent to command such a large army as this. I had said the same thing over and over again to the President and Secretary of War, and also that, if things could be satisfactorily arranged with General McClellan, I thought he could command the Army of the Potomac better than any other general in it " ("Report of the Committee on

* This was the situation—in a nutshell: McClellan, with one hundred and twenty thousand men, and having secured South Mountain by his cavalry, opposed Longstreet with forty-two thousand on one side of the mountain, and Stonewall Jackson with about as many on the other. McClellan's plan, known to the Government at Washington, was to attack and destroy Longstreet's army, then fall upon Jackson, and, having defeated both forces —conceded by the best critics to have been a perfectly feasible conclusion— to move upon Richmond, when the war would have indubitably ended then and there. At this juncture McClellan was superseded—for what reason?

the Conduct of the War," Vol. i, page 650). But things could not be satisfactorily arranged with General McClellan; he was known to be a Democrat of conservative opinions, and that was his disqualification, for, although it was known that he had served and would serve the country and the cause of the Union faithfully, it was also foreseen that the general who should terminate the war successfully would gain an overshadowing popularity with the people, and it was important to the party in power either that he should be in harmony with their political views, or be a man of such an accommodating disposition as to be easily bent to their purpose. It is improbable that General Burnside would have proved sufficiently pliable, but failure of success left him untried in that respect.*

After a delay of ten days at Warrenton, abandoning all of McClellan's plans, the march of the army was continued to the Rappahannock, down which stream it moved *via* Falmouth to a position opposite the town of Fredericksburg, which stands on the left or west bank of that river. Burnside tried to mask his movements by threatening an advance on Gordonsville; but Lee soon penetrated his design, and marched in a line almost parallel with his adversary. General Sumner's advance reached Falmouth

* Among other baseless fabrications concerning General Hancock, one relates that he conspired with others of the officers under McClellan's command to resist the Government at Washington, and retain that general in his position. A curious coincidence, in connection with this, exists in the fact that, while General Hancock reproved certain young officers who, in his presence, ventured to use threatening language in regard to McClellan's removal by saying sternly, "Gentlemen, we are serving no one man, we are serving our country," General McClellan himself, under similar circumstances, and at the same time, used almost the identical language employed by General Hancock. His words were, "Gentlemen, please remember that we are here to serve the interests of no one man. We are here to serve our country."

November 17th, and designed to cross the river to Fredericksburg; but, the bridges having been burned, he had only an artillery duel with the Confederate forces which were on the opposite bank. Our pontoons, by some neglect, had not arrived, and the army was kept in waiting for want of them for more than a week, until Lee had ample time to concentrate his forces at Fredericksburg in order to dispute the crossing of the river by Burnside's army.

The position of General Lee was a strong one, and he had time so to strengthen and to dispose of his forces as to make a direct assault upon it across a tide-water river an almost hopeless undertaking. The town of Fredericksburg is chiefly built of brick, and its site slopes gently up from the river to an elevation or ridge called Marye's Heights. These heights afforded commanding positions for the batteries of the enemy, and long ranges of stone fences running parallel with the line of defenses secured good protection for the infantry. In advance of these, earthworks were thrown up, extending at intervals to nearly a mile above the city and about three miles below it. No very active operations were commenced against Fredericksburg until the night of December 10th and morning of the 11th, when our army began throwing pontoon bridges over the river opposite and below the town. On the 13th, the army crossed in the face of a terrible fire from the enemy, and a fierce battle began. To the Second Corps, to which Hancock's division belonged, was allotted the task of storming the works of Marye's Heights, the powerful position already described just in the rear of the town, and which was defended by large masses of troops and many batteries of artillery. In the assault which followed, General Hancock led his division through such a fire as has rarely been encountered in warfare. The men forced their way with fearful loss within fifteen or twenty paces of the fatal stone wall at the foot of the Heights, but found it impossible to carry the position, although gallantly supported by other divisions of the Second Corps and other troops sent to aid them. Still they did not relinquish the ground, but held it under a murderous musketry and artillery fire, until late in the night, when they were relieved by fresh troops. Of this assault, an historian writes: "Braver men never smiled at death than those who climbed Marye's Hill that fatal day. Their ranks, even in the process of formation, were plowed through and torn to pieces by Rebel batteries, and, after at heavy cost they had reached the foot of the hill, they were confronted by a solid stone wall four feet high, from behind which a Confederate brigade of infantry mowed them down like grass, exposing but their heads to our bullets, and those only while thus firing. Never did men fight better, or die, alas! more fruitlessly, than did most of Hancock's division, especially Meagher's Irish brigade, composed of the Sixty-third, Sixty-ninth, and Eighty-eighth of New York, Twenty-eighth Massachusetts, and One Hundred and Sixteenth Pennsylvania. . . . Thus Hancock's and French's divisions were successively sent against those impregnable heights, guarded with batteries rising tier above tier, all carefully trained upon the approaches from Fredericksburg, while that fatal stone wall, so strong that even artillery could make no impression on it, completely sheltered Barksdale's brigade, which, so soon as our columns came within rifle range, poured into their faces the deadliest storm of musketry." (Greeley's "American Conflict," pages 344, 345.)

4

During the night of the 13th, or rather the morning of the 14th, at about two o'clock, General Burnside, commanding the army, visited General Hancock at his headquarters in Fredericksburg, to converse and advise with him on the events of the day, and just as he was leaving directed General Hancock to have his division in readiness to support an attack which he intended to make on the enemy's position on Marye's Heights at 9 A. M. that day; but the contemplated assault was not made, other counsels having prevailed.

General Hancock's official report of this battle includes a statement of the losses of his division, and illustrates the terrible nature of the fighting. It gives 5,006 men taken into action, of whom 2,010 were killed or wounded, and of these 156 were commissioned officers. Of General Hancock's personal staff, three were wounded, and four had horses shot under them, while the General himself had a narrow escape, a musket-ball having passed through his clothes, abrading the skin.

General Burnside's intention to renew the attack at Fredericksburg was so bitterly opposed by General Sumner and the other generals that he finally relinquished it. In his testimony before the Committee on the Conduct of the War, General Burnside states that he was induced by Sumner's protest to recall the order for this attack.

On the two days succeeding the battle, Sunday, 14th, and Monday, 15th, the troops laid on their arms, and during the night of the latter, protected from discovery by the noise produced by a peculiarly harsh and discordant gale, the army was withdrawn to the north side of the Rappahannock. The loss of the Union army in the fight at Fredericksburg was 12,321 killed, wounded, and missing, and the fact that one-sixth of this entire loss fell upon Hancock's division of 5,000 men shows what kind of work they did that day. The loss of the Confederates was 5,309 killed and wounded, the difference being accounted for by the fact that they fought from behind fences and breastworks. In the following month General Burnside ordered a movement across the Rappahannock and along its banks six miles above Fredericksburg. The divisions of Franklin and Hooker were put in motion in two parallel columns. On the 19th of January, 1863, a terrible storm of rain, which came up in the night and lasted two days, converted the country through the lines of the advance into "a continent of mud," deep, adhesive, and unmanageable. Still the columns struggled on in what is known in the history of the army as the "Mud March," and with incredible toil in corduroying, and dragging pontoons, artillery, and supply wagons over utterly impassable roads, they had neared the ford; but, seeing the hopelessness of the undertaking, and learning that Lee was ready to meet it, General Burnside recalled the army to its quarters.

Shortly after this General Burnside was relieved from command, and his resignation accepted, General Joseph Hooker being appointed by the President in his place.

The result of this change of commanders was to revive in the army the zeal and confidence which had certainly been considerably weakened under recent disasters, and from a feeling of doubt, generally prevalent, concerning the capacity of General Burnside.

CHAPTER IX.

AFTER his appointment to the command, General
Hooker wisely determined not to attempt any large operations during the winter season of impassable roads.
The "Mud March" had taught him and his generals that
there were other things to be overcome besides the enemy, and he spent three months in efforts to bring the
army into a condition of efficiency. Certain improvements in its organization were effected, such as abolishing
the "Grand Divisions," perfecting the several departments, consolidating the cavalry under able leaders and
improving its efficiency, and introducing corps badges,
for the double purpose of distinguishing to what corps a
soldier belonged and forming *l'esprit du corps*. The
ranks were filled up by recalling absentees, discipline and
drilling were maintained, and before the spring campaign opened, Hooker found himself at the head of 120,-
000 foot of all arms, and 12,000 well-appointed cavalry.

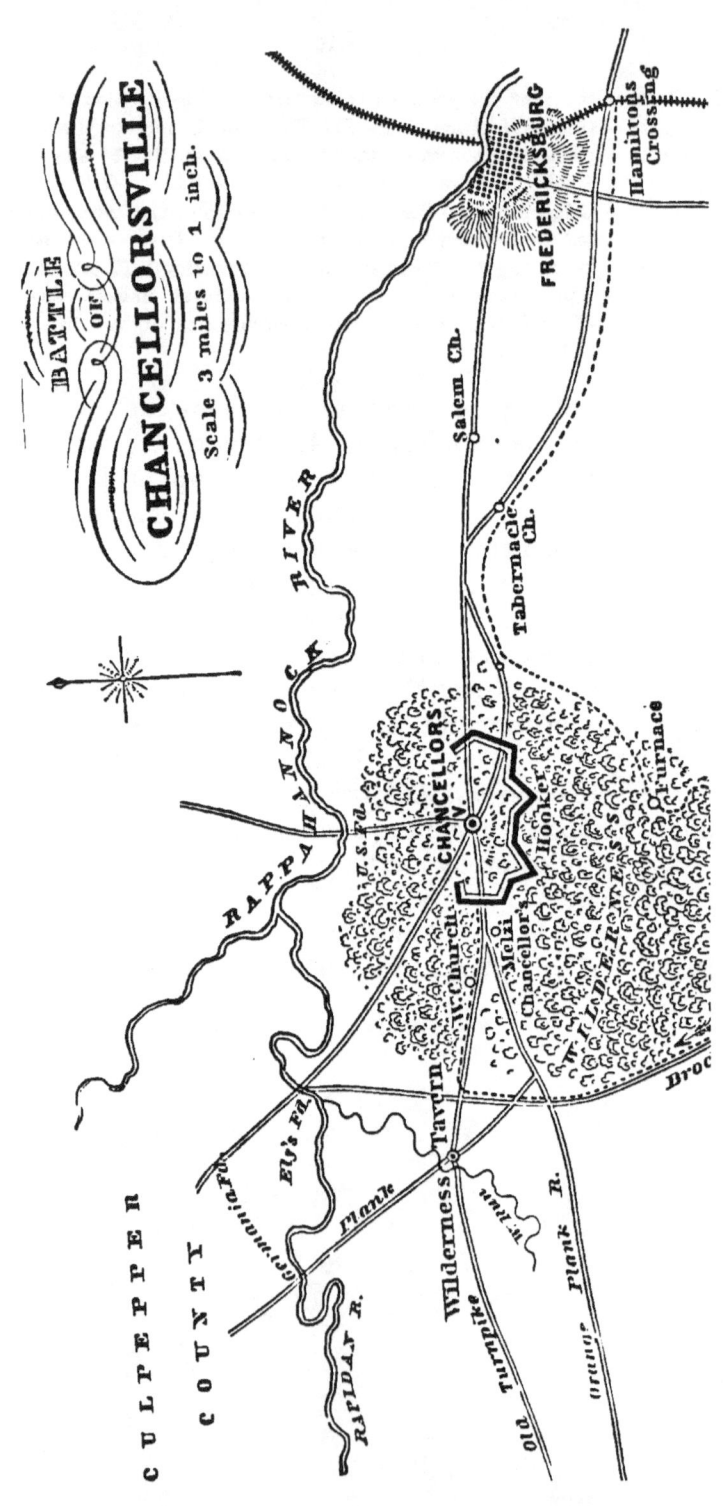

BATTLE OF CHANCELLORSVILLE

Scale 3 miles to 1 inch.

CULPEPPER COUNTY

RAPIDAN R.

RAPPAHANNOCK RIVER

Germania Fd.

Ely's Fd.

U.S. Fd.

Plank

Wilderness Tavern

Old Turnpike

Orange Plank R.

Plank R.

WILDERNESS

CHANCELLORSVILLE

Chancellors

McH. Church

Hooker

Chancellors Furnace

Brock

Salem Ch.

Tabernacle Ch.

FREDERICKSBURG

Hamilton's Crossing

The Confederate Army numbered scarcely half that force, as two divisions under Longstreet had been detached, and did not rejoin it until after the battle of Chancellorville.

Nearly due west from Fredericksburg, and eleven miles from that town and in the same county—Spottsylvania—there stands a large brick house, with a number of outbuildings, forming a little hamlet, called Chancellorville. It is on the western side of a wild and barren district, known as "The Wilderness." Lee's army had been lying during the winter along the Rappahannock, stretching for some miles east of Fredericksburg up that river nearly or quite to the mouth of the Rapidan, and had been strengthening the defenses along the river with a view of preventing its being crossed by the Union forces. Hooker's army rested upon the plains of Stafford, on the other side of the Rappahannock. General Hooker now formed the bold plan of marching up the river, crossing it and its tributary—the Rapidan— turning Lee's flank near Chancellorville, and sweeping him *en reverse*. On the 27th of April, 1863, his turning column was put in motion, consisting of the corps of Meade, Fifth; Couch, Second; Howard, Eleventh; and Slocum, Twelfth. The movement resulted in the battle usually called Chancellorville, which was attended by great loss of men, and resulted disastrously. The operations continued after our front crossing the river, from April 29th to May 6th. In this campaign General Hancock bore a conspicuous part. His division and that of French, both of the Second Corps, crossed the Rappahannock at the United States Ford, a little more than a mile below the point of affluence of the Rapidan, on April 30th.

On May 1, Hancock's division was thrown on the Fredericksburg turnpike to support Sykes's division, Fifth Corps, then moving to Fredericksburg along that road. Sykes was already engaged with the enemy; and Hancock, having formed his troops in a very advantageous position, was about to go into the attack, when both divisions were promptly ordered to retire from Chancellorville, much against the judgment of Generals Hancock and Couch, the latter of whom was the corps commander. Orders to fall back were repeated, however, but General Hancock was so loath to relinquish his ground that the advancing enemy had an opportunity of firing into the rear of his column as it made the backward march. Hancock was closely and hotly engaged on the two following days, May 2d and 3d, and successfully resisted all efforts of the enemy to break through his line. He had fixed his headquarters in the road just in front of the Chancellor house, one of the most exposed points on the whole field of battle, being constantly swept by the enemy's artillery. His horse was shot under him. At this point, on May 2, it was while leaning against a pillar of the house, close to Hancock's headquarters, that General Hooker was knocked down by a spent shot and rendered for a time insensible. Colonel N. A. Miles, Sixty-first New York Volunteers, who commanded the advanced line of Hancock's division on the Fredericksburg road, particularly distinguished himself on both the 2d and 3d of May, in repelling several fierce assaults made upon him by the enemy, and was dangerously wounded just after he had repulsed one of the fierce attacks on his line. General Hancock sent an aide to him with the message, " Tell Miles he is worth his weight in gold." Such prompt acknowledgment and warm commendation of handsome services was one of Hancock's characteristics, which greatly endeared him to both officers and men.

Hancock's division was the last to leave the field on the 3d, when our forces withdrew from the line which covered the roads concentrating at the Chancellorville house to the new position in the rear, which had been selected and prepared the previous evening. The division retired to this new line leisurely, dragging with it by hand the artillery of Lepine's Maine battery, which had been abandoned near the Chancellor house, after its officers, men, and horses had nearly all been killed or wounded.

The battle of Chancellorville was well planned, but was not well fought by the Union general. Possessing, no doubt, courage and many other elements of a good commander, Hooker was nevertheless not a great general. Had he possessed those qualities which are necessary to forecast a campaign in all its details, the results might have been different, and had not General Hooker, at a very critical moment during the action, been stunned and rendered insensible, as has already been related.

General Hancock, in his testimony before the Committee on the Conduct of the War, thus describes the retirement of our army: "My position was on the other side of the Chancellor house, and I had a fair view of this battle, and, although my troops were facing and fighting that way, the first lines referred to finally melted away and the whole front passed out; first the Third Corps went out, and there was nothing left on that part of the line but my own division; that is, on that extreme point of the line on the site of the Chancellor house, toward the enemy. I was directed to hold that position until a change of line of battle could be made, and was to hold it until I was notified that all the other troops had gotten off. This necessitated my fighting for a time both ways. I had two lines of battle, one facing toward Fredericksburg, and the other line behind that; and I had to face about the troops in the rear line to the right for the enemy who were coming on in that direction. I had a good deal of artillery, and, although the enemy masked their infantry in the woods very near me, and attempted to advance, and always held a threatening attitude, I judge that they had exhausted their troops, as they attempted no attack, although I remained for some time alone in this position with artillery all the time, some of my men of the rear line occasionally being shot by the enemy's infantry, and when the time came I marched off to my new position, about three quarters of a mile from the old position—the United States Ford, where the new line of battle had been laid out, and which we held until we crossed the river."

This withdrawal gave the enemy the roads leading to Fredericksburg, which they used to advance on Sedgwick and attack him.

The Chancellorville campaign was a failure. Our loss, including that of Sedgwick's corps, was 17,197 men killed, wounded, and missing; the Confederate loss was never ascertained, but it was probably not much less than ours, and, considering that among their mortally wounded was Lieutenant-General T. J. Jackson (Stonewall), their loss was greater. That general had loomed into an importance in the estimation of the South, and by the Confederate army, that caused his loss to be deplored by them as the greatest that could have befallen them.

This campaign terminated General Hancock's career as a division commander. The Second Corps returned

from Chancellorville to its former camp at Falmouth and
vicinity in front of Fredericksburg, where it remained
until the commencement of the campaign, which culminated at Gettysburg.   In the mean time, early in June,
1863, Couch relinquished the command of the Second
Corps, and General Hancock was placed at its head June
10, 1863.   On June 25th, while upon the march to Gettysburg, he was assigned to its permanent command by
orders of the President of the United States.

General Lee, having decided upon the bold measure
of carrying the war into the North, put his columns into
motion with that view, about a month after the affair at
Chancellorville.   He ascended the southern bank of the
river at Culpepper, and, after some movements, designed
to disguise his main purpose, threw his army northward,
and, in due time, crossed the Potomac, and turned through
Western Maryland into Pennsylvania.   The earlier movements of Lee's army were intended to induce Hooker to
withdraw from the line of the Rappahannock.   This last-
named general seemed to have been slow to believe that
his adversary really intended an invasion into Pennsylvania.   Lee had made great progress in his march, and
one of the columns had entered the Valley of the Shenandoah, while both were pressing toward the Potomac,
before Hooker moved from the Rappahannock.   Hill's
corps still occupied Fredericksburg, and the rest of Lee's
army was stretched along the route between that point
and the Potomac.   There is no doubt that General
Hooker discovered the intention of the Confederate
army in this northward movement, and that he wished
to take advantage of its long line by crossing the Rappahannock, cutting Lee's army in twain, destroying Hill's
corps, which formed its rear, and then pursuing and de-

stroying the other portions of it in detail. Indeed, General Hooker had suggested this plan to General Halleck and the President, but it had been rejected. He had now no alternative but to take his army back toward the capital, along the line so often traversed, *via* Warrenton, Cattell Station, Fairfax Station, and Manassas. Here he remained for several days, awaiting the unfolding of the enemy's purpose. So soon as Hill beheld the Union army disappear behind Stafford, he left his position at Fredericksburg, marched to join the other part of the Confederate army, and the entire force was soon thrown upon Pennsylvania. Jenkins, with his cavalry, followed as far as Chambersburg, carrying consternation to the unprotected people of Franklin, Cumberland, and the adjacent counties, and, on his return, bringing large numbers of cattle and horses, which he had gathered in those regions, and which formed a seasonable supply for his own and Ewell's forces, which met him at Hagerstown.

Meanwhile, Hooker could not cross the Potomac until he should become aware of his adversary's purpose, but, when sure of this, he marched with alacrity to overtake the invaders. At this time, Heintzelman commanded the Department of Washington, consisting of 36,000 men ; Schenck, the Middle District, including the region of Harper's Ferry ; while Dix was on the Peninsula with a considerable force. But, after Hooker crossed the Potomac, Halleck placed all these forces nominally under his control, though, inasmuch as the method, so constantly in vogue during the war, of directing the movements of armies from Washington was still popular, and as these movements were hampered by conflicting views, as well as from the need for men who were stationed at points where they were utterly useless, General Hooker, on the 27th of June, asked to be relieved from the command of the army, and on the 28th, a messenger arrived at his headquarters at Frederick, Maryland, with an order appointing Major-General George G. Meade in his place. The latter entered upon his responsible duties in a quiet and soldier-like manner, and the change of commanders occasioned no interruption in the progress of the army. By a variety of manœuvres, which need not here be detailed, it advanced in the direction of Gettysburg. Meanwhile some of Lee's forces had penetrated Pennsylvania as far as York, Carlisle, and the Susquehanna; but, upon the advance of the Federal army, these were called in and concentrated for a great field struggle. Those which were at Chambersburg crossed the South Mountain toward Gettysburg, and those that were nearer the Susquehanna converged upon the same point. This Lee probably did under the apprehension that Meade would cut off his communications. In fact, but for Meade's manœuvring, Lee would have crossed the Susquehanna and struck Harrisburg, and probably have made a dash upon Philadelphia. General Meade now saw that a great battle was inevitable, but could not foresee where it would occur. He caused careful examination of the topography of the country to be made, and, upon the whole, preferred in his own mind to receive battle on the line of Pipe-clay Creek, a stream running a few miles southeast of Gettysburg; but it was otherwise ordered. Buford's division of cavalry, being thrown out to the left of Meade's advancing army, proceeded in reconnoissance, occupied Gettysburg on June 30th, and pushed farther on north and west in the direction in which it was supposed Lee's army was advancing. The next day, General Reynolds was directed upon the same point, and, as Hill and Longstreet were approaching it, the hostile forces came in collision on the 1st of July, and on that day was fought the preliminary battle of Gettysburg.

CHAPTER X.

IT is not the purpose of this work to enter upon an accurate and minute description of the important battle of Gettysburg; it has been described ably and comprehensively, and our province is only to trace the career of General Hancock in this terrible and magnificent struggle, in which it is no injustice to others to say he bore a very conspicuous, and, largely, a controlling part. General Meade was the commander of the Union army, and deserves, and has received, high honor and commendation for the ability and efficiency with which he handled his forces. But it so happened that under his orders General Hancock selected the ground for the great conflict of the 2d and 3d July, and established that arrangement for the battle which was substantially maintained until the victory was won.

Before entering upon a narration of Hancock's operations during the battle of Gettysburg, it is proper to trace his movements from the time he assumed command of the Second Corps after the relief of General Couch.

Major-General D. N. Couch was relieved of the command
of the Second Army Corps on the 9th June, 1863, in pursuance of his personal request to the Secretary of War,
and General Hancock succeeded to the command.   There
was, perhaps, no other officer of the army so strong in the
confidence of the corps, or who could have succeeded
Sumner and Couch with so much satisfaction to the
troops.   Antietam, Fredericksburg, and Chancellorville
had raised his reputation as a division commander to the
highest point, and his appointment to the command of
the corps was one concerning which there could be no
question.   Indeed, it was contemplated, prior to General
Couch's retirement, to place General Hancock in command of the cavalry corps, and he was urged strongly by
the most conspicuous and able officers of the cavalry arm—
General John Buford, Colonel Grimes Davis, and others—
to accept the command.   General Hancock did not desire
this command, but finally agreed to accept it for the coming battle if the commander deemed it necessary.   Circumstances, however, occurred, making an immediate
change of commanders impracticable, and, before the matter was revived, the vacancy in the command of the Second Corps occurred.   General Caldwell succeeded General Hancock in the command of the First Division, Second
Corps, the other divisions being commanded by Generals
Gibbon and French.

On the night of the 13th and morning of the 14th of
June, 1863, the corps commenced its march, forming the
rear-guard of the Army of the Potomac, to confront Lee's
invasion into Pennsylvania.   It moved on the right flank
of the army by way of Acquia Creek, Dumfries, Wolf
Run Shoals, and Sangster's Station to Centreville.   This
march was devoid of particular incident, though the

first and second days were excessively fatiguing on account of the dust and heat. The corps remained at Centreville from the 13th to the 21st, when it moved across Bull Run to Thoroughfare Gap, to watch the passes in the mountains. It was withdrawn from that position on the 24th, and simultaneously the Confederate General Stewart's cavalry passed up the turnpike from New Baltimore to Gainesville, and at Haymarket fired a few shots from a battery into the flanks of the corps. The battery was rapidly driven off, and Stewart proceeded on the raid which had no other substantial result than to deprive Lee of his important services at Gettysburg at the most critical juncture.

The night of the 24th the corps camped at Gum Spring. General Abercrombie's troops from Centreville joined the corps at this point, and, as General Abercrombie was with it but one day, General Alexander Hays became the senior officer present with the Third Division, and fell to its command, General French having been relieved from the command of the Third Division on the 24th, and assigned elsewhere.

On the morning of the 25th the corps crossed the Potomac at Edward's Ferry. On the following day it moved to Sugar Loaf Mountain, and on the morning of the 27th to Monocacy Junction, near Frederick, Maryland. General Meade assumed command of the army on this day, relieving General Hooker. On the 29th the army was again in motion, the Second Corps reaching a point one mile beyond Uniontown at 10 P. M., where it halted. Here it remained until the morning of July 1st, when it marched to Tancytown, arriving there about 11 A. M. General Hancock, having ridden to General Meade's headquarters and reported to him in person, was

now made acquainted with the army commander's plan
to deliver battle on Pipe-clay Creek.

General Hancock had hardly returned to his command after this interview, when he received a communication from General Meade, announcing that General
Reynolds, commanding the left wing of the army, had
been killed or badly wounded in a conflict with the enemy in front of Gettysburg, and directing General Hancock to proceed to the front, and, in case of the truth
of General Reynolds's death, assume command of the
Eleventh, First, and Third Corps.

The loss of General Reynolds, especially at this time,
when General Meade relied upon his ability and soldierly
qualities, in view of the coming operations, was felt as a
most serious blow.

The following is a copy of the order directing General Hancock to proceed to the front and assume command of the troops assembled there:

> "HEADQUARTERS, ARMY OF THE POTOMAC,
> "*July* 1, 1863, 10 P. M.

" *Commanding Officer, Second Corps :*

"The Major-General commanding has just been informed that General Reynolds has been killed or badly
wounded. He directs that you turn over the command of
your corps to General Gibbon; that you proceed to the
front, and, by virtue of this order, in case of the truth of
General Reynolds's death, you assume command of the
corps there assembled, viz., the Eleventh, First, and Third
at Emmettsburg. If you think the ground and position
there a better one on which to fight a battle, under existing circumstances, you will so advise the General, and he
will order all the troops up. You know the General's

views, and General Warren, who is fully aware of them, has gone out to see General Reynolds."

"*Later*, 1.15 P. M.

"Reynolds has possession of Gettysburg, and the enemy are reported as falling back from the front of Gettysburg. Hold your column ready to move.

"Very respectfully, your obedient servant,

(Signed) "D. BUTTERFIELD,

"*Major-General, and Chief of Staff.*"

It will be observed that by this order General Meade placed General Gibbon in command of the Second Corps over the heads of his two seniors, Hays and Caldwell; that General Hancock was placed in command over his seniors—Generals Howard and Sickles—and that General Hancock was to advise General Meade whether the ground and position, under existing circumstances, was a "better one" on which to fight a battle, that all the troops might be ordered up. The copy of this order filed by General Meade before the Committee on the Conduct of the War differs by some error from the order received by General Hancock; and differs also in the same particular from the one filed with the same committee by General Butterfield, Chief of Staff of the Army of the Potomac, who signed the original order. In that the word "better" is placed in parenthesis, and the word "suitable," which does not occur in the copy received by General Hancock, is inserted immediately after it.

General Hancock called General Meade's attention to the fact that Generals Howard and Sickles ranked him. General Meade replied in substance that he could not help that; that General Hancock knew his views; that this was an emergency in which he could not stand on such a point, and that he had authority to assign to command those he deemed most suited for the occasion without regard to rank. This explains his action in reference to the assignment of General Gibbon over his seniors also.

General Hancock started for Gettysburg immediately upon receiving General Meade's order, turning over the command of the Second Corps to General Gibbon, accompanied by several of his staff-officers, and rode rapidly, closely scanning the ground on the route, as he had been instructed by General Meade to do with a view of noting the defensive positions which would be available, should that part of our force engaged at Gettysburg retire along that road. About half way between Taneytown and Gettysburg, an ambulance was met, accompanied by a single staff - officer, and bearing the body of General Reynolds.

As General Hancock passed along the road, he ordered all trains which would interfere with the movements of troops either way to march as rapidly as possibly to their destinations, so as to clear the road of obstruction.

About 3.30 P. M. he reached Cemetery Hill, where he met General Howard, and informed him that he had been ordered to assume command. General Howard acquiesced. No time was spent in conversation, the pressing duty of the moment being to determine our line of action, and to restore order among our troops, who were then retiring hurriedly through the town of Gettysburg, pursued by the enemy. Buford's cavalry, in an imposing array, was holding the open ground to the left and front of Cemetery Hill. General Buford himself was on Cemetery Hill with General Warren, where General Hancock met them for a moment. Generals Howard,

Warren, and Buford all gave their assistance in forming
our troops. In describing this particular moment, in the
progress of events, Swinton says ("Army of Potomac,"
page 334) : "As the confused throng was pouring through
Gettysburg, General Hancock arrived on the ground.
He had not brought with him his tried Second Corps,
but had ridden forward from Taneytown, under orders
from General Meade, to assume command and use discretionary power, either to retain the force at Gettysburg
or retire it to the proposed line of Pipe-clay Creek ; but
on his arrival he found a more pressing duty forced upon
him ; for it was clear that, if the flight of the shattered
masses of the First and Eleventh Corps was not stayed,
a great disaster must follow. In such an emergency it is
the personal qualities of a commander alone that tell.
If, happily, there is in him that mysterious but potent
magnetism that calms, subdues, and inspires, there results
one of those sudden moral transformations that are among
the marvels of the phenomena of battle. This quality
Hancock possesses in a high degree, and his appearance
soon restored order out of seemingly hopeless confusion
—a confusion which Howard, an efficient officer, but of
rather a negative nature, had not been able to quell."

Very soon the enemy's line of battle was seen advancing up the ravine between the town and Culp's Hill, southeast of the town. Wadsworth's division (First Corps) and
Hall's Fifth Maine Battery were sent at once to the western slope of Culp's Hill, which important position they
held during the entire battle. The brave Wadsworth was
by no means weakened or daunted by the day's work, but
was still full of fight. With reference to Ewell's advance
toward Culp's Hill on the evening of July 1, Lee's report
says : "General Ewell was therefore instructed to carry

the hill occupied by the enemy, if he found it practicable, but to avoid a general engagement until the arrival of the other divisions, which were ordered to hasten forward. In the mean time the enemy occupied the point which General Ewell designed to seize (Culp's Hill)." It will be seen, therefore, that the movements just narrated were very important ones. The lines having been established to deter the enemy from further advance, General Hancock dispatched his senior aide-de-camp, Major W. G. Mitchell, with a verbal message to General Meade, that "General Hancock could hold Cemetery Hill until nightfall, and that he considered Gettysburg the place to fight the coming battle." Major Mitchell left the battle-field (Cemetery Hill) about 4 P. M., and arrived at General Meade's headquarters between 6 and 7 P. M. Having delivered. General Hancock's message to General Meade in the presence of General Williams, Adjutant-General of the Army of the Potomac, General Meade replied, "I will order up the troops." The following is the disposition of troops as made by General Hancock on the evening of July 1st: The First Corps, except Wadsworth's division, which was posted as before stated, was on the right and left of the Taneytown road; the Eleventh Corps on the right of the Taneytown road on both sides of the Baltimore turnpike; Geary's division of the Twelfth Corps, having come up in advance of its corps commander, General Slocum, was ordered to occupy the high ground (Little Round Top) to the right of and near "Round Top," commanding the Gettysburg and Emmettsburg road, as well as the road to our rear.

CHAPTER XI.

THE Second Army Corps, which had been directed by General Meade to follow General Hancock to Gettysburg, had marched from Taneytown about 1.30 P. M. of the 1st, and bivouacked that night about three miles from Gettysburg, in a position to secure our left flank from any turning movement (around Round Top) by the enemy, or from any seizure of the road leading toward Taneytown from the direction of Emmettsburg. General Hancock directed a regiment of the Second Corps to be placed, on the evening of July 1st, at the bridge over Pipe-clay Creek, on the Taneytown road, so as to secure it from destruction, and to keep open our communications with the battle-field and to the rear.

By daylight on the morning of the 2d, General Hancock joined the Second Corps (which moved on to the field of Gettysburg), and formed it on the left of the Eleventh Corps, prolonging the line from the left of

Cemetery Hill toward Round Top until it connected with
the Third Corps. The divisions were posted from right
to left, in the order of Hays, Gibbon, and Caldwell.
Each division had one of its brigades in the rear of its
line in reserve. The light batteries of the corps were
posted from right to left, as follows : Woodruff's, Arnold's, Cushing's, Brown's, and Rorty's. The morning
was enlivened by some very sharp skirmishing, especially
on Hays's front; with this exception, and some irregular
artillery firing, the day passed in comparative quiet until
about 3 P. M., when the Third Corps (General Sickles)
advanced from its position in the line of battle toward
the "peach-orchard" and the Emmettsburg road. By this
movement the Third Corps lost connection on its right
and left flanks. It soon became heavily engaged with the
enemy. Its right flank was separated from the left of
the Second Corps, and in this interval General Gibbon,
commanding Second Division, Second Corps, placed the
Eighty-second New York and Fifteenth Massachusetts
regiments of infantry, and Brown's Rhode Island Battery.
The enemy's attack on Sickles forced him back, and, an
immediate call for reënforcements being made, General
Hancock was directed by the commander of the army
to send a division of the Second Corps to the assistance
of the Third, with orders to report to Major-General
Sykes, commanding Fifth Corps, whose troops were then
engaged on the left of the Third Corps. Caldwell's
division of the Second Corps was sent on this service.
Willard's brigade, Third Division, Second Corps, was sent
to the support of Birney's division, Third Corps, and two
regiments (Devereux's Nineteenth Massachusetts, and Mellon's Forty-second New York) to the assistance of Humphreys' division, Third Corps. At this juncture General

Hancock was informed by General Meade that General Sickles was disabled, and was instructed to take command of the Third Corps in addition to his own, and General Gibbon again succeeded to the command of the Second Corps. General Hancock led in person the brigade intended for Birney's support toward the left of the original line of battle of the Third Corps, and was proceeding with it to the front when he met General Birney, who told him that his troops had all been forced to the rear, abandoning the ground to which General Hancock was marching with Willard's brigade. Humphreys' division, Third Corps, was still in position, but, the enemy pressing him hard in front, and driving him at all points, he was forced back to the original line of battle, being placed by General Hancock on the line vacated by Caldwell's division, when it moved to General Sickles' support earlier in the fight.

In regaining this line General Humphreys suffered severe losses, but succeeded in preserving the organization of his command. The Nineteenth Massachusetts and Forty-second New York regiments, which, as before stated, had been sent to his support, had not arrived on his line when he commenced his retreat, but, observing that he was rapidly retiring, those regiments formed line of battle, delivered a few volleys, and then retired in good order, though suffering heavy losses. So closely were they pressed by the enemy that prisoners were captured by the retreating regiments. Brown's Rhode Island Battery and the regiments of Ward (Fifth Massachusetts) and Huston (Eighty-second New York), before mentioned, were still less fortunate. Having done good service in protecting General Humphreys' right, their left was exposed to the enemy's attack, and they were

forced back, losing both commanders and a large number
of other officers and men.   The battery was gallantly
served, but continued its fire so long that it could not be
entirely withdrawn, one gun falling into the enemy's
hands.   Captain Brown received a dangerous but not mortal wound.   Willard's brigade was placed by General Hancock on the line of battle at the point through which
Birney's troops had retired, and, as the enemy were following sharply, the brigade became almost immediately
engaged, losing heavily.   Colonel Willard was struck in
the face by a piece of bursting shell and killed, in General
Hancock's presence, at the moment when the General had given him his instructions.   The reënforcement
for which General Hancock had sent to General Meade
now began to come up, and our line was strengthened by
Doubleday's division and a portion of Robinson's division
(First Corps).   The enemy were then advancing along
nearly the entire front of General Hancock's line.   Gibbon's troops promptly checked the enemy's attack from
the direction of the brick house on the Emmettsburg road,
and the lost gun of Brown's battery was recaptured.

The Nineteenth Maine, Colonel Heath, bore a conspicuous part in this operation.   When it was seen that
the enemy were following the broken troops of the Third
Corps in great force, General Hancock dispatched Major
Mitchell, his senior aid, to General Meade for reënforcements.   Major Mitchell met General Meade just as the
latter was riding down the Taneytown road near his headquarters (a small white house), and delivered General
Hancock's request to him.   General Lockwood, with part
of his brigade (two regiments), was then marching down
that road, and the head of his column had just passed the
house mentioned.   General Meade said that those troops

should go to General Hancock, and sent one of his staff
with Major Mitchell to so inform General Lockwood.
When that officer received the orders from General
Meade, he asked Major Mitchell to point out the position he was required to move to, when Major Mitchell
told him to have the fence thrown down, just where the
head of his column had halted, and to move at once up
to the crest of the hill. This was promptly done; the
troops moved through the passage in the fence, formed
line, and, guided by Major Mitchell, who remained with
General Lockwood, moved up to the crest, and at once
came into action on the left of the troops of the Second
Corps. This part of our line was not continuous, owing
to Caldwell's division having been taken out of it, and
the breaking of Sickles' corps leaving a space which offered to the enemy a good opportunity to penetrate our
lines. While General Hancock was riding along the
line, approaching the position of the Second Corps, he
observed a Rebel regiment about penetrating one of the
intervals, firing as it advanced, Captain Miller, one of
the General's aides, who was riding at his side, being
wounded severely by its fire. Turning to one of our
regiments which was approaching in column of fours
to protect that point, General Hancock said to the commander, pointing to the Rebel flag: "Do you see those
colors?" "Yes, sir." "Well, capture them." The
commander smiled and said, "I will, General." The regiment charged as it was formed, in column of fours, in the
most gallant manner, dispersing the Rebel regiment and
capturing its colors and a number of prisoners. While
General Hancock was absent, wounded, after Gettysburg, he caused inquiry to be made with a view of ascertaining the regiment which had made this brilliant attack,

5

as he desired to recommend its commander for promotion. Knowing that several corps were represented at or near that portion of our line, he caused a circular letter to be sent to the different corps commanders to obtain the required information. In this letter he described the commander of the regiment and his horse. Strange to say, several claimants were found for the honor, but the regiment was in truth one of the General's own corps, the heroic First Minnesota.

In this attack, and the subsequent advance upon the enemy, that regiment lost seventy-five per cent. of its numbers. One of Stannard's Vermont regiments afterward advanced upon the right of the First Minnesota, and was instrumental in bringing off the abandoned guns of one of our batteries, from which the cannoneers had been driven, and which was then under the enemy's fire.

With the assistance of the reënforcements sent to him, General Hancock was speedily enabled to repulse the enemy, and to reëstablish the line as it had been before the Third Corps moved out toward the Emmettsburg road. Colonel Sherrill succeeded to Colonel Willard in command of the brigade of the Third Division, and with it made a gallant advance on the enemy's batteries to the right of the brick house. The One Hundred and Eleventh New York, Colonel McDougall commanding, bore a conspicuous part in this advance. The brigade lost fifty per cent. of its numbers, and showed by its gallant conduct on that field that its capture at Harper's Ferry the year before was not due to lack of mettle. Colonel Sherrill was killed the next day (the 3d), and Colonel McDougall being wounded, left the brigade in command of a lieutenant-colonel.

It is now time to follow the fortunes of Caldwell's

division (First), Second Corps. As it neared the line
General Sykes had been ordered to assume on the left of
the Third Corps, it was met by a staff officer of General
Sykes, and moved forward, part of the time at the double
quick, into the interval between the Third and Fifth
Corps, with orders to check and drive back the enemy.
The First Brigade, commanded by Colonel Edward E.
Cross, Fifth New Hampshire Volunteers, was in the advance, and drove the enemy in splendid style across the
wheat-field in its front. The Second and Third Brigades,
commanded by Colonel Patrick Kelly, Eighty-eighth New
York Volunteers, and Brigadier-General Zook, were also
put in to extend the line toward the Third Corps, and
likewise drove the enemy before them. The Fourth
Brigade, Colonel John P. Brooke commanding, was afterward directed to advance to relieve the First Brigade,
which was hard pressed. With his accustomed gallantry and energy, Brooke pushed his line farther to the
front than any other of our troops advanced during the
battle, and gained a position impregnable from an attack
in his front and of great tactical importance. Brooke
himself was slightly wounded. Having thus established
the line of his division, and having been reënforced by
Sweitzer's brigade of the Fifth Corps, General Caldwell
passed to the right with a view of making a connection
between his division and the left of the Third Corps,
but found all the troops there broken and retreating under the pressure of the enemy, and before Caldwell could
change front the enemy gained the ground on his right
and rear, and compelled his division to retire to a position
near the Taneytown road, where it remained until relieved by a part of the Twelfth Corps.

On returning to the Second Corps, on the evening of

July 2d, Caldwell took up position on the left of the other division of the corps, covering the ground vacated by the Third Corps, but not closely connecting with the Second Corps. The interval between his right and the left of Gibbon's division was filled by troops of the First Corps, which had been sent up during the day's battle to reën- force our line. It thus happened that Caldwell's division was separated, and took no very active part in repulsing the enemy's final assault on the 3d. Had the division resumed its proper place in the line when it returned from General Sykes on the 2d, the grand attack of the 3d would have been met entirely by the Second Corps, and its measure of glory would have been greater, if possible.

The losses of the First Division in its operations on the 2d were over twelve hundred ; its whole strength engaged being but a little over three thousand men. Two of its brigade commanders, Brigadier-General Zook and Colonel Cross, were killed, and a third, Colonel Brooke, was wounded. Colonel Richard P. Roberts, One Hundred and Fortieth Pennsylvania Volunteers, was also among the killed in that division.

Colonel Cross was an eccentric character, but an in- valuable soldier. He was a rigid disciplinarian, and used to say his regiment, the Fifth New Hampshire, *dared* not go back without orders. It would seem as if some one had neglected to give them their orders at Gettysburg, for that heroic regiment, numbering about one hundred and fifty muskets, had over one hundred casualties, and *the killed exceeded in numbers the wounded.*

If Colonel Cross ever knew fear, it was not known to others. He had been wounded severely several times, and was conspicuous on every field for his defiant bravery.

At Chancellorville, on the morning of May 3d, when our lines were about to be withdrawn, Colonel Cross made up his mind that the affair was "played out," as he expressed it, and, seating himself on the ground in front of his regiment, in the most composed manner, with the lid of a cracker-box for a desk, indited his report of the battle under a heavy fire of artillery. He had led an adventurous life before the war, one of its incidents having been a duel with Sylvester Mowry in Arizona.

Here occurred a curious instance of prevision of impending death. On the morning of the 2d, General Hancock said to Colonel Cross: "Colonel, I feel satisfied that to-day will bring you your promotion." The reply was: "General, this is my last day."

It was nearly dark on the 2d when the action had entirely ceased on the front of the Second Corps; and it was soon followed by very heavy firing on General Howard's line on Cemetery Hill. This firing seeming to come nearer and nearer, General Hancock directed General Gibbon to send Carroll's brigade of Hays's division to report to General Howard at once to reënforce him; and, hearing sharp firing at the same time still further to the right, on Slocum's line, and fearing that the troops which the latter had sent to his assistance had left him insufficient force, General Hancock ordered that two regiments should be sent to Slocum (Twelfth Corps). By some mistake these regiments also went to General Howard, instead of to their intended destination.

When Carroll's brigade arrived on Howard's front, the enemy had nearly carried the position. The artillerymen in Stewart's and Rickett's batteries ("B," Fourth United States Artillery, and "F," First Pennsylvania) were defending themselves with sponge-staffs and rammers, or whatever they could lay hands on, the bugler of Rickett's battery having had his brains knocked out by a trail-handspike in the hands of one of the enemy.

Carroll formed his line as best he could in the darkness, and with stentorian tones ordered the charge and swept the hill. It was thought afterward that the services rendered by Carroll's brigade were not so generously acknowledged, in General Howard's official report, as they should have been, and several letters were subsequently published on the subject, the point in controversy being, not how well Carroll's troops did, for as to this there was no question, but as to the pinch to which Howard was reduced when Carroll arrived to sustain him. General Howard himself admitted that affairs were critical, and the reënforcements unexpected—although it was afterward claimed that the brigade was sent in pursuance of a request from General Howard. But, in fact, the brigade was sent by General Hancock, solely upon his own motion and responsibility, when he heard the heavy firing at that point. General Howard may have sent a request to General Hancock for help, but, if so, it was not received, and was not the cause of his action in the premises. The brigade was retained during the remainder of the battle, as well as one of two regiments which, as has been stated, joined him by mistake.

CHAPTER XII.

On the evening of the 2d, after dark, while the firing still continued on Howard's and Slocum's front, a council of war was held at General Meade's headquarters, which General Hancock attended as commander of the left center of the army, General Gibbon being present as the immediate commander of the Second Corps, and General Birney as commander of the Third Corps.

The question was submitted to the council whether there should be any change in the position of the army. On this question the vote appears to have been unanimous to remain, though one or two generals present expressed the opinion that Gettysburg was not the place to fight the battle—or not an advantageous one.

The forenoon of the 3d passed in comparative quiet, as far as General Hancock's infantry was concerned, though the artillery was frequently and warmly engaged. The heavy and continuous firing in front of the Twelfth Corps indicated that the main efforts of the enemy were on that point.

From 11 A. M. until about 1 P. M. the silence was ominous, this being the interval of time when the enemy was placing his artillery and forming his lines for the grand attack on the third day. About the latter hour the cannonade opened upon our lines from one hundred and twenty guns, as if at a preconcerted signal. General Hancock was with General Meade and other general officers at that time, just in rear of the line of battle of the Second Corps, and was engaged in dictating an order to one of his staff, when the first shell fell into his group, killing one man and wounding several others. The shells now fell thicker and faster every moment, indicating plainly important impending events, and sending each one speeding to his post. General Hancock rode at once to the right of his line of battle, and from thence passed along it for a mile or more, with his staff and orderlies, under a furious fire, to its extreme left, in order to inspire confidence among his troops.

The batteries on our line responded promptly to the enemy's fire, but were greatly inferior in numbers, we having but about eighty guns in position at that time. Our artillery fire (in obedience to instructions from army headquarters) was not maintained as fully as it could have been, owing to the fact that our reserve ammunition was not abundant. General Hancock insisted that the enemy should be stoutly answered by the batteries on his line, and especially by those placed at our weakest points, which it was desirable should not be attacked, feeling confident that an infantry assault was impending against his lines, and because of the moral effect a cessation of our artillery fire would have upon our men. Nearly all of our ammunition, canister excepted, was expended. During this fire quite a number of caissons on our line were blown up—four in Thomas's battery alone, and the troops, especially the artillery, suffered severely during the cannonade, it being generally posted on the high ground in rear of the infantry. Its losses, in horses and material, were particularly great.

After the artillery firing had continued for an hour and three quarters, it slackened, and a strong line of the enemy's skirmishers immediately advanced from the fringe of woods beyond the Emmettsburg road, followed by an attacking column composed of about 18,000 infantry, led by Pickett's division in double line of battle, the brigades of Kemper and Garnett in front, and Armistead's brigade supporting. On his right was Wilcox's brigade, formed in column of battalions, and on his left Heth's division. As soon as the enemy's skirmishers made their appearance, General Hancock again rode along his lines to the right to encourage the troops, and to notify the commanders that the enemy was about to make his assault. It was quite remarkable that the General's favorite horse, one he had ridden in many battles, and always found reliable, became so terrified, just as the enemy's column was approaching our line, that it became utterly powerless, and could not be forced to move when the General wished to ride to the threatened point. He was therefore obliged to borrow a horse from one of his staff, Captain Brownson (son of Rev. Orestes Brownson), Commissary of Musters, Second Corps, dismounting that officer, and saying to him: "You can afford to have a horse of this kind, Captain, on such an occasion as this, but I can not."

Captain Brownson was a reliable and gallant·young officer, and was killed the following year at the battle of Ream's Station.

On arriving at the right of his line, he discovered that the troops across the Taneytown road, on Cemetery Hill, had been withdrawn during his absence, and fearing an attack at that point, from the manner in which the enemy's bullets were striking the fence in front as he passed by, he rode down to General Meade's headquarters, a few hundred yards, to ask that troops might be sent there at once from another command to fill the gap. Finding, however, that General Meade had left his headquarters, he rode to the point of assault, the troops cheering him as he passed by them along the lines. The assaulting column was then advancing rapidly. Our men evinced a striking disposition to withhold their fire for close quarters, and the enemy's advance had been for a time opposed only by an irregular artillery fire. Alex. Hays had several regiments posted well to the front behind stone walls, and on his extreme right was Woodruff's battery of light twelves. Whether the fire was closer here, or whether, as some claim, the troops in Pettigrew's command were not as well seasoned to war as Pickett's men, it is certain that the attack on Hays was very speedily repulsed. That it was pressed with resolution was attested by the dead and wounded on the field, which were as numerous on Hays's front as on any other part of it. The execution by the canister of Woodruff's battery at this point was very great. The enemy closed in toward their center to escape it, seeing which young Woodruff ordered a section to advance to secure an enfilade fire. While pointing to the proposed position, he was shot in the side and fell from his horse.

The mortal wound, however, did not prevent him from urging the execution of his order. On the left of the line, fire was first opened upon the enemy from two regiments of Stannard's Vermont brigade, First Army Corps, which were placed in a small grove some distance in front of and obliquely to the main line. Either to escape this fire, or for some other reason, the enemy's right closed in to their left, so that the center was urged forward against Gibbon's division by the pressure of both wings. Two regiments of Webb's brigade of that division, the Sixty-ninth and Seventy-first Pennsylvania Volunteers, were posted behind a low stone wall and breastwork of rail, hastily constructed on the slope toward the enemy. The rest of this brigade was behind the crest, some sixty paces in the rear, so posted as to enable them to fire over the heads of the two regiments in front. When the enemy's line had nearly reached the stone wall, the greater portion of the advanced regiments retired to the main line, but were rallied on the line in the rear by General Webb and his officers. It was thought at the time that this movement was due to the fact that these regiments were isolated from their brigade, and were posted on a down-hill slope. Whatever the reason, their partial retreat emboldened the enemy to push their advantage, numbers of them crossing our breastworks, led by General Armistead, who had the advance of the enemy's column. At this moment Cushing's guns, which were in advance of Webb's general line, seemed likely to fall into the hands of the enemy, and Lieutenant Cushing, their gallant commander, was instantly killed.

About this time General Gibbon was severely wounded. General Hancock passing along at this moment, Colonel

Devereux (Nineteenth Massachusetts Volunteers) begged to be permitted to move his regiment to the point of danger; General Hancock granted his request, and his regiment and Colonel Mellon's Forty-second New York were at once moved accordingly. Hall's brigade of Gibbon's division was also moved by the right flank (the enemy having been repulsed in his front), and was immediately followed by Harrow's brigade of the same division. These movements led to some confusion, owing principally to the fact that some of their men left their ranks while they were marching by the flank to fire at the enemy, and regimental organizations were, in a measure, lost. But individually all were firm.

Webb, Hall, Mellon, Devereux, and other gallant officers carried the men forward, and a color-sergeant of the Seventy-second Pennsylvania Volunteers advancing with his colors, the men pressed firmly on, and after a few moments of desperate fighting, almost breast to breast, the enemy's line was broken. They sought safety in flight, and threw themselves on the ground, as a means of surrender, to escape our fire. General Hunt, Chief of Artillery, Army of the Potomac, was also at the front of the assault at this time, and behaved with great personal gallantry; and Major Mitchell (General Hancock's Adjutant-General) and Lieutenant Haskell, both on horseback, were in the front rank of the troops engaged in this final struggle. General Hancock himself, seeing some troops unfavorably placed somewhat to the left and front, rode across to them; but, before reaching them, he met a small detachment which he supposed to be a decimated battalion of the Second Corps, which was firing into the enemy's flank. As it contained but fifteen or twenty files, he thought it too small to effect much, and ordered it to fall back to the line of the troops before mentioned (Stannard's Vermont brigade), telling the commander he would advance them altogether. From thence General Hancock passed along the front of Stannard's line (which was lying down in ranks), and behind it to the right, when he met General Stannard, and directed him to send two of his regiments to attack the enemy's right.

Turning again toward the point of assault, to which the enemy still adhered, General Hancock was shot from his horse. At the moment the General was hit, all of his staff officers were absent from him on other parts of the field, and he was accompanied only by his tried and faithful color-bearer, Private James Wells, Sixth New York Cavalry. The General was caught as he was falling from his horse by Lieutenants Hooker and Benedict, of General Stannard's staff. Major Mitchell, meanwhile, had ridden to Stannard's brigade and given an order in the General's name (but not knowing that the General had already given the order, or that he was present and wounded) to attack the enemy in flank.

In about fifteen minutes the Medical Director of the Second Corps, Surgeon M. A. Dougherty, arrived at the point where the General lay wounded, and immediately extracted from the wound several splinters of wood, some small pieces of lead, and a wrought-iron nail, which the ball had carried with it, as it passed through the General's saddle before it struck him. The nail wrapped itself around the ball, and the latter was flattened by striking the saddle and the bone of the General's thigh. Meanwhile, an ambulance had been sent for, and, after some time, the General was placed in it and removed to the field hospital of the Second Corps. A few moments after the General was shot, Major Mitchell joined him, and, as soon as he (General Hancock) saw that the enemy's assault was really broken—he could see the field by turning partly on his side, and raising himself on his elbow—he directed Major Mitchell to ride to General Meade with the following message : " Tell General Meade that the troops under my command have repulsed the enemy's assault, and that we have gained a great victory. The enemy is now flying in all directions in my front." Major Mitchell also informed General Meade that General Hancock had been dangerously wounded. General Meade returned the following reply to this message: " Say to General Hancock that I regret exceedingly that he is wounded, and that I thank him in the name of the country and for myself for the service he has rendered to-day."

As General Hancock was leaving the line of battle, he caused his ambulance to be stopped, while he dictated to Surgeon Dougherty, Medical Director, a note to General Meade, the substance of which was as follows : " We have won a victory, and nothing is wanted to make it decisive but that you should carry out your intention.* I have been severely, but I trust not seriously, wounded. I did not leave the field so long as there was a rebel to be seen upright."

No copy of this note was retained by General Han-

---

* This had reference to a previous conversation between Generals Meade and Hancock, in which General Meade had expressed his intention of putting in the Fifth and Sixth Corps, if Hancock was attacked. (See "Report of Committee on the Conduct of the War," vol. i, 1865, page 48, and General George Sykes's [Commander of Fifth Corps at Gettysburg] letter to editor of "Washington Chronicle," dated Fort Leavenworth, Kansas, December 9, 1856.)

GENERAL HANCOCK WOUNDED AT GETTYSBURG.

cock. It is presumed the original remained in General Meade's possession.

This ended General Hancock's connection with the memorable battle of Gettysburg. From the field hospital he was conveyed to the railway at Westminster, when he was placed in a car and carried to Baltimore, and from thence to Philadelphia, and finally to his father's house at Norristown, Pennsylvania.

It was at first supposed that his wound was caused by an explosive bullet; but after the battle it was discovered that the ball had passed through the pommel of the saddle the General had ridden, carrying with it the nail and piece of wood. The wound not healing kindly, was thoroughly probed six weeks afterward, when the ball was found to be imbedded in the General's thigh, near the bone, which it had injured badly. It was extracted after a painful operation by Surgeon L. M. Reed, Medical Director, Fifth Army Corps, Dr. William Corson of Norristown, Pennsylvania, General Hancock's family physician, and Surgeon George E. Cooper, United States Army. This wound has since given the General great pain and annoyance, but is now fully healed.

The casualties in the Second Army Corps during the great battle were 4,413, nearly 44 per cent. of all engaged. The "missing" numbered only 350 enlisted men, most of whom were captured from Caldwell's division, July 2d. Hays's division lost 1,382 men, Gibbon's 1,627, and Caldwell's 1,248.

The artillery brigade, consisting only of five batteries, lost 150 men and 250 horses. Three of the battery commanders were killed and one wounded. Of the killed, Woodruff and Cushing have been mentioned; the third was Rorty, commanding battery "B," First New York

Artillery, who was shot through the head while gallantly performing his duty. Besides those already mentioned were Colonel Denis O'Kane, Sixty-ninth Pennsylvania Volunteers; Colonel Max A. Thomans, Fifty-ninth New York Volunteers; Lieutenant-Colonel Steele, Seventh Michigan Volunteers; Lieutenant-Colonel Tschudy, Sixty-ninth Pennsylvania Volunteers; and Colonel Sherrill, One Hundred and Twenty-sixth New York Volunteers.

The prisoners captured numbered 4,500, exclusive of those secured by Caldwell's division on the 2d, of whom about one half fell to each of the two divisions engaged. Gibbon's division secured and turned in 12 stands of colors, and Hays's division 15 stands. The whole number of colors captured by the corps was 33; but several of them were secreted and disposed of as personal trophies.

CHAPTER XIII.

Gettysburg—Summing Up—General Lee's Intention to renew the Battle —Retreat of the Confederate Army—Killed and Wounded—Incidents of the Battle by an Eye-witness—Splendid Action of Hancock and his Staff—Longstreet's Advance—Magnificent Courage of the Southerners—The Philadelphia Brigade—Death of the Confederate General Armistead—General Hancock the Savior of Gettysburg.

THE battle of Gettysburg was one of the most magnificent of modern times. For three days the largest armies handled in modern warfare maintained a fierce and persistent struggle. More than 200 pieces of artillery, at intervals of this dreadful drama, belched forth missiles of destruction, and made the grand old hills tremble as with the thunders of heaven and the throes of volcanic fires. Never before had the horrible and the grand in human combat been blended in such sublime display. No painting, by either word or pencil, can adequately convey a conception of the stupendous features of this more than Titanic struggle. Each day every part of that extended battle-field presented terrible displays of the dread magnificence of war. But perhaps none was more sublimely impressive than the advance, on the third day, of Pickett's line of 18,000 men, in a tremendous charge upon that part of the Union line (the left center) held by the troops under Hancock's command. With the steady and solemn grandeur of the ocean's wave, they came sweeping on, undeterred by the storm of shell and grape and musketry which opened carnage gaps in their serried lines; and, although the North Carolinians, when they discovered that the force against which they were moving was not, as they had supposed, of unseasoned militia, like themselves, raised the cry "The Army of the Potomac!" and broke and ran, Pickett's brave Virginians pressed dauntlessly forward, rushed up the side of Cemetery Ridge, and fairly plunged into Hancock's line: "And Hancock, who had the day before turned the fortunes of battle in a similar emergency, again displayed those qualities of cool appreciation and quick action that had proved him one of the foremost commanders on the actual field of battle, and instantly drew together troops to make a bulwark against any further advance of the now exultant enemy." * This magnificent charge was repulsed with awful slaughter.

General Lee had thoughts of renewing the battle the next day, but found it impracticable; and he was reduced to the sad alternative of retreat, which involved the abandonment of the whole scheme of invasion, and all the bright hopes connected with it. He was convinced that the position of the Union army was impregnable. Still he did not hasten his retreat, but remained the whole of the next day (July 4th) in his position, somewhat retired, and sent off his impedimenta south and west. General Hancock believed that, if our troops had advanced on the evening of July 3d, with the Fifth and Sixth Corps, Lee's artillery would have been captured and his army destroyed.

Both armies sustained severe losses in this great conflict. On our side 2,834 were killed, 13,733 wounded,

* Swinton's "Army of the Potomac," p. 360.

and 6,643 missing—in all 23,210. No accurate account of the Confederate loss was ever obtained, but it was estimated at 36,000, of which number nearly 14,000 were prisoners.

In completing this account of the battle of Gettysburg, the following brief quotations will be found graphic and interesting. They are from the pen of Major-General St. Clair A. Mulholland, and were contributed to the Philadelphia "Times" of February 14, 1880. Describing a portion of the battle, the writer goes on as follows:

"Instantly the air was filled with bursting shells. The batteries that we had been watching for the last two hours going into position in our front did not open singly or spasmodically. The whole one hundred and twenty guns, which now began to play upon us, seemed to be discharged simultaneously, as though by electricity, and then for nearly two hours the storm of death went on. I have read many accounts of this artillery duel, but the most graphic description by the most able writer falls far short of the reality. No tongue or pen can find language strong enough to convey any idea of its awfulness. Streams of screaming projectiles poured through the hot air, falling and bursting everywhere. Men and horses were torn limb from limb; caissons exploded one after another in rapid succession, blowing the gunners to pieces. No spot within our lines was free from this frightful iron rain. The infantry hugged close the earth, and sought every slight shelter that our light earthworks afforded. It was literally a storm of shot and shell that the oldest soldiers there—those who had taken part in almost every battle of the war—had not yet witnessed. That awful rushing sound of the flying missiles, which causes the firmest heart to quail, was everywhere.

"At this tumultuous moment we witnessed a deed of heroism, such as we are apt to attribute only to the knights of the olden time. Hancock, mounted, and accompanied by his staff, Major Mitchell, Captain Harry Bingham, Captain Isaac Parker, and Captain E. P. Bronson, with the corps flag flying in the hands of a brave Irishman (Private James Wells, of the Sixth New York Cavalry), started at the right of his line, where it joined the Taneytown road, and slowly rode along the terrible crest to the extreme left of his position, while shot and shell roared and crashed around him, and every moment tore great gaps in the ranks at his side.

> " ' Stormed at with shot and shell
> Boldly they rode and well.'

"It was a gallant deed, and, withal, not a reckless exposure of life; for the presence and calm demeanor of the commander, as he passed along the lines of his men, set them an example, which an hour later bore good fruit, and nerved their stout hearts to win the greatest and most decisive battle ever fought on this continent. . . .

"At this moment silence reigned along our whole line. With arms at a 'right shoulder shift!' the division of Longstreet's corps moved forward with a precision that was wonderfully beautiful. It was now our turn, and the lines, that a few moments before seemed so still, now teemed with animation. Eighty of our guns opened their brazen mouths; solid shot and shell were sent on their errand of destruction in quick succession. We saw them fall in countless numbers among the advancing troops. The accuracy of our fire could not be excelled: the missiles struck right in the ranks, tearing and rending them in every direction. The ground over which they have passed is strewn with dead and wounded, but on they come. The gaps in the ranks are closed as soon as made. They have three quarters of a mile to pass exposed to our fire, and half the distance is nearly passed. Our gunners now load with canister, and the effect is appalling; but still they march on. Their gallantry is past all praise; it is sublime. Now they are within a hundred yards. Our infantry rise up, and pour round after round into these heroic troops. At Waterloo, the Old Guard recoiled before a less severe fire; but there was no recoil in these men of the South. They marched right on, as though they courted death. . . .

"At the most critical moment Hancock fell among his men, on the line of Stannard's Vermont brigade, desperately wounded; but he continued to direct the fight until victory was assured, and then he sent Major Mitchell to announce the glad tidings to the commander of the army. . . .

"Many noble officers and men were lost on both sides, and in the camp hospital they died in hundreds during the afternoon and night. The Rebel General Armistead died in this way. As he was being carried to the rear, he was met by Captain Harry Bingham, of Hancock's staff, who, getting off his horse, asked him if he could do anything for him. Armistead replied to take his watch and spurs to General Hancock, that they might be sent to his relatives. His wishes were complied with, General Hancock sending them to his friends at the first opportunity. Armistead was a brave soldier, with a chivalric presence, and came forward in front of his brigade, waving his sword. He was shot through the body, and fell inside of our lines. . . .

"On the morning of the 5th we found the enemy had

gone, and then what a scene! I think the fact was first
discovered by the troops on Culp's Hill, and what a cheer
went up! A cheer that swelled into a roar, and was
taken up by the boys on Cemetery Hill, rolled along the
crest to Round Top, and then back again. Cheers for the
Philadelphia Brigade, that stood a living wall against
which the hosts beat in vain. Cheers for Meade, the soldier 'without fear and without reproach,' who here began,
with a great victory, his illustrious career as commander
of the Army of the Potomac. Cheers for Hancock, who
had stemmed the tide of defeat on the first day, and selected the ground on which this glorious victory was
achieved; who, on the second day, had again stopped the
tide of Rebel victory, and restored our shattered lines;
and, on the third day, had met and repulsed the final assault, on which Lee's all was staked, and won the battle
that was really the death-blow of the rebellion."

An interesting incident in connection with General
Armistead's defection from the United States Army, at
the outbreak of the Rebellion, is related by General Hancock. It occurred at Los Angeles early in 1861. Armistead was there with Hancock, a captain and brevet major.
Virginia, his native State, called upon him to support her
cause, and, under the influence of this demand, he sided
with the Confederates. On leaving Los Angeles, he presented General Hancock with his major's uniform, saying that the latter "might some time need it." He also
placed in his hands for safe-keeping, and to be given to
his family if he should fall in battle, certain valuable private papers. These General Hancock sent to General
Armistead's sister (who had married a Union officer) at
the close of the war. Armistead also presented to Hancock a little prayer-book, which is still in the latter's pos-

session.   On a fly-leaf of the book is the following inscription: " Lewis A. Armistead.   Trust in God and
fear nothing."   It may be observed, by the way, that
General Hancock never needed the major's uniform ; he
skipped the grades from captain to brigadier-general.

CHAPTER XIV.

GENERAL HANCOCK, as has been already stated, returned to his father's house in Norristown, when unfitted
for active service by the severe wound which he received
at Gettysburg. It displays the nature of the popular
impression with regard to him, and particularly that of
his old friends and fellow townsmen in Norristown, that
General Hancock's painful journey from the field of battle was marked by expressions of popular interest all
along the route, and which culminated on his reaching
his childhood's home. The mode of his transportation
was in itself impressive. His form was extended upon a
stretcher placed upon the backs of the seats of the railway car, and was thus carried from Westminster to Baltimore, thence to Philadelphia, and from there to Norristown. His brilliant career had won the admiration of
his countrymen, and when the tidings of his wounding

spread abroad, universal sympathy was awakened, so that, wherever it was known that the wounded hero was passing, crowds flocked to obtain, if possible, a glance at the shattered form of one so celebrated. When he arrived at the Norristown station, he was met by a large detachment of the invalid guards, who tenderly placed him upon their shoulders and bore him along the streets to his parental home. As they passed along, crowds of the citizens of his native town gazed with silent and respectful sympathy upon the man who had gone from their midst a sprightly boy, and was now returned to them wounded and shaken, but bearing the highest military rank, the well-earned measure of brilliant heroism in many a battle. We can imagine but inadequately the mingled feelings of tenderness, pride, and gratitude with which that noble father and gentle mother would receive under such circumstances the son of their love and admiration. Nor can we fully conceive of the tide of thrilling memories that would crowd upon the General when he found himself lying helpless in the home of his boyhood, surrounded by so many of the companions of his youth.

But careful surgical attention, and the vigor of a sound constitution, produced slow but sure convalescence, and, although the wound was not entirely healed, and continued to give him serious trouble for many years, he eventually became entirely qualified for renewed active service in the field. Meanwhile, his enforced retirement was rendered less irksome by the many kind attentions which he received from his fellow citizens, expressions of their estimation of his character and public services. Among these was the presentation by some of the citizens of Norristown of an elegant service of plate (gold and silver) with the following inscription and device:

6

Surmounting the inscription was the badge of the Second Corps, the trefoil, or three-leaf clover. Such a token of regard, costly and valuable in itself, was doubly so coming from the companions of his boyhood, reversing in his case the proverb, that men are not apt to be honored in their own country and among their own kindred. Not only at Norristown, but in Philadelphia, in New York, and at West Point, he was greeted with enthusiastic manifestations of popular regard, when he was so far restored as to visit those places. His reception at his old military school at West Point was peculiarly cordial. There he had the gratification to meet the aged chieftain, General Scott, who highly complimented him upon the brilliancy of his services, and expressed the pride he felt in one who bore his name so gloriously.*

As soon as General Hancock was able to endure the journey, he set out to join his wife and children at Longwood, near St. Louis. In a letter to his father written at that place, dated October 12, 1863, he says:

"I threw aside my crutches a few days after my arrival,

---

* A letter is still in existence which was written by Captain, now General Hancock, to Lieutenant-General Scott, dated Los Angeles, California, March 1, 1861, in which the Captain expresses the most patriotic sentiments, deprecates the Secession movement, and intimates a wish that he may be permitted to render some service to the Union cause. Lieutenant-General Scott was at that time Commander-in-Chief of the army.

and now walk with a cane. I am improving, but do not yet walk without a little roll. My wound is still unhealed, though the doctors say it is closing rapidly; I find some uneasiness in sitting long in my chair, and can not yet ride. The bone appears to be injured, and may give me trouble for a long time. I am busy trimming up the forest trees in the lawn of 'Longwood,' which covers nearly eleven acres. . . . Allie and the children send their best love to you and mother. Please give my best love to mother.

"I remain, as ever, your affectionate son,

"WINFIELD S. HANCOCK."

While it is impracticable to detail here all of the manifestations of public regard, which, at about this time, were tendered to General Hancock, room must be made for mention of a few of these instances.

In February, 1864, the Select and Common Councils of Philadelphia passed the following resolutions:

"*Resolved*, By the Select and Common Councils of the City of Philadelphia, that the thanks of the citizens of Philadelphia are eminently due and are hereby tendered to Major-General Hancock, for his brilliant services in the cause of the Union, during the present unholy Rebellion against the authority of the Government and people of the United States.

"*Resolved*, That the use of Independence Hall be granted to General Hancock for the reception of his friends, and in order to afford the citizens of Philadelphia an opportunity to testify their personal regard for him, and their appreciation of his gallantry and patriotism.

"*Resolved*, That the Mayor of Philadelphia and the

Presidents of Councils be requested to carry these resolutions into effect; and that the Clerks of Councils be requested to furnish a copy of the same to General Hancock.

" ALEXANDER J. HARPER,

" *President Common Council.*

" JAMES LYND,

" *President Select Council.*

"Attest: WM. F. SMALL,

" *Clerk of Common Council, February 18, 1864.*

"Approved: ALEXANDER HENRY, *Mayor.*"

These resolutions were duly transmitted to General Hancock, and their receipt was acknowledged by him, under date of February 22d, in a graceful letter, accepting the tender of Independence Hall for a reception to his friends. In this letter the General said: "I am deeply sensible of the honor thus conferred, and do not feel at liberty, for many reasons, to decline the honor of a public reception, notwithstanding the doubt I may have as to my right, by accepting, to lay claim to such a testimonial. If I possess any such claims, it is due to the brave soldiers who have fought under my command, very many of whom are citizens of Philadelphia. To receive congratulations which may reflect credit upon them will be a sufficient reason for my acceptance. It will show them that their countrymen are not unmindful of their military services, and will stimulate them to greater deeds of heroism." The reception was held in Independence Hall on the afternoon of February 25, 1864, and was a most impressive occasion.

At about the same period the "Union League" of Philadelphia presented General Hancock with a handsome silver medal, struck in commemoration of its gratitude and admiration for his eminent public services.

Here may also be properly introduced the following resolution of Congress, passed unanimously by both Houses, and approved April 21, 1866. It was a recognition by the representatives of the entire country of the distinguished part borne by General Hancock in the battle of Gettysburg. The joint resolution of January 28, 1864, to which reference is herein made, omitted, by some strange inadvertence, to make any mention of the name of Winfield Scott Hancock:

"*Resolved*, by the Senate and House of Representatives, That in addition to the thanks heretofore voted by joint resolution, approved January 28, 1864, to Major-General George G. Meade, Major-General O. O. Howard, and to the officers and soldiers of the Army of the Potomac, for the skill and heroic valor which, at Gettysburg, repulsed, defeated, and drove back—broken and dispirited—the veteran army of the Rebellion : the gratitude of the American people and the thanks of their representatives in Congress are likewise due and are hereby tendered to Major-General Winfield Scott Hancock, for his gallant, meritorious, and conspicuous share in that great and decisive victory."

On March 2, 1864, General Ulysses S. Grant, who had captured Vicksburg, Mississippi, after a continuous siege, lasting from May 22 to July 4, 1863, and who, on this latter date, had been commissioned major-general in the United States Army, received his commission as lieutenant-general, and, on March 17, 1864, assumed command of the Union forces in Virginia, of which forces the Army of the Potomac was now reorganized into three corps : the Second, under Major-General Winfield Scott

Hancock; the Fifth, under Major-General Governeur K. Warren; and the Sixth, under Major-General Sedgwick, General Meade being still in chief command. " The three corps commanders," says Swinton, " were men of a high order of ability, though of very diverse types of character. Hancock may be characterized as the ideal of a soldier. Gifted with a magnetic presence and a superb personal gallantry, he was one of those lordly leaders who, upon the actual field of battle, rule the hearts of troops with a potent and irresistible mastery. Warren, young in the command of a corps, owed his promotion to the signal proofs he had given, first as Brigadier, then as Chief Engineer, and, latterly, as the temporary commander of the Second Corps. Sedgwick, long the honored chief of the Sixth Corps, was the exemplar of soldierly obedience to duty."

General Hancock, who had reported for duty at Washington on the 15th of December, 1863, proceeded thence to the headquarters of the Second Corps, then lying in winter cantonments on the Rapidan, near Stevensburg, Virginia, and resumed the command of the corps. He remained there a few weeks, when he was summoned to Washington, and requested by the authorities there to make a tour to some of the Northern States on recruiting service for the Second Corps. He was successful in securing large accessions to his corps, and, when these duties had been completed, rejoined the Army of the Potomac in March, 1864, and resumed his command. Soon after his return to the army, the reorganization, already alluded to, was effected, and the Second Corps was reënforced by adding to it two divisions of the Third Corps, the latter being discontinued. The three divisions constituting the Second Corps were consolidated into two;

and, as finally arranged, the divisions and brigades of the Corps were as follows:

First Division, Brigadier-General F. C. Barlow.
    First Brigade, Colonel N. A. Miles.
    Second Brigade (Irish), Colonel T. A. Smythe.
    Third Brigade, Colonel R. Frank.
    Fourth Brigade, Colonel J. R. Brooke.

Second Division, Brigadier-General John Gibbon.
    First Brigade, Brigadier-General A. S. Webb.
    Second Brigade, Brigadier-General J. P. Owens.
    Third Brigade, Colonel S. S. Carroll.

Third Division, Major-General D. B. Birney.
    First Brigade, Brigadier-General J. H. Ward.
    Second Brigade, Brigadier-General Alexander Hays.

Fourth Division, Brigadier-General J. B. Carr.
    First Brigade, Brigadier-General G. Mott.
    Second Brigade, Colonel W. R. Brewster.

    Inspector-General and Chief of Staff, Lieutenant-Colonel C. H. Morgan.
    Chief of Artillery, Colonel J. C. Tidball.

It will be observed that General Gibbon had rejoined his division, and that General Caldwell had been relieved from the command of the First Division, which was given to General F. C. Barlow. The latter was not a stranger to the division, having commanded one of the most distinguished regiments in it, the Sixty-first New York Volunteers, until severely wounded at Antietam, September 17, 1862. Immediately after the opening of this campaign, Brigadier-General Mott assumed command of the Fourth Division.

A few days before the opening of the campaign, the Second Corps was reviewed by General Grant. Over 30,000 men, the greater number of them veterans, marched by on that occasion, and presented, perhaps, the finest parade ever witnessed in the Army of the Potomac. But in less than one year this corps alone lost by the casualties of war, not only the vast numbers that had marched proudly by General Grant, but nearly 10,000 more, its casualties amounting to upward of 35,000 men, or about one-third of the entire forces operating against Richmond.

When the campaign of 1864 opened, the Confederate army, under General Lee, occupied the bluff ridges which skirt the south bank of the Rapidan, a position strong by nature, and so strengthened by works as to make a direct attack upon him impracticable. He could only be drawn from it by a turning movement. His left would have been more easily flanked; but that process would have carried Grant's army too far from its base of supplies. He determined, therefore, to cross the Rapidan by its lower fords, and turn Lee's right. Grant's original programme was to gain his adversary's rear, and he had given instructions to this effect to his corps commanders; but, as we shall see, the resistance to his progress by the enemy prevented the carrying out of this plan, and brought on the battles of the "Wilderness." Instead of retreating out of the region called by this name, Lee resolved to give battle in it.

The Wilderness is an extensive tract of table-land which stretches from the south bank of the Rapidan southward. It is seamed with ravines, and, with the exception of a few small clearings, is covered with a dense growth of dwarf timber and underbrush. The forward movement from the Union camps was commenced about midnight of the 3d of May, 1864.

Not to enter upon full details of these engagements, the operations of General Hancock are pertinent, and will be given with only such other material as shall render the narrative intelligible.

CHAPTER XV.

The Wilderness—Crossing the Rapidan—The Enemy in Force—Forming the Line of Battle—Attack of the Second Corps—Close Quarters in the Woods—Nightfall, and Cessation of Fighting—Brigadier-General Hays killed—A Serious Loss.

THE Second Corps moved from its camp on the night of May 3d, with between 29,000 and 30,000 men and officers fit for duty, embracing eighty-four regiments of infantry, and a brigade of artillery, consisting of nine batteries. During the campaign, about twenty-five regiments were added to the Corps, making the number of its regiments one hundred and nine.*

Crossing the Rapidan on the morning of the 4th at Ely's Ford, the Corps forming the left column of the army marched to Chancellorville and bivouacked for the night, General Hancock's headquarters being established at the edge of the small peach orchard from which his division, just one year and a day before, had drawn from the field by hand Lepine's Fifth Maine Battery, after it had lost all of its officers, cannoneers, and horses. The gallant young Kirby, who had been placed temporarily in command after its officers had been disabled, received his death-wound while in command of this battery. The bones of horses and half-buried dead were yet visible here and there on the field.

* Included in this reënforcement were Tyler's division of heavy artillery, then acting as infantry, and the "Corcoran Legion."

Lee had offered no opposition to the crossing of the river by the Union army. One hundred thousand men, with their enormous train of 4,000 wagons, were passed over the Rapidan without molestation. Why he made no resistance is not clear. But it is probable that he was willing that this vast mass of men and impedimenta should become entangled in the Wilderness, in hope that he might destroy or capture them. It was bold forbearance.

At 5 A. M. on the 5th, the Second Corps took up its line of march for Shady Grove Church, where the left of the army was to have rested, had the movement been uninterrupted.

The advance of the column was nearly an hour's march beyond Todd's tavern, when, at 9 A. M., hearing firing to the right, General Hancock halted, as the enemy had been discovered in some force on the Wilderness turnpike, and two hours later received orders from General Meade to move up the Brock road to its intersection with the Orange plank road. Birney's division, then in the rear, formed the head of the column in the retrograde march.

General Hancock preceded his troops to the point indicated, where he found General Getty, with his division of the Sixth Corps, who had secured and held possession of the Orange plank road and the Brock road after a hard fight. On his backward march from Todd's tavern, General Hancock met the reserve artillery of the army, which had followed his column from Chancellorville, and advised its commander to return with it to that point, as the movement of the Second Corps then in progress would leave him unprotected by the infantry, and from Chancellorville he could move up on either the Orange plank road or the old Wilderness turnpike.

The head of Birney's division arrived on the ground about 2 P. M., and the troops formed at once in two lines of battle on Getty's left, along the Brock road. Mott's and Gibbon's divisions followed immediately, forming in succession in two lines on Birney's left. Frank's brigade of Barlow's division was stationed at the junction of the Brock and Catharpen roads, and the remainder of the First Division was established on some high cleared ground in front of the Brock road, forming the left of our line. This elevated ground commanded the country for some distance to the right and left, and was the only point on our line of battle where artillery could have any effective range, and, indeed, the only ground on which it could be brought into battery. The whole artillery brigade was therefore massed with Barlow's division, except Dow's Sixth Maine Battery and one section of Rickett's F Company, First Pennsylvania. Dow was posted on the second line on Mott's left. The section of Rickett's battery was placed on the plank road under the orders of General Getty, who had been hotly engaged, and repulsed the enemy. Upon General Hancock's arrival, General Getty informed him that he momentarily expected an attack from the two divisions of Hill's corps, known to be immediately in the Wilderness, a few hundred yards in his front; and to meet this antici- .pated assault General Hancock at once ordered breastworks of logs and earth to be built along his entire front line of battle; subsequently a line of breastworks was also thrown up along the second line.

The formation of the lines was accomplished slowly on account of the narrowness of the Brock road (it was only wide enough for a column of fours), the density of the forest on either side of it, and the fact that it was impracticable to get the artillery out of the way of the infantry until the cleared ground, before mentioned, was reached.

At 2.15 P. M. General Hancock received a dispatch from Major-General Meade (commanding the Army of the Potomac), which stated that the enemy held the Orange plank road nearly to its junction with the Brock road (the point just referred to), and directing him to attack with his own troops and Getty's division, and to endeavor to connect with Warren (Fifth Corps) on the Orange plank road, also stating that Griffin's division of the Fifth Corps had been driven back on the Orange pike, and that Warren's left, Crawford's division, was within one mile of Parker's store. Fifteen minutes later another dispatch was received by General Hancock from army headquarters, stating that the enemy's infantry had driven our cavalry down the Orange plank road from Parker's store, and that a portion of A. P. Hill's corps was then moving on that road toward the intersection of the Brock road which Getty's troops were then holding. The same dispatch stated that Getty had been ordered to drive the enemy back on the Orange plank road, but that he might not be strong enough to do so, and General Hancock was directed to move out to support Getty toward Parker's store, to drive the enemy beyond that point, and to hold it and to unite with General Warren's left.

When these dispatches reached General Hancock, the greater portion of his command was marching up the Brock road from Todd's tavern, and was not yet in position to attack. General Hancock himself rode back along the column to hasten its movements, which, for reasons before given, were necessarily slow.

Between 3 and 4 P. M. orders were sent to General

Hancock from army headquarters to attack with Getty's division, and to support the advance with the entire Second Corps; but at this hour Birney's division (the leading one) was the only one formed, and it was therefore impracticable to execute the order at that moment.

At 4.15 P. M. General Getty moved out his division, on either side of the Orange plank road, under direct orders from General Meade, received while General Hancock was along the Brock road hurrying up his troops. When General Hancock returned to the junction of the Brock and Orange plank roads, he learned from General Getty that he was directed to attack without waiting for the Second Corps, and had already ordered his troops to advance. General Hancock told him that he regretted that he could not have waited until the Second Corps was up and formed, but he would reënforce him at once on his right and left, and support him as rapidly as possible.

Getty had not advanced more than three hundred paces into the dense wood when he encountered the enemy's line of battle, and the fight at once became so fierce that General Hancock ordered Birney forward with his own and Mott's division to Getty's assistance, although the formations which General Hancock had hoped to have completed before advancing to the attack were not yet perfected.

Birney moved into action on Getty's right and left, and a section of Rickett's Pennsylvania Battery advanced along the plank road just in rear of the infantry line.

The importance of General Hancock's design of having his attacking force thoroughly in hand before he assailed the enemy's line became very evident now, for the battle at once assumed such proportions that it was not easy to push reënforcements in sufficiently fast to sustain it.

At 4.30 P. M. Carroll's brigade, of Gibbon's division, was hurried into the fight on the right of the plank road, Owen's brigade, same division, following closely.

The "Irish Brigade," Colonel Thomas Smythe (who was the last general officer killed during the war), Second Delaware Volunteers, commanding, and Colonel John R. Brooke's brigade, both of Barlow's division, made a forcible attack on the enemy's right, and drove it back some distance.

The battle raged furiously until it became too dark to see (about 8 P. M.). The lines were very close together, at some points not more than fifty paces apart, and the thickets were so dense and tangled that it was impossible for the commanders to see how the battle was going, or to obtain any insight into the enemy's plans or intentions. The section of Rickett's battery which had gone into action on the plank road when Getty and Birney advanced suffered most severely in men and horses from the enemy's musketry. At one time it was captured, but was gallantly retaken by a detachment of the Eighth Ohio and Fourteenth Indiana regiments, of Carroll's brigade. It was then replaced by a section of Dow's Sixth Maine Battery. No decided advantage remained with either party when night set in, save that Smythe and Brooke had driven the enemy's right, as before stated, his left remaining firm, notwithstanding the fierce onset of our troops. His line, however, was in great confusion.

Among the killed during this day's battle was Brigadier-General Alexander Hays (a Pennsylvanian by birth), one of the most chivalrous and intrepid soldiers that ever wore a sword. He was a heroic leader of troops in battle, and his loss was irreparable to the Second Corps.

At Gettysburg, at Bristow's Station, at Mine Run, he had led his division, colors in hand, in full view of the enemy, where he was a mark for a thousand rifles, only to meet death in these tangled thickets, where his personal example could hardly be seen or felt by more than a single battalion.

CHAPTER XVI.

DURING the night of the 5th, General Hancock received orders to renew his attack on the morning of the 6th at 5 A. M. He was cautioned to look out for his left flank, and was informed that his right would be relieved by an attack of Wadsworth's division of the Fifth Corps and two divisions of the Ninth Corps under General Burnside. Getty's division, Sixth Corps, remained under General Hancock's orders.

Before the attack was commenced on the morning of the 6th, General Hancock was informed from army headquarters that Longstreet was passing up the Catharpen road to attack his flank. We shall see that this information had a decided effect upon the course of the action, and preparations were at once made for Longstreet's reception. Barlow's division was placed in position to oppose him, and the artillery was posted to cover the road leading from the Catharpen to the Brock road, along which it was supposed Longstreet would advance. A strong skirmish line was also thrown out covering the Brock road. These dispositions were made under the supervision of Major-General Gibbon, who commanded the left of General Hancock's line (his own and Barlow's divisions), and General C. H. Morgan, General Hancock's Chief of Staff.

General Birney was placed in command of the right (Third and Fourth divisions, Second Corps, and Getty's division, Sixth Corps).

At 5 A. M.—the hour appointed—Birney moved to the attack along the Orange plank road with his own, Mott's, and Getty's divisions. Carroll's and Owen's brigades of Gibbon's division followed in his support.

The battle at once opened, Birney assaulting with great vigor, and, after a bloody contest at close quarters with musketry alone, the enemy's line was broken at all points, and he was driven in confusion through the forest for about one and a half miles with much slaughter. The troops, having been thrown into some disorder by their long advance under fire through the dense thickets, were now halted by General Birney's orders to readjust the lines, General Birney personally informing General Hancock on the field of the necessity for this halt. About this hour Webb's brigade of Gibbon's division relieved Getty's division, Sixth Corps, which had lost very heavily. Getty's division reformed along the Brock road. At 7 A. M. General Hancock sent an aide to General Gibbon to order in a division upon the enemy's right to fight up toward the Orange plank road. The intended movement did not, however, take place in force.

Subsequent events made it plain that an attack by Barlow's entire division, at that time one of the most powerful in the army, if it had not resulted in the com-

plcte overthrow of the enemy, would at least have prevented the subsequent turning of Mott's left flank. We
shall see how the anticipated attack of Longstreet still
further paralyzed General Hancock's left wing.

At 8 A. M. Stevenson's division of the Ninth Corps
reported to General Hancock, at the intersection of the
Brock and plank roads, and reënforced Birney. Wadsworth's division of the Fifth Corps went into action on
the right of the plank road about the same hour, connecting with General Birney's line.

About this time General Hancock was notified from
army headquarters that General Burnside had pushed
forward nearly to Parker's store, and would attack with
two divisions across General Hancock's front to relieve
his troops.

Meantime the enemy made some demonstrations on
the left, which were the source of considerable uneasiness, until the receipt of a dispatch from army headquarters stating that General Sheridan with a division of
cavalry had been ordered to attack Longstreet (who was
supposed to be advancing in that direction).

At 8.50 A. M. Birney's, Stevenson's, Mott's, and Wadsworth's divisions, with Webb's, Carroll's, and Owen's
brigades of Gibbon's division, again advanced along the
Orange plank road, and the battle was resumed with more
fierceness and determination than ever, if that were possible. The action at this point had hardly been recom-
menced when the left flank was seriously threatened, the
enemy pressing forward their skirmishers, and opening
with their artillery, as if an advance was intended there.
Rapid firing was heard also in the direction of Todd's tavern, which was thought to be General Sheridan's troops attacking Longstreet there. To strengthen this impression,

one of those incidents, trivial in themselves, but which lead sometimes to great results, occurred. One of General Hancock's staff, who was engaged in constructing a defensive line across the Brock road on the left, hearing the firing in the direction of Todd's tavern, rode out for a mile and a half, to examine the country and to get what information he could concerning the state of affairs. Through an opening in the woods he saw a column of infantry moving, and, though not able to satisfy himself absolutely as to whether they were Confederate or Union soldiers, the officer reported the movement to General Hancock. It being certain that the troops seen were infantry, and that they were moving from the direction of Todd's tavern, General Hancock thought there was little room to doubt that it was Longstreet's column, and Brooke's brigade of Barlow's division was at once thrown into the works which had been constructed.

The column seen afterward proved to be a body of convalescents sent from "Convalescent Camp," near Alexandria, Virginia, to join their regiments. They had followed the route of the Second Corps across the Rapidan, and blundered down from Chancellorville to Todd's tavern at that inopportune moment, whence they retraced their steps by the Brock road into our lines. Their uniforms being gray with dust rendered it difficult at a distance to distinguish them from the Confederates.

Two other brigades, Leasure's, of the Ninth Corps, and Eustis's, of the Sixth, had come up and reported in the mean time to General Hancock, and were held in readiness to support Barlow, should they be required at that point.

The troops thus disposed of could have been spared (as it afterward turned out) to have reënforced the attack along the plank road, for Longstreet about this time abandoned his anticipated flank march, and came in to the assistance of Hill, who had been thoroughly used up. It was ascertained that General Sheridan had had an encounter with Stewart's cavalry.

About 10 A. M. another incident occurred on General Hancock's right, which drew off a portion of his attacking force at a critical hour of the day—General Meade sending him word that a brigade of the Fifth Corps (Cutler's) had fallen back out of the woods, considerably disorganized, reporting heavy losses, and that the enemy's skirmishers were within half a mile of General Warren's headquarters. General Meade stated that he had no troops which he could use to check this advance of the enemy, and directed General Hancock to take the necessary measures at once. General Birney was accordingly ordered to send two brigades to restore the line of the Fifth Corps, where it was reported broken on Warren's left. A short time afterward General Birney informed General Hancock that he had reëstablished connection with the Fifth Corps and restored the lines where Cutler had fallen back. It was at this time, while General Hancock was about to renew his advance along the plank road with a column of 20,000 men under Birney, and while he was receiving dispatches from his extreme left attributing the firing in that direction (Todd's tavern) to Longstreet, that the latter commenced his assault to relieve Hill's shattered corps.

Striking Frank's brigade of Barlow's division (on Mott's left), which had lost severely in the early part of the day, and had nearly exhausted its ammunition, Longstreet forced it rapidly back, and then, encountering the left of Mott's division, compelled it in turn to retire.

This vehement onset by Longstreet caused disorder among the troops, and, although General Hancock made great efforts to hold his advanced position along the plank road by *refusing* the left of his line, he was unable to do so on account of the disorganization of the troops before referred to, and the nature of the field, which prevented him from seeing or being seen for more than a few rods. The personal bravery and example which, on the heights at Gettysburg or on the bloody slope at Fredericksburg, might be seen by and restore confidence to thousands, on this field narrowed to the view of a single regiment.

It should be stated here that our troops had been for many hours previous to Longstreet's advance under a murderous musketry fire; many valuable officers whom they had been accustomed to follow had been lost; and that they had advanced a long distance through dense thickets where their formation had been partly broken. The weather also was excessively hot, and the men suffered from want of water.

General Hancock now ordered General Birney, who was in immediate command of this portion of our lines, to withdraw his troops from the forest, where it was almost impracticable to adjust the lines, and to reform them in our breastworks along the Brock road, our original line of battle. The enemy followed closely, but did not immediately assail our line—probably owing to the fact of Longstreet having been wounded at this moment.

To gain time, and to check the enemy, should he attempt to carry our breastworks while our lines were being reformed, General Hancock directed Colonel Leasure's brigade of the Ninth Corps to advance and sweep the thickets and woods along the front of our line to the right toward the Orange plank road, keeping his right about one hundred paces from our breastworks, to attack the enemy's right flank, if in position. These instructions were carried out by Colonel Leasure with great promptness and success. Forming his brigade at right angles to our line of breastworks, he marched across the entire front of Mott's and Birney's divisions, crossing the Orange plank road, and encountering, as he proceeded, what he believed to be a brigade of the enemy' forces, which fell back in disorder without engaging him. After he had very fully and intelligently executed General Hancock's orders, he resumed his position on our right in the line of battle.

During this morning's battle Colonel Carroll was shot through the arm. General Hancock meeting him, and supposing he was on his way to the hospital, asked him who would command his brigade during his absence. Carroll replied with some spirit that he " had not yet given up the command of his brigade, and was not yet done fighting."

No further movements of importance took place on either side until a few minutes after 4 P. M. (our efforts in the mean time being exerted to rearrange and perfect our lines), when the enemy advanced in force under the command of Lee in person, pushing forward until he came to the edge of the slashed timber, less than one hundred paces from our breastworks, when he halted and continued a heavy musketry fire. Though his fire was heavy, but little execution was done among our troops, owing to our breastworks and the conformation of the ground; but, after about thirty minutes of this work had passed, some of our men began to waver, and finally a portion of Mott's division and part of Ward's brigade of Birney's division in the first line gave way in considerable disorder.

General Hancock made great exertions to rally the men, and numbers of them were returned to the line of battle.

As soon as the break in our lines above referred to occurred, the enemy pressed forward, and some of his men reached our breastworks and planted their colors on them.

At this moment General Birney, who was standing just in rear of the section of Dow's battery, at the cross-roads, turned to Colonel Carroll, whose brigade was in two lines just on the right of the plank road, saying: "Carroll, you must put your brigade in there and drive the enemy back." With the promptness which always characterized that officer, when ordered against the enemy, he moved his brigade by the left flank across the plank road until opposite the point abandoned by our troops, and then by the right flank in double time, retaking the line with ease, and with the loss of a few men, the enemy falling back, suffering severely under the withering fire which our troops now poured into their ranks. On the opposite (left) flank of the break in our lines, reënforcements were promptly sent by General Gibbon, Brooke's brigade of Barlow's division having been just anticipated by Carroll's reaching the breastwork first and driving the enemy back. A portion of Dow's Sixth Maine battery on Mott's line handsomely assisted in the repulse of the enemy. It delivered a most destructive fire at short range as the enemy rushed for our works, and was served with admirable steadiness and gallantry.

The confusion among a portion of Mott's and Birney's divisions, on this occasion, was increased very much, if not indeed originated, by our front line of breastworks having caught fire just before the enemy made his advance, the fire having been communicated to it from the woods in front (the battle-ground of the previous day and that morning), which had been burning for some hours. The breastworks on this part of the line were built of dry logs, and just at the moment of the enemy's advance were a mass of flames, the fire extending for several hundred yards to the right and left. The intense heat and smoke, which a prevailing wind blew directly into the faces of our men, prevented them from firing over the parapet, and, at some points, even drove them from the line.

No incident of the war has been more persistently or grossly misrepresented than this affair. Many histories of the battle of the Wilderness—notably Greeley's, Coppee's, and Anchor's—make this the fiercest and most successful attack by the enemy during the day, and state that the tide was only turned in our favor by troops sent by General Grant, when, in truth, except for the breaking of Ward's brigade of Birney's division, and some of Mott's troops, the assault would not have been considered of the first magnitude among the many engagements in which the Second Corps had taken part.

General Hancock had received an order to attack again at 6 P. M., but that order was countermanded when General Meade was informed of the attack of Longstreet on General Hancock's lines. Between 6 and 7 P. M. General Hancock was summoned to headquarters of the army for consultation. While on his way thither, he was called upon for troops to help General Sedgwick (Sixth Corps), whose line had been broken by the enemy. Getty's division (then commanded by Wheaton, in consequence of General Getty having been wounded) was at once sent to its own corps.

The night of the 6th and the morning of the 7th

7

passed without material incident, except that early on the morning of the 7th a reconnoissance was made under General Birney's direction, which discovered that the enemy did not hold the Orange plank road for a long distance in our front.

At 9 A. M. on the 7th a dispatch to General Hancock from army headquarters informed him that the movements of the enemy indicated an attack on his own or General Warren's lines, but the day passed with only some slight skirmishing.

At daylight on the morning of the 8th, in accordance with orders from army headquarters, General Hancock withdrew his corps from its position on the Brock road, and covered the rear of the army during its movements toward Spottsylvania Court-house.

CHAPTER XVII.

In concluding his official report of this great battle, General Hancock says, as follows:

"I am aware that I have given but a meager sketch of the part taken by the troops under my command in the battle of the Wilderness. The nature of the country in which that battle was fought is well known. It was covered by a dense forest, almost impenetrable by the troops in line of battle, where manœuvring was an operation of extreme difficulty and uncertainty.

"The undergrowth was so heavy that it was scarcely possible to see more than a hundred paces in any direction —no movements of the enemy could be observed until the lines were almost in collision. Only the roar of the musketry disclosed the position of the combatants to those who were at any distance, and my knowledge of what was occurring on the field, except in my immediate position, was limited, and was necessarily derived from reports of subordinates commanding.

"The casualties of service then, and subsequently, have rendered it impossible for me to obtain the official reports of many of the gallant officers who took a prominent and distinguished part in that great battle. Major-General Birney, Brigadier-Generals Wadsworth, Stevenson, and Hays are dead. General Barlow is in Europe, and Generals Ward and Owens are out of service. I have applied to General Getty for his report, but have not yet received it. Looking at the action after so long a time has elapsed, it seems that the expected movement of Longstreet upon the left flank on the morning of the 6th had a very material effect upon the result of the battle. I was not only cautioned officially that the movement was being made, but many incidents narrated in the body of this report, such as the skirmishing and artillery firing on General Barlow's flank, the heavy firing in the direction of Todd's tavern, where Sheridan was to attack Longstreet, and the report of the infantry moving on the Brock road from the direction of Todd's tavern, confirmed me in the belief that I would receive a formidable attack on my left. This paralyzed a large number of my best troops, who would otherwise have gone into action at a decisive point on the morning of the 6th.

"Had Frank's brigade been supported that morning by the remainder of Barlow's division, the result must have been very disastrous to the enemy, in his then shattered condition.

" From accounts from Confederate sources it is now known that our fierce attack along the Orange plank road, on the 6th, had broken Hill's corps to pieces, and that Longstreet was recalled from the Cartharpen road to retrieve the disaster which had overtaken Hill, while Stuart, with his cavalry, was directed to attack our left.

"I am not aware what movements were made by General Burnside near Parker's store on the morning of the 6th, but I experienced no relief from the attack I was informed he would make across my front—a movement long and anxiously waited for.

"The late Major-General Birney acquitted himself with great honor during the battle. His command made a splendid and irresistible advance on the 6th, in which he entirely overthrew the enemy in his front.

"Major-General Gibbon commanded the left of my line. The troops of his division were sent to the right during the severe fighting along the plank road, on the 5th and 6th, when they were under the command of General Birney.

"Brigadier-General Barlow, commanding First Division, Second Corps, was under the immediate command of General Gibbon during the battle on the extreme left of my line. He performed important services. His division, which had charge of the support of nearly all of my artillery, did not go into action as a whole, but each of his brigades was engaged at different periods on the 5th and 6th.

"Brigadier-General Mott, commanding Fourth Division, Second Corps, was under the command of General Birney during the operations of the 5th and 6th. He displayed his accustomed personal gallantry on the field.

"Brigadier-General Getty, commanding Second Division, Sixth Corps, was under my command on the 5th and 6th. He was severely wounded while engaged with the enemy on the morning of the 6th. Brigadier-General Wheaton succeeded him in command. His troops fought with great bravery on both days.

"Brigadier-General Alexander Hays, that dauntless soldier, whose intrepid and chivalric bearing on so many

battle-fields had won for him the highest renown, was
killed at the head of his brigade on the 5th.

"Brigadier-General Wadsworth, whose brilliant example and peerless courage always had such an inspiriting
effect upon his soldiers, fell while leading them against
the enemy on the morning of the 6th.*

"Commanding First Brigade, Gibbon's Division,
Brigadier-General Alexander Webb ; Colonel (now Brigadier-General) Thomas A. Smythe, commanding the Irish
Brigade of Barlow's division ; and Colonel (now Brigadier-General) John P. Brooke, commanding Fourth Brigade of Barlow's division ; are entitled to high praise for
the manner in which they led their troops into action.

"Colonel (now Brigadier-General) S. S. Carroll, whose
services and gallantry were conspicuous throughout the
battle, received a painful wound on the 5th, but refused
to retire from the field or to give up his command.   He
particularly distinguished himself, on the afternoon of the
6th, by the prompt and skillful manner in which he led
his brigade against the enemy, when he had broken the
line of Mott's and Birney's troops.

"Colonel (now Brigadier-General) N. A. Miles, commanding First Brigade of Barlow's division, checked several attempts of the enemy to advance on my left.   In
these encounters General Miles displayed his usual skill
and courage.

"Major Henry L. Abbott, Twentieth Massachusetts

---

* When General Wadsworth reported to General Hancock, at the junction of the Brock and Orange roads on the morning of the 6th, he looked
worn out physically. He was then an old man, but his gallant heart was
full of energy and courage. General Hancock placed him in command of
the troops on the right of the plank road, where his division went into
action, and he was killed there, on his line of battle, not long after he left
General Hancock's side. His body fell into the enemy's hands.

Volunteers, was mortally wounded while leading his regiment, in the heat of the contest, on the morning of the 6th. This brilliant young officer, by his courageous conduct in action, the high state of discipline in his regiment, his devotion to duty at all times, had obtained the highest reputation among his commanding officers. His loss was greatly deplored.

"Brigadier-General Webb speaks highly of the conduct of Colonel (now Brigadier-General) Bartlett, of the Fifty-seventh Massachusetts Volunteers, whose regiment was associated in action with Webb's brigade for a short time on the 6th."

The following tabulated statement shows the number of casualties occurring in the Second Corps, save those of one regiment, the Fourteenth Indiana, which were not reported during this great battle:

COMMAND.	KILLED.		WOUNDED.		MISSING.		TOTAL.		Loss.
	Commanding Officers.	Enlisted Men.	Commanding Officers.	Enlisted Men.	Commanding Officers.	Enlisted Men.	Commanding Officers.	Enlisted Men.	
Corps Hdqrs...			1				1		
Art'y Brigade..		1		9		3		13	
1st Division....	9	130	21	637	3	107	33	874	
2d Division.....	7	118	40	593	2	108	49	819	
3d Division.....	14	250	83	1490	6	130	103	1870	
Total	30	499	145	2729	11	318	186	3576	3762

This list shows *only* the casualties in the Second Corps, and does not embrace those of the troops of the other corps commanded by General Hancock on the field —portions of the Fifth, Sixth, and Ninth Corps, and heavy artillery. At one time, during the second day's battle, he commanded not less than 60,000 men.

Thus, for two days, this fierce struggle continued between these contending hosts, both buried, as it were, in the chaparral of the Wilderness. It was a terrible scene, unlike any other battle known to history. There was no opportunity for strategy or for the application of skill in manœuvring, for even brigade commanders could not gain a full view of their commands; much less could the commanding generals see the armies whose terrible struggles they ought to have controlled. Even spectators of the fight could see little of it, and could only judge by the ear, from the cheer of the Federals, or the yell of their enemies, and the roar of musketry, where the fighting was the fiercest, and, as the sounds advanced or receded, to which side the advantage leaned.

When Saturday, the 7th, dawned upon that unique Wilderness battle-field, both armies were weary, bleeding, and exhausted. Ten thousand dead and wounded men added gloom and horror to that naturally gloomy wilderness, while other phases of the dread débris of war on every hand shocked the eye and sickened the heart. Neither commander seemed disposed to assume the aggressive, so that, with the exception of a severe but indecisive conflict of cavalry forces near Todd's tavern, there was no renewal of the battle on the 7th. The battle of the Wilderness was a drawn battle; neither side could claim decided advantage, although the Union loss was the greater in killed and wounded, especially so in the loss of gallant and valuable officers. It had been a battle of simple "hammering"; artillery was of little use; cavalry could scarcely be employed at all, on account of the dense woods and underbrush; and the conflict was with the musket and the bayonet—stern and terrible struggle beneath the shades of that mysterious wilderness, which concealed from one portion of the combatants what the others were doing.

It had been General Grant's intention, in crossing the Rapidan, to turn Lee's right flank, and get between him and Richmond. His purpose was arrested by the battle of the Wilderness; but, so soon as it was over, he resumed his purpose, and turned his columns in that direction, marching on Spottsylvania Court-House. General Lee, of course, aimed to foil the plans of his adversary, and marched in the same direction by the roads* nearly parallel with that upon which Grant's army marched—the Brock road, and a few miles west of it.

* His chief column marched along the road leading from Parker's store to Spottsylvania Court-House.

CHAPTER XVIII.

SPOTTSYLVANIA COURT-HOUSE, in the vicinity of which
the battle which bears its name was fought, is some fifteen miles southeast from the central portion of the location of the Battle of the Wilderness, in the direction of
Fredericksburg, and is in the same county with the latter
town. The features of the region around it are of the
same general character, but the country is more open and
free from forest and underbrush. Two inconsiderable
rivers, the Po and the Nye, traverse the district, flowing in a general southeast course, and at a distance from
each other varying from six to ten miles. The court-
house is more than half way from the nearest point on
the Po to the nearest on the Nye.

The purpose to march to Spottsylvania was formed
early on Saturday, the 7th of May; but the march of the
column did not begin until after the immense trains had
been withdrawn from their positions near the battle-field,
and sent to Chancellorville *en route*, there to park for the
night. This motion of the trains let Lee know that his

GENERAL HANCOCK AT SPOTTSYLVANIA.

enemy was about to withdraw in some direction, but gave him no clew to the objective point.

The order of march placed the Fifth Corps (General Warren) in the advance, with instructions to move rapidly and seize Spottsylvania Court-house. Hancock's corps was to follow on the same (Brock) road, while Sedgwick and Burnside were to march by an exterior route *via* Chancellorville. But General Lee, having directed Anderson, now commanding Longstreet's corps, to march out for purposes of observation, that officer started about ten o'clock at night, and finding no good place to encamp, on account of the woods being on fire, pressed on and anticipated Warren in taking Spottsylvania Court-house.

Warren marched at 9 P. M. on the 7th, but was delayed an hour and a half at Todd's tavern by the cavalry escort of General Meade being in the way. Next morning, at three o'clock, he was again detained by the cavalry division of General Merritt, which the day before had been fighting Stuart; and, when they at length gave the road, Warren's column advanced, and, after indescribable difficulties in removing barricades, two brigades of Robinson's division, that had been deployed in line of battle, entered the clearing two miles from the Court-house, and advanced over the plain; but, before they had gone far, they were met by a murderous fire of musketry from the enemy.

Wearied with the battle of the preceding day, and worn out by the hard and sleepless night of marching, annoyed, too, as they had been by Stuart's cavalry, it was not to be wondered at that the men faltered. They fell back to the woods; their general (Robinson) was severely wounded; and it was with some difficulty the men were rallied and reformed. Griffin's division, which had ad-

vanced to Robinson's right, was received with a similar
severe fire, and wavered and fell back. Thus began the
fierce and protracted battle of Spottsylvania; and we
proceed to detail the part borne in that series of terrible
struggles by General Hancock.

As already intimated, orders for the movement of the
Army of the Potomac from the Wilderness had been
issued on the 7th of May. The army was to move by
its left flank. In this operation, Hancock's corps (the
Second) was to follow the Fifth (Warren's). During the
night of the 7th the troops slept upon their arms, along
the Brock road, behind the breastworks; and the poor
fellows had need of better rest. They had been marching and fighting so long, and with scarcely any opportunity of taking food, that they were almost exhausted.
But the conduct of this corps, under all the trying circumstances in which it was placed—called, as it was, to
march and fight continuously for twelve successive days
—illustrates the wondrous courage and endurance of the
American soldier, and also the incalculable value of thorough organization and drill as elements of prowess in an
army. One reason why Hancock's men could do and
endure so much was that he bestowed great attention
upon the complete *preparation* of the *individual* soldier
for his work, and also upon the thorough *organization* of
his corps, from the platoon to the division, in every movement, separate and combined, that might render them
wary and provident in the camp and on the march, and
effective in the field. Careful of their comfort and their
health, he won their love and attachment; and, such was
their perfect confidence in his great military ability,
that they would do anything for him that was possible.
And he was very happy in having subordinate com-

manders who seconded his efforts for the good of the corps and the perfection of its *morale*.

About 10 o'clock at night Generals Grant and Meade came along the lines to Hancock's headquarters, at the intersection of the Brock and the Orange roads, and remained there until near morning of the 8th.

The Second Corps was to have moved at 10 or 11 P. M. on the night of the 7th, following Warren's corps; the latter corps occupied the road until daylight, so that the head of General Hancock's column did not move until after that hour.

The Second Corps moved to Todd's tavern, arriving at that place about 9 o'clock A. M., relieving Gregg's division of cavalry there. Barlow's and Mott's divisions were placed in position to cover the Brock and Catharpen roads, Birney being held in reserve, and preparations were made by intrenching the lines to receive the enemy, in case he attempted an advance in that direction. It was also necessary to hold strongly the roads centering at Todd's tavern, as a protection to the heavy artillery and trains following the army in its movements toward Spottsylvania.

About 11 A. M. on the 8th Colonel N. A. Miles, with his brigade of Barlow's division, one brigade of Gregg's cavalry, and a battery, made a reconnoissance on the Catharpen road toward Corbin's bridge. When this force had reached a point within a half mile of the bridge, the enemy opened upon it with artillery from the high ground on the opposite side of the Po River. Miles at once formed line, opened upon the enemy with his battery, retaining his position until 5.30 P. M., when General Hancock sent orders directing him to return to Todd's tavern. As Miles's command was put in motion

in that direction, he was attacked by Mahone's brigade of
Hill's corps, then on the march to Spottsylvania. As
soon as the firing between Miles and Mahone was heard
by General Hancock, he sent a brigade of infantry to
support our troops, and ordered that others should be
held in readiness to move to their assistance, if required,
at the same time directing Miles to retire slowly upon
our main line.   Miles, as usual with him, carried out
his instructions with spirit and success, repelling handsomely two attacks made by the enemy, and inflicting
considerable loss on him.

In the mean time, at 1.30 P. M., General Meade directed General Hancock to send a division of his corps
to a point about midway between Todd's tavern and
Spottsylvania, as a support to the Fifth (Warren's) and
Sixth (Sedgwick's) corps.   General Gibbon's division
was sent on this service.   At 7.50 P. M. Burton's brigade
of heavy artillery reported for duty to General Hancock,
by order of General Meade.   It was massed in rear of
the line of battle of the Second Corps, and was withdrawn from that position later in the evening by order
from army headquarters.

On the morning of the 9th there were some indications of an advance by the enemy on our lines; but no
fighting occurred, save that the Confederate sharpshooters
were very active, and early in the day their deadly aim
brought down a distinguished victim, in the person of
General Sedgwick, the brave and beloved commander
of the Sixth Corps.   He was shot in the face while rally-
ing some of his men for wincing at the zip-zipping of
the enemy's bullets, and died instantly.   This was a great
loss to the Union army.   He was a model soldier, of
great skill, and of lion-hearted courage.   He was sorely

lamented by his brother officers and by the whole army. He was a native of Connecticut.

At noon Birney and Barlow moved their divisions to a point which connected them with Gibbon on the high clear ground overlooking the Po, between Todd's tavern and Spottsylvania Court-house, Mott remaining to hold the roads centering at Todd's tavern. Burton's brigade of heavy artillery, which had again been sent to report to General Hancock, was also stationed there.

During the afternoon the enemy's wagon train was observed from our line of battle (the line of Birney's, Gibbon's, and Barlow's divisions) on the opposite side of the Po, on the Block House road, moving toward Spottsylvania. Our batteries shelled it sharply, and forced it to take another road.

The river (Po) was examined with a view of crossing it, and at 6 P. M., in pursuance of orders from General Meade, Birney's, Barlow's, and Gibbon's divisions were directed to force the passage.

Brooke's brigade of Barlow's division had the advance in this movement. The south side of the stream was held by the enemy with only a small force of cavalry and a section of artillery, but the crossing was extremely difficult, owing to the depth of the water and the dense undergrowth on the banks of the river.

Brooke pushed forward rapidly, driving the enemy back, and seizing the cross roads between Glady Run and the Po. Birney crossed the river higher up, where he was stoutly resisted. Gibbon crossed below Barlow, and met with no opposition. The troops were now thrown rapidly forward along the Block House road in the direction of the wooden bridge over the Po; but night came on before they could reach that point.

General Hancock was anxious to have seized this bridge and recrossed the river before ordering a halt, but the skirmishers could not be kept moving through the thick wood in the darkness, although a portion of them reached the river, which was ascertained to be too deep for fording at that point. He was therefore compelled to suspend movements until the following morning.

During the afternoon of the 9th, Mott's division was withdrawn from Todd's tavern (by order of General Meade), and moved to a position in front of Spottsylvania, on the left of Wright's (Sixth Corps).

On the evening of the 9th, General Hancock directed three bridges to be thrown over the stream: one at the point at which Brooke had crossed, one (a pontoon) where Gibbon had passed over, and a third a short distance lower.

At daybreak on the morning of the 10th, a close reconnoissance was made of the wooden bridge across the Po, on the Block House road, with the intention of forcing a passage over it, if it should be practicable to do so. The reconnoissance discovered the enemy in force on the opposite side, in earthworks which covered the bridge and its approaches. After a careful survey of the position had been made, General Hancock concluded not to attempt to carry the bridge by assault, but ordered Brooke's brigade of Barlow's division to a point higher up the stream (where a reconnoissance had been made by Lieutenant-Colonel Morgan, General Hancock's Chief of Staff), to ascertain if a crossing could be effected there. To cover Brooke's movement, three or four regiments of Birney's division were sent out on the Andrews's tavern road.

Brooke soon forced a crossing, after a sharp contest,

at a point about one mile above the wooden bridge, and discovered the enemy's intrenched line occupied by infantry and artillery, running parallel to and a short distance from the stream. Colonel Hamill, Sixty-sixth New York Volunteers, distinguished himself in this affair.

While these movements were in progress, General Meade informed General Hancock that he designed assaulting the enemy's works on Laurel Hill, in front of General Warren's (Fifth Corps) position, near Alsop's house. General Hancock was instructed to move two of his divisions to the left, to take part in the assault, and to assume command of the troops which were to participate in it.

Gibbon's and Birney's divisions were at once moved to the north bank of the stream, and massed in rear of Warren's corps, leaving Barlow to hold the ground on the south side of the Po. General Hancock accompanied the two former divisions, and proceeded to reconnoitre the ground on which the attack was to be made.

While Birney was withdrawing from the south side of the river, the regiments which he had ordered out some distance to the front, toward Andrews's tavern, to cover Brooke's movements, were attacked near Glady Run and driven in, and, as they retired, the skirmishers of Barlow's division became sharply engaged in turn, and it now became evident that the enemy was advancing in force upon Barlow's position.

We now quote as follows from General Hancock's official report, describing what followed:

" The Major-General commanding [Meade], having received this information, and not desiring to bring on a battle on the south side of the Po, directed me to withdraw Barlow's division to the north bank of the river at once, and to give my personal supervision to the movement.

"I immediately joined General Barlow, and instructed him to prepare his command to recross the river, on the bridges we had laid in the morning. The enemy was then driving in his skirmishers. The withdrawal of Barlow's troops commenced about 2 P. M. Two of his brigades—Brooke's and Brown's — occupied an advanced position in front of the Block House road, between it and the Po. Miles's and Smythe's brigades were formed along that road; the left resting on a sharp crest, within a few hundred paces of the wooden bridge. In rear of this line, a broad, open plain extended to the point where our pontoon bridge was thrown across the river. General Barlow, anticipating an advance of the enemy, had constructed a line of breastworks parallel to the Block House road, a short distance in front of it, and had made other necessary dispositions to receive him.

"When I directed General Barlow to commence retiring his command, he recalled Brooke's and Brown's brigades, and formed them on the right of Miles's and Smythe's brigades, on a wooded crest, in rear of the Block House road, about one hundred paces in rear of the line of breastworks. As soon as Brooke's and Brown's brigades had occupied this position, Miles and Smythe were ordered to retire to the crest in front of our bridges on the south bank of the Po. Here they formed line of battle, throwing up hastily a light line of breastworks, of rails and such other materials as they could collect on the ground. In a few minutes they were prepared to resist the enemy, should he overpower Brooke and Brown, and attempt to carry the bridges. I directed that all the bat-

teries on the south side of the river, save Arnold's A,
First Rhode Island Battery, should cross to the north
bank, and take position commanding the bridges. These
dispositions had scarcely been completed, when the enemy,
having driven in the skirmishers of Brooke's and Brown's
brigades, pressed forward and occupied the breastworks
in front of them; then, advancing in line of battle supported by columns, they attacked with great vigor and
determination, but were met by a heavy and destructive
fire, which compelled them to fall back at once in confusion, with severe losses in killed and wounded. Encouraged, doubtless, by the withdrawal of Miles's and
Smythe's brigades from our front line, which it is supposed they mistook for a forced retreat, they reformed
their troops, and again assaulted Brooke's and Brown's
brigades. The combat now became close and bloody. The
enemy, in vastly superior numbers, flushed with the an-
ticipation of an easy victory, appeared to be determined
to crush the small force opposing them, and, pressing forward with loud yells, forced their way close up to our
lines, delivering a terrible musketry fire as they advanced.
Our brave troops again resisted their onset with undaunted
resolution; their fire along the whole line was so continuous and deadly that the enemy found it impossible to
withstand it, but broke again and retreated in the wildest
disorder, leaving the ground in our front strewed with
their dead and wounded. During the heat of this contest the woods on the right and rear of our troops took
fire; the flames had now approached close to our line,
rendering it almost impossible to retain the position
longer.

   " The last bloody repulse of the enemy had quieted
them for a time, and, during this lull in the fight, General

Barlow directed Brooke and Brown to abandon their positions, and retire to the north bank of the Po—their right and rear being enveloped in the burning wood, their front assailed by overwhelming numbers of the enemy. This withdrawal of the troops was attended with extreme difficulty and peril; but the movement was commenced at once, the men displaying such coolness and steadiness as is rarely exhibited in the presence of dangers so appalling. It seemed, indeed, that these gallant soldiers were devoted to destruction. The enemy, perceiving that our line was retiring, again advanced, but was again promptly checked by our troops, who fell back through the burning forest with admirable order and deliberation, though, in doing so, many of them were killed and wounded—numbers of the latter perishing in the flames. One section of Arnold's battery had been pushed forward by Captain Arnold during the fight, to within a short distance of Brooke's line, where it had done effective service. When ordered to retire, the horses attached to one of the pieces, becoming terrified by the fire, and unmanageable, dragged the gun between two trees, where it became so firmly wedged that it could not be moved. Every exertion was made by Captain Arnold and some of the infantry to extricate the gun, but without success. They were compelled to abandon it. This was the *first gun ever lost by the Second Corps.*

"Brooke's brigade, after emerging from the wood, had the open plain to traverse between the Block House road and the Po. This plain was swept by the enemy's musketry in front, and by their artillery on the heights above the Block House bridge, on the north side of the river.

"Brown's brigade, in retiring, was compelled to pass

through the entire wood in its rear, which was then burning furiously, and, although under a heavy fire, it extricated itself from the forest, losing very heavily in killed and wounded. Colonel Brown crossed the river some distance above the pontoon bridge, forming his troops on the right of Brooke, who had also crossed to the north bank on the pontoon bridge. I feel that I can not speak too highly of the bravery, soldierly conduct, and discipline displayed by Brooke's and Brown's brigades on this occasion. Attacked by an entire division of the enemy (Heth's), they repeatedly beat him back, holding their ground with unyielding courage until they were ordered to withdraw, when they retired with such order and steadiness as to merit the highest praise. Colonel James A. Beaver, One Hundred and Forty-eighth Pennsylvania Volunteers, and Lieutenant-Colonel D. L. Stryker, Second Delaware Volunteers, are particularly mentioned by Colonel Brooke for marked services and conspicuous courage. The enemy regarded this as a considerable victory, and General Heth published a congratulatory order to his troops, endorsed by General Hill and General Lee, praising them for their valor in driving us from our intrenched lines. Had not Barlow's fine division, then in full strength, received imperative orders to withdraw, Heth's division would have had no cause for congratulation. There were no more than two brigades of Barlow's division engaged at any one time. When General Barlow commenced withdrawing his troops, I had directed General Birney to move his division to the right, and occupy the heights on the north bank of the Po commanding our bridges, in order to cover Barlow's crossing. The artillery, under command of Colonel J. C. Tidball, Commander of Artillery, Second Corps, was

placed in position for the same purpose. As soon as
Brooke's and Brown's brigades had crossed the Po, General Barlow directed Colonel Smythe, commanding Second Brigade, to march his command across the pontoon
bridge, and take position immediately on the north side,
where his fire would sweep the bridges, in case the enemy
designed forcing a passage. Miles's brigade was thus left
to cross last, and to tear up the bridges at that point.

"I had sent a detachment to destroy the upper bridge
when the withdrawal was determined upon. The enemy,
now seeing a few regiments remaining on the south bank,
attempted to cross the open plain in their front, but were
at once driven back by General Miles's troops and our
artillery on the heights. A furious artillery fire was also
opened by the enemy's batteries on the heights above the
wooden bridge over the Po. Our batteries replied with
a well-directed fire, which speedily silenced them, explod-
ing one of their caissons, and forcing them to withdraw
their guns. Miles's brigade now crossed to the north
bank, taking up the pontoon bridge, and thoroughly destroying the other. The enemy made no attempt to cross
the stream."

General Hancock now directed Birney to return with
his division to Warren's right, to take part in the contemplated assault on Laurel Hill, Barlow's division remaining on Birney's right, in the position it had taken when
it had crossed the river.

General Hancock was not able to return to Warren's
front until 5.30 P. M., and then found an assault in progress against the enemy's works by the Fifth Corps (Warren's) and Gibbon's division of the Second Corps. This
assault was made by General Warren in accordance with

orders he had received from General Meade, General
Warren having reported the circumstances then favorable,
during General Hancock's absence on the south side of
the Po supervising the withdrawal of Barlow's division.

The position held by the enemy was the crest of a
densely wooded hill, crowned with earthworks, his front
being swept by the fire of his artillery and infantry.
The approach to the position was obstructed by a dense
growth of low cedars, forming, with their sharp, inter-
lacing branches, a natural abatis.   The troops made a
gallant struggle for a time, and even entered the works
at one or two points, but were driven out, and finally
wavered and fell back.   Gibbon's loss was quite heavy
in this assault.   A few moments after it was known that
this assault had failed, General Hancock received orders
from General Meade directing him to make another attack at the same point at 6.30 P. M.   Preparations for this
advance had just been completed, when General Hancock
was ordered to defer the movement, in case the troops
were not already in motion, and to send a heavy force to
the right of Barlow's division to check a column of the
enemy reported to have passed the Po, and to be moving
against our right flank.

Instructions for the execution of this order were
scarcely given by General Hancock when it was countermanded by General Meade, and he was directed to proceed with the attack on the enemy's position in his front
at Laurel Hill, as previously directed.   The assault was
then made under General Hancock's orders by the Fifth
Corps and portions of Gibbon's and Birney's divisions of
the Second Corps.

The troops encountered the same obstructions which
had forced them back when they had assailed this point

under General Warren's orders at 5 p. m., and they were again compelled to retire with considerable loss. A good deal of confusion prevailed in Ward's brigade of Birney's division. The heavy firing did not cease until near 8 p. m. Mott's division (Second Corps), then in position on the left of the Sixth Corps (some distance to the left of the point of assault at Laurel Hill and to the left of the Fifth Corps), also participated in the general attack at 5 p. m.

During the operations of the 10th, in front of Laurel Hill, the gallant and esteemed Medical Director of the Second Corps, Surgeon A. M. Dougherty, was struck by a piece of a shell which burst among the staff of General Hancock. The same shell passed through the corps flag, which always accompanied the General on the field, and tore it almost to shreds.

CHAPTER XIX.

The Second Corps had no serious fighting on the
11th. At 4 P. M. of that day General Hancock received
the following order from army headquarters:

"Headquarters, Army of the Potomac, *May* 11, 1864, 4 P. M.

"General : You will move as soon after dark as it
can be done, without attracting the enemy's attention, the
divisions of Birney and Barlow, with which, and Mott's
division, you will assault the enemy's line from the left
of the position now occupied by General Wright, and
between him and General Burnside. The position occupied by General Mott, or the left of it, near Hicks's house,
would be a suitable point. This assault should be made
at 4 P. M., as promptly as possible. There are two roads
by which you can move. Gibbon's division can not be
moved without giving notice to the enemy. He will be
moved before daylight, and, if he can possibly be spared,
he will be sent to you.

(Signed) "George G. Meade, *Major-General.*
"Major-General Hancock, *Commanding Second Corps.*"

8

It will be admitted that, considering the late hour at which the order was received, and the consequent impossibility of making the necessary examination of the position to be assailed, there was little hope for such brilliant success as followed. On the application of General Hancock to army headquarters, to have the ground pointed out to him, so that he could determine his route of march accurately, Colonel Comstock was sent to designate the point at which the assault was to be made. Arriving at General Hancock's headquarters, that officer, accompanied by three of General Hancock's staff, set out to decide upon the exact point at which the enemy's lines should be assailed. Unfortunately Colonel Comstock missed his way, and, after riding many miles, the party found themselves on General Burnside's lines (Ninth Corps), beyond the point of intended assault. Colonel Comstock took a survey of the angle (the one which General Hancock carried the next morning) from the hill opposite the Lendrum house, but gave no indication that it was to be the point of attack. It was nearly dark before the party arrived at the " brown house." Here General Mott was found, but, as before stated, could tell but little about the ground. An attempt made by him that day to drive in the enemy's pickets, for the purpose of gaining some information, had partly failed, and nothing remained to be done but to add to the little learned from him, and his field officer of the day, by inspecting so much of the ground as was held by our pickets.

It was barely possible, before night set in, to select the line for the formation of the corps, and, it being too dark to see more, the officers of General Hancock's staff returned to him as rapidly as their horses could carry them, to report the information gained by them.*

At 10 p. m. Birney's and Barlow's divisions were put in motion, guided by Major Mendell, of the Engineers. The night was pitchy dark, the road narrow and bad, and the rain falling heavily. The march, under these circumstances, was made with great difficulty. The column moved very close to the enemy's line, and was in constant danger of a collision. The men were worn out from constant fighting and marching (they had been under fire every day since the 5th of May), and almost slept on their feet, as they dragged along at the slow pace such a column is obliged to maintain under such circumstances.

At one point, where the command was closing up on the head of the column, a runaway pack-mule, bursting suddenly through the sleepy ranks of these nervous and worn-out men in the darkness, seemed to threaten a general stampede, and, at another, the accidental discharge of a musket startled the column into the temporary belief that the corps had come in contact with the enemy's line.

About midnight, the head of the column arrived at the "brown house" (in front of the point to be attacked), near which it was proposed to form the troops. Passing

* Before General Hancock moved to Spottsylvania on the 11th, he asked General Meade if he had any accurate information concerning the enemy's position, to which General Meade replied "No," and that he only understood that a certain house, designated on the map as the "white house" (pointing it out to General Hancock) was inside of the enemy's lines. When General Hancock arrived at the "brown house," he drew a line on the map between the latter and the "white house," then drew a perpendicular to that line, determined its bearing by the compass, and on that line established the troops. Fortunately, the "white house" stood just where General Meade understood it to be, and the troops struck the "salient" when they advanced.

as quietly as possible over a slight line of rifle-pits, which
had been thrown up there by General Mott's command,
our troops moved close up to our picket line (about twelve
hundred yards distant from the enemy's intrenchments),
where our formation for the attack was made.   Gibbon's
division in the mean time came up and joined Mott at
the "brown house," so that General Hancock had his
whole corps for the work before him.   Lieutenant-Colonel Merriam, Sixteenth Massachusetts Volunteers, field
officer of the day of Mott's division, having some knowledge of the ground, rendered invaluable assistance to General Hancock in the formation of the troops.   He fell,
mortally wounded, the next morning, greatly regretted.
Lieutenant - Colonel Willian and Captain Thompson of
General Mott's staff also gave assistance; but the principal labor of the formation fell upon General Hancock
and the three officers of his staff (Colonel C. H. Morgan,
Chief of Staff, Second Corps, and Captains Mitchell
and Wilson, Aides-de-camp) who had reconnoitered the
ground the previous evening with Colonel Comstock, of
General Grant's staff.   Between our lines and the enemy's
works the ground ascended sharply, and was thickly
wooded, with the exception of a cleared space about four
hundred yards wide, extending to the enemy's position,
in front of the Lendrum house, and curving to the right
toward the salient of his works.   A small rivulet ran
parallel to and just in front of our line.

The formation for the assault was as follows: Barlow's
division in two lines of battalions in mass (across the clear
space before mentioned), Brooke's and Miles's brigades
in front, Brown's and Smythe's brigades in the second
line, each regiment doubled on the center, with very
close intervals.

Birney formed on Barlow's right in two deployed lines. In his front was marshy ground (the small rivulet mentioned above), and a dense wood of low pines. Mott formed in rear of Birney, and Gibbon in reserve.

It was almost daylight when General Hancock had completed these preparations. A heavy fog delayed the advance until half past four, when the word was given. At this moment General Birney rode up to General Hancock, and said his men could not pass the swamp and small stream directly in front. "General, *you must pass it*," said General Hancock. Birney passed the obstacle, and pushed forward, keeping up well with Barlow, who was now pressing up the slope in quick time, but without firing a shot, marching over the enemy's pickets, who stood in silent wonder and bewilderment as they were enveloped in this solid mass of twenty thousand men who suddenly came upon them through the dense fog.

From the high ground surrounding the Lendrum house the enemy's picket reserve opened a galling fire upon Barlow's flank, mortally wounding, among others, Lieutenant-Colonel D. L. Stryker, Second Delaware Volunteers, who had highly distinguished himself on the 10th.

Our heavy column moved on regardless of this annoyance, but General Hancock, having brought up General Carroll's brigade, Second Division, to cover Barlow's right flank, that officer (Carroll) promptly attacked the picket reserve of the enemy at the Lendrum house, which resisted stoutly, and received pretty rough treatment from Carroll's men for having fired into the rear of our column long after it had broken through their picket line and passed their position.

As soon as the curve in the clearing permitted Bar-

low's men to see the red earth of the enemy's intrenchments at the salient, the mercurial temperament of the
gallant Irish Brigade of that division no longer allowed
them to be silent; they gave a ringing cheer, and the
whole division, spontaneously taking the "double quick,"
rushed at the formidable works under a scorching fire
from the enemy's musketry and artillery, which opened
along his whole line.   Nothing now could check our column.   Tearing away the abatis with their hands, the
men sprang over the breastworks, bayoneting or beat-
ing to the earth with clubbed muskets the desperate
resisting enemy.   Birney entered the salient about the
same time with Barlow, and in a few moments we had
possession of nearly a mile of line, upward of 4,000
prisoners of Johnson's division of Ewell's corps, twenty
pieces of artillery, with horses, caissons, and material
complete, several thousand stand of small arms, and more
than thirty battle flags.   Among our prisoners were
Major-General Edward Johnson and Brigadier-General
George Stuart.*

The celebrated "Stonewall" brigade was taken almost entire.   The enemy retreated in great disorder and
confusion.   The interior of the intrenchments was filled

* The story of the meeting of General Hancock and General George
Stuart has been told in various ways.   What actually happened was, that
General Hancock supposed from his action that General Stuart was about
to offer his hand, and accordingly extended his, designing at the same time
to comfort him somewhat in his painful situation by giving him news of
his wife, whom General Hancock had met a few days before in Wash
ington.   He had known her from childhood, and had attended their wed-
ding.   But General Stuart refused to take his outstretched hand, whereupon General Hancock said: " General, if you did not design to take my
hand, you should not have acted as though you did.   Such an affront
should not be put upon me before my officers and soldiers.   Had I not mis-
interpreted your action, I would not have offered you my hand."

with dead, most of whom were killed by our men with the bayonet when they rushed into the works; their bodies, at many points in the salient, were piled one upon another.

Our troops could not be held in hand after the capture of the intrenchments, but pursued the enemy through the wood in the direction of Spottsylvania, until they encountered a new line of works and heavy reënforcements of infantry, which were now coming with all speed to aid Johnson, the rebel commander, that officer having applied for them during the night before, under the belief that he would be assailed on the morning of the 12th, having heard the march of the column as it came on the ground.*

They were too late to save him, however; but they compelled our troops to retire to the captured line of works on the right and left of the salient, which, in the mean time, General Hancock had occupied by his reserves. This was effected not a moment too soon, for the enemy were prompt to attempt to retrieve their misfortunes, and pushed heavy reënforcements into the gap. General Hancock, however, firmly held the captured line. About 6 A. M. the head of Wright's Sixth Corps came on the field, and took position to the right of the salient. General Hancock had previously sent for troops to put in on his right to check the enemy, who were pressing forward there, and seemed likely to pass to his rear, between him and the Fifth Corps. Mott now joined the Sixth Corps

---

* It is well to say here that General Johnson was not "surprised" by us on the morning of the 12th. He has since stated to General Hancock that he was looking for our attack, and had called his men up earlier than usual to be ready for us. They had been dismissed from the ranks, and were cooking breakfast when our advance was made.

at the salient, on Wright's left; Birney joined Mott; and then came Gibbon and Barlow in succession.

Simultaneously with the arrival of the Sixth Corps the enemy renewed his vehement efforts to recapture his line, pressing his line of battle up to the very breastworks, and planting his colors on the side opposite ours, only separated by the parapet, the two lines firing into each other's faces for hours. So fierce was this cross-fire that the forest was mown down like grass, and trees fourteen inches in diameter were hewn to the ground by Minie balls. The enemy never exhibited greater bravery or resolution. At 8 p. m. they pressed Wright so fiercely that he called urgently on General Hancock for aid, and Brooke's brigade of Barlow's division was sent to him, although it had taken a foremost part in the assault of the morning, had suffered most seriously during the several hours it had already been engaged, and had been withdrawn from the line of battle temporarily to replenish its ammunition. It was, however, the only brigade available at that moment.

It relieved a portion of Wheaton's command on Wright's front line, where it was called upon to stand the brunt of the fight, until its ammunition was again exhausted.

After some hours it was returned to General Hancock, but fearfully reduced in numbers.

One section of Brown's battery was placed in the line on the left of the salient, and was able to hold its position there, where it did good service; but a section of Gillis's battery, Fifth United States Artillery, which was pushed up to the line at the salient (where it fired canister into the enemy's ranks), was speedily disabled, and lost so heavily in horses and men that it was soon withdrawn. Artillery was also placed on the knoll to the right and front of the Lendrum house, about three hundred yards from the salient, where they fired constantly over our troops into the enemy's lines. Between this point and the works was another knoll, which soon came to be known as "dangerous ground"—the enemy's bullets which cleared the parapet sweeping it clean. It was then that Major Bingham, while riding with General Hancock, took a fancy to dismount and tighten his saddle-girth, but was unable to finish the operation by reason of a Minie ball passing through his leg. Near the same spot, earlier in the morning, while Major Mitchell was pointing out to General Wright the position for the troops of the Sixth Corps, the latter was struck by a piece of shell and hurled several feet, fortunately with no worse injury than a severe contusion.

Early in the morning (about the time that General Hancock's troops carried the works at the salient) Burnside's corps (the Ninth), which was in position some distance to Hancock's left, made a slight demonstration; but as it made no impression on the enemy, and gave no relief or assistance to Hancock, we make no further mention of it.

During the afternoon Cutler's and Griffin's divisions of the Fifth Corps came on the field.

The enemy continued his desperate efforts to regain his lost works, and the battle raged incessantly along the whole line, from the right of the Sixth Corps to Barlow's left, throughout the day and until midnight of the 12th, when his firing ceased, and his troops were withdrawn from Hancock's front.*

* General Hancock placed Brigadier-General Thomas W. Egan in command at the salient during the night, with instructions to hold it against all

A cold, drenching rain fell during the battle, in which the troops were under a deadly musketry fire for nearly twenty hours. When the firing ceased, about midnight, the exhausted men lay down in the mud in the intrenchments, and slept among thousands of the dead and wounded.

Our losses in killed and wounded were, of course, heavy in such a day's work as this, but we had given the enemy a stunning blow, and had defeated him most signally. His losses during the day, in killed and wounded and prisoners, could not have been less than ten thousand men, and were probably much greater.

General Hancock had fixed his headquarters for the day at the Lendrum house, a point much exposed to the enemy's fire. During the morning, while Generals Wright, Hancock, and Gibbon were sitting in the yard near the house, their heads inclined toward each other, in earnest conversation, a Minie ball passed between the three heads, without hitting either, and buried itself with a spiteful "spud" in the side of the house.

Here may properly be related an incident which naturally possessed great interest to the Confederates, and which is one among the many vivid occurrences which made the history of this fierce encounter. The story was told at a reunion of the Army of Northern Virginia, which took place in Richmond, Virginia, in the winter of 1877, and is given as related by Colonel James H. Skinner, of the Confederate Army, an eye-witness:

"Our infantry not only encountered with cheerfulness all the trials and hardships of the camp and of the march, but in the fierce encounters of battle displayed a

attempts from the enemy. He could not have selected one from his whole command who could have held it more stoutly and gallantly.

proud self-reliance to which the annals of other wars and
other armies can scarce furnish a parallel. Let one notable instance, out of many, suffice for illustration. It was
on the memorable morning of the 12th of May, 1864, in
the battle of Spottsylvania Court-house. In the early
dawn our army had suffered a fearful disaster. An assault by Hancock's corps had broken our lines and swal-
lowed up almost a division, including the larger part of
the famous Stonewall brigade. Early's division was
forthwith summoned to retrieve, if possible, our loss, and
to reëstablish our lines, through the gap in which the enemy were pouring. It was an appalling crisis in our affairs, which called for the presence and direction of our
noble Commander-in-Chief. He placed himself in front
of the division, as though intending to lead the charge in
person. Traces of anxiety could be read, or at least fancied, on even his uniformly calm and imperturbable brow.
Our own tried and trusted chief of division was that day
commanding a corps, but the mantle of an Early could
not have fallen on worthier shoulders than those of the
heroic John B. Gordon. The line, divining General
Lee's purpose, insisted that he should abandon it; each
heart felt that in his life the fortunes of the Confederacy
were, under God, bound up. This brave division, though
it would have gloried to distinguish itself under the immediate leadership of its Commander-in-Chief, was unwilling to do so at the necessary hazard of his invaluable
life. They knew that, led by Gordon—as they frequently had done under Early—they could and would accomplish all that lay in the power of men, and, therefore,
from the ranks the cry arose, 'General Lee to the rear!'
This is the incident to which General Lee himself reluctantly referred, and locates in the battles around Spottsyl-

vania Court-house. He yielded to the demand of his
men, who had, no doubt, by this time, inspired him with
the fullest confidence, and by the hand of General Gordon his horse was led through an opening made in Captain James Bumgardner's company, the color company
of the Fifty-second Virginia infantry, the regiment which
your speaker had the honor to command. General Gordon immediately thereafter gave to the division the order
to charge, and with a wild yell it sprang forward."

CHAPTER XX.

AT daylight on the 13th it was found that the enemy
had withdrawn to his second line of intrenchments, about
half a mile in the rear of those we had captured. As
soon as this was reported to General Meade, he directed
General Hancock to throw forward a reconnoitring force,
to ascertain the strength and exact position of the enemy,
if practicable. General Hancock instructed General Gibbon to make the advance from his point. He selected
Owen's brigade for the service. It is sometimes dangerous to have a high reputation for skill and bravery, and
Colonel Carroll found it so on this occasion; for, General
Owen not being in command at the time, General Gibbon resolved to send Carroll out on the reconnoissance in
command of his brigade.

It so happened that, when Gibbon met Carroll and told
him what he proposed to do, the latter was on his way
to the hospital. The wound he had received in the Wilderness had become very painful and offensive for lack
of proper care, and the exhausting labor of the past week
had so reduced him that the surgeon insisted on his

spending a few days in the field hospital. Too proud and high-spirited to tell his division commander on what errand he was sent, Carroll turned back and moved out with Owen's brigade, his own in support. In the sharp encounter with the enemy which followed, a break occurred in the line, and Carroll rushed to the spot to restore order, and had his unhurt arm terribly shattered at the elbow by a Minie ball. The lines were very close, and Carroll clearly saw the man who shot him, and had a moment to wonder where he should be hit. This was the last occasion when Colonel Carroll met the enemy. His severe wounds entirely disabled him for many months, though he recovered sufficiently to command a division in the Veteran Corps, which General Hancock was organizing when the war closed. No army ever contained a more intrepid soldier.

May 13th and 14th passed without serious fighting.

May 15th, in accordance with orders from General Meade, Barlow's and Gibbon's divisions were withdrawn from the line of works captured on the 12th, and marched to a position near the Fredericksburg and Spottsylvania road. Birney remained in the works to cover the right of Burnside's corps.

On the 17th Brigadier General R. O. Tyler's division of heavy artillery and the " Corcoran Legion " (infantry) joined the Second Corps, a reënforcement of about eight thousand men.*

The same day—17th—General Hancock received orders from army headquarters to move back to the works

---

* The material of these regiments was excellent, and they were well-disciplined and completely equipped; but they were not inured to war like the veterans they had come to replace. The " Corcoran Legion " was assigned to Gibbon's division.

he had captured on the 12th, and to assault the enemy at daylight on the 18th in the intrenched line occupied in front of that position. The Sixth Corps was to form on his right, and attack at the same hour.

At dark on the 17th General Hancock's troops were in motion, and were in the position designated for the attack before daylight the next morning. At 11 A. M. Gibbon and Barlow moved to the attack, their troops formed in lines of brigades. Our artillery, which was posted on the works captured on the 12th, fired over the heads of the troops. Birney's and Tyler's divisions were held in reserve.

The enemy was posted in a strongly intrenched line, screened by a forest, about one half mile in front of and parallel to the works taken on the 12th. His position was strengthened by heavy slashings and abatis. As our troops neared this line, they were received by a hot fire of musketry and artillery, which made great slaughter in our ranks. They pushed on, however, until they reached the edge of the abatis, which, with the galling fire, stopped their progress. They made many gallant attempts to penetrate the enemy's position, but without success.

Finding that he was losing quite seriously, and that the enemy's works were too strong to be carried by his force, General Hancock informed General Meade of the condition of affairs, and was at once instructed by him to withdraw from the assault. This was accomplished, the enemy making no attempt to leave his works and attack us, and our troops again occupied the lines in front of the Lendrum house. The " Corcoran Legion," which, as before stated, joined the Second Corps on the 17th, was specially marked for good conduct. It lost seventy in killed and wounded. General Wright attacked at the same time, but without success.*

During the night of the 18th, Barlow's, Birney's, and Gibbon's divisions marched to a point near Anderson's mill, on the Nye River, Tyler's division remaining in position on the Fredericksburg and Spottsylvania road, near the Harris house.

May 19th, General Hancock received instructions from General Meade, directing him to prepare to move toward Bowling Green, on the Richmond and Potomac Railroad.

At 5 P. M., while preparations for this march were in progress, heavy musketry firing was heard in the direction of Tyler's division. It was soon found that Ewell's corps of the enemy had passed the Nye in front of Tyler, and was making a determined attack upon him. Birney was at once hurried to his support, and Gibbon and Barlow were put in readiness to move up to sustain him, if required. General Hancock at once rode to the fight, and found Tyler hotly engaged in front of the Fredericksburg and Spottsylvania road. As soon as Birney's troops came on the ground, two brigades were thrown into action on Tyler's right. Some troops of the Fifth Corps, notably Cutler's brigade, had also been sent to reënforce Tyler, on his left, and these were put in. The contest was a severe one, and continued until

---

* In ordering this assault, it was perhaps supposed that the Second Corps would be urged to greater effort to repeat its renowned achievements of the 12th on the same ground; but such was not the case. Large numbers of the dead of that day were still unburied, and, having been exposed to a burning sun for nearly a week, presented a hideous and sickening sight, and such a stench arose from the field as to make many of the officers and men deathly sick. In fact, all the circumstances were such as to dishearten, instead of encouraging, the men.

about 9 P. M., when the enemy's lines were driven back and broken at all points, and Ewell retreated rapidly across the Nye. His loss in this engagement was heavy in killed and wounded. He left about four hundred prisoners in our hands. This was the first action in which Tyler's troops had taken part. They conducted themselves very handsomely.*

In concluding his official report of these operations, General Hancock writes as follows:

" This action terminated the operations of my command; and during the second epoch of the campaign the losses in the Second Corps, in the several severe battles which this epoch embraces, were as follows:

COMMAND.	KILLED.		WOUNDED.		MISSING.		TOTAL.		AGGREGATE.
	Commanding Officers.	Enlisted Men.	Commanding Officers.	Enlisted Men.	Commanding Officers.	Enlisted Men.	Commanding Officers.	Enlisted Men.	
Corps Hdqrs....			2				2		2
Art'y Brigade...		14	3	30	1	2	4	46	50
1st Division....	30	376	88	1715	11	369	129	2460	2589
2d Division.....	16	142	38	731	2	100	56	973	1029
3d Division.....	26	230	76	1275	5	175	107	1680	1787
Total......	72	762	207	3751	19	646	298	5159	5457

" From the commencement of the campaign the troops under my command marched and fought almost constantly. They had not had a single day's rest since

---

* Tyler's men had taken off their knapsacks as they went into action, and the fine clothes and many comforts, fresh from Washington, exposed, attracted the attention of Birney's old veterans as they passed, and, notwithstanding the rapidity with which they were moving, it was observed that a vast number of coats, shoes, etc., changed owners, and that Tyler's men were not so fatigued on the long marches afterward by the weight of their knapsacks.

the 2d of May. Their conduct was such as to merit the highest praise. They encountered the dangers, privations, and fatigues incident to such arduous and perilous services with unshaken fortitude and intrepid valor.

"Major-General Birney, commanding Third Division, and Brigadier-General (now Brevet Major-General) Barlow, commanding First Division, are entitled to high commendation for the valor, ability, and promptness displayed by them during the operations included in this epoch of the campaign. The magnificent charge made by their divisions, side by side, at Spottsylvania, on the 12th of May, stands unsurpassed for its daring courage and brilliant success.

"Brigadier-General (now Major-General) Gibbon, then commanding Second Division, and Brigadier-General (now Brevet Major-General) Mott, commanding the Fourth Division, until it was consolidated with Birney's division, merit high praise for the manner in which they handled the troops commanded by them.

"Brigadier-General (now Brevet Major-General) Webb, commanding First Brigade, Second Division, was severely wounded while gallantly leading his troops at Spottsylvania, May 12th.

"Colonel (now Brevet Major-General) Miles, performed marked and distinguished services, especially at Catharpen road, on the 8th, and at the battle of the Po, on the 10th, and at Spottsylvania, on the 12th and 18th of May.

"Colonel Coons, Fourteenth Indiana Volunteers, Lieutenant-Colonel D. L. Stryker, Second Delaware Volunteers, and Lieutenant-Colonel Merriam, Sixteenth Massachusetts Volunteers, three brave and able officers, were killed while leading their men into action, during the storming of the enemy's works at Spottsylvania, on the morning of the 12th of May. Many other gallant officers and soldiers of my command exhibited rare and conspicuous valor and devotion during the battles described in this report whose names are unmentioned here, owing to the almost total absence of detailed reports from my subordinate commanders. Lieutenant-Colonel (now Brigadier-General) C. H. Morgan, my Chief of Staff, deserves especial mention for distinguished services, which were particularly meritorious and valuable at Spottsylvania, from the assistance he gave me in selecting the ground for the formation of the troops before the assault.

"In the preliminary examination of the ground, and in the disposition of the troops for the assault, Major (now Lieutenant-Colonel and Brevet Brigadier-General) W. G. Mitchell, A. D. C., assisted General Morgan.

"Surgeon (now Brevet Lieutenant-Colonel) A. N. Dougherty, Medical Director, Second Army Corps, behaved with great gallantry. He was wounded at Spottsylvania on the 10th of May.

"Major H. H. Bingham, Judge Advocate, Second Army Corps, conducted himself with his usual conspicuous gallantry. He received a severe wound while courageously performing his duty at Spottsylvania, on the 12th of May."

There is an old adage to the effect that it is the "willing horse that is worked to death." None of the troops in the Army of the Potomac got much rest during these bloody days, but the record seems to show that General Hancock was marching or assaulting without as much intermission as fell to the lot of some others. On the 9th of May the Second Corps had moved from Todd's tavern, fording the Po, and having marched in the dark through the woods as far as the Block House bridge, the men bivouacked, supperless, and in their wet clothes. On the 10th, Barlow's division fought the desperate combat on the Po. Birney and Gibbon twice assaulted on Warren's right, and Mott attacked near the "brown house." On the night of the 11th the corps moved to the "brown house," and assaulted the enemy's intrenched lines at 4.30 A. M. on the 12th, without previous rest or food, and remained fiercely engaged with the enemy for twenty hours. On the 13th, a heavy reconnoissance was made, and the 14th was passed in sharp skirmishing. On the morning of the 15th the corps moved again; was in motion all night of the 17th, preparatory to the attack of the 18th; was again marching all night of the 18th, withdrawing from the lines and massing at the Anderson house; and now, on the third consecutive night, it was proposed to send it on a flank march of over twenty miles, to attack "vigorously" in the morning.

Quotations from General Hancock's reports, giving commendatory notice of conspicuous gallantry or other meritorious action in his subordinate officers, are given a prominent place in this work, that the reader may appreciate a noteworthy feature of his character. A just recognition of the value of those who serve never fails to add dignity to the character of those who command.

CHAPTER XXI.

THE order for the march to Bowling Green and Milford Station was as follows:

"HEADQUARTERS, ARMY OF THE POTOMAC,
May 19, 11½ P. M., 1864.

"MAJOR-GENERAL HANCOCK, *Commanding Second Corps*:

"The Major-General commanding directs that you move with your corps to-morrow at 2 A. M. to Bowling Green and Milford Station, *via* Guinea's Station, and take position on the right bank of the Mattapony, if practicable. Should you encounter the enemy, you will attack him vigorously, and report immediately to these headquarters, which you will keep advised of your progress from time to time.

"Brigadier-General Torbert, with a cavalry force and a battery of horse artillery, is ordered to report to you for duty. An engineer officer and guide will be sent to you. Canvas pontoons will likewise be put at your disposal.

(Signed)   "A. A. HUMPHREYS,
"*Major-General, Chief of Staff.*"

At once, upon receipt of this order, General Hancock directed a reconnoissance of the route of march by one of his staff with the headquarters escort, which was made as far as Guinea's Station, and, the location of the enemy's signal stations being obtained, the hour of march was changed, at General Hancock's suggestion, to 11 P. M., so as to permit those stations to be passed as far as possible before daylight. The corps moved accordingly, and at break of day on the 21st the head of the column reached Guinea's Station, from which place Torbert drove the enemy's cavalry videttes. The troops reached Bowling Green at 10 A. M. At Milford Station, just beyond Bowling Green, our cavalry found the enemy in rifle-pits, on the north side of the Mattapony, prepared to dispute the crossing. Before the infantry could get up, Torbert had dislodged this force (a part of Kemper's old brigade of infantry), capturing about sixty prisoners, and saving the bridge from serious injury. Barlow's division crossed as soon as it came up, the other divisions following, and a strong position was taken up on the high land about one mile from the river.

The cavalry was pushed to the front to give timely notice of any movement of the enemy in our direction, in which case General Hancock had made all necessary preparations to attack. Considering the enemy might concentrate against this flanking column before Warren, who was moving up the telegraph road, should come within supporting distance, a strong line of breastworks was thrown up along our front.

The position was so powerful naturally, and so much strengthened by breastworks and slashing timber in front, that we were willing to undertake its defense against any force of the enemy. The troops were greatly exhausted at the conclusion of this day's work, and were harassed again at night by a groundless alarm among some of the new regiments of the corps. Fortunately, the next day —the 22d—was a day of rest.*

At 5 A. M., on the 23d, the corps moved toward the North Anna—Birney's division in advance—and about midday reached the banks of that river, finding the cavalry of our advance skirmishing briskly with the enemy. Birney formed a line across the telegraph road, Gibbon across the railroad, Tyler being posted in reserve. The long lines of the enemy's jaded troops could be seen on the opposite side of the river, forming simultaneously with ours, and a sharp artillery fire was opened on them, compelling them to take cover in the woods in the rear, and in the intrenchments which they had already pre-

---

* It is to be noted that the course now being pursued by General Hancock, in accordance with his orders from headquarters, was a part of the flank movement planned by General Grant after Spottsylvania, and which was to be a repetition of that by which he had withdrawn—advancing—from the Wilderness. Meanwhile, Lee's army was moving in a parallel line with the Union force, having the inside track, and keeping in the advance. It was, in fact, a race between these two vast columns, under the inspiration and guidance of skilled and experienced leaders, and forms in its history a most interesting and exciting event.

The march of the armies extended through one of the most beautiful and highly cultivated regions of the "Old Dominion," and one hitherto unscathed by the fiery breath of war. The land was dotted with those fine old Virginia homesteads, whose stately elms shadowed the hospitable mansions, and all of whose surroundings reminded the observer of the ancient Colonial times, their broad acres recalling the baronial domains of old England.

The object of the rival generals was to reach and cross the next important stream (the North Anna) each before his adversary. The marches of the 21st and 23d of May had brought our army near to the desired goal—the north bank of the North Anna—only to find the enemy strongly posted on its south bank, and ready to dispute its passage.

pared to meet such a contingency as this. They held
also a small earthwork on the north bank of the river,
forming a bridge head to protect the county bridge. The
enemy was quickly pressed back, until Gibbon's skirmishers reached the river on the left, and Birney's reached the
strip of land between Long Creek and the river, on which
the bridge head was placed. Birney succeeded in getting
a brigade over the creek, and making such a reconnoissance of the position as to satisfy himself that it could be
taken; and having reported this to General Hancock, he
was directed to make the attempt. This was a little before four o'clock; it was half past six, however, before
the arrangements for the assault were completed.

At that hour Egan's and Pierce's brigades of Birney's
division, led by their gallant commanders, charged from
different points over an open field, several hundred yards
in width, carrying the works with scarcely a check, and
driving the enemy pell-mell across the river. No official
report of this brilliant affair was ever submitted by General Birney; but this injustice was in part remedied by the
fact that General Hancock was on the ground, and recorded
what he saw in his own official report, in which he says:
"I have seldom witnessed such gallantry and spirit as
the brigades of Egan and Pierce displayed." Rare, but
well-merited praise! The artillery under Colonel Tidball was warmly engaged during this assault. A section
of Arnold's Rhode Island Battery was in action within
close musketry range, and lost its gallant young commander, Lieutenant Hunt, who was mortally wounded.
The enemy made numerous and determined efforts to
burn the bridge as they fell back over the river, and at
intervals during the ensuing night, but were frustrated
by the vigilance of Birney's pickets. They succeeded,

however, in burning the railroad bridge. Birney's division crossed the river at 8 A. M. the next day, and occupied the abandoned works about the Fox house, after driving off the enemy's pickets. The pontoon bridges were thrown across below the railroad bridge, on which Barlow's and Gibbon's divisions crossed and formed on Birney's left, which placed the entire corps (save Tyler's division, left in reserve at the captured bridge head) on the south side of the river.

The impression evidently prevailed at army headquarters that the enemy would not hold the line of the North Anna, but was falling back through Hanover Junction; and General Hancock was directed to cross his trains as soon as practicable and be prepared to move at once. This impression was wide from the truth, however, for the enemy at this point held one of the most powerful and peculiar positions of the campaign. The line was in the shape of a V, the flanks resting on a natural obstacle, and the point of the V on the river. Hancock crossed to the left of the point, and Warren to the right of it. All efforts to shake Lee's hold on the river and unite our several wings were futile. Warren and Hancock could reënforce each other only by recrossing the river, marching several miles, and crossing again.

It is possible that Lee was only prevented from attacking one or the other (Hancock or Warren) by the hope that the assault which had characterized the previous part of the campaign on our part would be renewed by General Grant at this point, and also by our bold movement in crossing to his side of the river.

Warren was attacked while getting into position, but was not seriously molested thereafter. Smythe's brigade of Gibbon's division had a smart encounter with the

9

enemy on the evening of the 24th. The enemy pressed our advanced posts heavily for a short time, but gained no advantage.

May 25th and 26th passed without events of importance to the Second Corps, the troops being engaged in destroying the railroad toward Milford, on the 26th. During that night he withdrew to the north bank of the North Anna, destroying the railroad and county bridges.

About 10 A. M. on the 27th the corps moved from the North Anna over the county and old stage roads, and camped that night about three miles from the Pamunky River.

The march from Anderson's mill (commencing on the 21st at daybreak) to Bowling Green and Milford, and then to North Anna, was made very rapidly, and required great exertions from the officers and men. Their conduct was marked by their usual bravery and devotion to duty, in the severe contests which occurred during this epoch.

The following list shows (partially) the loss in the Second Corps from 21st to 27th May, inclusive:

| COMMAND. | KILLED. | | WOUNDED. | | MISSING. | | AGGREGATE. |
	Commanding Officers.	Enlisted Men.	Commanding Officers.	Enlisted Men.	Commanding Officers.	Enlisted Men.	
Corps Hdqrs							
Art'y Brigade......		1		3			4
1st Division........	1	20	3	61		10	95
2d Division	5	40	4	158		34	241
3d Division	2	31	8	151		11	203
Total*.......	8	92	15	373		55	543

* The casualties of the Fourth and Eighth Ohio Volunteers, Fourteenth Indiana Volunteers, and First Delaware Volunteers are not included in the above table.

May 28th, the corps crossed the Pamunky and took position between the Fifth and Sixth Corps. The cavalry, under General Sheridan, were hotly engaged at this time in our immediate front at Hawes's shop. On the 29th, at midday, Barlow's division moved out on the Hanover Court-house road, to make a reconnoissance. The enemy's dead, killed in the cavalry engagement of the day before, were found in considerable numbers along the road and through the woods, but Barlow did not encounter the enemy until he struck his cavalry skirmishers at the forks of the Cold Harbor and Hanover Court-house roads. The skirmishers of the First Division speedily dispersed the cavalry force, and the division pushed on till the works of the enemy, well manned, were developed on Swift Creek, a tributary of the Tolopotomy. Barlow reporting the enemy in such force that it would probably require a general engagement to dislodge him, General Hancock at once ordered up Gibbon and Birney, whose divisions formed respectively on Barlow's right and left. On the left, on Gibbon's front, the enemy's skirmish line of rifle-pits was handsomely carried by Brooke's brigade of Barlow's division, assisted by Owen's brigade, Gibbon's division. Our line at once advanced to the captured position. During the day the skirmishing was incessant, with some losses, and many acts of gallantry were performed in developing the enemy's line, which was very strongly posted, the greater part of his front being protected by a marsh. Our artillery was chiefly posted along the ridge on which the Sheldon house stands.

About 3 P. M. the Sixth Corps moved up and took position on the right of the Second. A short time after— 7 P. M.—General Meade directed General Hancock to attack the enemy "as soon as he could find a suitable place," in order to relieve Warren, then pressed by the enemy. The saving clause in the order could have been taken advantage of by a less vigorous soldier than General Hancock, for darkness would have set in before any examination could have been made. But the object stated left, to a man of Hancock's mind, no alternative, and, without waiting to look for "a suitable place," knowing that to be of service the attack must be made promptly, he ordered Barlow to advance at once, and with equal promptitude Barlow sent Brooke forward with his brigade. This excellent and energetic soldier pushed on over obstacles that would have deterred many others, and succeeded in capturing the strongly intrenched line in his front, and with it a few prisoners. As this occurred some time after dark, no immediate advantage could be taken of it.

On the morning of the 31st, Birney was directed to cross Swift Run and assail the enemy's advanced line on the right of the Richmond road. This movement was successfully executed, and the intrenchments carried. Gibbon and Barlow pushed close up to the enemy's lines in their fronts, but found the position too strong to admit of successful assault. The remainder of this day and the 1st of June passed with heavy skirmishing, but no engagement of importance occurred.

The losses on the Tolopotomy, as the position of the corps on the 29th, 30th, and 31st of May, and 1st of June was designated, were quite severe in the aggregate, but were not reported separately.

Early on the morning of June 1st Wright's corps was withdrawn from our right toward Cold Harbor, and Birney's division was therefore withdrawn from the south side of the Run. During the day the skirmish line was sharply engaged, but no heavy fighting occurred.

On the night of June 1st the corps withdrew from the position of Tolopotomy Creek, under orders to mass near army headquarters; but that order was suddenly changed, and instructions were given to push on to Cold Harbor with all speed.

In General Meade's orders for this movement, he says: "You must make every exertion to move promptly, and reach Cold Harbor as soon as possible. At that point you will take position to reënforce Wright on his left, which it is desired to extend to the Chickahominy. Every confidence is felt that your gallant corps of veterans will move with vigor and endure the necessary fatigue."

The night was intensely hot and close, and the dust was suffocating, but the wishes of General Meade would have been more than carried out, had it not been for the unfortunate mistake made by one of his staff sent to guide the column. This officer, an excellent soldier by the way, knowing General Hancock's anxiety to reach Cold Harbor at the earliest moment, undertook to lead the column by a "short cut" through a wood road, forgetting the adage "that the longest way round is often the shortest way home." After traversing this wood for some distance, the road grew so narrow that the artillery caught between the trees and was eventually obliged to turn back, and, it being very dark at the time, the infantry moved on some distance without discovering the break in the column in the rear, and the result was much confusion. General Hancock put his staff at work to remedy the evil as far as possible, and after great exertions the corps was reunited; but all hope of reaching Cold Harbor before daybreak was gone, and it was not until near 7 A. M. that the corps began to arrive at that point, and then in an ex-tremely exhausted condition.

While the troops were struggling in the woods in the night, General Meade had ordered General Hancock to attack at once on reaching Cold Harbor, and endeavor to interpose between the enemy's right and the Chickahom-iny, and to secure a crossing of that stream.

CHAPTER XXII.

THE unfortunate delay which prevented the Second Corps from reaching Cold Harbor at the time anticipated, and the fatigued condition of the men after their exceptionally toilsome journey, rendered an immediate assault on the enemy inexpedient, and the orders for the attack were suspended until 5 P. M. of June 2d, and finally until 4.30 A. M. of the 3d. The corps was formed as follows: on Wright's left, Gibbon's division crossing the Mechanicsville road, Barlow on his left. Birney's division, which had been left to support Smith's Eighteenth Corps in front of Moody's house, came up at 2 P. M. on the 2d, and was posted in rear of Barlow's left.

All the ground required in taking positions was wrested from the enemy by heavy skirmish lines and sharp fighting.

There was little opportunity after the troops got into position to make the close examination of the ground which was desired; but every effort was made to get information of the enemy's position. It was found that he held a sunken road in front of Barlow's division, which, if protected on the flanks and well manned, might prove as disastrous to the First Division as the sunken road and stone wall at Fredericksburg and the sunken road at Antietam to the troops which assaulted them. Little could be learned of the enemy's main line in front of Barlow, on account of the dense growth of low pines which effectually screened it. In Gibbon's front the information gained was even more scant.

Barlow's division was formed for the assault in two deployed lines: the brigades of those tried and ever-faithful leaders, Brooke and Miles, in the first line, and those of Byrnes and McDougall in the second. Gibbon had a similar formation for his first line, which consisted of Tyler's and Smythe's brigades, while those of McKeen and Owen were in close column of regiments in the second line. The gallant McKeen had been taken from his regiment to command one of General Gibbon's brigades in the First Division, a few days before, when the heavy artillery division (Tyler's) was broken up.

Birney was ordered to support Barlow's advance, whose point of attack was a small house on a prominent point, notable for the fact that our artillery held it for a long time against Stonewall Jackson, on the day of the battle of Gaines's Mill, in 1862.

At the appointed hour, on the morning of the 3d, the divisions of Barlow and Gibbon moved to the assault. Barlow had a severe struggle at the sunken road, where he found the enemy posted, but succeeded in dislodging him, and followed him closely into his works, under a heavy fire from artillery and musketry. At the moment of entering the works, Brooke was struck in the abdomen by a canister shot, and very seriously wounded, an irreparable loss at this critical moment. The troops, for a time, held possession of the works, seizing three guns and capturing one color and about three hundred prisoners. Colonel L. O. Morris, who assumed command of Brooke's brigade when the latter was wounded, turned the captured guns upon the enemy, and endeavored to get them to work; but the occasion now demanded other efforts, for the enemy's reserve was rapidly approaching, and, unfortunately, Barlow's second line was not near enough to sustain the first. Miles made desperate efforts to hold that portion of the line he had taken, but was forced back by an enfilading fire of artillery. Barlow's men did not, however, retreat in confusion. With a gallantry rarely exhibited under such circumstances, a part of his line, particularly the One Hundred and Forty-eighth Pennsylvania regiment, Colonel Beaver commanding, faced to the enemy within a short distance of his line, and held their ground until they had constructed, with their bayonets and hands, a cover which enabled them to hold on permanently. The line so held was not more than thirty to forty paces from the enemy at one point.

In this battle Colonel Byrnes, Twenty-eighth Massachusetts Volunteers, commanding the Irish Brigade, Second Corps, which had been brought up in support, received a mortal wound. He was a brave and promising young officer. Colonel Morris, Sixty-sixth New York Volunteers, another valuable and gallant officer, was shot through the heart.

On the right Gibbon was still more severely handled. The difficulties of the ground in his front were such that no rapid advance could be made, and the men were, therefore, longer exposed to the fire. His advance was made a little later than Barlow's, owing to delay in forming one of his brigades. His line was unfortunately cut in two by a marsh by which, as it widened as they advanced, the parts were more and more separated. Notwithstanding the obstacles of the ground, however, Gibbon's troops pushed close up to the enemy's works, but not in such strength and order as to enable them to go further. The officers and men behaved intrepidly. Colonel McMahon, One Hundred and Sixty-fourth New York Volunteers, bore his colors in his own hands to the enemy's works, planting them on the parapet, where he fell, pierced by many bullets, and expired in the enemy's hands, losing his colors with honor. The gallant McKeen (Eighty-first Pennsylvania Volunteers), commanding a brigade of Gibbon's division, fell mortally wounded, just in front of the breastwork. He was shot in the stomach, and suffered intense agony. Seeing that he would probably be left to die between the lines of battle, it was reported that he begged his adjutant to kill him, and thus end his pain.

Colonel Haskell, Thirty-sixth Wisconsin Volunteers, whose courage and mettle had been formerly so conspicuously shown at Gettysburg and on other fields, succeeded to the command of McKeen's brigade, but had hardly ridden out to his line when he was shot through the head. Colonel Porter, Eighth New York Heavy Artillery, was also among the killed in this onslaught, and General Tyler was dangerously wounded and carried from the field.

But Gibbon's troops did not retire in disorder. Repelled, but not routed, they, too, held a position close to the enemy. Smythe's brigade even made a second attack, but failed to effect a lodgment, because, as stated in General Gibbon's report, of a blunder on the part of the commander of the brigade ordered to Smythe's support.

Birney's division took no part in the assault. It was not near enough to be brought up in time to take part in Barlow's attack. General Hancock was with Barlow's division during the assault. Offensive movements on our part ceased with the repulse of Smythe's second advance.

About this time General Grant visited General Hancock on the battle-field, and inquired how the fight had gone. General Hancock informed him that we had been repulsed, and had lost very severely, especially in valuable and distinguished officers, whom it would be hard to replace, and that the Second Corps had received a blow from which it would be difficult to recover—mentioning McKeen, Haskell, McMahon, Byrnes, and others. After some conversation, General Grant asked General Hancock whether he thought another assault would be likely to succeed. General Hancock replied that he was of the opinion that it would not; but that he would send to his division commanders and get their views on the subject, which he at once did. All of the division commanders were of the opinion that we could not carry the enemy's line by another attack.

General Grant then said that he would like General Hancock to have his troops in readiness to advance again against the enemy's works in the course of the morning, but also said that the advance should not be made unless further orders to that effect were received from himself or General Meade. General Grant then rode to another part of our lines. General Hancock at once gave the necessary orders to his division commanders to have their troops in readiness, in case he was ordered to make another attack. No such orders reached him, however, from General Grant or General Meade, but about 9 A. M. General Hancock received the following:

"HEADQUARTERS, ARMY OF THE POTOMAC,
June 3, 1864, 8.45 A. M.

"MAJOR-GENERAL HANCOCK : I send you two notes from Wright, who thinks he can carry the enemy's main line if he is relieved by attacks of the Second and Eighteenth Corps; also, that he is under the impression that he is in advance of you. It is of the greatest importance no effort should be spared to succeed. Wright and Smith are both going to try again, and, unless you consider it hopeless, I would like you to do the same.

(Signed)   "GEORGE G. MEADE, *Major-General.*"

From prisoners captured, General Hancock knew when he received the above note that Bushrod Johnson's entire division had come up and reënforced the enemy in their works in his front, and did not therefore consider we had any hope of success in another attack. How far the first attacks of Smith and Wright had been pushed does not appear in any published accounts of the battle, but we have never heard that any other troops than those of the Second Corps penetrated the enemy's lines or secured any trophies. General Wright's impression that he was in advance of the Second Corps was due, no doubt, to the direction of the line, for, as we have seen, the Second Corps line was almost in contact with that of the enemy, both in Barlow's and Gibbon's fronts, and so remained until the army moved to the James River.

An assault by the Second Corps had never been a trifling affair. Blood always followed the blow. An idea of the desperate fighting during this day's battle may be formed from the fact that the official report showed the losses in the Second Corps to be over three thousand men and officers, and this when only the two smallest divisions of the corps were actually engaged.

General Hancock had seen the young men whom he had trained to war and educated to command—on whom he relied in emergencies, and some of whom he had learned to love with a sincere affection—struck down in quick succession, in their chivalrous efforts to add another victory to our arms. He knew that the unlimited devotion of his men was capable of still further sacrifice, but he recoiled from sending them again to useless slaughter. It has been stated in Swinton's "Army of the Potomac," and since in various publications, that the *order* was actually given for a second assault at Cold Harbor on the morning of June 3d, but that, when it reached the troops in regular succession through division, brigade, and regimental commanders, no man stirred.

Whether such an occurrence was possible in any body of troops in the Army of the Potomac may well be questioned; certainly it was an impossibility and an absurdity when ascribed to the Second Corps. Leaving out of view the men like Barlow, Mott, Smythe, Miles, and many others, whom no danger could daunt, nor any considerations deter from prompt compliance with orders to advance, even if certain death seemed to await them, those who know General Hancock know also that, in such a contingency as is narrated by Swinton, he would have ridden to the front line and forced the men against the enemy.

About 10.40 A. M., on the 3d, after it was seen that we could not carry the enemy's lines, Birney's division was sent to the support of the Fifth Corps (Warren's), at

Moody's house, on the right of the Eighteenth Corps, where it remained until the 5th.

In the evening, just before dark, the enemy attacked both Barlow's and Gibbon's lines, but were easily repelled.

Early on the morning of the 4th Gibbon's sharp-shooters found the body of Colonel McKeen, and secured his watch and papers, but his body was so close to the enemy's line that they were unable to remove it. This day was characterized by very heavy artillery firing and a repetition of the attempt on Barlow's and Gibbon's lines in the evening.

Colonel L. O. Morris, Seventh New York Heavy Artillery, who had fallen to the command of Brooke's brigade, after that officer was wounded on the 3d, was killed this day in the trenches by one of the enemy's sharpshooters. Colonel James A. Beaver, One Hundred and Forty-eighth Pennsylvania Volunteers, succeeded him in command of the brigade.

Regular approaches against the enemy having now been decided upon, work to that end was begun by the One Hundred and Forty-eighth Pennsylvania Volunteers, Barlow's division, and on Gibbon's front.

On the 5th, about 5 P. M., Colonel Lyman, of General Meade's staff, and Major Mitchell, aide to General Hancock, carried out a flag of truce on the Mechan-icsville road, which was met by Major Wooten, of the Eighteenth North Carolina Infantry. General Lee being absent from his headquarters, no reply was received to the dispatch borne by Colonel Lyman until nearly ten o'clock. The flag was again put out the following morning, with a letter from General Grant to General Lee, but it was not until the 7th that an arrangement was effected for a cessation of hostilities from 6 to 8 P. M., for the purpose of burying the dead and succoring the wounded between the lines.

While holding the lines at Cold Harbor, General Hancock insisted upon retaining his headquarters in the very exposed location selected on the morning of his arrival. Unable to conceal his anxiety during the heavy firing which occurred each night, the General would call for his horse and ride rapidly toward that point of the line where the firing was heaviest. On one of these occasions his absence from his headquarters seemed remarkably providential. He had hurried off, accompanied by one or two of his staff, and, while the remainder were having their horses brought up, a shell came whistling into headquarters' camp, and struck the Assistant Provost Marshal of the corps, Captain Alexander McCune, who was standing in the door of General Hancock's tent, carrying off one of his legs below the knees, a wound from which he died a few days after.

When Birney's division rejoined the corps of the Fifth, it extended our line to the left nearly to the Chickahominy.

The corps remained in position, taking part in the siege operations at Cold Harbor, until the night of June 12th, when it took up the march for James River, glad to lose sight of the ground where it had met such losses. It had, in fact, received an almost mortal blow at Cold Harbor, and never again in that campaign recovered its full force.

A story was current in the army about this time that General Hancock, upon being asked where the Second Corps was, replied that "it lay buried between the Rapidan and the James."

This reply might have been made without any great

exaggeration, for it had lost in battle the flower of its
strength. The average loss for a period of about thirty
days was over 400 men daily. It was not in numbers
only, however, that the blow was so grievously felt.
Between these rivers the corps had suffered terribly in
the loss of its leaders—the men whose presence, experience, and example were worth many thousands of men.
Hays, Abbott, Merriam, Carroll, Webb, Brown, Coons,
Stryker, Tyler, Byrnes, McMahon, Brooke, Haskell, Mc-
Keen, Porter, the Morrises, and many other leaders of
troops in battle were dead or gone from the corps by
reason of wounds; and, although there were many other
brave and efficient officers left, the places of those who
had been taken could not be filled, as the right men, unfortunately, are not always in the right places, and, in
fact, are frequently unknown, until circumstance and experience have developed them.

CHAPTER XXIII.

THE change of base to the James River in front of an enemy who had exhibited such consummate ability was a delicate and hazardous movement; but General Grant, assisted by his able subordinates, accomplished it with much skill and with entire success. We have not space for the details of the whole process, but must be content with describing the movements of the forces under the immediate command of General Hancock. This we are enabled to do with exactness, aided by the kindness and scholarly ability of General C. H. Morgan, late Chief of Staff of the Second Corps, whose narrative has been kindly placed at our service.

The march across the Peninsula (fifty-five miles) occupied two days, and was admirably conducted by every part of the army, Lee making no attempt to interfere with the withdrawal of the Union forces. The point on the James which the army struck was below Harrison's Landing. Delay was occasioned by the non-arrival of pontoons; but, as we shall see, other means were supplied for transporting his troops over the river. The details of his movement are as follows.

Barlow's division marched out of the lines at Cold Harbor at 11 P. M., June 12th, followed in succession by Gibbon and Birney. The lines were so close, and the picket firing had been so incessant for many days, that its cessation on our part was sufficient of itself to notify the enemy that we were moving. It was, therefore, an operation of great delicacy to disengage ourselves from this position without a contest. The movement was happily accomplished, however; and some time after the divisions had marched, the picket line was quietly withdrawn and joined to the corps by Colonel Hamill, Sixty-sixth New York Volunteers, field officer of the day of the Second Corps—an officer who, from his coolness and other soldierly qualities, was especially adapted for such delicate service—assisted by Captain W. P. Wilson, A. D. C., whom General Hancock had detailed for duty with Colonel Hamill on that occasion.

After a weary night-march the corps reached Jones's Bridge over the Chickahominy. At this point Birney's division took the lead, and the column proceeded toward the James River, bivouacking at Wilcox Landing, between five and six o'clock that evening.

A few minutes past ten o'clock the next morning, the transports were in readiness to begin crossing the troops to Windmill Point, on the south bank of the James. A bridge of boats was constructed at a lower point on the river, on which other corps of the army crossed.

General Hancock established his headquarters at the landing, to superintend the transfer, and so energetically was it pushed that, despite the somewhat limited means at command, the three divisions and four batteries of the corps were landed on the south bank at Windmill Point, ready to move by 6.30 A. M. on the 15th.

During the night of the 14th General Hancock received the following instructions from General Meade :

"General Butler has been ordered to send to you at Windmill Point sixty thousand (60,000) rations. So soon as they are received and issued, you will move your command by the most direct route to Petersburg, taking up a position where the City Point Railroad crosses Harrison's Creek, at the cross roads indicated at this point, and extend your right toward the mouth of Harrison's Creek, where we now have a work."

We quote these instructions in full, because the march of the Second Corps and the hour of its arrival at Petersburg had a very decided bearing on the fate of that city, and formed the subject of considerable controversy at the time.

Early on the morning of the 15th, General Hancock issued his orders of march, directing Birney's division to move at 9 A. M., or as soon thereafter as it had drawn its rations. At 6.30 A. M. General Hancock notified General Meade that the rations had not arrived, and at 7.30 A. M. General Meade replied that the corps should move without its rations, leaving an officer to conduct the transport to some suitable point on the Appomattox. But it chanced that, just as this order was received, General Hancock was informed that the rations had arrived and were being unloaded—this report being made by the engineer officer charged with the repair of the wharf at which the transport was to land. General Hancock was therefore authorized to go on with the issue, and it was not until an hour later that word reached him that the report concerning the arrival of the rations was erroneous, the officer who made it having seen a transport from City Point go to the wharf, and surmised the rest. As soon as this was ascertained, the ration details were recalled, and the column ordered to move. (It may be mentioned here that the transport arrived about noon, and, as she drew eleven feet of water, could not have unloaded at any wharf on the south side.) General Hancock remained on the north bank, hurrying forward the embarkation of his ammunition and artillery, until the last-mentioned order was received, when he crossed the river and joined his troops. His having been in the saddle almost night and day since the 3d of May had caused the wound he had received at Gettysburg to become much irritated and inflamed, threatening, in fact, to compel him to quit the field for a time. He was now, in consequence, obliged to travel in an ambulance, leaving his chief of staff to conduct the column.

A map had been furnished General Hancock from army headquarters for his guidance, on which the designated position of the corps at Harrison's Creek was traced in colored crayon. According to the map, Harrison's Creek was about four miles from Petersburg, in the direction of City Point. As is now well known, the position indicated had no existence, and Harrison's Creek was within the enemy's lines.

The order to move was given at 9.15 A. M. by signal telegraph, and also transmitted at the same hour by the hands of a staff officer; but, to add to the chapter of accidents, the boat in which the staff officer took passage grounded, and he was delayed thirteen minutes, while the signal dispatch miscarried entirely. If we describe these incidents with some minuteness, we hope it may not therefore be inferred that we attach any great importance to them, for the corps could have moved at half past six with one day's rations, had it been so ordered, or had General Hancock surmised that he was an element in any important combination made by the Lieutenant-General, or that any attack was to be made on Petersburg that day. As it was, the column moved at 10.30 A. M. The country was pretty thoroughly swept of its white inhabitants, who had fled at the approach of our army, and the roads had from disuse ceased to have the appearance of highways.

Some negro guides were procured, but neither they nor the occasional white people found could give any information concerning Harrison's Creek.

It was finally determined that the map was worse than useless as a guide. The day was very hot, and but little water was found on the route, causing the men to suffer severely. No delays occurred, however, after the march began, and about 3 P. M. Birney's division was within six miles of Petersburg, on the Prince George Court-house road. Here it was decided, from information gleaned from negroes, that the speediest method of getting to the position the corps was ordered to take was to march to old Court-house, and thence by a cross road to the line behind Harrison's Creek. Accordingly Birney and Gibbon were turned in the direction of Old Court-house, while Barlow, who was in their rear, took a shorter road from Powell's Creek to Old Court-house, followed by the train.

Random artillery firing had been heard at intervals during the march, and, as the column turned from the direct road to Petersburg, the firing — without being heavier than that from a single battery—became brisk enough to cause the question to be presented to General Hancock's mind, whether or not he should march toward the guns. Inquiry at the houses in the vicinity showed that Kautz's division of cavalry with several guns had passed toward Petersburg in the morning, and the firing was naturally attributed to a reconnoissance or raid by the cavalry, and General Hancock therefore decided to adhere to his original instructions. He had a right to suppose that if any enterprise had been set on foot which might require his coöperation, he would have been informed thereof, in order that he might direct the march of his troops with intelligence. General Hancock's surprise may therefore be imagined when, at half past five, as the head of his column was about a mile from Old Court-house, he received the following dispatch from Lieutenant-General Grant, addressed to General Gibbon or any division commander of the Second Corps:

"Some of my staff, who came up from Fort Powhatan, report not having seen the Second Corps marching as they passed. Orders were sent for the corps to march early this morning, and General Meade reported that the orders were sent at 6 A. M. [It has been seen that these orders were modified by consent of General Meade, on account of the rations, which had been ordered to the corps.] Use all haste in getting up. Smith carried the outer works at Petersburg to-day, and may need your assistance. This order is intended for the whole Second Corps and directed to you, supposing you to have the advance. Communicate it to all the division commanders and to General Hancock, and push forward as rapidly as possible. Commissary stores are now being loaded into wagons, and will reach you some time to-night on the road.

(Signed)   "U. S. GRANT, *Lieutenant-General.*"

Fortunately the head of the column at this time was nearly opposite the Middle Road leading to Petersburg, and was at once turned in that direction.

One of General Barlow's staff had brought the above order to General Hancock (it had reached General Barlow, instead of General Gibbon), and word was sent back by him that the leading divisions had marched for Petersburg, and that, if Barlow would take a cross road in the same direction, he would be met at the City Point Railroad crossing, and shown to his position. Staff officers were dispatched by General Hancock to General Smith, to ascertain the situation and to find the roads by which the troops would probably move in taking position, General Hancock himself, notwithstanding the condition of his wound, insisting upon mounting his horse and going to the front, though he was in such excruciating pain as to be unable to bear riding faster than a walk.

General Hancock's wound, received at Gettysburg, continued to give him great trouble and annoyance during the campaign, and, although he continued with his command, he was obliged to travel in an ambulance a great portion of the time. His habit, on the march, was to remain in his ambulance at the head of his column until in the vicinity of the enemy, when he mounted his horse, and there remained until the fighting was over. During the whole of the summer of 1864 he was daily attended by a surgeon on account of his wound, which at that time was much irritated, and discharging more or less all the time—small portions of the bone at times passing from it.

While in front of the enemy's works at Petersburg, Virginia, in June, 1864, when the troops were constantly under fire, and the General was obliged to be mounted nearly all of the time, both day and night, his wound became so inflamed and dangerous that, as will be hereafter seen, he was compelled to relinquish command of the corps for a few days (June 17th, after the bloody fight of that day was over), and turned it over to his next in rank. He did not, however, leave the field, but continued with the troops, and again assumed command of the corps, June 27th, finding himself much relieved by the discharge of quite a large piece of bone from the wound.

He continued to suffer from this wound during all the rest of the war.

Half an hour after the receipt of the dispatch from the Lieutenant-General, the following was received from General Smith:

"HEADQUARTERS EIGHTEENTH CORPS, *June* 15, 1864.
(*No hour.*)

" MAJOR-GENERAL HANCOCK (or GIBBON):

"GENERAL: General Grant has authorized me to call on you to hurry forward to Petersburg, to aid in its capture. At present I do not suppose there is much infantry force there, but the wide open spaces along my entire front, and the heavy artillery fire of the enemy, have prevented me from attempting any assault, and from getting my artillery into position to do any service. If the Second Corps can come up in time to make an assault to-night after dark, in vicinity of Norfolk and Petersburg Railroad, I think it may be successful. But to-night is the last night, as General Lee is reported crossing at Chapin's Bluff. Please inform me by bearer when the head of your column may be expected here. My left is at the Jordan Point road. Respectfully,

(Signed)   " WILLIAM F. SMITH,
" *Major-General Commanding.*"

At 6.30 P. M. the head of General Hancock's column (Birney's division) had arrived at the Bryant house, on Bailey's Creek, about one mile in rear of Hinck's division of the Eighteenth Corps. Gibbon followed closely, and both divisions were massed at that point, with instructions to move up as soon as they could ascertain where their assistance was needed.

General Hancock, in the mean time, sought General Smith on the field, and met him on his line just at dusk. In the interview which followed, General Hancock tendered to General Smith the use of Gibbon's and Birney's divisions for any further operations General Smith might desire to make, telling him in substance that it was too dark for him (General Hancock) to make any examination of the position, and as General Smith had acquired familiarity with the situation, by having been in front of the works during the afternoon, he should know best what ought to be done.

At General Smith's request the two divisions were brought up, and relieved the troops of the Eighteenth Corps in the captured works, between the Friend and Dunn houses, embracing nearly, if not quite all, of the captured line, Gibbon taking the right of the Prince George road, and Birney the left. It was about 11 P. M. when this operation was completed.

The failure of the Second Corps to arrive "in time" was given in the "New York Tribune," a day or two after, as the reason why Petersburg was not taken on the 15th June. It must be clear, from the narrative we have given, that the hour of arrival of the Second Corps was as soon after General Grant's dispatch was received as possible.

That General Hancock was under no responsibility

10

to go to Petersburg before the receipt of that dispatch must be equally apparent. Feeling aggrieved at the charges referred to, as they evidently came from an official origin, General Hancock applied for a court of inquiry, and then the remarkable fact was developed that not even General Meade, the Commander of the Army of the Potomac, knew that Petersburg was to be attacked.

In endorsing General Hancock's application, General Meade says, "Had either General Hancock or myself known that Petersburg was to be attacked, Petersburg would have fallen."

General Hancock was thoroughly impressed with the importance of gaining every foot of ground which could be seized in the direction of the Appomattox. After midnight, on the 15th, therefore, he sent the following instructions to Generals Gibbon and Birney:

"If there are any points on your front commanding your position, now occupied by the enemy, the Major-General commanding directs that they be taken at or before daylight, preferably before, as it is desirable to prevent the enemy from holding any points between us and the Appomattox. It is thought there are one or two such points. General Barlow will soon be up, and will mass on Gibbon's left."

This dispatch was delivered to Generals Gibbon and Birney between 1 and 2 A. M. on the 16th. Barlow's division had missed its road from Old Church, and, for some reason not easily understood, had marched toward City Point, until it was stopped by one of General Hancock's staff, and the column placed on the Petersburg road—too late, however, to enable the division to get on the field that evening (the 15th). It bivouacked about three miles in the rear, and came up early the next morning.

In regard to the manner in which the instructions we have just quoted were carried out, it may be said that nothing was done during the night. The enemy's pickets were firing briskly while Gibbon and Birney were relieving the troops of the Eighteenth Corps, and the commander reported that the darkness prevented the necessary examination to determine whether or not the enemy occupied any positions in front such as were spoken of in General Hancock's note.

The General rode to the line of the Second Division soon after daybreak, and found the enemy's pickets within pistol-shot of the intrenchments. A staff officer, who was sent to Birney's front, passed through his line and out toward the Avery house, without seeing any of Birney's pickets, but saw the enemy forming line of battle to the right, and in front of that point, seizing the large redoubt in that vicinity, and stealing, an hour after daylight, the very ground Burnside and Barlow afterward assaulted with such heavy loss. The troops of the enemy seen were evidently coming in great haste from Petersburg, the column being stretched out in such manner as to indicate that the march had been hurried.

During the temporary absence of both General Grant and General Meade on the morning of the 16th, General Hancock was instructed to take command of all the troops then in front of Petersburg, and to push forward a reconnoissance to determine a suitable place for an assault which it was proposed to make at 6 P. M. Barlow's division had been meanwhile formed on Birney's left, and Burnside's corps, which came up later, had massed on Barlow's left, under instructions to assist in the assault, or in case the enemy should attack our lines.

The reconnoissance was made by Birney on the left of the Prince George Court-house road. General Meade arrived while it was in progress, and it was decided that the attack should be made toward the Hare house on Birney's front. This reconnoissance led to a very animated skirmish and artillery fire, which continued to the time set for the assault. The burden of the attack fell upon Barlow's and Birney's divisions. Gibbon was, however, engaged, and two brigades of the Eighteenth Corps and two of the Ninth were used as supports. It was evident that Lee's veterans had arrived, for the spirited attacks of Birney and Barlow failed to break the enemy's line, though it was forced back some distance. General Barlow led one of his assaults, cap in hand, but his example was in vain. He was bravely seconded by his officers, many of whom were shot down. The gallant Colonel Patrick Kelly, Eighty-eighth New York Volunteers, commanding the Irish Brigade, was killed at the head of his command while cheering them on. He was a most faithful, intrepid, and reliable soldier. Colonel James A. Beaver, One Hundred and Forty-eighth Pennsylvania Volunteers, commanding the Fourth brigade of Barlow's division, was seriously wounded at the head of his command, leaving that brigade in the hands of its fourth commander within a fortnight. The skirmish and artillery fire continued much of the night, as at Cold Harbor.

The 17th passed without an assault by the Second Corps, although the troops were engaged at intervals during the day in checking the attempt of the enemy to feel our lines. Burnside made a successful assault in the morning from Barlow's left, capturing several guns and

some prisoners. He attacked again in the evening un-
successfully, in which attack Barlow participated, losing
largely, particularly in prisoners. These assaults were
made against the positions taken up by the enemy late on
the previous morning, as already described. By night of
the 17th General Hancock's wound had become so irritated and painful as to compel him temporarily to relinquish the command of his corps, which was turned over
to the next senior, Major-General Birney.

CHAPTER XXIV.

THE history of the bloody assaults, made on the 18th under General Birney's orders, has never been written. At daylight he pushed forward a strong skirmish line on the right and left of the Prince George Court-house road, and found that the enemy had withdrawn from the positions they held the night before, to the new line beyond the Hare house. It is very evident that it was not then supposed at army headquarters that the purpose of the enemy in holding their advanced ground so tenaciously was to permit the construction of the new line, which Lee held so long and successfully afterward, for at 7 A. M. the following was sent to General Birney:

"HEADQUARTERS, ARMY OF THE POTOMAC,
"*June* 18th, 7 A. M.

"MAJOR-GENERAL BIRNEY: I have received your dispatch and Hoke's man. There is every reason to believe the enemy have no regularly fortified line between the one abandoned and Petersburg; but, if time is given them, they will make one. I have moved the whole army forward, and directed the commanding officers on your right and left to communicate with you. It is of great importance the enemy should be pressed, and, if possible, forced across the Appomattox. I can not ascertain whether there is any force in our front but Beauregard's, consisting of Hoke's, Ransom's and Johnson's (Bushrod) divisions. They can not be over 30,000, and we have 55,000. If we can engage them before they are fortified, we ought to whip them.

(Signed) "GEO. G. MEADE."

General Birney pushed on until he developed the works of the enemy, and, between 10 and 11 A. M., reported to General Meade that their position was strong; that artillery could not assist in attacking them ; and that he (Birney) was ready to assault when Martindale and Neill (commanding troops of the Eighteenth Corps on the right of the Second) were ready.

General Meade directed that the attack should be made at 12 M., by headquarters time ; that the column of assault should be strong, well supported, and vigorously pushed, and should advance without firing until it had penetrated the enemy's lines. The main assault was made by Gibbon's division in two lines, and it must have been made "on time," for at 12.20 P. M. General Pierce, then commanding a brigade in Gibbon's division, reports that the assault has been repulsed, and a postscript to the same dispatch announces the wounding of Pierce himself.

General Birney, however, determined to renew the assault, and, on notifying General Meade of this intention, received the following reply :

"You will attack again as you propose with the least

possible delay. The order of attack this morning required strong columns of assault. Please conform to
this. General Martindale is about advancing again, and
needs your coöperation. Select your own point of attack,
but do not lose any time in examination."

Martindale's previous advance to a crest occupied by
the enemy met with little opposition. He secured about
forty prisoners. We give one more dispatch from General Meade, to show the persistence with which he attempted to force the lines of Petersburg on the 18th.

"HEADQUARTERS, ARMY OF THE POTOMAC,
"*June* 18, 1864.

"MAJOR-GENERAL BIRNEY: I have sent a positive
order to Generals Burnside and Warren to attack, at all
hazards, with their whole force. I find it useless to appoint an hour to effect coöperation, and I am therefore
compelled to give you the same order. You have a large
corps, powerful and numerous, and I beg you will at
once, as soon as possible, assault in a strong column. The
day is fast going, and I wish the practicability of carrying the enemy's line settled before dark.
(Signed)   "GEO. G. MEADE,
"*Major-General.*"

Birney's next attempt was made from the Hare house
on Mott's front, with two columns formed in columns of
regiments. Mott took the measures most likely to lead
to success. The First Maine Heavy Artillery, nearly one
thousand strong, was in his command, and, as it was a new
regiment, composed of exceptionally good material, and
had not yet become disheartened by repeated and unsuc-
cessful assaults, Mott determined that it should lead the

attack, and, if it gained any advantages, the old, tried regiments in the rear should secure and retain them. The First Maine made a most gallant advance. They charged, without firing, across an open field about three hundred and fifty yards in width, but failed to penetrate the enemy's lines, leaving over six hundred in killed and wounded. The veteran regiments in the rear, who, as Mott said, "had seen the wolf and bore his scars," did not persist in the assault.

Barlow's division had its full share in the assaults made this day on the immediate right of the Ninth Corps and left of Mott's division, but the details of the movements are not known. The mortality list, however, speaks for itself.

At 5 P. M. General Meade had become satisfied that it was impracticable to carry the enemy's lines, but his last dispatch shows how firmly he had set his soul upon the attempt.

"HEADQUARTERS, ARMY OF THE POTOMAC,
"5 P. M., *June* 18, 1864.

"MAJOR-GENERAL BIRNEY: Sorry to hear you could not carry the works. Get the best line you can, and be prepared to hold it. I suppose you can not make any more attacks, and feel satisfied all has been done that can be done.

(Signed) " GEORGE G. MEADE,
" *Major-General Commanding.*"

Here ended the long list of terrible and bloody assaults, inaugurated at Spottsylvania, in which the Army of the Potomac was hurled against the enemy's lines; to be seized at every rebound, and hurled again and again, until all opposition was beaten down by the mere shock of impact.

On the 19th the army was busily engaged in strengthening its position by breastworks. On the 20th the Second Corps was relieved from the lines by the Sixth and Ninth Corps, and massed in rear of the left center. This going "in reserve" was an old joke in the corps. As long ago as Gettysburg, when it was announced that the Second Corps would be in reserve, a brisk little Irishman in the Irish Brigade created much merriment among his comrades by his dry observation, " Yis, resarved for the hard fighting." Accordingly, no surprise was felt when the morning saw the corps on the move across the Norfolk Railroad and Jerusalem plank road, where it took up Warren's line and extended it to the Williams house— this being the first of the extensions to the left in front of Petersburg which had for their object the cutting of the Weldon and Lynchburg Road. This road was the line of supply, both of men and of provisions, for Lee's army. It connected Richmond with North Carolina, and was also a line of retreat. Hence the importance of controlling it. Barlow's division had the left, and pushed to within two miles of the Weldon Road, skirmishing with the enemy's cavalry. He was relieved by the Sixth Corps, which, on the night of the 21st, took up the line from the left of the Second Corps to the Williams house.

On the night of the 21st General Birney was ordered to move forward, in connection with the Sixth Corps, to more closely envelope the enemy's line. The left being the exposed flank, General Birney directed that it should preserve its connection with the Sixth Corps, and make its progress correspond with General Wright's right. General Meade, becoming impatient at the delay to which this methodical arrangement gave rise, ordered each corps to move forward independently of the other. The enemy were already feeling the right of the Sixth Corps line, and as Birney swung forward, in obedience to General Meade's orders, he left this firing to his rear and to his left. Barlow was on that flank, and had a lively appreciation of the danger attending the movement. He therefore moved one brigade on his left by the flank, ready to form line at once, should his left be threatened. There was no trouble until about three o'clock in the afternoon of the 22d, when Barlow's left was thrown into confusion by an attack of the enemy, who had penetrated through the gap between the Second and Sixth Corps. The giving way of his left, and consequent advance of the enemy, forced Barlow's whole division hastily back to its original position. The enemy burst upon him just as his line was reëstablished, but was met so vigorously by Miles that the attack here was almost immediately abandoned.

The enemy now pushed down the line, striking the other divisions in turn as their left flanks were exposed, and attacking also in front, until the entire line had been thrown back on its original ground, with a loss of several hundred prisoners and four guns—the latter belonging to McKnight's Pennsylvania Battery, on Gibbon's front. McKnight made a brave effort to save his guns, and to recapture them, but the enemy succeeded in running the guns over the broken parapet and drawing them off. The recapture of these guns was earnestly desired, none ever having been lost by the corps up to that time, excepting one of Arnold's Battery at the Po. General Gibbon offered to General Pierce (commanding a brigade in the Second Division, on whose line the guns were taken) all the assistance he might require; but that officer was of the opinion that the task was almost hopeless, and no determined effort was made.

For some reason, the loss of brigade and regimental commanders had been exceptionally great in the Second Corps, and, though we have not the data for comparison, we are confident that no other corps was nearly so unfortunate in this respect.

General Meade issued orders for Birney and Wright to attack at half past three on the morning of the 23d; subsequently changing the hour to seven o'clock, he took post at the Sixth Corps headquarters in the morning. How far Wright moved we have never learned, but Barlow's skirmishers were advanced far enough to show that the enemy was behind rifle-pits, " as full as they could be got "; and upon hearing this, General Meade countermanded the order for the attack.

By the 27th General Hancock, though still suffering, was so far recovered as to permit him to resume command.

On the night of the 11th of July the Second Corps vacated its breastworks, and massed near the Williams house, and on the following day went into camp in rear of the Fifth Corps, General Hancock fixing his headquarters in the yard of the shot-riddled building, on the Norfolk road, known as the "deserted house."

The Sixth Corps had been sent to Washington on the 9th, to meet Early's movements in that direction. The narrow escape of Washington on this occasion determined General Grant to recommend the consolidation of the four departments near Washington into one, to be commanded by an officer who could be trusted in all emergencies. The concentration of troops in the Valley rendered that an important command, and as it was under-

stood that General Meade was not averse to a more independent command than that of the Army of the Potomac,
it was contemplated to transfer him to the Shenandoah.
General Hancock was to succeed to the Army of the
Potomac, and General Gibbon to the Second Corps.
Action was delayed in the matter, but after General
Sheridan's first successes the project was renewed (the
President giving his assent), at Hampton Roads; but
when the time had arrived to put the intent into execution, Mr. Lincoln thought a change would be unwise,
while Sheridan (who had just won a battle) was doing
"so well." General Hancock did not take any part in
this matter, although informed of it by General Meade,
nor did he express himself upon it.

On July 23d General Birney gave up his division
(Third, Second Corps), to take command of the Tenth
Army Corps, in the Army of the James, to which he
had been assigned, on the recommendation of Generals
Meade and Hancock, among others. He had rendered
marked service during the campaign, service which was
generously and freely recognized by General Hancock.
Birney and Mott represented the remains of the gallant
old Third Corps, which had won such distinction under
Heintzelman, Hooker, Phil Kearney, Sickles, Berry, and
other distinguished commanders. This corps deserves
special credit for its conduct at Chancellorville and Gettysburg.

The losses of the Second Corps from the crossing of
the James until July 26th were very heavy, as will be
seen from the following table taken from General Hancock's official report : *

---

* The number, being more than six thousand men, amounted to nearly
one fourth the entire loss of the corps during the war.

COMMAND.	KILLED.		WOUNDED.		MISSING.		AGGREGATE.
	Commanding Officers.	Enlisted Men.	Commanding Officers.	Enlisted Men.	Commanding Officers.	Enlisted Men.	
Corps Hdqrs.........							
Art'y Brigade........	1	3		10		3	17
1st Division.........	17	249	53	1006	29	922	2276
2d Division.........	12	161	44	805	32	907	1961
3d Division.........	26	250	73	1256	15	377	1997
Total*.........	56	663	170	3077	76	2209	6251

* The casualties of the Eighth Ohio Volunteers and First Delaware Volunteers are not included in the above table.

CHAPTER XXV.

GENERAL Lee's lines of defense had been strengthening every day, and on the 1st of July were deemed impregnable, the Union engineers declaring that to take them by assault was utterly impracticable. A chain of redans, infantry curtains of bold construction, and rifle-pits swept clear round his position, while every approach was obstructed by abatis, stakes, and other obstacles. Richmond was similarly defended.

After two weeks of unavailing effort to carry the defenses of Petersburg by strategy and assault, it was manifest that they could only be reduced by regular siege.

A vast system of earthworks was constructed, which by the end of July were in condition to begin operations against the enemy, either by assault or by flanking the Confederate lines. Underground approaches to the lines of the enemy, and even under some points thereof, were dug, and it was resolved to make an assault in front of Burnside's position, parts of which were but one hundred and fifty yards from the enemy's front. A fort of the enemy projected beyond his average front, and Burnside,

on his own responsibility, had run an underground approach, starting from a ravine out of sight of the enemy,
and laid a mine under this work. It was intended to explode this mine, then open artillery fire, and make an
assault upon the enemy through the chasm expected to
be made by the explosion. The mine failed to explode
the first time it was fired. Lieutenant Jacob Douty and
Sergeant Henry Rees, of the Forty-eighth Pennsylvania,
bravely ventured in to ascertain the cause of failure, and,
relighting the fuse, the mine exploded, tossing the fort
and its garrison of 300 men into the air, and creating a
chasm 150 feet long by 60 wide and 30 deep. As it was
Burnside's mine, and in front of his position, the assaulting column was taken from his corps.

Burnside threw forward a division of colored troops,
which advanced beyond the crater made by the explosion,
charged, and was driven back into the crater, and there
all were huddled together in confusion. All order was
lost, and personal safety became the only impulse; the
enemy began to pour in upon them shot and shell; and
that hapless chasm became an appalling slaughter-house.

The enemy made an assault, which, in sheer despera-
tion, was repulsed, and then thousands began to dart out
of this slaughter-pen, and race at topmost speed into their
own lines. Our loss in this "miserable affair," as Grant
called it, was 4,400 killed, wounded, and prisoners; the
enemy's 1,000, including the 300 blown up in the fort.

These operations in front of Petersburg were very
wearing to the men of the army. The weather was intensely hot, water difficult to procure, the dust was almost
insufferable, especially to troops in motion, and the labor
of mining and constructing earthworks was overpowering.
On the afternoon of July 26th the Second Corps marched

toward Deep Bottom, *via* Point of Rocks and Bermuda Hundred, in obedience to orders from General Grant. General Hancock's instructions were to move rapidly from Deep Bottom to Chapin's Bluff, and to take and hold a position which would prevent the enemy from crossing at that point; while General Sheridan, with his cavalry, moved to the Virginia Central Railroad, and operated toward Richmond. Beyond this, General Hancock's movements were to be contingent upon General Sheridan's success, the main object being the destruction of the railroads north of Richmond, with the hope also of taking that city.

There were two bridges over the James at Deep Bottom, the bridge heads being held by Foster's brigade of the Tenth Corps. Naturally, for the purposes indicated, the cavalry would cross by the lower bridge and the infantry by the upper. On arriving at General Foster's headquarters, however, General Hancock ascertained that the enemy had so hemmed in Foster at the upper bridge, and were so strongly fortified, that it was doubtful if an advance in that direction would be successful. After studying the situation, and obtaining General Meade's consent to the change, he (General Hancock) determined to throw his infantry across the lower bridge, turn the enemy's flank, while General Foster threatened the position in front, and let the cavalry pass out in that direction. The infantry commenced crossing the bridge, which was thickly covered with hay to prevent the tread of the men and horses being heard in the enemy's lines, between 2 and 3 A. M. on the 27th, and was massed behind a belt of timber on the north bank near the bridge head. The cavalry followed immediately. Soon after daylight General Hancock ordered an advance. On the right the skirmish line of the Third Division, consisting of the Ninety-ninth and One Hundred and Tenth Pennsylvania Volunteers, was thrown out toward the New Market and Malvern Hill road, and, having become briskly engaged with the enemy, it was found necessary to reënforce it by the Seventy-third New York Volunteers. In the center, Barlow's skirmish line of Miles's brigade, composed of the One Hundred and Eighty-third Pennsylvania, Twenty-eighth Massachusetts, and Twenty-sixth Michigan Volunteers, commanded by Colonel Lynch, One Hundred and Eighty-third Pennsylvania, and accompanied by General Miles in person, engaged the enemy. Miles, ever on the alert, seized the opportunity afforded by the ground, which partly protected and concealed his advance, and by skillful disposition succeeded in throwing his skirmish line upon the enemy's rifle-pits, which were weakly held at that point, drove him back, and captured four twenty-pounder guns with their caissons. The skirmishers of General Foster had joined in this advance. Gibbon's skirmishers had been thrown out toward Four Mile Run, and as the enemy fell back his division took the advance in pursuit.

A battery, which opened fire on our right opposite General Mott, was speedily driven away by our artillery and Mott's skirmishers, and retreated by a cross road to the New Market and Long Bridge road.

When our advance arrived at Bailey's Creek, the enemy was found posted in well-constructed earthworks, with abatis, apparently well manned, in a position of unusual natural strength, the creek itself being an obstacle which could not well be passed by a line of battle, and the intervening ground being perfectly open to the enemy's fire. A close examination established the fact that the chance of a successful assault was doubtful, and an attempt was made to turn the position.

In the mean time the cavalry under General Sheridan moved over to the New Market and Long Bridge road, in the direction of Malvern Hill, gaining, by spirited charges, some high ground on our right, the possession of which, it was hoped, would be advantageous; but it did not prove so, as it was discovered that the enemy's flank was sharply refused to the left at Flusser's mill.

While Gibbon's division held the New Market and Malvern Hill road, Mott's and Barlow's divisions were thrown forward to the New Market and Long Bridge road, connecting with the cavalry. Barlow made a strong reconnoissance of the enemy's line, but failed in his purpose of uncovering his flank.

During the day some of our gunboats, stationed in the James River, threw their immense shot and shell over our lines into the enemy's intrenchments. About 3 P. M. General Grant visited the field, but General Hancock did not meet him. Having examined the position, he left a note for the latter, in which he stated that he had ridden along the line for some distance, and did not see that much was likely to be done, but still desired the cavalry to pass out if possible, his intention being that it should raid on the enemy's communications. His information was that seven brigades of infantry and a small force of cavalry were opposed to General Hancock during the night of the 27th.

The enemy received reënforcements from the south side of the river. Birge's brigade, Tenth Corps, of Butler's Army, about twenty-six hundred men, reported to General Hancock early on the morning of the 28th, and relieved Gibbon's division from its advanced position on

the New Market and Malvern Hill road. Gibbon then
massed in rear of our line of battle, in reserve. General
Sheridan was placed under General Hancock's orders, it
having been decided that he should advance up the Central or Charles City road, if either could be opened.

About 10 A. M., on the 27th, the following dispatch
was received by General Hancock, sent by General
Meade:

"CITY POINT, 9.10 P. M., *July 26th.*

"The position now occupied by Hancock would give
Sheridan no protection in returning by the way of Bottom's Bridge. I do not want him to go, unless the
enemy is driven into Chapin's Bluff or back to the city;
otherwise, he would be compelled to return north of the
Chickahominy, and it would be two or three weeks before
his cavalry would be fit for other service.

"I do not want Hancock to attack intrenched lines;
but I do want him to remain another day, if he can, with
the assistance of the cavalry, turn the enemy's position
and drive him away. It looks to me as if the cavalry
might move well out and get in rear of the enemy.

(Signed)   "U. S. GRANT,
                   "*Lieutenant-General.*"

The enemy had been discovered moving in strong
force to General Hancock's right as early as 8 A. M., and
it was evident that he was assuming the offensive. The
fire of our gunboats was directed upon the enemy by
signals, and forced him to change his route of march.
About 10 A. M. the enemy advanced against our cavalry,
not only on the New Market and Long Bridge road, but
also on the Charles City road. Gregg was forced in on
the latter, with the loss of one gun, while Torbert was

driven back on the cross road, connecting the roads leading by Ruffin's house, and the led horses and artillery of the cavalry seemed almost in the grasp of the enemy, when General Sheridan, by a brilliant charge (his men dismounted), drove him back in confusion for over a mile, capturing several colors and about two hundred prisoners. The prisoners belonged to Kershaw's division of infantry.

Gibbon's division had been hurried up to support General Sheridan, but the latter had disposed of the matter before Gibbon's arrival.

Anticipating now a more determined attack, General Hancock changed the disposition of the troops, taking a position along the New Market and Malvern Hill road, and posting artillery to prevent the enemy from cutting him off from the river.

General Hancock received repeated dispatches informing him that the enemy was concentrating against him, but no further demonstrations were made, save that our cavalry skirmishers were somewhat pressed. Generals Grant and Meade visited the line during the afternoon, and instructed General Hancock to send Mott's division that night to Petersburg, with instructions to report to General Ord, to relieve the Eighteenth Corps in the intrenchments. General Hancock continued holding his position at Deep Bottom with the remaining divisions of his corps, Birge's brigade of the Tenth Corps, and the cavalry, until the night of the 29th, when, having attracted to his front a large portion of Lee's army, it is supposed that General Grant concluded it to be a favorable time to assault the enemy's lines at Petersburg. General Hancock was now instructed to return to that point with the two divisions of his corps; and, accordingly, soon after dark on the 29th, he withdrew his entire command from Deep Bottom, Birge's brigade returning to the Tenth Corps, and General Sheridan crossing the Appomattox at Broadway Landing, to carry out special instructions received by him from Lieutenant-General Grant. Hancock pushed on, throughout a most weary and trying night-march of upward of twenty miles, in which the energies of the troops were taxed almost beyond endurance, to the position held by the Ninth and Eighteenth Corps in front of Petersburg, arriving there on the morning of the 30th, in time to witness the explosion of the "mine."

In the report of the operations at Deep Bottom by General Hancock, Colonel Biles, Ninety-ninth Pennsylvania Volunteers, and Colonel Lynch, One Hundred and Eighty-third Pennsylvania Volunteers, are specially mentioned for good conduct.

On the very day of the mine explosion General Grant ordered the cavalry and a corps of infantry to start on a new expedition—a raid on the Weldon Railroad. The Second Corps ("Hancock's cavalry," as the men then styled it) was the one designated. There was, however, a limit to the endurance of both men and horses, and it being represented by General Hancock that the corps was not in a condition to move at once on such service, and Gregg making a similar representation concerning his horses, the expedition was temporarily suspended.

CHAPTER XXVI.

THE expedition to destroy the Weldon Railroad, to
which allusion was made at the close of the last chapter,
was intrusted by General Grant to other hands than
was at first designed, and was eventually carried out with
success.

The Second Corps meanwhile remained at its camp
in the neighborhood of the " deserted house," as a reserve
in connection with the operations against Petersburg.
During this time and until the 12th of August General
Hancock was engaged in the duty of presiding over the
court of inquiry, that had been ordered by the President
to investigate the mine operation, which had resulted so
unfortunately for the Union army.

On the date last mentioned the corps was directed to
move to City Point, the design being to send a second
expedition to Deep Bottom, with the view of diverting
Lee's attention to some extent from Petersburg, and thus
enabling a more advantageous prosecution of the siege
of that stronghold.

The Second Corps bivouacked on the night of the 12th at City Point, and on the 13th the embarkation commenced, General Hancock proceeding to Deep Bottom in a tug-boat, accompanied by General Ingalls, Chief Quartermaster of the Army of the Potomac, to arrange for disembarking the troops. The fleet which conveyed this expedition consisted of sixteen vessels, ocean and river steamers, some of them drawing thirteen feet of water. A good deal of miscalculation was made in the planning of this expedition, and it failed in its chief intention—that of effecting a surprise of the enemy. General Birney, with the Tenth Corps, was already at Deep Bottom, where, after considerable delay, he was joined by the Second Corps, and the entire force immediately went into action.

On the 16th a fierce attack was made by General Birney, General Gregg (D. McM.), as a diversion, being ordered to push up the Charles City road with his cavalry and Miles's brigade.

The assault was made by Terry's division, led with marked gallantry by General Terry in person, on a point just above Flusser's mills, driving the enemy out of his works, and capturing three colors and between two and three hundred prisoners. An attack was made on the enemy on Terry's right in the mean time by Brigadier-General Birney's division of colored troops and Craig's brigade of Mott's division. The men acquitted themselves brilliantly, Colonel Craig being unfortunately killed.

At this point heavy reënforcements joined the enemy, who assailed us in turn, dislodging our troops from their works. Meanwhile, Gregg and Miles were having a lively fight on the Charles City road at Deep Creek, over which stream Gregg charged in column of fours through a ravine, driving the enemy in all directions, and pursuing him at a gallop for a mile and a half. Colonel John Irvin Gregg, commanding a brigade in General D. Mc. M. Gregg's division, which made the charge, was severely wounded in this affair. An important incident in the occurrence was the killing of General John R. Chambliss, the officer in command of the enemy's forces. He was shot through the body while endeavoring to recall his men. On his person was found a valuable map of Richmond and its defenses. His body was sent to the rear and buried within our lines.

Gregg and Miles now pushed on rapidly to within about six miles of Richmond, where they came upon intrenchments, and, the enemy shortly appearing in strength, they were forced to return to Deep Creek.

This brought the movement to August 17th. Continuous skirmishing occurred on the following day, but no heavy fighting, and at noon of that day, with the consent of General Grant, a flag of truce in the hands of Major Mitchell, of General Hancock's staff, was sent into the enemy's lines, to propose a cessation of hostilities. Major Mitchell succeeded in getting his flag recognized, and a truce was arranged, during which the dead of both sides were removed from between the lines, the body of General Chambliss being exhumed and delivered to his people.

On the morning of the 18th, General Barlow being obliged to relinquish the command of his division on account of ill health, General N. A. Miles succeeded him. In the afternoon of this day General Birney was attacked by the enemy in force, the latter being handsomely repulsed. In the mean time General Hancock's expeditionary force was being gradually reduced, orders from head-

11

quarters requiring him to send portions of it back to Petersburg, and on the 20th he was ordered to withdraw his command from Deep Bottom, and return by Point of Rocks to its old camps in front of Petersburg.

The casualties in the Second Corps attending this (second) expedition to Deep Bottom amounted in the aggregate to nine hundred and fifteen killed and wounded. The expedition was not as successful as had been hoped, but it caused General Lee to detach in the direction of the north side of the James a considerable force, thus weakening for the time his strength at Petersburg, and enabling General Grant to extend his left flank toward the Weldon Railroad. This road, as already stated, was an important avenue of Lee's communication with the South, and to cut it was General Grant's object. The expedition for this latter purpose was intrusted to the charge of General Warren, who began his operations on the morning of the 18th of August, while General Hancock was yet on the north side of the James.

The desired object was handsomely accomplished, the Weldon Road being captured and held at Ream's Station, but on the day following this the right center of our line was suddenly attacked and cut by a powerful column, but rallied, and reënforcements fortunately coming up to General Warren's aid, the position was regained and held, in spite of two other attacks, though with very large loss.

Returning to the lines before Petersburg on the morning of August 21st, after a dreary and fatiguing night-march over terrible roads, General Hancock's men were allowed to remain in camp only long enough to make coffee. The First and Second Divisions were then ordered to the vicinity of the Strong house, to slash timber and complete the defensive line. Finally this command was ordered to move on to the Gurley house, in the rear of the Fifth Corps, at which position they bivouacked in the mud, General Hancock and his division commanders sleeping on the ground in the midst of a pouring rain.

The next morning both divisions were placed on fatigue duty, repairing the roads. The First Division was now set to work completing the task which had been begun by General Warren of destroying the Weldon Railroad, and on the afternoon of the following day had accomplished this as far as Ream's Station, while the Second Division followed in support. Here slight intrenchments existed, and these were now occupied by Miles's division. They were, however, badly constructed, both sides being exposed to an enfilading and reverse fire, while the salient had been thrown out beyond a deep cut in the railroad, which seemed to separate that part of the line from the rest by an almost impassable obstacle. In these imperfect works, as it turned out, the two smallest divisions of the Second Corps (about six thousand strong) aided by a part of General D. McM. Gregg's cavalry, dismounted, were to fight one of the sharpest engagements of the war against a force exceeding them nearly three times in numbers.

At about half past ten on the night of the 24th of August, General Hancock received the following dispatch:

"HEADQUARTERS, ARMY OF THE POTOMAC,

"8 P. M., *August* 24, 1864.

"MAJOR-GENERAL HANCOCK, *Commanding Second Corps:*

"Signal officers report large bodies of infantry passing south from their intrenchments by the Halifax and Vaughan roads. They are probably destined to operate against General Warren or yourself, most probably against

your operations. The Commanding General cautions you
to look out for them.

   (Signed) "A. A. HUMPHREYS,

      "*Major-General, Chief of Staff.*"

  To this dispatch General Hancock replied, requesting
to know, if possible, the number of the enemy seen
marching, and the time; stating also, that if the enemy
was undertaking an operation against him, he did not desire to separate his forces so far—referring to the fact of
his instructions directing him to destroy the railroad as far
as Rowanty Creek, eight miles beyond Ream's Station.*

  At daylight on the 25th General Hancock directed
Gregg to make a reconnoissance with part of his cavalry,
to ascertain what was in his front. Meanwhile the work
of tearing up the railroads was suspended. A squadron
of cavalry, sent out by Gregg, reported on their return
that they had driven in the enemy's pickets at two
points on the Vaughan road without developing any apparent increase of strength. Accordingly the work of
tearing up the railroad was pushed on, but had progressed
but little, when our pickets were driven in by a sharp attack by the enemy, and Gibbon's division was withdrawn
from this duty, and ordered back to take post in the works,
where it occupied the left of our infantry line. Telegraphic communication having been opened from army
headquarters to Ream's Station, dispatches to and fro
were sent by these means. At this time, however, General Meade sent a dispatch to General Hancock by one of
his staff officers, announcing that he had ordered Mott to

---

 * In reply to this dispatch, General Hancock was informed that the number of the enemy seen marching out of their intrenchments was estimated
at 8,000 or 10,000; the time of leaving their works about sunset.

send all his available force to Ream's Station, and to take a battery with him, the officer in command to report to General Hancock on his arrival. He also authorized General Hancock to exercise his judgment as to withdrawing his command and assuming position on the left and rear of Warren, or any other position he might select. To this dispatch General Hancock replied that he was already engaged and could not withdraw, and that night could only tell what would come forth. This dispatch, it will be seen, was sent by an aid, being dated at 1 p. m., August 25th, although the telegraph line had been opened and used by General Hancock as early as 11.45 a. m. As late as 2.40 p. m. General Meade sent another dispatch to General Hancock by a messenger, informing the latter that he had ordered Wilcox's division of the Ninth Corps to move forward to Hancock's support by the Jerusalem plank road, and remain on it at a point about five miles from Ream's Station until ordered up by General Hancock. The dispatch closed as follows :

"I hope you will be able to give the enemy a good thrashing. All I apprehend is his being able to interpose between you and Warren. You must look out for this.
        (Signed)   " GEO. G. MEADE."

In the mean time Miles's pickets, on the Dinwiddie road, near Ream's Station, had already been driven in by a vigorous attack by the enemy in some force.

It was unfortunate that the reenforcements sent by General Meade were dispatched by way of the Jerusalem plank road, about ten miles around, and ordered to stop at a point five miles distant from General Hancock, when the open road along the railway, a distance of less than three miles, was available. It will also be remembered that General Hancock, with 6,000 infantry and 2,000 cavalry, most of the latter on picket duty, was now to confront a force of about 18,000 of the enemy's infantry and cavalry.*

* Some time after the battle of Ream's Station—after the war had closed, in fact—General Hancock was informed, by a Confederate officer who had the best means of knowing the facts, that their force consisted of about all the cavalry they had in the Army of Northern Virginia, and all they could draw from the Valley, commanded by General Wade Hampton; also, three divisions of infantry of four brigades each under Lieutenant-General A. P. Hill, who commanded all of their forces engaged. These brigades were made up from different divisions of General Lee's army for the occasion, and consisted of all the troops they could spare from the Petersburg line.

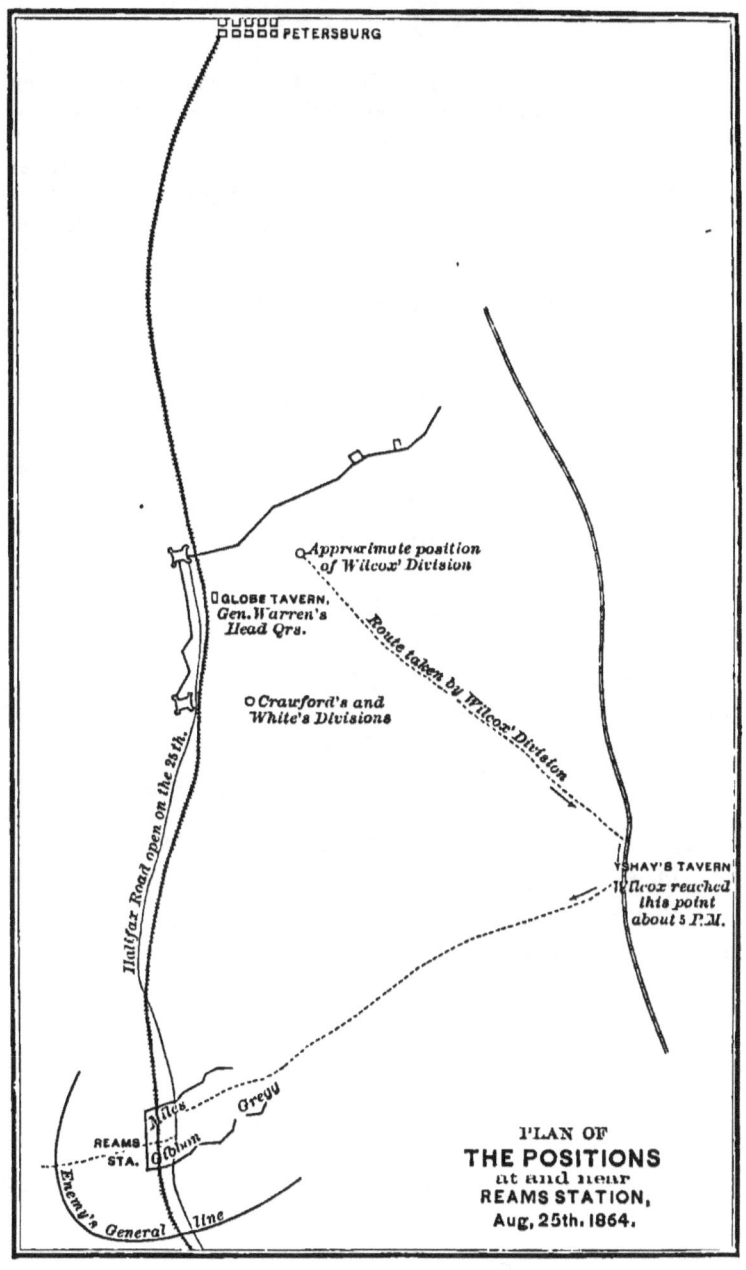

PETERSBURG

○ *Approximate position of Wilcox' Division*

▢ GLOBE TAVERN,
Gen. Warren's Head Qrs.

○ *Crawford's and White's Divisions*

Route taken by Wilcox' Division

Halifax Road open on the 25th.

SHAY'S TAVERN
Wilcox reached this point about 5 P.M.

Miles
Gregg
REAMS STA.
Gibbon

Enemy's General line

PLAN OF
THE POSITIONS
at and near
REAMS STATION,
Aug, 25th, 1864.

CHAPTER XXVII.

IN answer to the dispatch from General Meade, General Hancock replied as follows:

> "HEADQUARTERS, SECOND ARMY CORPS,
> "*August* 25, 1864, 4.15 P. M.

"GENERAL MEADE: I have just received your dispatch by Captain Rosecrantz. I fear it will be too late to have Wilcox come for any practical purposes, as he is between four and five miles off now; still, I shall order up his division. Had the division come down the railroad, it would have been here in time. I desire to know, as soon as possible, whether you wish me to retire from this station to-night, in case we get through safe.

(Signed) "W. S. HANCOCK,
"*Major-General.*"

In the mean time General Hancock sent a staff officer to order up Wilcox's division. While the occurrences just described had taken place, artillery had been posted by the Confederate General Hill to attack our intrenchments at Ream's Station in reverse, and a heavy fire was opened by those batteries. After about fifteen minutes of artillery fire, the enemy assaulted Miles's lines, where a break occurred, this point being held by three New York regiments, largely made up of substitutes and new recruits.

In describing these works, it will be remembered, mention was made of the salient which was separated from the remainder of the line by a deep cut in the railroad; in this salient had been placed Brown's Rhode Island Battery and Sleeper's Massachusetts Battery, and, as a reserve, a small brigade of the Second Division. When the break in our lines took place, the two batteries mentioned fell into the enemy's hands, after having been gallantly served until the last moment. Murphy's brigade of the Second Division was driven out, but the other brigade (Rugg's) was captured almost *en masse*. Another battery (McKnight's), stationed to the right and rear of the break, was also captured, after doing good execution. The faulty construction of this part of the line exposed Gibbon's division to a musketry fire in reverse, and, though ordered forward to retake our line, at the first fire from the enemy our men retired ingloriously to the breastworks.

General Hancock's horse was shot under him here while he was endeavoring to remedy this unfortunate state of affairs. In fact, at this juncture, only the most extraordinary efforts on the part of General Hancock, assisted by Generals D. McM. Gregg and Miles, prevented the disaster from assuming the most serious proportions. Miles rallied a portion of his own regiment, the Sixty-first Volunteers, and succeeded in recapturing McKnight's battery and a considerable portion of the line, his small attacking force being reorganized, as it became dissipated, by parties collected by Generals Hancock and Miles and their staff officers. General Hancock is described as having exposed himself much more than the humblest soldier in his command, in his efforts to restore the fortunes of the day ; not only was his horse shot under him, but another ball cut his bridle rein in two, and his corps flag, which always followed him closely, was pierced by five balls, while another struck the staff. One of his staff officers, Captain Brownson, Commissary of Musters, heretofore creditably mentioned, was now mortally wounded while conducting some men he had rallied to the front. He was a brave and valuable young officer. This attack, which threatened to cut the road in rear of Miles's position, was checked by a heavy flank fire from Gregg's cavalry on our extreme left, enabling Gibbon to reëstablish his line in time to cover the endangered road.

The conspicuous services which were rendered by General D. McM. Gregg with his command and one regiment of Spear's cavalry, during this day and particularly at this point, can not be overestimated. He checked the pursuit of Gibbon's men, and saved that portion of our line from an overwhelming disaster.

A new line was at length established, and General Hancock confined his further efforts to holding this position. General Wilcox had not come up, and it was decided not to resume the offensive.

This was the first occasion during the war when General Hancock experienced the bitterness of defeat. Never before had he seen his corps fail to respond to the utmost when he had called upon them personally for a supreme effort. He could no longer conceal from himself that his once mighty corps retained but the shadow of its former strength and vigor. Struck to the heart by these new impressions, he rode up to one of his staff, covered with dust and begrimed with powder and smoke, and placing his hand on the officer's shoulder said, "Colonel, I don't care to die, but I pray to God I may never leave this field."

Darkness was now fast closing in. Still no reënforcements had arrived, and as the position was untenable, unless the works could be retaken, General Hancock gave orders for withdrawal from the field. Previous to this, however, he sent for his three division commanders, and asked each one if he could retake the lines he had lost. Miles replied he could, that he had already retaken a part; Gregg said he could retake his without difficulty, as it was a mere cover to General Gibbon's flank; but General Gibbon stated that his division was so shattered and dispersed that he could not retake his line. General Hancock then directed that as soon as it was dark the withdrawal should commence, and this was successfully accomplished. General Hancock sent his adjutant-general, General Francis A. Walker, to convey orders to the troops, but General Walker rode into the enemy's lines and was captured. It was learned from him after his release that the enemy left the field at the same time with our force, fell back six miles, and encamped.

The losses of the two divisions of the Second Corps engaged in the battle of Ream's Station amounted in the aggregate to 2,198 killed and wounded, about equally divided between Gibbon's and Miles's divisions.

The following dispatch is pertinent at this point :

"HEADQUARTERS OF THE ARMY OF THE POTOMAC,
"*August* 25th, 1864, 11 P. M.

"DEAR GENERAL: No one sympathizes with you

more than I do in the misfortunes of this evening.
McEntee gave me such a good account of affairs up to
the time he left, and it was then so late, I deferred going
to you as I had intended.　If I had had any doubt of your
ability to hold your lines from a direct attack, I would
have sent Wilcox with others down the railroad; but my
anxiety was about your rear, and my apprehensions were
that they would either move around your left or interpose between you and Warren.　To meet the first contingency I sent Wilcox down the plank road; for the second,
I held Crawford and White.　I thought it likely, not
trying you, they might attack Warren, and wished to
leave him until the last moment some reserves.　I am
satisfied you and your command have done all in your
power, and, though you have met with a reverse, the
honor and escutcheon of the Old Second are as bright
as ever, and will on some future occasion prove that it is
only when enormous odds are brought against them that
they can be swerved.　Don't let this matter worry you,
because you have given me every satisfaction.

"Truly yours,　　GEORGE G. MEADE,
(Signed)　　　　　"*Major-General Commanding.*
" To MAJOR-GENERAL HANCOCK, *Commanding Second Corps.*"

It is no small proof of General Hancock's military
skill that he was able to extricate himself from a position
in which destruction seemed almost inevitable, and not
only this, but that he should have inflicted such punishment upon the overwhelming forces of his adversary as
to make it almost a drawn battle, which is shown by the
fact that the enemy left the field immediately after the
Union forces retired.

CHAPTER XXVIII.

On the day after the battle of Ream's Station, one of the two divisions engaged in that fight was massed near the Jones house, and the other at the Avery house. Mott's division still remained in the intrenchments before Petersburg. Everything continued quiet up to the beginning of September, excepting such skirmishing as happened along the picket lines of the two armies, and in which but little advantage remained to either side.

On the 16th of September occurred the famous raid of Hampton's cavalry to our rear at Coggin's Point, resulting in the capture of the beef herd of our army, consisting of 2,500 cattle. For days afterward the enemy's pickets were very facetious on the subject of beef, as, indeed, they had a right to be.

On the night of September 24th the First and Second Divisions, Second Corps, relieved the Tenth Corps in the intrenchments from the right of Mott's division to the

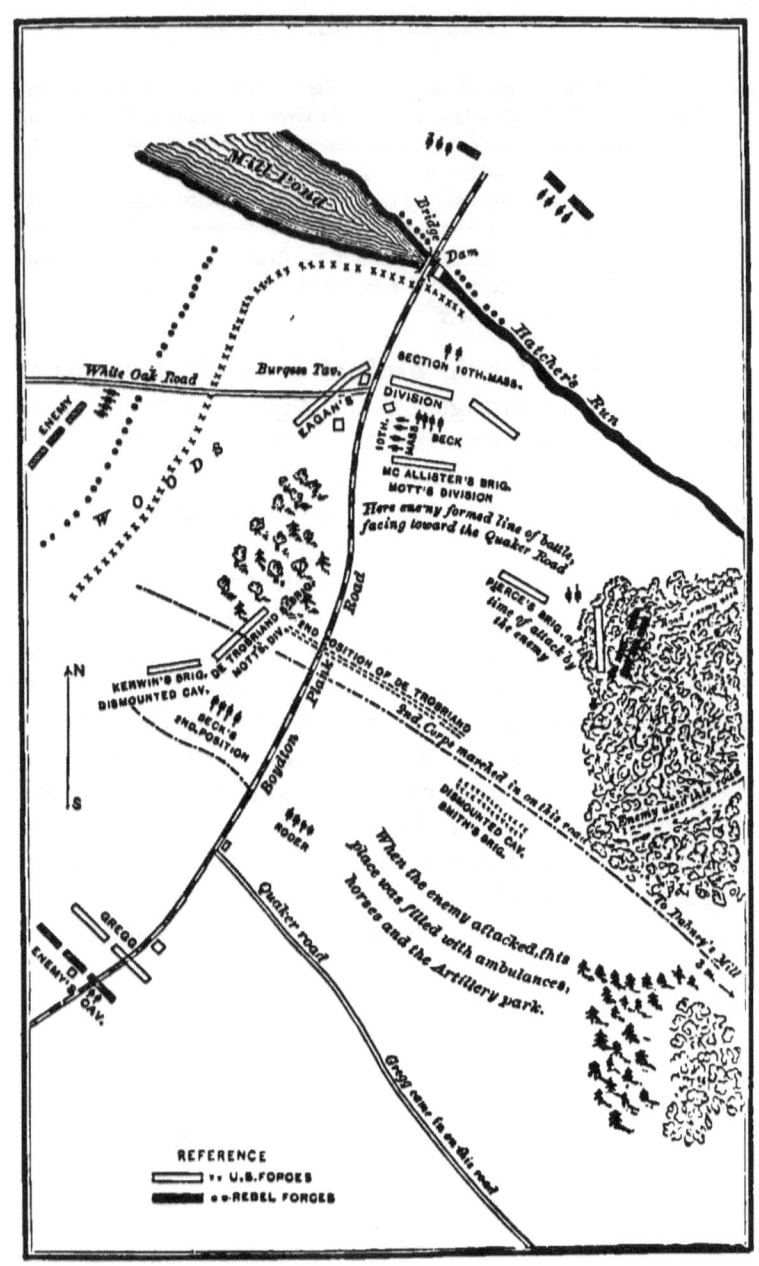

PLAN—BATTLE OF BOYDTON ROAD.

Appomattox, and on the night of the 30th of September the latter division was drawn out of the works, leaving the First and Second Divisions to cover the entire space of over three miles from beyond the plank road to the river.

No operations of importance occurred until the 21st of October, when General Hancock was informed that Lieutenant-General Grant desired a formidable movement made with a view of seizing and holding the South Side Railroad.

On the morning of the 25th the Second and Third Divisions were massed ready to move, General Egan being in command of the Second Division, and General Smythe of his brigade. In order that the nature of the movement proposed by the Lieutenant-General may be clearly understood, so much of the order as elucidates this is here given:

"On the afternoon of the 26th inst. (Wednesday), Major-General Hancock, commanding Second Corps, will move the divisions of his corps, now in reserve, to the Vaughan road just outside the line of rear intrenchments. They will take routes well to the rear, so as to avoid the observation of the enemy, and every precaution will be taken during the night to conceal the movement. At 2 P. M. of the 27th General Hancock will move by the Vaughan road across Hatcher's Run, pass by Dabney's mills, and Wilson & Arnold's steam saw-mill, on the Boydton plank road, across the open country to the Claiborne road, near its intersection with the White Oak road, and, recrossing Hatcher's Run near the Claiborne road bridge, will take the road running northeast from the vicinity of the bridge to the South Side Railroad, and endeavor to seize a commanding position. General Gregg's cavalry will form a part of General Hancock's command, and will move on his left. General Hancock will probably be able to reach the Boydton plank road by the time General Parke attacks the enemy's right between Claypole's and Hatcher's Run.

"General Gregg will concentrate his cavalry on the afternoon of the 26th inst. (Wednesday) at some point toward the left, convenient for crossing Hatcher's Run by the first route below that used by Hancock's infantry, and which shall not disclose the movement to the observation of the enemy. Every precaution will be taken to conceal the movement. His pickets from the vicinity of the plank road westward will be relieved in time to accompany him on the morning of the 27th. Upon concentrating his command, he will report to Major-General Hancock.

"General Gregg will move on the morning of the 27th, not later than two o'clock, across Hatcher's Run below the Second Corps, and move on the left of the infantry, probably using the Quaker road as far as the Boydton plank. His route must be governed by that of the Second Corps.

"Major-General Parke, commanding Ninth Corps, will move at such hour on the morning of the 27th as will enable him to take the right of the enemy's infantry, between Hatcher's Run and their new works at Hawke's and Dabney's, at the dawn of day. It is probable that the enemy's line of intrenchments is incomplete at that point, and the Commanding General expects, by a secret and sudden movement, to surprise them and carry their half-formed works. General Parke will therefore move and attack vigorously at the time named, not later than half past five, and, if successful, will follow up the enemy closely, turning toward the right. Should he not break the enemy's line, General Parke will remain confronting them until the operations on the left draw off the enemy.

"Major-General Warren, commanding Fifth Corps, will, if practicable, move simultaneously with the Ninth Corps, and proceed to the crossing of Hatcher's Run below the plank road bridge, from which point he will support the Ninth Corps, and, if the attack is successful, follow up the enemy on the right of the Ninth Corps.

"Should General Parke fail to break the enemy's line, General Warren will cross Hatcher's Run and endeavor to turn the enemy's right by recrossing at the first practicable point above the Boydton plank road, keeping on the right of Hancock. He will then turn toward the plank road and open the plank road bridge."

On the afternoon of the 26th the two divisions, Mott's and Egan's, numbering between 6,000 and 7,000 men, moved out along the line of intrenchments to the Weldon Railroad, bivouacking near Fort Du Chesne. The enemy's videttes were encountered on the Vaughan road, but did not contest our advance. Egan advanced so energetically that by daylight he was ready to attempt the crossing of Hatcher's Run. Smythe's brigade was deployed, and advanced in fine style, carrying the works at a run.

As soon as Egan's division had crossed the stream, he pushed forward to Dabney's mill. Mott followed the Vaughan road for a mile or so, and then marched by a cross road to Dabney's mill. Gregg had crossed Hatcher's Run without difficulty, and the sound of his guns was now heard on the left, growing more and more distinct. The infantry now pushed rapidly on toward the Boydton road, arriving in sight of it just as the rear of the enemy's wagon train was crossing the bridge over

Hatcher's Run at Burgess's mill.   The enemy at once opened fire upon Hancock's column with a section of artillery from the hill, on the south side of the run, near Burgess's tavern.   Their fire was speedily silenced, however, by Beck's battery.   General Hancock did not consider it prudent to continue his march to the White Oak road while any of the enemy remained south of the run, and therefore ordered Egan to move toward the bridge and drive them over it.   Gregg was now coming up by the Quaker road, and one of his brigades was sent forward to relieve Egan, while Mott was directed to advance toward White Oak road bridge.

Before his column was well under way, however, General Hancock received an order from General Meade in person to halt at the plank road, Generals Grant and Meade having then arrived upon the field.   The latter informed General Hancock that Crawford's division, Fifth Corps, was working its way up the run, and requested General Hancock to extend his line to the right, in order to make the desired connection with Crawford's troops.   The change of orders was owing to the Fifth and Ninth Corps not having broken through the enemy's lines, as originally designed in the programme laid out for the movement.   General Grant determined to end this operation there.

Accordingly two brigades of Egan's division were deployed on the right of the plank road, the line afterward extending further to the right by the deployment of two regiments, but without meeting Crawford's troops, which were afterward discovered to be about three fourths of a mile from the extreme right of Hancock's line.   Meanwhile the enemy was, showing considerable activity in the front and on the left.   Egan drove their dismounted cavalry across the run by a charge of Smythe's brigade, which was very handsomely made, capturing one gun. Very soon afterward a vigorous artillery fire was opened upon Egan from the heights on the north bank of the run and an enfilading fire from a battery on his left, which had crossed the stream at the White Oak bridge. It was impracticable to capture or drive off the enemy, but Beck, with four of his guns, maintained an unequal contest with it most gallantly, until relieved by Granger's Tenth Massachusetts Battery.

As soon as General Hancock had learned the location of Crawford's division, Generals Grant and Meade left the field, the latter expressing a desire that General Hancock should hold his position until the following morning, when he was to retire by the same road on which he had come.

Sharp firing on the right, opposite Pierce's brigade, now excited General Hancock's apprehension, and, two regiments having been sent into the woods to ascertain the cause, a large force of the enemy was discovered. It had been sent by Lee, under the immediate command of General Heth, to meet General Hancock's column, which was threatening his communication. A part of this force had crossed the run between Crawford and Hancock, and marched by a wood road through a dense forest toward the Boydton plank road. Pierce's two regiments were at once overrun by numbers, and fell back in confusion upon the remainder of the brigade, closely followed by the enemy, whose force consisted of three brigades. The result of this was that the brigade was obliged to fall back to the plank road before it could reform. This movement of the enemy brought them in close view of the clearing in the angle between the plank road and the line of march of the Second Corps, which was filled with ambulances, led horses, artillery, and all the impedimenta generally found in the rear of an army, promising an easy and valuable capture. Fortunately De Trobriand's brigade of Mott's division was so placed as to be able to open fire upon the enemy immediately, and Roder's battery extricated itself from the mass of ambulances, wagons, loose horses, etc., came into battery, and opened fire. Smith's brigade of Gregg's cavalry was dismounted, and moved up to aid De Trobriand. Kerwin's brigade, also dismounted, came into line on the left. In the mean time, however, the enemy found themselves suddenly attacked in the rear, the result of a masterly movement under direct orders of General Hancock. At the first sound of the enemy's attack on Pierce, he had sent his aide-de-camp, Major Mitchell, to General Egan, to direct him to abandon the assault against the heights on the north bank of the stream, and to face about and assail the enemy with his whole force. When Major Mitchell reached General Egan, he found that that officer was already in motion to attack the force of the enemy in his rear. The latter, being entirely oblivious of the presence of Egan's troops, were struck with amazement when he swept down upon their flank with Smythe's and Willett's brigades of his own division, and McAllister's brigade of Mott's division. The attack was made with such irresistible force that the enemy were driven in great confusion from the field, leaving two colors and nearly one thousand prisoners, besides the guns which had been lost at the first advance upon Pierce. When Major Mitchell attempted to return to General Hancock after having delivered his message to General Egan, he found the enemy in possession of the Boydton plank road, whereupon, procuring the Thirty-sixth Wisconsin Volunteers from Rugg's brigade of the Second Division, Major Mitchell advanced against the enemy, and drove them from the road, capturing about two hundred prisoners and one color.

General Egan's attack was followed up immediately by General Hancock with De Trobriand's brigade of Mott's division and Kerwin's brigade of dismounted cavalry, thus placing the enemy between two fires and adding to his confusion and loss.

In the mean time, and nearly simultaneously with the enemy's attack on Pierce, they commenced pressing heavily against our left, where Mott's skirmishers became sharply engaged, and a number of men and several valuable officers were lost.   Indeed, hardly had Egan succeeded in his attack, when General Hancock was obliged to send all of the dismounted cavalry back to General Gregg, who was attacked by five brigades of cavalry under General Wade Hampton.   Gregg met his attack with great resolution, and succeeded in repelling Hampton, although he did not effect this until after dark.

One of Gregg's regiments, the First Maine Cavalry, was under orders to proceed home to be mustered out of service, but went into action voluntarily and participated in Hampton's repulse.

By this time the situation was rather mixed.   The enemy were in force in our front, and their artillery was firing upon us from three directions—in fact, from all directions, excepting the narrow road on which the corps had marched from Dabney's mill and the Quaker road, and Hampton had pushed so far up the plank road in our rear that his shot passed entirely over Gregg's line and into our front line of infantry, which was engaged in an opposite direction. Renewed efforts were made at this time to reach Crawford's right, by extending our skirmish line, but without success. Captain Harry Bingham, sent to communicate with General Warren or Crawford, was captured by the enemy, and as, strange to say, the fire at Boydton road was not heard by General Warren, owing to the dense wood intervening and the skirmishing on his own front, the chance for reënforcement was slim.

General Hancock was now informed by dispatch from General Meade that the signal officer reported the enemy concentrating against him, but that his orders to remain until the following morning were unchanged. General Meade, of course, did not then know of the battle which had taken place as soon as he left the field. This question, whether to remain upon the field until morning or withdraw during the night, now appealed to General Hancock's judgment and soldierly instinct with great force. One element which entered materially into this question was the fact that Hancock had moved in the morning by order without his reserve ammunition, which had been directed by General Meade to be placed on pack mules, and to await the movements of the Ninth and Fifth Corps, and then to be sent to General Hancock at the South Side Railroad. The conflict of the day had so drained the quantity of ammunition on hand as to seriously cripple the troops, this being particularly the case with the cavalry and artillery. The only connection with the main body of the army was by a narrow wood road to Dabney's mill, and this was not only seriously threatened by the enemy, but the rain was rapidly rendering it almost impassable, so that already it became a question of doubt whether the ammunition, which was thirteen miles in the rear, could be brought up and issued in time for a fight in the morning.

General Meade now sent a dispatch to General Hancock, authorizing him to withdraw during the night, if he thought proper to do so, and informed him that Ayres's division of the Fifth Corps had been sent to his support, and was halted for the night at Armstrong's mill; also that, if he (General Hancock) could attack successfully in the morning, with the assistance of Ayres's and Crawford's divisions, he desired him to do so. Of course these instructions only served to add to General Hancock's embarrassment, and to render him more reluctant to abandon his position; but, the responsibility being put upon him, and the doubtful question as to the ammunition having to be taken into consideration, he determined at last upon withdrawal. General Meade, at a late hour of the night, sent word to General Hancock that he concurred in this conclusion.

General Hancock had at this time under his command the entire cavalry force of the Army of the Potomac (General Sheridan had two thirds of the cavalry originally belonging to the Army of the Potomac with him in the Shenandoah Valley), and he considered the risk of sacrificing this body on the following morning (for want of ammunition) too great to be assumed, when such a disaster could be avoided by quitting the field that night.

It is proper to state here that General Hancock's advance at Boydton road was within three and a half miles of the bridge on the South Side Railroad, which point could readily have been seized by Hancock's troops, but for the orders which he had received to suspend the movement. The battle of Boydton road occurred after General Hancock would have had ample time to have reached the South Side Road, had he not been halted to fight it when he was; as matters turned out, he probably would have been overwhelmed, had he proceeded to the railroad, for the enemy, not being occupied by an attack of the Fifth and Ninth Corps, would have been free to have concentrated all their strength against him.

General Hancock having decided to withdraw from the field, no time was lost in insuring the safe execution of the movement. At 10 P. M. the order was given for the withdrawal to commence, Mott moving first, Egan following, but halting at Dabney's mill to protect the withdrawal of Crawford's division of Warren's corps. He then joined Mott's division, which had massed and waited for him after crossing Hatcher's Run, when both divisions returned to the lines in front of Petersburg, October 28, 1864.

Gregg marched off the field on the Quaker road about half past ten o'clock, and the pickets were withdrawn about 1 A. M. on the 28th.

It has since been learned that the Confederates remained on the battle-field all night, and so increased their force that they would have attacked General Hancock on the morning of the 28th with fifteen thousand infantry and all of Hampton's cavalry.

In his official report of this battle, General Hancock personally acknowledged the services of his subordinates, particularly Brevet Major-General Mott and Brigadier-General Gregg, commanding the cavalry. He recommended General Egan for the appointment of brevet major-general, which was afterward made, for his distinguished services and marked gallantry on this occasion. Major and Brevet Lieutenant-Colonel W. G. Mitchell, Senior Aide-de-Camp, was highly commended in General Hancock's report, reference therein being made to General Egan, who had spoken in high terms of his services and of his example to the troops, particularly for effecting, at the head of the Thirty-sixth Wisconsin Volunteers, Captain Farwell commanding, the capture of about two hundred prisoners and one color.   In continuation, General Hancock says : " I have had occasion to acknowledge the services of Major Mitchell in every action in which I have been engaged during the war.   He always finds an opportunity for increasing his reputation for bravery and high soldierly qualities.   I hope the brevet appointment of colonel for which I have heretofore recommended him may be conferred upon him."   Colonel McAllister, Eleventh New Jersey Volunteers, commanding a brigade ; Lieutenant C. H. Morgan, Assistant Inspector-General and Chief of Staff ; Lieutenant W. B. Beck, Fifth United States Artillery ; and many others, were mentioned in honorable terms.

Although the general plan for seizing the South Side Railroad failed, the cause of failure being readily discernible, the battle of Boydton road goes down in history as a most brilliant engagement, conducted under specially difficult and embarrassing circumstances.   At the time it was planned, General Hancock was informed that a force of twenty thousand infantry would be given him for the operation, to be composed of troops from General Butler's army, in addition to those of his own corps, yet, when the official orders were issued, he found that he was to have only the two small divisions, Second and Third, of the Second Corps, as his force of infantry, with which to make the movement.

The losses of General Hancock's command in this battle aggregated 1,482 killed, wounded, and missing.

Hardly does the history of the war exhibit an instance of more brilliant generalship than that displayed by

Hancock on this occasion; the management of the action was most creditable to his skill and to the able handling of his troops in the very difficult combination of circumstances amid which he was placed. His position was isolated, his force entirely unequal to that of the enemy, and the failure to reënforce or even to supply his command with ammunition was to the last degree embarrassing. Nothing but consummate self-possession, rapid and comprehensive combinations, and indomitable energy could have extricated his command.

CHAPTER XXIX.

THE engagement at the Boydton road was the last
occasion on which General Hancock had the honor to direct in battle any part of the Second Army Corps. In
connection with his command of this magnificent corps,
one feature of the great popularity which General Hancock enjoyed among his troops is explained by the nature of his official reports as a brigade, division, and
corps commander, in the generous and complete description therein supplied of the services of those who were
under his command, and the liberal and complimentary
notice of such officers and men as specially distinguished
themselves.

It is a fact that the many thousands of men who returned to civil life at the close of the war, who had followed Hancock through Williamsburg, Antietam, Fredericksburg, Chancellorville, Gettysburg, and across that
great battle-field from the Rapidan to Petersburg—when

12

every step was taken in blood—carried with them memories that can never be effaced; and that so long as he and they live, will he remain their ideal of a leader.

A responsible writer in the "United Service Magazine," May, 1866, stated that the Second Corps embraced on its rolls the names of upward of 200,000 men; that it lost 70,000 men in battle; that it captured nearly, or quite, a hundred colors, and as many guns as any other corps ever took from the enemy, excluding those captured at fortified cities and places; that, at the first Fredericksburg, it lost 4,300 men, one third of the loss of the army; at Antietam, 5,200 men, one third of the loss of the army; at Gettysburg, 4,400 men; and, in the campaign from the Rapidan to the surrender of Lee's army, about 38,000 men, being one third the entire loss. An additional and emphatic illustration of the terrible destruction in this corps exists in the fact that, between May 3 and October 27, 1864, it lost thirty-seven brigade commanders, killed, wounded, and missing (there being only two of the latter), an average of about four brigade commanders to each brigade in the course of six months' fighting. [The Second Corps started with eleven brigades, and in a few days, on account of losses, was reduced to nine.]

About the middle of November, 1864, General Hancock desired to avail himself of a short leave of absence, as there were then no movements being made against the enemy; but, in reply to an intimation to that effect, he was informed by General Meade that the Secretary of War had made a proposition to General Grant which might render a leave unnecessary. A subsequent interview with General Grant disclosed the fact that the Secretary of War had inquired whether the services of

General Hancock could be spared for the winter, with a view of raising and organizing a corps of veterans from those soldiers who had served two years and had been honorably discharged. This proposition being made to General Hancock, he accepted it, and, being consulted as to his successor in command of the Second Corps, recommended for that position Major-General Humphreys, Chief of Staff of the Army of the Potomac.

In taking leave of the Second Army Corps, General Hancock issued the following order:

"HEADQUARTERS SECOND ARMY CORPS, BEFORE PETERSBURG,
"*November* 26, 1864.
"GENERAL ORDERS, No. 44:

"SOLDIERS OF THE SECOND CORPS: In obedience to instructions which direct me to another field of duty, I transfer the command of this corps to Major-General A. A. Humphreys, United States Volunteers.

"I desire at parting with you to express the regret I feel at the necessity which calls for our separation.

"Intimately associated with you in the dangers, privations, and glory which have fallen to your lot during the memorable campaign of the past two years, I now leave you with the warmest feelings of affection and esteem.

"Since I have had the honor to serve with you, you have won the right to place upon your banners the historic names of 'Antietam,' 'Fredericksburg,' 'Chancellorville,' 'Gettysburg,' 'Wilderness,' 'Po,' 'Spottsylvania,' 'North Anna,' 'Cold Harbor,' 'Petersburg,' 'Ream's Station,' 'Boydton Road,' and many other contests.

"The gallant bearing of the intrepid officers and men of the Second Corps, on the bloodiest fields of the war, the dauntless valor displayed by them in many brilliant

assaults on the enemy's strongest positions, the great
number of guns, colors, prisoners, and other trophies of
war captured by them in many desperate combats, their
unswerving devotion to duty, and heroic constancy under
all the dangers and hardships which such campaigns en-
tail, have won for them an imperishable renown and the
grateful admiration of their countrymen. The story of
the Second Corps will live in history, and to its officers
and men will be ascribed the honor of having served
their country with unsurpassed fidelity and courage.

"Conscious that whatever military honor has fallen
to me during my association with the Second Corps, has
been won by the gallantry of the officers and soldiers
that I have commanded, I feel that in parting from them
I am severing the strongest ties of my military life.

" The distinguished officer who succeeds me is entitled to your entire confidence. His record assures you
that, in the hour of battle, he will lead you to victory.

"WINFIELD S. HANCOCK,
" *Major-General of Volunteers.*"

We give also the order of General Humphreys in assuming command of the Second Corps.

"HEADQUARTERS SECOND ARMY CORPS, *November* 26, 1864.
" GENERAL ORDERS, No. 45:

"In compliance with, and by authority of orders
from the headquarters of this army, I assume command
of the Second Corps.

"It is natural that I should feel some diffidence in
succeeding to the command of so distinguished a soldier as
Major-General Hancock.

"I can only promise you that I shall try to do my
duty, and preserve your reputation unsullied, relying

upon you to sustain me by that skill and courage which you have so conspicuously displayed on so many fields.

"A. A. HUMPHREYS,
"*Major-General of Volunteers.*"

General Hancock arrived at Washington November 27, 1864, and at once began the enlistment and organization of the First Veteran Corps. There were many difficulties in the way, and it is doubtful if any other officer in the service would have succeeded as well as he did. In the first place, the number of honorably discharged men of the two years' service was much smaller than was counted on by the War Department, the greater number of them having returned to the field in other organizations. Particularly was this the case with officers. Great care was also necessary in the selection of officers from those who presented themselves for admission to the First Veteran Corps. The State regulations controlling "bounties" also interfered with enlistments in this organization, very small bounties being offered by the general Government.

Although the enlistment resulted in securing about 10,000 men, General Hancock (in view of the fact that the spring operations about the Potomac were about to commence) applied for orders returning him to the Second Corps in the field, and received the assent of the Secretary of War; but late in February he was sent for by General Halleck, and asked to repair to Winchester, Virginia, and take command of the Army of the Shenandoah, in the Middle Military Division. General Sheridan, who then held that command, was about moving from Winchester with a large force of cavalry, and it was not proposed to assign General Hancock permanently to the command until the result of Sheridan's movements should be known. A conference ensued at the office of the Secretary of War, between the President, the Secretaries of War and State, Mr. Wilson, Chairman of the Senate Military Committee, and General Halleck, General Hancock being present. During this conference the Secretary of War promised that he would relieve the General from Winchester within ten days, but, there being comparatively few troops there, if General Hancock took command at that point, the enemy would suppose his command was large. On this promise of the Secretary of War, the General consented to go, Mr. Stanton thanking him warmly for yielding.

It was supposed at the war office at this time that the enemy designed a sudden movement up the "valley" during General Sheridan's absence, from the fact that Lee's cavalry was supposed to be picketing the Rappahannock, indicating a threat against Washington, similar to Early's movement of a previous date. General Hancock arrived at Winchester and relieved General Sheridan on Monday night, February 26, 1865, the latter officer starting on the following morning on his expedition down the "valley" with a large cavalry force.

Mr. Stanton at once began sending troops to General Hancock, and in three weeks he had (taking the disposable troops in his command and those sent to him) about 30,000 men available for a movement. Being allowed to select his commanders to a certain extent, he gathered about him at Winchester those tried and trusty young officers, Egan, Brooke, Carroll, and others, each in command of a powerful division.

The Middle Military Division embraced at this time the Army of the Shenandoah, the Department of Washington, General Augur commanding; the Department of Maryland, commanded by General Lewis Wallace; the Department of Pennsylvania, Major-General Cadwallader commanding; and the Department of West Virginia.

The returns, including the Army of the Shenandoah, showed a total of almost 100,000 men for duty within the limits of General Hancock's command.

The latter now bent all his energies to organizing and equipping a force as powerful as possible from the mass of his command, and, without leaving any points uncovered, found himself able to move with about 25,000 infantry, 3,000 cavalry, and a proper complement of artillery.

The following extract from a dispatch from the Secretary of War will show how General Hancock's labors were appreciated:

"I am very much gratified by your energy in organizing and administering the military force of your important command. Your dispatch of this evening to General Halleck vindicates my judgment in assigning you to that position, and shows that you could not in any other render service so valuable and urgent to the Government. I would be glad to have a detailed report of the force and its location, a thing I have never been able to procure. For what you have done already, you have the thanks of this department.

(Signed) "EDWIN M. STANTON."

It was arranged subsequently, and after the forcing of the lines at Petersburg, that, if Lee fell back on Lynchburg, Hancock was to march his army against him at that point; and, if Lee joined Joseph E. Johnston, Hancock's troops were to be sent to Sherman by shipping. The rapid march of events, however, rendered either of these movements unnecessary, and the only duty remaining to General Hancock in the "valley" was to force the surrender and to receive the paroles of the partisan troops in that region.

On the night of April 14, 1865, Abraham Lincoln, President of the United States, was assassinated in Ford's Theatre, Washington, D. C., by J. Wilkes Booth. On April 22d, orders were issued at Washington transferring General Hancock's headquarters to that city, and two days after his arrival there he received the following instructions from the War Office, these being the orders which led to what connection General Hancock had with the trial of the conspirators against the President and the subsequent execution of some of them :

"War Department, Washington City, *April 25, 1865.*

"General : Your headquarters having been established in Washington, you will please consider yourself specially charged with the security of the Capital, the public archives, and the public property therein, and with the necessary protection to the President, the officers of the Government, and the loyal citizens. The following subjects are especially recommended to your attention.

"1st. The condition of the forts and defensive works.

"2d. The organization, proper discipline, and management of an adequate military force, to act as a mounted military police at all times, day and night, within the city, for the purpose of guarding against assassination, and of arresting offenders.

"3d. You are also directed to give special attention to the employment of your force in the arrest of the persons who were recently engaged in the murder of President Lincoln, and the attempted assassination of the Secretary of State, taking all proper measures for their detection and to prevent their escape.

"4th. All other matters essential to the security and peace of your command.

"In the absence of Lieutenant-General Grant you will report to the Secretary of War, daily, for any instructions he may have to give.

"You will acknowledge the receipt of these instructions.

"Your obedient servant,

(Signed)   "EDWIN M. STANTON,

                                              "*Secretary of War.*

"MAJOR-GENERAL W. S. HANCOCK, *Division Commander,*
    "HEADQUARTERS MIDDLE MILITARY DIVISION."

The duties with which General Hancock was charged during the exciting period following Mr. Lincoln's death were perhaps not always agreeable. It is well known, to those conversant with the true condition of affairs, that for several days the Government really rested upon the shoulders of Mr. Stanton; and that, in the exciting state of anxiety and doubt, almost amounting to bewilderment, his strong will dominated over all; and, in calling General Hancock to the Capital at that time, the Secretary gave the strongest proof of the high esteem in which that officer was held by him.

At this point reference may be properly made to the following facts: The official report of Lieutenant-General Grant, made public in the fall of 1865, drew from General Hancock a letter, dated Baltimore, December 16, 1865, and addressed to Colonel T. S. Bowers, Assistant Adjutant-General, Washington, D. C., in which General Hancock took exception to Lieutenant-General Grant's report, alleging that therein the Second Army Corps, and he as its commander, had not received exact justice in the relations of the battles and engagements in which they had been concerned.   The letter was lengthy, and named in detail such battles and engagements, besides certain meritorious services of commanders and other officers, and drew from Lieutenant-General Grant a handsome response in acknowledgment and explanation, comprised in a letter from the Assistant Adjutant-General under date December 18, 1865.   In this communication it was explained that no intentional omission was made in Lieutenant-General Grant's report, its necessary limits comprehending the movements of armies instead of corps.   This letter concluded as follows: " He (Lieutenant-General Grant) directs me to say that such omission arose from no lack of appreciation of the gallant services rendered by yourself and your command during that campaign—services not surpassed by those of any corps in the Army of the Potomac."

It should be observed in this connection that, at the time when General Grant wrote his report, he had not received many of the subordinate reports from General Meade.

The entire loss by casualties in the Second Corps from May 5, 1863, until October 28, 1864, aggregated 28,520 men, of whom 3,932 were killed, 17,201 wounded, 7,387 missing.

Although General Hancock was in Washington in command of the Middle Military Division, comprising in all about 100,000 men, during the trial and execution of the prisoners charged with the assassination of President Lincoln, he was not a member of the military commission which tried Mrs. Surratt, nor had he anything whatever to do with her trial, nor any responsibility for the finding of the court, nor for the sentence imposed.

The troops that guarded the prisoners, including Mrs. Surratt, were, of course, under General Hancock's command, being a portion of the forces stationed within his division; and when the orders for the execution were issued by the President of the United States, those orders were directed to General Hancock, as the highest officer present in command, according to invariable military usage when military sentences are to be executed. The orders for this execution were transmitted by General Hancock through the proper channels to the governor of the military prison, General Hartranft, who had custody of the prisoners. A writ of *habeas corpus* was issued by Judge Wylie, of the United States District Court, in the case of Mrs. Surratt, returnable at 10 A. M. on the day of the execution. General Hancock formally transmitted the writ by the hands of the Secretary of War to the President of the United States for his ʼaction. The President suspended the writ, and directed General Hancock, as military commander, to cause the executions to be proceeded with, as originally ordered. General Hancock, accompanied by the Attorney-General of the United States, appeared before Judge Wylie in the United States District Court, and returned the writ to the Judge, and the latter released him (Hancock) from attendance upon the court, and, for reasons assigned, declined to take any further action in the case. The civil authorities being prohibited from further interference, the military were obliged to proceed under the orders of the President, Commander-in-Chief of the Army of the United States. Any different action would have been absurd and indefensible, as well as futile. Executive officers in military service are not responsible for the findings or acts of military courts, nor for illegal or unjust sentences, nor are civil executive officers. A sheriff is bound by his oath of office to execute the sentence of a court, whatever may be his private opinion of the justice of that sentence; much less can a military officer refuse to execute legal the order of his superior. To hold General Hancock responsible in any particular for the death of Mrs. Surratt is an absurdity which no person familiar with law, either civil or military, will sustain. Indeed, it is in evidence from his very acts that General Hancock did all within his power with a view to saving Mrs. Surratt. Thinking it possible that other writs or a reprieve might be issued, addressed to him, he went to the arsenal where the prisoners were confined, and remained there until the last moment. Not only this, but he stationed couriers at positions along the streets leading from the White House to the arsenal, for the purpose of having conveyed to him instant intelligence if any favorable orders should be issued. No such orders were issued, and the executions proceeded under the direction of General Hartranft, governor of the prison, who had been appointed a special provost marshal general to attend the military commission, and execute its mandates and sentences.

Early on the morning of the execution of Mrs. Surratt, the daughter of the prisoner visited General Hancock and asked his advice. He counseled her to repair to the Executive mansion and throw herself upon the mercy of the President; and subsequently, after the return of the writ of *habeas corpus*, when it became evident that there was no hope of pardon or reprieve, he notified Miss Surratt of the fact. As Mrs. Surratt was a Roman Catholic, many persons supposed that the adherents to that faith would deeply sympathize with her unhappy fate, and experience a feeling of resentment against General Hancock on account of his nominal connection with her execution. Such an apprehension did great injustice to the intelligence and fairness of the priesthood and laity of that church, assuming, as it did, that they would condemn a public official for fulfilling his public duty under the orders of his superiors. It is a fact that the priesthood and members of the Roman Catholic communion, from the archbishop down, attached no blame to General Hancock for the part he bore in the painful transaction in question.

The Archbishop of Baltimore, at this time the highest Catholic official in the United States, gave every assurance that he had never censured General Hancock for the merely perfunctory part with which the latter was intrusted in the Surratt tragedy. On the contrary, his Grace the Archbishop, Rev. T. B. Walter—Mrs. Surratt's spiritual adviser—and other friends during this unhappy occasion, expressed their appreciation of the General's delicacy and kindness during the progress of the trial and execution.

Thus much of statement in regard to the Surratt case would seem to be proper and pertinent in this place, in view of certain interested and unfounded accusations concerning the connection therewith of General Hancock.

CHAPTER XXX.

THE Middle Military Division, of which General Hancock was in command, having been discontinued, and the Middle Military Department established, he was appointed to the latter, and assumed command July 30, 1865. At that time, or just after the close of the war, the department contained a large number of troops, and it became a part of his duty to superintend and direct the mustering out of the volunteer service, which work was satisfactorily accomplished.

His headquarters were in Baltimore, a city which all through the war had been in a chronic exasperated condition, the leading citizens sympathizing with the South. But so ably and judiciously did General Hancock administer the affairs of his command that much of this feeling was soon removed. He treated all questions with justice and impartiality, and won the respect and confidence of the majority of all classes of the citizens. His dignified presence, courtly manners, and wise and magnanimous administration of affairs did much to restore the era of confidence and kind feeling, and marked the General as one who was as skillful in promoting public interests in peace as he was brilliant and energetic in war.

Orders from the War Department, dated August 6, 1866, released General Hancock from the military command of the Middle Military Department and transferred him to that of the Department of Missouri, with his headquarters at Fort Leavenworth, Kansas.

Sectional feeling was very bitter in Missouri at that time, and the public peace was threatened. It required all the wisdom, address, and personal magnetism of General Hancock to repress the combative tendencies of the people during the election which occurred about this time, though he gave the whole weight of his influence to the civil authorities in their efforts to preserve the peace and maintain the law. In fact, it was at this time and under the peculiar difficulties which surrounded him, both in Maryland and in Missouri, that General Hancock began to be noted for the spirit of true patriotism, and the courageous adherence to the essence of constitutional law, which continued to characterize his connection with administrative authority thereafter.

During the fall of 1866 and the ensuing winter, some of the Indian tribes inhabiting portions of Kansas and the Indian Territory (Department of Missouri), became restless and turbulent, and their relations to our Government demanded immediate adjustment. This was especially true of the Cheyennes, and also of the Kiowas, Apaches of the plains, and Arrapahoes. The Cheyennes are a very warlike tribe, which at this time roamed at large between the Arkansas and Platte Rivers. This region was traversed by the main roads leading to Colorado and New Mexico, the intended route of the Kansas

Pacific Railroad—eastern division—then in process of construction. Depredations were committed almost daily by the Indians, stages were stopped and robbed, settlers were despoiled on their farms, murdered, and burned on the funeral pyres of their destroyed houses, and travelers on the roads were murdered and mutilated, until matters came to such a pass that travel was suspended across that portion of the plains, except by stages carrying strong guards of soldiers, or by trains with heavy escorts.

The Indians made open threats to post commanders and others that, when the " grass grew " in the spring of 1867, they would clear the country of the whites, and stop the progress of the Kansas Pacific Railroad.

With a view to taking measures to avert a general Indian war and massacre, General Hancock was directed (March 14, 1867) by Lieutenant-General Sherman to organize a force out of the troops serving in his department, and approach to the country of the Cheyennes, Kiowas, and Arrapahoes, and notify them that there was to be war or peace ; and, if they preferred the latter, they must cease from their outrages upon travelers and their depredations against the white settlers.

In compliance with these instructions, General Hancock marched from Fort Riley, Kansas, March 26, 1867, with a force of cavalry, infantry, and artillery, amounting to about fourteen hundred men. He reached Fort Larned, Kansas, near the mouth of the Pawnee Fork and within a few miles of the Arkansas River, on April 7, 1867.

On the 12th of that month General Hancock held a council with some of the leading Cheyenne chiefs, at which he explained fully and explicitly the views and intentions of our Government toward the Indians. On the 14th, two days later, General Hancock, for the purpose of again talking with the prominent chiefs at their village, moved with his command from Fort Larned to a point on the Pawnee Fork, situated about twenty-five miles above the post. An Indian village was near this point, and the command encamped within one mile and a half of it, the village being occupied by Cheyennes and a large band of Sioux. Stringent orders were given by the General that the Indians should not be disturbed either in their persons or property. The latter had, however, resolved on war, and during the night of the 14th, although they had promised to meet the General in council on the following day, they abandoned their village. They hastened northward toward the Smoky Hill and Republican Rivers, attacked the mail stations on the Denver Road and working parties on the Kansas Pacific Railway, killing and wounding a number, running off stock, and committing other depredations. As soon as General Hancock learned that the Indians had abandoned their village, he sent General Custer after them with a force of cavalry, with orders to overtake, and, if possible, bring them back. General Custer followed them rapidly for two days, but did not come up with them, they having crossed the Smoky Hill River on the morning of the 16th, eight hundred strong, and entered upon the series of outrages already mentioned.

General Hancock in the mean time remained in his camp awaiting information; and, on hearing of the conduct of the Indians by official report of General Custer, and knowing that by these murders and depredations the war, which had been actually in progress for more than a year, was being continued with renewed ferocity, he gave orders for the destruction of their village, as a punishment for their treachery and bad faith, and for the murders which they had willfully and gratuitously committed. A few old people and sick, who had been left behind in the village by the Indians, were taken in charge under the General's orders and were properly cared for.

This Indian war was vigorously prosecuted by General Hancock with the small force at his command during the remaining period of his continuance in the Department of the Missouri, that is, until September, 1867, when he left the command of that department.

During that summer General Hancock organized a force of mounted volunteers, about twenty-five hundred strong, in the neighboring States and Territories, and, adding to this all the regular troops under his command, conducted the war with such success that he eventually conquered a peace without unnecessary cruelty and with comparatively slight loss to our arms. The war did not finally close until the winter of 1868–'69, being continued by General Sheridan after he relieved General Hancock, many lives being lost during its continuance, much property destroyed, and the settlement of the country retarded and travel over the plains suspended.

The official records show that General Hancock, during his command in the Indian country, did all that was possible to preserve peace with the Indians, and that it was not until the murders and outrages, treacherously undertaken by them, had been committed, that he punished them by destroying their village.

Pursuant to orders from the President of the United States, General Hancock relinquished the command of the Department of the Missouri on the 12th of September, 1867, and shortly after proceeded to New Orleans, where he assumed command of the Fifth Military District, comprising the States of Louisiana and Texas.

The considerations which prompted this appointment were highly complimentary to the General, who had, in every position in which his services had been employed, exhibited so much foresight, moderation, firmness, practical wisdom, and administrative ability, that the cabinet turned to him as the man most eminently qualified to harmonize the discordant elements of society in the South, and restore the regular operation of the law. In Maryland and Missouri his influence had been so benign and so efficient as to promise similar results in this new field of civic-military operations.

He set out for New Orleans immediately upon transferring the Department of Missouri to General Phil Sheridan, but at St. Louis was met by a telegram from the President ordering him to Washington, where he remained for some days in conference with the national authorities concerning the command to which he was going, after which time he returned to St. Louis.

He finally arrived at New Orleans and assumed command of the district on the 29th of November, relieving General Mower. General Hancock had meanwhile carefully considered the subject of the reconstruction of the Southern States under the acts passed by Congress, and had concluded upon his own duty in the premises and determined upon his course.

Here it is proper to give the " Reconstruction Acts," so called, under which those appointed to command in the States recently in rebellion were authorized and empowered to act.

(From " U. S. Statutes at Large," Volume XIV, Chapter CLIII.)

CHAPTER CLIII.—*An Act to provide for the more efficient Government of the Rebel States.* (*Passed March 2d, 1867.*)

Whereas, no legal State government or adequate protection for life or property now exists in the rebel States of Virginia, North Carolina, South Carolina, Georgia, Mississippi, Alabama, Louisiana, Florida, Texas, and Arkansas; and whereas it is necessary that peace and good order should be enforced in said States until loyal and republican State governments can be legally established; therefore,

Be it enacted by the Senate and House of Representatives of the United States of America in Congress assembled, That said rebel States shall be divided into military districts, and made subject to the military authority of the United States as hereinafter prescribed, and for that purpose Virginia shall constitute the first district; North Carolina and South Carolina the second district; Georgia, Alabama, and Florida the third district; Mississippi and Arkansas the fourth district; and Louisiana and Texas the fifth district.

SEC. 2. *And be it further enacted,* That it shall be the duty of the President to assign to the command of each of said districts an officer of the army, not below the rank of brigadier-general, and to detail a sufficient military force to enable such officer to perform his duties and enforce his authority within the district to which he is assigned.

SEC. 3. *And be it further enacted,* That it shall be the duty of each officer assigned as aforesaid, to protect all persons in their rights of person and property, to suppress insurrection, disorder, and violence, and to punish, or cause to be punished, all disturbers of the public peace and criminals; and to this end he may allow local civil tribunals to take jurisdiction of and to try offenders, or, when in his judgment it may be necessary for the trial of offenders, he shall have power to organize military commissions or tribunals for that purpose, and all interference under color of State authority with the exercise of military authority under this act shall be null and void.

SEC. 4. *And be it further enacted,* That all persons put under military arrest by virtue of this act shall be tried without unnecessary delay, and no cruel or unusual punishment shall be inflicted, and no sentence of any military commission or tribunal hereby authorized, affecting the life or liberty of any person, shall be executed until it is approved by the officer in command of the district, and the laws and regulations for the government of the army shall not be affected by this act, except in so far as they conflict with its provisions: *Provided*, That no sentence of death under the provisions of this act shall be carried into effect without the approval of the President.

SEC. 5. *And be it further enacted*, That when the people of any one of said rebel States shall have formed a constitution of government in conformity with the Constitution of the United States in all respects, framed by a convention of delegates elected by the male citizens of said State twenty-one years old and upward, of whatever race, color, or previous condition, who have been resident in said State for one year previous to the day of such election, except such as may be disfranchised for participation in the rebellion or for felony at common law, and when such constitution shall provide that the elective franchise shall be enjoyed by all such persons as have the qualifications herein stated for electors of delegates, and when such constitution shall be ratified by a majority of the persons voting on the question of ratification who are qualified as electors for delegates, and when such constitution shall have been submitted to Congress for examination and approval, and Congress shall have approved the same, and when said State, by a vote of its legislature elected under said constitution, shall have adopted the amendment to the Constitution of the United States, proposed by the Thirty-ninth Congress, and known as Article Fourteen, and when said article shall have become a part of the Constitution of the United States, said State shall be declared entitled to representation in Congress, and senators and representatives shall be admitted therefrom on their taking the oath prescribed by law, and then and thereafter the preceding sections of this act shall be inoperative in said State: *Provided*, That no person, excluded from the privilege of holding office by said proposed amendment to the Constitution of the United States, shall be eligible to election as a member of the convention to frame a constitution for any of said rebel States, nor shall any such person vote for members of such convention.

SEC. 6. *And be it further enacted*, That, until the people of said rebel States shall be by law admitted to representation in the Congress of the United States, any civil governments which may exist therein shall be deemed provisional only, and in all respects subject to the paramount authority of the United States at any time to abolish, modify, control, or supersede the same; and in all elections to any office under such provisional governments all persons shall be entitled to vote, and none others, who are entitled to vote, under the provisions of the fifth section of this act; and no person shall be eligible to any office under any such provisional governments who would be disqualified from holding office under the provisions of the third article of said Constitutional amendment.

SCHUYLER COLFAX,
Speaker of the House of Representatives.
LA FAYETTE S. FOSTER,
President of the Senate, pro tempore.

(From "U. S. Statutes at Large," Vol. XV, Chapter VI.)

CHAPTER VI. *An Act supplementary to an Act entitled, "An Act to provide for the more efficient Government of the Rebel States," passed March second, eighteen hundred and sixty-seven, and to facilitate Restoration.*

Be it enacted by the Senate and House of Representatives of the United States of America in Congress assembled, That, before the first day of September, eighteen hundred and sixty-seven, the commanding general in each district defined by an Act entitled, "An Act to provide for the more efficient government of the Rebel States," passed March second, eighteen hundred and sixty-seven, shall cause a registration to be made of the male citizens of the United States, twenty-one years of age and upward, resident in each county or parish in the State or States included in his district, which registration shall include only those persons who are qualified to vote for delegates by the act aforesaid, and who shall have taken and subscribed the following oath or affirmation: "I, ———, do solemnly swear (or affirm), in the presence of Almighty God, that I am a citizen of the State of ———; that I have resided in said State for ——— months next preceding this day, and now reside in the county of ———, or the parish of ———, in said State (as the case may be); that I am twenty-one years old; that

I have not been disfranchised for participation in any rebellion or civil war against the United States; nor for felony committed against the laws of any State, or of the United States; that I have never been a member of any State legislature, nor held any executive or judicial office in any State and afterward engaged in insurrection or rebellion against the United States, or given aid or comfort to the enemies thereof; that I have never taken an oath as a member of Congress of the United States, or as an officer of the United States, or as a member of any State legislature, or as an executive or judicial officer of any State, to support the Constitution of the United States, and afterward engaged in insurrection or rebellion against the United States, or given aid or comfort to the enemies thereof; that I will faithfully support the Constitution and obey the laws of the United States, and will, to the best of my ability, encourage others so to do, so help me God "; which oath or affirmation may be administered by any registering officer.

Sec. 2. *And be it further enacted*, That, after the completion of the registration hereby provided for in any State, at such time and places therein as the commanding general shall appoint and direct, of which at least thirty days' public notice shall be given, an election shall be held of delegates to a convention for the purpose of establishing a constitution and civil government for such State loyal to the Union; said convention in each State, except Virginia, to consist of the same number of members as the most numerous branch of the State legislature of such State in the year eighteen hundred and sixty, to be apportioned among the several districts, counties, or parishes of such State by the commanding general, giving to each representation in the ratio of voters registered as aforesaid as nearly as may be. The convention in Virginia shall consist of the same number of members as represented the territory now constituting Virginia in the most numerous branch of the legislature of said State in the year eighteen hundred and sixty, to be apportioned as aforesaid.

Seo. 3. *And be it further enacted*, That at said election the registered voters of each State shall vote for or against a convention to form a constitution therefor under this act. Those voting in favor of such a convention shall have written or printed on the ballots by which they vote for delegates, as aforesaid, the words " For a Convention," and those voting against such a convention shall have written or printed on such ballots the words "Against a Convention." The persons appointed to superintend said election, and to make return of the votes given thereat, as herein provided, shall count and make return of the votes given for and against a convention, and the commanding general, to whom the same shall have been returned, shall ascertain and declare the total vote in each State for and against a convention. If a majority of the votes given on that question shall be for a convention, then such convention shall be held as hereinafter provided; but if a majority of said votes shall be against a convention, then no such convention shall be held under this act: *Provided*, That such convention shall not be held unless a majority of all such registered voters shall have voted on the question holding such convention.

SEC. 4. *And be it further enacted*, That the commanding general of each district shall appoint as many boards of registration as may be necessary, consisting of three loyal officers or persons, to make and complete the registration, superintend the election, and make return to him of the votes, list of voters, and of the persons elected as delegates by a plurality of the votes cast at said election; and upon receiving said returns he shall open the same, ascertain the persons elected as delegates, according to the returns of the officers who conducted said election, and make proclamation thereof; and if a majority of votes given on that question shall be for a convention, the commanding general, within sixty days from the date of election, shall notify the delegates to assemble in convention, at a time and place to be mentioned in the notification, and said convention, when organized, shall proceed to frame a constitution and civil government according to the provisions of this act, and the act to which it is supplementary; and, when the same shall have been so framed, said constitution shall be submitted by the convention for ratification to the persons registered under the provisions of this act at an election to be conducted by the officers or persons appointed or to be appointed by the commanding general, as hereinbefore provided, and to be held after the expiration of thirty days from the date of notice thereof, to be given by said convention; and the returns thereof shall be made to the commanding general of the district.

SEC. 5. *And be it further enacted*, That if, according to said returns, the constitution shall be ratified by a majority of the votes of the registered electors, qualified as herein specified, cast at said election, at least one half of all the registered voters voting upon the question of such ratification, the president of the convention shall transmit a copy of the same, duly certified, to the President of the United States, who shall forthwith transmit the same to Congress, if then in session, and if not in session, then immediately upon its next assembling; and if it shall moreover appear to Congress that the election was one at which all the registered and qualified electors in the State had an opportunity to vote freely and without restraint, fear, or the influence of fraud; and if the Congress shall be satisfied that such constitution meets the approval of a majority of all the qualified electors in the State, and if the said constitution shall be declared by Congress to be in conformity with the provisions of the act to which this is supplementary, and the other provisions of said act shall have been complied with, and the said constitution shall be approved by Congress, the State shall be declared entitled to representation, and senators and representatives shall be admitted therefrom as therein provided.

SEC. 6. *And be it further enacted*, That all elections in the States mentioned in the said " Act to provide for the more efficient Government of the Rebel States," shall during the operation of said act, be by ballot; and all officers making the said registration of voters and conducting said elections shall, before entering upon the discharge of their duties, take and subscribe the oath prescribed by the act approved July second, eighteen hundred and sixty-two, entitled "An Act to prescribe an Oath of Office": *Provided*, That if any person knowingly and falsely take and subscribe any oath in this act prescribed, such person so offending and being thereof duly convicted, shall be subject to the pains, penalties, and disabilities which by law are provided for the punishment of the crime of willful and corrupt perjury.

SEC. 7. *And be it further enacted*, That all expenses incurred by the several commanding generals, or by virtue of any orders issued or appointments made by them, under or by virtue of this act, shall be paid out of any moneys in the treasury not otherwise appropriated.

SEC. 8. *And be it further enacted*, That the convention for each State shall prescribe the fees, salary, and compensation to be paid to all delegates and other officers and agents herein authorized or

13

necessary to carry into effect the purposes of this act not herein otherwise provided for, and shall provide for the levy and collection of such taxes on the property in such State as may be necessary to pay the same.

SEC. 9. *And be it further enacted*, That the word "Article," in the sixth section of the act to which this is supplementary, shall be construed to mean "section."

SCHUYLER COLFAX,

Speaker of the House of Representatives.

B. F. WADE,

President of the Senate, pro tempore.

(From Vol. XV, "U. S. Statutes at Large," Chapter XXX.)

CHAPTER XXX. *An Act supplementary to an Act entitled "An Act to provide for the more efficient Government of the Rebel States," passed on the second day of March, eighteen hundred and sixty-seven, and the Act supplementary thereto, passed on the twenty-third day of March, eighteen hundred and sixty-seven.*

Be it enacted by the Senate and House of Representatives of the United States of America in Congress assembled, That it is hereby declared to have been the true intent and meaning of the act of the second day of March, one thousand eight hundred and sixty-seven, entitled "An Act to provide for the more efficient Government of the Rebel States," and of the act supplementary thereto, passed on the twenty-third of March, in the year one thousand eight hundred and sixty-seven, that the governments then existing in the Rebel States of Virginia, North Carolina, South Carolina, Georgia, Mississippi, Alabama, Louisiana, Florida, Texas, and Arkansas were not legal State governments; and that thereafter said governments, if continued, were to be continued subject in all respects to the military commanders of the respective districts, and to the paramount authority of Congress.

SEC. 2. *And be it further enacted,* That the commander of any district named in said act shall have power, subject to the disapproval of the General of the Army of the United States, and to have effect till disapproved, whenever in the opinion of such commander the proper administration of said act shall require it, to sus-pond or remove from office, or from the performance of official duties and the exercise of official powers, any officer or person holding or exercising, or professing to hold or exercise, any civil or military office or duty in such district under any power, election, appointment, or authority derived from, or granted by, or claimed under, any so-called State or the government thereof, or any municipal or other division thereof; and upon such suspension or removal such commander, subject to the disapproval of the General as aforesaid, shall have power to provide from time to time for the performance of the said duties of such officer or person so suspended or removed, by the detail of some competent officer or soldier of the army, or by the appointment of some other person, to perform the same, and to fill vacancies occasioned by death, resignation, or otherwise.

SEC. 3. *And be it further enacted,* That the General of the Army of the United States shall be invested with all the powers of suspension, removal, appointment, and detail granted in the preceding section to district commanders.

SEC. 4. *And be it further enacted,* That the acts of the officers of the army already done in removing in said districts persons exercising the functions of civil officers, and appointing others in their stead, are hereby confirmed: *Provided,* That any person heretofore or hereafter appointed by any district commander to exercise the functions of any civil office, may be removed either by the military officer in command of the district, or by the General of the Army. And it shall be the duty of such commander to remove from office as aforesaid all persons who are disloyal to the Government of the United States, or who use their official influence in any manner to hinder, delay, prevent, or obstruct the due and proper administration of this act and the acts to which it is supplementary.

SEC. 5. *And be it further enacted,* That the boards of registration provided for in the act entitled "An Act supplementary to an Act entitled 'An act to provide for the more efficient government of the Rebel States,' passed March two, eighteen hundred and sixty-seven, and to facilitate restoration," passed March twenty-three, eighteen hundred and sixty-seven, shall have power, and it shall be their duty, before allowing the registration of any person, to ascertain upon such facts or information as they can obtain, whether such person is entitled to be registered under said act, and the oath required by said act shall not be conclusive on such question, and no person shall be registered unless such board shall decide that he is entitled thereto: and such board shall also have power to examine, under oath (to be administered by any member of such board), any one touching the qualification of any person claiming registration; but in every case of refusal by the board to register an applicant, and in every case of striking his name from the list as hereinafter provided, the board shall make a note or memorandum, which shall be returned with the registration list to the commanding general of the district, setting forth the grounds of such refusal or such striking from the list: *Provided*, That no person shall be disqualified as member of any board of registration by reason of race or color.

SEC. 6. *And be it further enacted*, That the true intent and meaning of the oath prescribed in said supplementary act is (among other things), that no person who has been a member of the Legislature of any State, or who has held any executive or judicial office in any State, whether he has taken an oath to support the Constitution of the United States or not, and whether he was holding such office at the commencement of the rebellion or had held it before, and who was afterward engaged in insurrection or rebellion against the United States, or given aid or comfort to the enemies thereof, is entitled to be registered or to vote; and the words " executive or judicial office in any State " in said oath mentioned shall be construed to include all civil offices created by law for the administration of any general law of a State, or for the administration of justice.

SEC. 7. *And be it further enacted*, That the time for completing the original registration provided for in said act may, in the discretion of the commander of any district, be extended to the first day of October, eighteen hundred and sixty-seven; and the boards of registration shall have power, and it shall be their duty, commencing fourteen days prior to any election under said act, and upon reasonable public notice of the time and place thereof to revise, for a period of five days, the registration lists, and upon being satisfied that any person not entitled thereto has been registered, to strike the name of such person from the list, and such person shall not be allowed to vote. And such board shall also, during the same period, add to such registry the names of all persons who at that time possessed the qualifications required by said act who have not been already registered : and no person shall, at any time, be entitled to be registered or to vote by reason of any executive pardon or amnesty for any act or thing which, without such pardon or amnesty, would disqualify him from registration or voting.

SEC. 8. *And be it further enacted,* That section four of said last-named act shall be construed to authorize the commanding general named therein, whenever he shall deem it needful, to remove any member of a board of registration and to appoint another in his stead, and to fill any vacancy in such board.

SEC. 9. *And be it further enacted,* That all members of said board of registration, and all persons hereafter elected or appointed to office in said military districts, under any so-called state or municipal authority, or by detail or appointment of the district commanders, shall be required to take and to subscribe to the oath of office prescribed by law for officers of the United States.

SEC. 10. *And be it further enacted,* That no district commander or member of the board of registration, or any of the officers or appointees acting under them, shall be bound in his action by any opinion of any civil officer of the United States.

SEC. 11. *And be it further enacted,* That all the provisions of this act and of the acts to which this is supplementary shall be construed liberally, to the end that all the intents thereof may be fully and perfectly carried out.

SCHUYLER COLFAX,
Speaker of the House of Representatives.

B. F. WADE,
Speaker of the Senate, pro tempore.

Fully acquainted with the nature of these acts, General Hancock was guided in his after course by his own judgment, sense of duty, and conscientious interpretation of the Constitution and the law. While on the steamboat which was carrying him to New Orleans, he drew up in his own handwriting the military order which has since become celebrated as "Order No. 40," and of which the following is an exact copy:

"HEADQUARTERS, FIFTH MILITARY DISTRICT,

"NEW ORLEANS, LA., *November* 29, 1867.

"GENERAL ORDERS, No. 40.

"I. In accordance with General Orders, No. 81, Headquarters of the Army, Adjutant-General's Office, Washington, D. C., August 27, 1867, Major-General W. S. Hancock hereby assumes command of the Fifth Military District, and of the Department composed of the States of Louisiana and Texas.

"II. The General Commanding is gratified to learn that peace and quiet reign in this department. It will be his purpose to preserve this condition of things. As a means to this great end he requires the maintenance of the civil authorities, and the faithful execution of the laws as the most efficient under existing circumstances.

"In war it is indispensable to repel force by force, to overthrow and destroy opposition to lawful authority; but when insurrectionary force has been overthrown and peace established, and the civil authorities are ready and willing to perform their duties, the military power should cease to lead, and the civil administration resume its natural and rightful dominion. Solemnly impressed with these views, the General announces that the great principles of American liberty are still the inheritance of this people, and ever should be. The right of trial by jury, the *habeas corpus*, the liberty of the press, the freedom of speech, the natural rights of persons, and the rights of property must be preserved.

"Free institutions, while they are essential to the prosperity and happiness of the people, always furnish the strongest inducements to peace and order. Crimes and offenses committed in this district must be left to the consideration and judgment of the regular civil tribunals, and those tribunals will be supported in their lawful jurisdiction.

"Should there be violations of existing laws which are not inquired into by the civil magistrates, or should failures in the administration of justice be complained of, the cases will be reported to these headquarters, when such orders will be made as may be deemed necessary.

"While the General thus indicates his purpose to respect the liberties of the people, he wishes all to understand that armed insurrection or forcible resistance to the law will be instantly suppressed by arms."

CHAPTER XXXI.

It will have been seen by reference to the Reconstruction Acts, that under those laws General Hancock had now
become the absolute ruler of two great States—Louisiana
and Texas—he had power to remove civil magistrates
and suppress the local tribunals, to establish military commissions and suspend the civil laws ; such were the unlimited and dangerous powers conferred upon the military
commanders of the several districts in the Southern country by those unparalleled acts under which they were to
perform their functions. It is just to observe here that,
had President Lincoln lived, no such laws as these would
have been enacted, for it is known that he had indicated
the theory of reconstruction which he designed to carry
out, and which he certainly would have carried out. His
theory, as announced by himself, was that the States
which attempted to secede had not succeeded in getting
out of the Union, that the rebellion was a failure, that
our brave armies had preserved the Union, and that, when

the military power of the Confederacy was broken, the several States which had for a time swerved from their course in our national system, fell back naturally into their normal orbits, and were to be treated as States and members of the National Union. All he insisted upon, and all he believed Congress had a right to exact, was obedience to the Constitution and to the laws of the United States, for the future guarantee of which he required State pledges, and the placing of such men in authority as would promote future loyalty to the General Government. He certainly never dreamed of reducing the seceded States to a territorial condition, or of treating them as conquered countries whose destinies would be arbitrarily determined by the central Government, irrespective of the provisions of the Constitution, and regardless of those principles which Americans had always held to be fundamental in free governments. The President never swerved from the conviction "that free governments derived their just powers from the consent of the governed," and, had he lived, the harsh measures which the extreme radicals in Congress adopted would never have been inaugurated.

President Johnson was disposed to carry out the known plans of his predecessor, and attempted to do so, but various causes conspired to embarrass and thwart his efforts, one of these being that, as a Southern man, he had not the full confidence and coöperation of the extreme wing of the Republican party; another that he had not the strong hold which his predecessor had upon the confidence and affection of the country, and hence could not exert the power that could readily have been exercised by Mr. Lincoln.

J. Wilkes Booth proved himself the worst enemy the

South ever had, by assassinating the only man who could have restored the Union upon constitutional principles; for by that fatal shot he opened the way for bringing to the front the most violent partisans, who for a time absorbed the national authority and influence, and swayed the fortunes of the country according to their own interests and their own desires.

It will be remembered that, previous to the time General Hancock assumed command at New Orleans, Congress had parceled out the South into a number of military districts, and appointed over each a military governor clothed with despotic powers, which we have described. This action of Congress seemed to be based upon the assumption that the Southern people had forfeited all their constitutional liberties, and were not entitled to any of the civil rights of freemen. This doctrine was openly avowed upon the floors of Congress, in the press, and elsewhere, notwithstanding that it was palpably at war with all ideas of political advancement, and with the very principles of our own Revolution, and upon which we became an independent country. On such a foundation were enacted the harsh and unreasonable laws we have quoted, and which were generally enforced throughout the South; but, as has been indicated in his "General Order No. 40," and as was the case during his control of affairs in Louisiana and Texas, General Hancock gave a liberal interpretation to these laws, in strict conformity with Section 11, of the Act last quoted, which was passed after General Hancock left the Fifth Military District, his first action, in issuing the order in question, being to proclaim that the Constitution had not perished amid the clash of arms, but was still the fundamental law of the whole land and the palladium of the civil rights of all the people.

Here, and in reference to this remarkable order, it is to be observed that it elicited many expressions of approbation from different parts of the country, only one of which we are able to give in this place, written by Hon. J. S. Black, of Pennsylvania, on the day following the date of the issuing of General Orders, No. 40, or immediately after the knowledge of the nature of this order had reached Washington by telegraph. It is as follows:

"WASHINGTON, *November* 30, 1867.

"MY DEAR GENERAL: This moment I read your admirable order. I am much engaged, but I can not resist the temptation to steal time enough from my clients to tell you how grateful you have made me by your patriotic and noble words. Yours is the most distinct and most emphatic recognition which the principles of American liberty have received at the hands of any high officer in a Southern command. It has the very ring of the Revolutionary metal. Washington never said a thing in better taste or at a better time. It will prove to all men that 'peace hath her victories not less renowned than those of war.'

"I congratulate you, not because it will make you the most popular man in America, for I dare say you care nothing about that, but it will give you through all time the solid reputation of a true patriot and a sincere lover of your country, its laws, and its government; this, added to your brilliant achievements as a soldier, will leave you without a rival in the affections of all whose good will is worth having, and give you a place in history which your children will be proud of.

"This acknowledgment from me does not amount to much, but I am expressing only the feelings of millions, and expressing them feebly at that. With profound respect,

"Yours, etc.,

(Signed)   "J. S. BLACK."
"Major-General W. S. HANCOCK."

The determination to leave all public or private grievances, which should be brought before him in his command, to the civil authorities, and to restrain the military power from unnecessary interference with them, which General Hancock had formed when he undertook the command, and had expressed in his Order No. 40, was carried out in practice in every case that came before him. Quotations from certain of his orders indicating this are pertinent:

"HEADQUARTERS, FIFTH MILITARY DISTRICT, NEW ORLEANS,
"LOUISIANA, *December* 4, 1867.
"SPECIAL ORDERS, No. 202.

"*Extract.*

. . . .

"II. Paragraph III of Special Order No. 188, from these headquarters, dated November 16, 1867, issued by Brevet-General Mower, removing P. R. O'Rourke, Clerk of Second District Court, Parish of Orleans, for malfeasance in office, and appointing R. L. Shelley in his place, is hereby revoked, and P. R. O'Rourke is reinstated in said office. If any charges are set up against the said O'Rourke, the Judicial Department of the Government is sufficient to take whatever action may be necessary in the premises.
"By command of MAJOR-GENERAL HANCOCK."
[Official.]

"HEADQUARTERS, FIFTH MILITARY DISTRICT,
"NEW ORLEANS, *December* 5, 1867.
"SPECIAL ORDERS, No. 203.
"*Extract.*

. . . .

"II. The true and proper use of the military power, besides defending the national honor against foreign nations, is to uphold the laws and civil government, and to secure to every person residing among us the enjoyment of life, liberty, and property. It is accordingly made by act of Congress the duty of the commander of this district to protect all persons in those rights, to suppress disorder and violence, and to punish, or cause to be punished, all disturbance of the public peace, and all crimes.

"The Commanding General has been informed that the administration of justice, and especially of criminal justice, in the courts, is clogged, if not entirely prostrated, by the enforcement of Paragraph No. II, of the Military Order No. 125, current series, from these headquarters, issued on the 24th of August, 1867, relative to qualifications of persons to be placed on the jury list of the State of Louisiana. To determine who shall and who shall not be jurors appertains to the legislative power, and until the laws in existence regulating this subject shall be amended or changed by that department of the civil government, which the constitution of all the States vests with that power, it is deemed best to carry out the will of the people as expressed in the last legislative act upon this subject. The qualification of a juror under the law is a proper subject for the decision of the courts.

"The Commanding General in the discharge of the trust reposed in him will maintain the just power of the judiciary, and is unwilling to permit the civil authority and laws to be embarrassed by military interference; and, as it is an established fact that the administration of justice in the criminal tribunals is greatly embarrassed by the operation of Paragraph No. II, Special Orders, No. 125, current series, from these headquarters, it is ordered that this said order, with said paragraph, which relates to the qualifications of persons to be placed on the jury list, be, and the same is hereby revoked, and that trial by jury be henceforth regulated and controlled by the Constitution and civil laws, without regard to any military orders heretofore issued.

"By command of MAJOR-GENERAL HANCOCK."

[Official.]

Another extract, this time from Special Orders, No. 211, sustains the jurisdiction of the civil courts over the rights of private property. It is as follows:

.   .   .   .

"IV. Paragraph III, of Special Orders, No. 197, current series, from these headquarters, issued by Brevet-General J. A. Mower, in the matter of the estate of D. B. Staats, is hereby revoked. The local tribunal possesses ample power for the protection of all parties concerned."

Another, being Special Order No. 213, secures the

purity of elections and forbids military interference at the polls. It is as follows:

. . . .

"In compliance with the supplementary Act of Congress of March 23, 1867, notice is hereby given that an election will be held in the State of Texas, on the 10th, 11th, 12th, 13th, and 14th days of February, 1868, to determine whether a convention shall be held and for delegates thereto, to frame a 'constitution' for the State under said Act.

. . . .

"IX. Military interference with elections, unless it shall be necessary to keep the peace at the polls, is prohibited by law, and no soldiers will be allowed to appear at any polling place unless as citizens of the State they are registered as voters, and then only for the purpose of voting.

"X. The sheriff and other peace officers from each county are required to be present until the election shall be completed, and are made responsible for good order."

The Hon. E. Heath, Mayor of New Orleans, having addressed a communication to the General, requesting his intervention in State suits against the city on its notes, the General directed his secretary for civil affairs to transmit his (the General's) reply. In this reply the General respectfully declines interfering in the way desired, and assigns reasons for so declining. These reasons are briefly:

"1. An order would be in effect a stay law in favor of the city, which under the Constitution could not be enacted by the legislature of the State, while the commander of the district ought not to assume such an authority.

"2. This debt, though illegal at first, had been legalized by the legislature, and the city was bound to pay it.

"3. The inability to pay, which was assigned as a reason for asking military interference, was no valid reason, for all debtors might plead the same.

"4. That as the taxes due the city could not be seized by her creditors, there was no necessity for the intervention invoked."

In the matter of the trial of offenses against the laws of the State by military commissions, General Hancock took equally wise and conservative ground. He was urged by Judge Noonan, by Governor Pease, and others of the State of Texas, to appoint military commissions to try three prisoners, Wall, Thatcher, and Pulliam, charged with murder. Earnest reasons were urged for his acquiescence in their request, but the General refused to use military power in cases where civil tribunals could perform their functions, and in a well-considered response assigned reasons for the refusal. This paper is an admirable one. It recites the acts of Congress under which his intervention was invoked, and shows that, although these gave a military commander in a certain condition of things power to punish criminals and all disturbers of the public peace, under the same section is declared, "To that end he may allow local civil tribunals to assume the jurisdiction, and try offenders."

The paper further sets forth that the power to organize military commissions for the trial of criminals was an extraordinary power, and should be exercised only when the local civil tribunals are unable or unwilling to enforce the laws against crime.

He further urged that the State government of Texas, organized under the authority of the United States, was then in the full exercise of its powers, the courts in full operation, no unwillingness had been shown by them to perform their duties, nor were there any obstructions in the way of enforcing the laws by civil authority. Under such circumstances there were no good grounds for the exercise of the extraordinary power vested in the commander to organize military commissions for the trial of the persons named. The paper went on to say, "It must be a matter of profound regret to all who value constitutional government, that there should be occasions in times of civil commotion when the public good imperatively requires the intervention of military power for the repression of disorders in the body politic, and for the punishment of offenses against existing laws, framed for the preservation of social order; but that the intervention of this power should be called for or even suggested by civil magistrates when the laws are no longer silent, and civil magistrates are possessed of all the powers necessary to give effect to the laws, excites the surprise of the commander of the Fifth Military District. In his view, it is an evil example, and full of danger to the cause of freedom and good government, that the exercise of the military power through military tribunals, created for the trial of offenses against civil law, should ever be permitted when the ordinary powers of the existing State governments, if faithfully administered, are ample to the punishment of offenders."

The General concluded by assuring the authorities that, if they had not force enough to retain the prisoners until they could be tried, he (the General) would supply it upon proper application, and that, if there were not citizens of Texas in sufficient number and of proper qualifications to furnish officers for enforcing the laws of the State, it would then become necessary for the commander of the Fifth District to exercise the powers vested in him by the acts of Congress, but until such was shown to exist it was not his purpose to interfere.

General Hancock was also applied to, to set aside elections by the people which were alleged to be irregular, and to assume the appointing power himself; but, in a letter written by his direction, he declined to interpose his authority, and advised that, in case there were vitiating irregularities in elections, they be referred to the people to rectify by a new election.

Governor B. F. Flanders had, on the 11th of December, 1867, addressed a communication to General Hancock, suggesting that, in the exercise of his powers as commander of the district, he should remove from office certain officials—the police jury—for alleged malfeasance in office. In reply General Hancock reminded the Governor that removals from office were not to be made without judicial investigation, and that the courts of justice could very easily furnish relief for the evils complained of.

In view of these applications to him as commander for the exercise of judicial functions, General Hancock, on the 1st of January, 1868, issued General Orders, No. 1. The following is a quotation from this order:

" Applications have been made at these headquarters, implying the existence of an arbitrary authority in the Commanding General touching purely civil controversies. One petitioner solicits this action, another that, and each refers to some special consideration of grace or favor which he supposes to exist, and which should influence the department. The number of these applications. . . makes it necessary to declare that the administration of civil justice appertains to the regular courts. The rights of litigants do not depend upon the views of the General; they are to be judged and settled according to the laws. Arbitrary power, such as he has been urged to assume, has no existence here. It is not found in the laws of

Louisiana or of Texas; it can not be derived from any act of Congress. It is restrained by the Constitution. . . . The Major-General commanding takes occasion to repeat that, while disclaiming judicial functions in civil cases, he can suffer no forcible resistance to the execution of processes of the courts."

General Hancock had been applied to by Chief Engineer Henry Van Vleet, of the New Orleans, Mobile, and Chattanooga Railroad Company, to issue a certain order in behalf of the said company. In declining to issue such an order, the General, in his reply, dated January 2, 1868, says:

"The order asked for embraces questions of the most important and delicate nature, such as the exercise of the right of eminent domain, the obstruction of navigable rivers or outlets, etc., and it appears to him very questionable whether he ought to deal with questions of that kind; nor is it clear that any benefit could result to the company from such an order."

After suggesting that the State of Louisiana was the proper authority to grant the request, the General declined to take action in the matter, but offered, if it was desired, to send the papers to the Secretary of War.

Pages might be filled with the recital of the arduous and complicated and delicate duties which General Hancock was now called upon to perform in the difficult problem which he was required to solve in the administration of the affairs of the Fifth Military District. Every species of order was sought from him; and, had he chosen to use the almost absolute power conferred upon the district commanders, as some others did, he might have made history very rapidly, and of a very sensational character; but he met every issue that was raised, and every attempt that was made upon him, with that cool and calm judgment, keen foresight, and unswerving regard for the law and the right which have always characterized him. Civil issues he left to the civil tribunals, and his entire administration demonstrated that he was resolved, as far as possible, to keep the military subordinate to the civil power; that he sought the peace and quiet of the district, the welfare of its people, and the good of the whole country. The civil record of General Hancock in his wide and important command was as wise, conservative, and beneficent as his military record had been glorious. His orders during his administration surprise one by their exhibition of a thorough familiarity with the great principles of law and civil polity, such as would not be expected in a professional soldier. He always seemed to have an intuition, in the most critical crisis, of the right thing to be done, and his execution was as skillful and as effective as his perceptions were clear, comprehensive, and correct.

The nature of the Reconstruction Acts has been sufficiently set forth, and the character of the administration which was expected of the commanders who were appointed to carry out the provisions of these in the Southern States has been sufficiently indicated by what has been shown of the nature of the demands made upon General Hancock. In the appointment to the command of most of the Southern military districts, sufficient care had been taken to ensure the proper carrying out of the wishes of those who had succeeded in framing and passing the Reconstruction Acts. Happily for the communities over which General Hancock was called to rule, here was at least one man who determined to uphold constitutional liberty and the rights of the citizen under the laws. Hancock was a man too magnanimous and too just to do otherwise; and, accordingly, when appointed military Governor of Texas and Louisiana, he put the most merciful interpretation upon the Reconstruction Laws, and administered the affairs of his district in such a manner as to promote the happiness of the people, and to reconcile them to the Government of the United States. But this course did not suit the men who enacted those laws, and who had grasped control at Washington. Moreover, it was beginning to be perceived that General Hancock was becoming popular with the people. A presidential election was about to occur, and it was not impossible that he should become a formidable impediment in the way of the schemes of the ultra radicals, or a dangerous rival to those ambitious men who craved the nomination to that high office. Altogether, the controlling powers at Washington were not satisfied with the quiet, conservative, orderly, and energetic manner in which Hancock was administering the government of the district under his command, or rather permitting the civil authorities to administer it. This was not according to their programme of restoration; and, when they learned, moreover, to their deep regret, that General Hancock's wise and conciliatory administration was winning him golden opinions —not only from the people placed under his control, but from all rightly judging persons the country over— they determined upon his removal. The course followed to this end was characteristic of those who had it in charge. General Garfield, the Chairman of the Committee on Military Affairs of the House of Representatives, introduced a bill to reduce the number of major-generals in the army, with the avowed purpose of ousting General Hancock. The bill, however, was never pressed to its passage, those friendly to it fearing that it would excite a public demonstration in favor of the persecuted officer. A safer method was adopted, which was to effect, by petty and humiliating interference with General Hancock's jurisdiction and administration in the Fifth Military District, the purpose which his enemies were unable to accomplish by legitimate means. A constant succession of harassing acts followed, designed to practically humiliate General Hancock before the people whom he was sent to govern, and to invalidate his acts of government, the persistent and obvious course of which action not unnaturally made a profound impression upon General Hancock, so that about this time he wrote to a friend in Congress as follows : ". . . . I hope to be relieved here soon. The President is no longer able to protect me, so that I may expect one humiliation after another until I am forced to resign. I am prepared for any event. Nothing can intimidate me from doing what I believe to be honest and right."

Soon afterward he wrote the following official letter :

" HEADQUARTERS FIFTH MILITARY DISTRICT,
"NEW ORLEANS, LA., *February* 27, 1867.

" *To* BREVET MAJOR-GENERAL L. THOMAS, *Adjutant-General, U. S. A., Washington, D. C.*

" GENERAL : I have the honor to transmit herewith copies of my correspondence with the General-in-Chief in reference to my recent action concerning the removal from office of certain aldermen in the city of New Orleans, made by me 'for contempt of the orders of the district commander.' I request that the same may in an appropriate manner—as explanatory of my action, and for his information—be laid before his Excellency the President of the United States, with this my request to be relieved from the command of this military district, where it is no longer useful or agreeable for me to serve. When relieved, should the exigencies of the service permit, it would be most in accordance with my inclinations to be sent to St. Louis, Mo., there to await further orders.

" I am, very respectfully, your obedient servant,
" W. S. HANCOCK,
" *Major-General*."

On the 16th of March, 1868, he was relieved of his command at New Orleans.

CHAPTER XXXII

New Orleans—The Pease Correspondence—Message of President Johnson to both Houses of Congress—Letter of General Hancock on the Freedmen's Bureau—Commendatory Article in the "Southern Review."

SHORTLY before the close of his administration at New Orleans, General Hancock received from Governor Pease, of Texas, a letter referring to a previous application for the appointment of military commissions to try offenders in that State, and defining the reasons for that application. In reply to this communication General Hancock wrote his justly celebrated letter upon that subject, and we append both as illustrating the difficulties of General Hancock's position, and the soundness of his political principles, the loftiness of his character, the clearness of his judgment, the manliness of his patriotism, and the profundity of his statesmanship.

"EXECUTIVE OF TEXAS, AUSTIN, TEXAS,
"*January* 17, 1868.

"BREVET-LIEUTENANT-COLONEL W. G. MITCHELI.,
"*Secretary of Civil Affairs.*

"SIR: Your letter of the 28th of December, 1867, was received at this office on the 11th instant. I think it my duty to reply to some portions of it, lest my silence should be construed into an acquiescence in the opinions expressed therein, in regard to the condition of Texas, and the authority of the Civil Provisional Government now existing here.

"I dissent entirely from the declaration that 'the State government of Texas, organized in subordination to the authority of the United States, is in the full exercise of all its proper powers.' The act of Congress, 'to provide for a more efficient government of the Rebel States,' expressly declares in its preamble, that no legal State government, or adequate protection of life or property, now exists in Texas, and it is necessary that peace and good order should be enforced in said State, until a loyal and republican State government can be legally established. It then provides that Texas shall be subject to the military authority of the United States, and shall constitute a part of the Fifth Military District.

"It also directs the President to assign to the command of that district an officer of the army not below the rank of brigadier-general, and to detail a sufficient military force to enable such officer to perform his duties and enforce his authority; and makes it the duty of such officer to protect all persons in their rights of person and property; to suppress insurrection, disorder, and violence, and to punish or cause to be punished all disturbers of public peace and criminals; and to this end he may allow local civil tribunals to take jurisdiction of and try offenders; or, when in his judgment it may be necessary for the trial of offenders, he shall have power to organize military commissions or tribunals for that purpose; and also declares that interference under color of State authority with the exercise of military authority of said act shall be null and void.

"This Act further provides that, until the people of Texas shall be by law admitted to representation in the

Congress of the United States, any government that may exist therein shall be deemed provisional only, and in all respects subject to the paramount authority of the United States, at any time to abolish, modify, control, or supersede the same.

" The Supplementary Act of July 19, 1867, declares it to have been the true intent and meaning of the original Act and the Supplementary Act of the 23d of March, 1867, that the government then existing in Texas was not a legal State government, and that thereafter said government, if continued, was to be continued subject in all respects to the military commander of the District, and the paramount authority of Congress.

" The reasonable construction of these provisions of the Act of Congress referred to, would seem to be, that Texas is placed under a military government, of which the chief officer is the commander of the Fifth Military District; and that whatever civil government there is in Texas is provisional only, subject to said military commander and the paramount authority of Congress, and exists only by their sufferance, as a part of the machinery through which the military authority of the United States is exercised.

" This construction is supported by the acts of the successive commanders of the Fifth Military District and their correspondence with this office from the time they first assumed command in March, 1867, until quite recently. They have exercised the right of removing and appointing at their pleasure the officers of this civil provisional government (with the exception. of the few that are appointed by the Governor), and of filling by appointment all vacancies in offices heretofore filled by election by the people of Texas. They have also, at pleasure, exercised the right to abolish, modify, control, and supersede the laws heretofore enacted, as well as the proceedings and judgments of the courts. They have also, at their pleasure, made arrests for violations of the criminal laws.

"It is true that they have permitted the officers of this civil provisional government, except the Legislature, to perform their duties as prescribed by the laws of Texas, but in subordination to their orders and the laws of the United States.

"I am at a loss to understand how a government, without representation in Congress, and without any militia force, with such limited powers, and those subject to be further limited and changed at pleasure by the military commander of the District, can with any propriety be called a State government organized in subordination to the authority of the Government of the United Sates and in full exercise of all its proper powers.

"I also dissent from the declaration that, 'at this time the country is in a state of profound peace.' Texas cannot properly be said to be in a state of profound peace. It is true that there no longer exists here any organized resistance to the authority of the United States; but a large majority of the white population who participated in the late rebellion are embittered against the Government by their defeat in arms and loss of their slaves, and yield to it an unwilling obedience only because they feel that they have no means to resist its authority. None of this class has any affection for the Government, and very few of them have any respect for it. They regard the legislation of Congress on the subject of reconstruction as unconstitutional and hostile to their interests, and consider the government now existing here under the authority of the United States as an usurpation upon their rights.

14

They look upon the enfranchisement of their late slaves, and the disfranchisement of a portion of their own class, as an act of insult and oppression.

"This state of feeling toward the Government and its acts, by a large majority of the white population who have heretofore exercised the political power of Texas, combined with the demoralization and impatience of restraint by civil authority that always follow the close of great civil wars, renders it extremely difficult to enforce the criminal laws in those portions of the State which are most densely occupied, and often impossible to do so in those parts of the State which are sparsely settled. A knowledge of this state of affairs induces many to redress their fancied wrongs and grievances by acts of violence.

"It is a lamentable fact, that over one hundred cases of homicide have occurred in Texas within the last twelve months, while not one tenth of the perpetrators have even been arrested, and less than one twentieth of them have been tried.

"Within the last few months United States officers and soldiers have been killed while in the discharge of their duties, and in no case have those who committed these offenses been tried or punished. In these cases the most strenuous efforts were made by the military authorities to arrest the guilty parties, but without success, although they were well known.

"It often happens, that, when the civil officers of a county are disposed to do their duty and endeavor to make arrests, they are unable to do so, because they are not properly sustained by the citizens of the county, and when arrests are made, a large proportion of the offenders escape from custody, because there are no secure jails for their confinement, and the county authorities have not the means to pay for proper guards. Several cases have come to my knowledge, in which sheriffs failed entirely to arrest parties who had been indicted, although they remained in the county for months.

"Grand juries often fail to find indictments when they ought to do so, and petit juries as often fail to convict offenders in cases where the evidence is conclusive. Hence it results that, in many cases, offenders escape punishment when the magistrates and sheriffs do their duty.

"It is by no means charged that all who took part in the rebellion participate in or approve the many outrages and acts of violence which are perpetrated in Texas without punishment. A large majority disapprove and deplore this state of affairs; few of them, however, give any active aid in the enforcement of the criminal laws.

"All good citizens feel and acknowledge that there is but little security for life in Texas, beyond what each man's personal character gives him. Many loyal citizens have expressed the opinion that it would have a good effect upon the community, if some of the perpetrators of aggravated crimes—like that in Uvalde County, where the difficulty of keeping the prisoners in confinement rendered it highly probable that they would escape, and where the sparseness of population made it so difficult to procure a jury, that it was considered almost certain that the parties would never be tried by the civil courts—should be brought before a military commission. In this opinion I fully concur; and it was for this reason that I made the recommendation.

"The condition of affairs here was much worse before the establishment of the present military government than it has been since. The fear of an arrest by the military authorities and a trial by a military commission has had some effect in deterring lawless men from the commission of crime. But I am constrained to say that, since the publication of General Orders, No. 40, of 29th November, 1867, from Headquarters, Fifth Military District, there has been a perceptible increase of crime and manifestation of hostile feelings toward the Government and its supporters.

"It is an unpleasant duty to give such a recital of the condition of the country. But the reports and correspondence on file in the offices of the Freedmen's Bureau and of the military commanders in Texas, since the close of the rebellion, will prove the truth of what is stated here.

"In my communications with the previous commanders of the Fifth Military District, orally and in writing, I have frequently given them my views in regard to the powers of the present civil provisional government of Texas, and also in regard to the condition of affairs here, and the great difficulty and sometimes impossibility of executing the laws for the prevention and punishment of crime and the preservation of the public peace.

"If all these matters had been known to the Commanding General of the Fifth Military District, his surprise might not have been excited that a civil magistrate of Texas, who is desirous to preserve peace and good order and to give security to person and life, should have applied to him, as the chief officer to whom the government of Texas is entrusted by the laws of the United States, to do by military authority what experience has proved can not be effectually done by the civil officers of Texas, with the limited means and authority with which they are invested by law. I am, sir, with great respect,

"Your obedient servant,

"E. M. PEASE."

HEADQUARTERS FIFTH MILITARY DISTRICT,
NEW ORLEANS, LA., *March* 9, 1868.

To His Excellency E. M. PEASE, *Governor of Texas.*

SIR: Your communication of the 17th January last was received in due course of mail (the 27th January), but not until it had been widely circulated by the newspaper press. To such a letter—written and published for manifest purposes—it has been my intention to reply as soon as leisure from more important business would permit.

Your statement, that the act of Congress "to provide for the more efficient government of the Rebel States" declares that whatever government existed in Texas was provisional; that peace and order should be enforced; that Texas should be part of the Fifth Military District, and subject to military power; that the President should appoint an officer to command in said district, and detail a force to protect the rights of person and property, suppress insurrection and violence, and punish offenders, either by military commission, or through the action of local civil tribunals, as in his judgment might seem best, will not be disputed. One need only read the act to perceive it contains such provisions. But, how all this is supposed to have made it my duty to order the military commission requested, you have entirely failed to show. The power to do a thing, if shown, and the propriety of doing it, are often very different matters. You observe you are at a loss to understand how a government, without representation in Congress or a militia force, and subject to military power, can be said to be in the full exercise of all its proper powers. You do not reflect that this government, created or permitted by Congress, has all the powers which the act intends, and may fully exercise them accordingly. If you think it ought to have more powers, should be allowed to send members to Congress, wield a militia force, and possess yet other powers, your complaint is not to be preferred against me, but against Congress, who made it what it is.

As respects the issue between us, any question as to what Congress ought to have done has no pertinence. You admit the act of Congress authorizes me to try an offender by military commission, or allow the local civil tribunals to try, as I shall deem best; and you can not deny the act expressly recognizes such local civil tribunals as legal authorities for the purpose specified. When you contend there are no legal local tribunals for any purpose in Texas, you must either deny the plain reading of the act of Congress, or the power of Congress to pass the act.

You next remark that you dissent from my declaration, "that the country (Texas) is in a state of profound peace," and proceed to state the grounds of your dissent. They appear to me not a little extraordinary. I quote your words: "It is true there no longer exists here (Texas) any organized resistance to the authority of the United States, but a large majority of the white population who participated in the late rebellion are embittered against the Government, and yield to it an unwilling obedience." Nevertheless, you concede they do yield it obedience. You proceed:

"None of this class have any affection for the Government, and very few any respect for it. They regard the legislation of Congress on the subject of reconstruction as unconstitutional and hostile to their interests, and consider the government now existing here under authority of the United States as a usurpation on their rights. They look on the emancipation of their late slaves and the disfranchisement of a portion of their own class as an act of insult and oppression."

And this is all you have to present for proof that war and not peace prevails in Texas; and hence it becomes my duty—so you suppose—to set aside the local civil tribunals, and enforce the penal code against citizens by means of military commissions.

My dear sir, I am not a lawyer, nor has it been my business, as it may have been yours, to study the philosophy of statecraft and politics. But I may lay claim, after an experience of more than half a lifetime, to some poor knowledge of men, and some appreciation of what is necessary to social order and happiness. And for the future of our common country, I could devoutly wish that no great number of our people have yet fallen in with the views you appear to entertain. Woe be to us whenever it shall come to pass that the power of the magistrate—civil or military—is permitted to deal with the mere opinions or feelings of the people.

I have been accustomed to believe that sentiments of respect or disrespect, and feelings of affection, love, or hatred, so long as not developed into acts in violation of law, were matters wholly beyond the punitory power of human tribunals.

I will maintain that the entire freedom of thought and speech, however acrimoniously indulged, is consistent with the noblest aspirations of man and the happiest condition of his race.

When a boy, I remember to have read a speech of Lord Chatham's, delivered in Parliament. It was during our Revolutionary War, and related to the policy of employing the savages on the side of Britain. You may be more familiar with the speech than I am. If I am not greatly mistaken, his lordship denounced the British Government—his government—in terms of unmeasured bitterness. He characterized its policy as revolting to every sentiment of humanity and religion; proclaimed it covered with disgrace, and vented his eternal abhorrence of it and its measures. It may, I think, be safely asserted that a majority of the British nation concurred in the views of Lord Chatham. But who ever supposed that profound peace was not existing in that kingdom, or that government had any authority to question the absolute right of the opposition to express their objections to the propriety of the king's measures in any words, or to any extent they pleased? It would be difficult to show that the opponents of the Government in the days of the elder Adams, or Jefferson, or Jackson exhibited for it either "affection" or "respect." You are conversant with the history of our past parties and political struggles touching legislation on alienage, sedition, the embargo, national banks, our wars with England and Mexico, and can not be ignorant of the fact that for one party to assert that a law or system of legislation is unconstitutional, oppressive, and usurpative is not a new thing in the United States. That the people of Texas consider acts of Congress unconstitutional, oppressive, or insulting to them, is of no consequence to the matter in hand. The President of the United States has announced his opinion that these acts of Congress are unconstitutional. The Supreme Court, as you are aware, not long ago decided unanimously that a certain military commission was unconstitutional. Our people everywhere, in every State, without reference to the side they took during the rebellion, differ as to the constitutionality of these acts of Congress. How the matter really is, neither you nor I may dogmatically affirm.

If you deem them constitutional laws, and beneficial to the country, you not only have the right to publish your opinions, but it might be your bounden duty as a citizen to do so. Not less is it the privilege and duty of any and every citizen, wherever residing, to publish his opinion freely and fearlessly on this and every question which he thinks concerns his interest. This is merely in accordance with the principles of our free government; and neither you nor I would wish to live under any other. It is time now, at the end of almost two years from the close of the war, we should begin to recollect what manner of people we are; to tolerate again free, popular discussion, and extend some forbearance and consideration to opposing views. The maxims, that in all intellectual contests truth is mighty and must prevail, and that error is harmless when reason is left free to combat it, are not only sound, but salutary. It is a poor compliment to the merits of such a cause, that its advocates would silence opposition by force; and generally those only who are in the wrong will resort to this ungenerous means. I am confident you will not commit your serious judgment to the proposition that any amount of discussion, or any sort of opinions, however unwise in your judgment, or any assertion or feeling, however resentful or bitter, not resulting in a breach of law, can furnish justification for your denial that profound peace exists in Texas. You might as well deny that profound peace exists in New York, Pennsylvania, Maryland, California, Ohio, and Kentucky, where a majority of the people differ with a minority on these questions; or that profound peace exists in the House of Representatives, or the Senate, at Washington, or in the Supreme Court, where all these questions have been repeatedly discussed, and parties respectfully and patiently heard. You next complain that in parts of the State (Texas) it is difficult to enforce the criminal laws; that sheriffs fail to arrest; that grand jurors will not always indict; that in some cases the military acting in aid of the civil authorities have not been able to execute the process of the courts; that petit jurors have acquitted persons adjudged guilty by you; and that other persons charged with offences have broke jail and fled from prosecution. I know not how these things are; but, admitting your representations literally true, if for such reasons I should set aside the local civil tribunals, and order a military commission, there is no place in the United States where it might not be done with equal propriety. There is not a State in the Union—North or South—where the like facts are not continually happening. Perfection is not to be predicated of man or his works. No one can reasonbly expect certain and absolute justice in human transactions; and if military power is to be set in motion, on the principles for which you would seem to contend, I fear that a civil government, regulated by laws, could have no abiding place beneath the circuit of the sun.   It is rather more than hinted in your letter, that there is no local State government in Texas, and no local laws, outside of the acts of Congress, which I ought to respect; and that I should undertake to protect the rights of persons and property in *my own way* and in an *arbitrary manner.*   If such be your meaning, I am compelled to differ with you.   After the abolition of slavery (an event which I hope no one now regrets), the laws of Louisiana and Texas existing prior to the rebellion, and not in conflict with the acts of Congress, comprised a vast system of jurisprudence, both civil and criminal.   It required not volumes only, but libraries to contain them.   They laid down principles and precedents for ascertaining the rights and adjusting the controversies of men, in every conceivable case.   They were the creations of great and good and learned men, who had labored, in their day, for their kind, and gone down to the grave long before our recent troubles, leaving their works an inestimable legacy to the human race. These laws, as I am informed, connected the civilization of past and present ages, and testified of the justice, wisdom, humanity, and patriotism of more than one nation, through whose records they descended to the present people of these States.   I am satisfied, from representations of persons competent to judge, they are as perfect a system of laws as may be found elsewhere, and better suited than any other to the condition of this people, for by them they have long been governed.   Why should it be supposed Congress has abolished these laws?   Why should any one wish to abolish them?   They have committed no treason, nor are hostile to the United States, nor countenance crime, nor favor injustice.   On them, as on a foundation of rock, reposes almost the entire superstructure of social order in these two States.   Annul this code of local laws, and there would be no longer any rights, either of person or property, here.   Abolish the local civil tribunals made to execute them, and you would virtually annul the laws, except in reference to the very few cases cognizable in the Federal courts. Let us for a moment suppose the whole local civil code annulled, and that I am left, as commander of the Fifth Military District, the sole fountain of law and justice.   This is the position in which you would place me.

I am now to protect all rights and redress all wrongs.   How is it possible for me to do it?   Innumerable questions arise, of which I am not only ignorant, but to the solution of which a military court is entirely unfitted.   One would establish a will, another a deed; or the question is one of succession, or partnership, or descent, or trust; a suit of ejectment or claim to chattels; or the application may relate to robbery, theft, arson, or murder.   How am I to take the first step in any such matter?   If I turn to the acts of Congress I find nothing on the subject.   I dare not open the authors on the local code, for it has ceased to exist.

And you tell me that in this perplexing condition I am to furnish, by dint of my own hasty and crude judgment, the legislation demanded by the vast and manifold interests of the people!   I repeat, sir, that you, and not Congress, are responsible for the monstrous suggestion that there are no local laws or institutions here to be respected by me, outside the acts of Congress.   I say, unhesitatingly, if it were possible that Congress should pass an act abolishing the local codes for Louisiana and Texas—which I do not believe —and it should fall to my lot to supply their places with something of my own, I do not see how I could do better than follow the laws in force here prior to the rebellion, excepting whatever therein shall relate to slavery.   Power may destroy the forms, but not the principles of justice; these will live in spite even of the sword.   History tells us that the Roman Pandects were lost for a long period among the rubbish that war and revolution had heaped upon them, but at length were dug out of the ruins—again to be regarded as a precious treasure.

You are pleased to state that, "since the publication of (my) General Orders, No. 40, there has been a perceptible increase of crime and manifestation of hostile feeling toward the Government and its supporters," and add that it is "an unpleasant duty to give such a recital of the condition of the country."

You will permit me to say that I deem it impossible the first of these statements can be true, and that I do very greatly doubt the correctness of the second.   General Orders, No. 40, was issued at New Orleans, November 29, 1867, and your letter was dated January 17, 1868.   Allowing time for Order No. 40 to reach Texas and become generally known, some additional time must have elapsed before its effect would be manifested, and a yet further time must transpire before you would be able to collect the evidence of what you term "the condition of the country"; and yet, after all this, you would have to make the necessary investigations to ascertain if Order No. 40 or something else was the cause. The time, therefore, remaining to enable you, before the 17th of January, 1868, to reach a satisfactory conclusion on so delicate and nice a question must have been very short. How you proceeded, whether you investigated yourself or through third persons, and if so, who they were, what their competency and fairness, on what evidence you rested your conclusion, or whether you ascertained any facts at all, are points upon which your letter so discreetly omits all mention, that I may well be excused for not relying implicitly upon it; nor is my difficulty diminished by the fact that, in another part of your letter, you state that ever since the close of the war a very large portion of the people have had no affection for the Government, but bitterness of feeling only. Had the duty of publishing and circulating through the country, long before it reached me, your statement that the action of the district commander was increasing crime and hostile feeling against the Government, been less painful to your sensibilities, it might possibly have occurred to you to furnish something on the subject in addition to your bare assertion.

But what was Order No. 40, and how could it have the effect you attribute to it? It sets forth that "the great principles of American liberty are still the inheritance of this people and ever should be, that the right of trial by jury, the *habeas corpus*, the liberty of the press, the freedom of speech, and the natural rights of person and property must be preserved." Will you question the truth of these declarations? Which one of these great principles of liberty are you ready to deny and repudiate? Whoever does so avows himself the enemy of human liberty and the advocate of despotism. Was there any intimation in General Orders, No. 40, that any crimes or breaches of law would be countenanced? You know that there was not. On the contrary, you know perfectly well that while "the consideration of crime and offences committed in the Fifth Military District was referred to the judgment of the regular civil tribunals," a pledge was given in Order No. 40, which all understood, that tribunals would be supported in their lawful jurisdiction, and that "forcible resistance to law would be instantly suppressed by arms." You will not affirm that this pledge has ever been forfeited. There has not been a moment, since I have been in command of the Fifth District, when the whole military force in my hands has not been ready to support the civil authorities of Texas in the execution of the laws. And I am unwilling to believe they would refuse to call for aid if they needed it.

There are some considerations which, it seems to me, should cause you to hesitate before indulging in wholesale censures against the civil authorities of Texas. You are yourself the chief of these authorities, not elected by the people, but created by the military. Not long after you had thus come into office, all the judges of the Supreme Court of Texas—five in number—were removed from office, and new appointments made : twelve of the seventeen district judges were removed, and others appointed. County officers, more or less, in seventy-five out of one hundred and twenty-eight counties, were removed, and others appointed in their places. It is fair to conclude that the executive and judicial civil functionaries in Texas are the persons whom you desired to fill the offices. It is proper to mention, also, that none but registered citizens, and only those who could take the test oath, have been allowed to serve as jurors during your administration. Now, it is against this local government, created by military power prior to my coming here, and so composed of your personal and political friends, that you have preferred the most grievous complaints. It is of them that you have asserted they will not do their duty; they will not maintain justice; will not arrest offenders; will not punish crimes; and that, out of one hundred homicides committed in the last twelve months, not over ten arrests have been made ; and by means of such gross disregard of duty you declare that neither property nor life is safe in Texas.

Certainly you could have said nothing more to the discredit of the officials who are now in office. If the facts be as you allege, a mystery is presented for which I can imagine no explanation. Why is it that your political friends, backed up and sustained by the whole military power of the United States in this district, should be unwilling to enforce the laws against that part of the population lately in rebellion, and whom you represent as the offenders? In all the history of these troubles, I have never seen or heard before of such a fact. I repeat, if the fact be so, it is a profound mystery, utterly surpassing my comprehension.   I am constrained to declare that I believe you are in very great error as to facts.   On careful examination at the proper source, I find that at the date of your letter four cases only of homicides had been reported to these headquarters as having occurred since November 29, 1867, the date of Order 40, and these cases were ordered to be tried or investigated as soon as the reports were received.   However, the fact of the one hundred homicides may still be correct, as stated by you.   The Freedmen's Bureau in Texas reported one hundred and sixty; how many of these were by Indians and Mexicans, and how the remainder were classified, is not known, nor is it known whether these data are accurate.

The report of the commanding officer of the District of Texas shows that since I assumed command no applications have been made to him by you for the arrest of criminals in the State of Texas.

To this date eighteen cases of homicides have been reported to me as having occurred since November 29, 1867, although special instructions had been given to report such cases as they occur.   Of these, five were committed by Indians, one by a Mexican, one by an insane man, three by colored men, two of women by their husbands, and, of the remainder, some by parties unknown—all of which could be scarcely attributable to Order No. 40.   If the reports received since the issuing of Order No. 40 are correct, they exhibit no increase of homicides in my time, if you are correct that one hundred had occurred in the past twelve months.

That there has not been a perfect administration of justice in Texas, I am not prepared to deny.

That there has been no such wanton disregard of duty on the part of officials as you allege, I am well satisfied.   A very little while ago you regarded the present officials in Texas as the only ones who could be safely trusted with power.   Now you pronounce them worthless, and would cast them aside.

I have found little else in your letter but indications of temper, lashed into excitement by causes which I deem mostly imaginary; a great confidence in the accuracy of your own opinions, and an intolerance of the opinions of others; a desire to punish the thoughts and feelings of those who differ from you; and an impatience which magnifies the shortcomings of officials who are perhaps as earnest and conscientious in the discharge of their duties as yourself; and a most unsound conclusion that, while any persons are to be found wanting in affection or respect for the government, or yielding it obedience from motives which you do not approve, war, and not peace, is the status, and all such persons are the proper subjects for military penal jurisdiction.

If I have written anything to disabuse your mind of so grave an error, I shall be gratified. I am, sir, very respectfully,

Your obedient servant,

W. S. HANCOCK,
Major-General Commanding.

It would seem that General Hancock's letter should have convinced every fair and law-loving man that it was wiser far to restore the civil tribunals to the effective administration of the existing laws than to inaugurate the dangerous expedient of military commissions which denied to accused persons the right of trial by jury, and the other forms of law which are such essentials of the civil administration of justice.

By all that has been written here in the nature of history, and by the character of the orders issued by General Hancock, and of the requests and demands made upon him, it will be seen that the administration of the affairs of the Fifth Military District was no sinecure, either for its commander or his staff. It was, on the contrary, perplexing and laborious, and the perpetual demands made upon him for intervention, even in cases which he had referred to the civil tribunals and proper official functionaries, called for close attention and excessive labor, even as regarded the mere correspondence; and perhaps no part of General Hancock's very active life was more wearing and vexatious than the few months passed in New Orleans. But certainly no portion of it, not even excepting the brilliant campaigns in which he won so much honor, exhibited more true greatness of mind, or a broader extent and variety of knowledge and of administrative capacity. This portion of his career gained the confidence and elicited the applause of all fair and patriotic minds throughout the country, excepting only those whose personal and political schemes were thwarted by his unswerving adherence to the principles of honor, rectitude, and fair dealing.

On the 18th of December, 1867, the following message was sent by the President of the United States to both Houses of Congress. It displays certainly in what estimate the services of General Hancock were held by the highest executive authority in the land:

Gentlemen of the Senate and of the House of Representatives:

An official copy of the order issued by Major-General Winfield S. Hancock, commander of the Fifth Military District, dated headquarters in New Orleans, Louisiana, on the 29th day of November, has reached me through the regular channels of the War Department, and I herewith communicate it to Congress for such action as may seem to be proper in view of all the circumstances.

It will be perceived that General Hancock announces that he will make the law the rule of his conduct; that he will uphold the courts and other civil authorities in the performance of their proper duties, and that he will use his military power only to preserve the peace and enforce the law. He declares very explicitly that the sacred right of the trial by jury and the privilege of the writ of *habeas corpus* shall not be crushed out or trodden under foot. He goes further, and, in one comprehensive sentence, asserts that the principles of American liberty are still the inheritance of this people, and ever should be.

When a great soldier, with unrestricted power in his hands to oppress his fellow men, voluntarily foregoes the chance of gratifying his selfish ambition, and devotes himself to the duty of building up the liberties and strengthening the laws of his country, he presents an example of the highest public virtue that human nature is capable of practicing. The strongest claim of Washington to be "first in war, first in peace, and first in the hearts of his countrymen," is founded on the great fact that in all his illustrious career he scrupulously abstained from violating the legal and constitutional rights of his fellow citizens. When he surrendered his commission to Congress, the President of that body spoke his highest praise in saying that he had "always regarded the rights of the civil authorities through all dangers and disasters." Whenever power above the law courted his acceptance, he calmly put the temptation aside. By such magnanimous acts of forbearance he won the universal admiration of mankind, and left a name which has no rival in the history of the world.

I am far from saying that General Hancock is the only officer of the American army who is influenced by the example of Washington. Doubtless thousands of them are faithfully devoted to the principles for which the men of the Revolution laid down their lives. But the distinguished honor belongs to him of being the first officer in high command south of the Potomac, since the close of the civil war, who has given utterance to these noble sentiments in the form of a military order.

I respectfully suggest to Congress that some public recognition of General Hancock's patriotic conduct is due, if not to him, to the friends of law and justice throughout the country. Of such an act as his at such a time it is but fit that the dignity should be vindicated and the virtue proclaimed, so that its value as an example may not be lost to the nation.

ANDREW JOHNSON.

WASHINGTON, D. C., *December* 18, 1867.

The effect of this message upon Congress was, of course, of the slightest; it served, however, to put on record, from its highest public exponent, the deep and wide-spread public opinion which was slowly formulating itself toward a consummation of result, the nature of which will appear farther on in these pages.

As a further contribution to the history of this period of General Hancock's career we insert the following letter:

HEADQUARTERS FIFTH MILITARY DISTRICT,
NEW ORLEANS, LA., *February 24, 1868.*

MAJOR-GENERAL O. O. HOWARD, *Commissioner of Bureau Refugees, Freedmen, and Abandoned Lands, Washington, D. C.:*

GENERAL: Referring to the report of Captain E. Collins, Seventeenth Infantry, sub-assistant commissioner of the bureau, refugees, freedmen, and abandoned lands, at Brenham, Texas, dated December 31, 1867, and transmitted by you for my information, I have the honor to state that I do not understand how any orders of mine can be interpreted as interfering with the proper execution of the law creating the bureau. It is certainly not my intention that they should so interfere. Anything complained of in that letter, which could have lawfully been remedied by the exercise of military authority, should have received the action of General Reynolds, who, being military commander, and also Assistant-Commissioner for Texas, was the proper authority to apply the remedy, and to that end was vested with the necessary power.

A copy of the report of Captain Collins had already been forwarded to me by General Reynolds, before the receipt of your communication, and had been returned to him on January 16, with the following endorsement: "Respectfully returned to Brevet Major-General J. J. Reynolds, commanding District of Texas.

"This paper seems to contain only vague and indefinite complaints, without specific action as to any particular cases. If Captain Collins has any special cases, of the nature referred to in his communication, which require action at these headquarters, he can transmit them, and they will receive attention."

No reply has been received to this—a proof either of the non-existence of such special cases, or of neglect of duty on the part of Captain Collins in not reporting them. It is and will be my pleasure, as well as duty, to aid you, and the officers and agents under your direction, in the proper execution of the law. I have just returned from a trip to Texas. While there, I passed through Brenham twice, and saw Captain Collins, but neither from him nor from General Reynolds did I hear anything in regard to this subject, so far as I recollect.

There are numerous abuses of authority on the part of certain agents of the bureau in Texas, and General Reynolds is already investigating some of them.

My intention is to confine the agents of the bureau within their legitimate authority, so far as my power as district commander extends; further than that, it is not my intention or desire to interfere with the Freedmen's Bureau. I can say, however, that, had the district commander a superior control over the freedmen's affairs in the district, the bureau would be as useful, and would work more harmoniously, and be more in favor with the people. At present there is a clashing of authority. I simply mention the facts without desiring any such control.

The Reconstruction Acts charge district commanders with the duty of protecting all persons in their rights of person and property; and to this end authorize them to allow local civil tribunals to take jurisdiction of and try offenders; or, if in their opinion necessary, to organize a military commission or tribunal for that purpose.

They are thus given control over all criminal proceedings for violation of the statute laws of the States, and for such other offenses as are not by law made triable by the United States courts. The Reconstruction Acts exempt no class of persons from their operation, and the duty of protecting *all* persons in their rights of person and property, of necessity, invests district commanders with control over the agents of the bureau, to the extent of at least enabling them to restrain these agents from any interference with or disregard of their prerogatives as district commanders.

The district commanders are made responsible for the preservation of peace and the enforcement of the local laws within their districts; and they are the ones required to designate the tribunals before which those who break the peace and violate these laws shall be tried.

Such being the fact, many of the agents of the bureau seem not to be aware of it. In Texas some are yet holding courts, trying cases, imposing fines, taking fees for services, and arresting citizens for offenses over which the bureau is not intended by law to have jurisdiction.

General Reynolds is aware of some of these cases, and is, as I have already mentioned, giving his attention to them.

In Louisiana this state of affairs exists to a less extent, if at all. I am, General, very respectfully,

Your obedient servant,

W. S. HANCOCK,

Major-General U. S. Army, Commanding.

It was in the neighborhood of the time to which we have now arrived that it became matter of public conversation that some misunderstanding had arisen between General Grant and General Hancock. That such, to a certain extent, was the case, is as much a matter of history as any other portion of this book. Into the nature and causes of this temporary disagreement it is unnecessary to enter here. Gossip is not history. It is only necessary to say that these eminent soldiers sometimes differed upon pending questions, and with regard to the proper conduct of high official functions, and that their good understanding was for a time disturbed. In relation to this, General Hancock once remarked to a friend: "The differences which arose between General Grant and myself were mainly, if not entirely, due to misrepresentations and exaggerations of the language and conduct of both of us." Time and better information afterward removed the mistaken impressions which had been formed, and the published remarks of General Grant and the frequent expressions in private of General Hancock give ample assurance that these ceased to exist.

In conclusion of so much of this history as refers to the Fifth Military District, we will quote here from an article entitled "The Civil Record of General Hancock," published in the "Southern Review," for October, 1871 :

"Absolutely refusing to comply with all such petitions (asking for arbitrary use of his military powers), he respects the rights of the people one and all, and confines the exercise of his unlimited powers within the sacred bounds of constitutional law and justice. We hail him, therefore, as a second Washington, whom no amount of temptation can seduce from the path of conscious rectitude. He would offend the powers that be, and will disgust his friends, if necessary, but he will not violate his own sense of right and justice and mercy. He is, in fact, one of the few men who, in the history of our race, have shown themselves as firm and noble in the administration of civil justice—as brave and heroic in the conduct of their military campaigns. Hancock is a just man; a simple, massive, and heroic character, as calm and dispassionate in the formation of his opinions as he is firm and inflexible in his adherence to them. He is not to be driven from his convictions of right, because in the formation of them his great aim has been not exaltation of self, but his country's good. . . .

"We admire this memorable state paper (letter to Governor Pease), because it stands out so grandly above the darkness of evil times and an almost universal defection of principle, like some memorial of the olden time, when the regard for justice and the liberties of the people had a fixed abode in the hearts of statesmen."

CHAPTER XXXIII.

FROM New Orleans General Hancock was appointed
to the command of the Division of the Atlantic, which
command he assumed March 31, 1868. This division was
composed of three military departments, namely, the Department of the Lakes, that of the East, and that of Washington. The first embraced the States of Ohio, Michigan,
Indiana, Illinois, and Wisconsin, with General John
Pope commanding, headquarters at Detroit; the second,
the New England States, New York, New Jersey and
Pennsylvania, General Irvin McDowell commanding,
headquarters, New York; and the third the District of
Columbia, Maryland, and Delaware, General E. R. S.
Canby commanding, headquarters at Washington.

The year 1868 is memorable in the life of General
Hancock, for the reason of its being the occasion of his
being named as a prominent candidate for the Democratic nomination for the Presidency of the United
States. The Republican convention had met on the
20th of May of that year, and had nominated General
Ulysses S. Grant for President, and Hon. Schuyler Colfax for Vice-President. The Democratic convention

assembled in the city of New York, July 4th. The balloting at this convention presented some strange political phenomena. There were twenty-one several ballots, Horatio Seymour (who was ultimately nominated, in company with the Hon. Francis P. Blair, of Missouri, for Vice-President) received no votes until the fourth ballot, when he received nine, and he gained no increase on this until the last ballot, when he received 317; the highest vote received by Mr. Pendleton was on the eighth ballot, $156\frac{1}{2}$; the highest received by Mr. Hendricks was 162. General Hancock began with $33\frac{1}{2}$, rose to $131\frac{1}{2}$, and concluded, on the 18th ballot, with $144\frac{1}{4}$. There were fewer than fifteen names before the convention.

The campaign which followed the two conventions was exciting, the conclusion being the election of General Grant by a popular vote of 3,015,071, against 2,709,613 cast for Horatio Seymour, the electoral vote being 214 to 80.

It had never been General Hancock's habit to indulge in campaign work; opportunities of voting, even, are rare for army officers, but he always maintained his citizenship in Pennsylvania—as he does to this day. He could hardly, then, have been expected to enter with much vigor or personal effort into the canvass of 1868. A different view from this, however, appeared to strike the radical journals of the time, for they bruited about the assertion that General Hancock was dissatisfied with the result of the National Democratic convention, and was personally inactive in the canvass for this reason. This gratuitous charge General Hancock would not in the least have seen fit to take into consideration, but that a warm personal friend of his, S. T. Glover, Esq., an eminent lawyer of St. Louis, addressed to him a letter of inquiry upon the subject. To this letter the General replied, and we give below the entire correspondence as reprinted from the "National Intelligencer" (Washington, D. C.), of July 29, 1868.

"St. Louis, Missouri, *July* 13, 1868.

"MAJOR-GENERAL HANCOCK: I deem it proper to direct your attention to statements made by the radical press to the effect that you are greatly dissatisfied with the results of the National Democratic convention. The object of these statements is to create an impression that you do not acquiesce in the judgment of the convention, that your friends do not, and, in consequence, Seymour and Blair will not have their cordial support. I wish you to know, General, that I have taken the liberty to pronounce these statements false, and to assure those who have spoken with me on the subject that nothing could cause you more regret than to find your friends, or any of them, less earnest in supporting the ticket which has been nominated than they would have been had your name stood in the place of Governor Seymour's.

"I am, very sincerely, your friend,

"S. T. GLOVER."

REPLY OF GENERAL HANCOCK.

"Newport, Rhode Island, *July* 17, 1868.

"S. T. GLOVER, Esq., *St. Louis, Missouri:*

"MY DEAR SIR: I am greatly obliged for your favor of the 13th instant. Those who suppose that I do not acquiesce in the work of the National Democratic convention, or that I do not sincerely desire the election of its nominees, know very little of my character. Believing, as I verily do, that the preservation of constitutional government eminently depends on the success of the

Democratic party in the coming election, were I to hesitate in its cordial support I feel I should not only falsify my own record, but commit a crime against my country. I never aspired to the Presidency on account of myself. I never sought its doubtful honors and certain labors and responsibilities merely for the position. My only wish was to promote, if I could, the good of the country, and to rebuke the spirit of revolution which had invaded every sacred precinct of liberty. When, therefore, you pronounced the statements in question false, you did exactly right. 'Principles and not men' is the motto for the rugged crisis in which we are now struggling.

"Had I been made the Presidential nominee I should have considered it a tribute, not to me, but to principles which I had proclaimed and practiced; but shall I cease to regard these principles because, by the judgment of mutual political friends, another has been appointed to put them in execution? Never! Never!

"These, sir, are my sentiments, whatever interested parties may say to the contrary; and I desire that all may know and understand them. I shall ever hold in grateful remembrance the faithful friends who, hailing from every section of the country, preferred me by their votes, and other expressions of confidence, both in and out of the convention, and shall do them all the justice to believe that they were governed by patriotic motives; that they did not propose simply to aggrandize my personal fortunes, but to serve their country through me, and that they will not now suffer anything like personal preferences or jealousies to stand between them and their manifest duty. I have the honor to be, dear sir,

"Very respectfully yours,
"WINFIELD S. HANCOCK."

General Hancock's report to the War Department for 1869 was very brief, as no military operations of importance occurred. On the 20th of March of that year, by General Orders, No. 10, Headquarters of the Army, General Hancock was relieved from the command of the Division of the Atlantic by General George G. Meade, and was ordered to the Department of Dakota. But being at this time a member of the "Dyer Court of Inquiry,"* then in session at the city of Washington, General Hancock did not proceed to the northwest to assume command of his new department until May 17, 1869.

The duties devolving upon the General in this command chiefly consisted in preserving peace and order among the numerous warlike Indian tribes inhabiting portions of the territory embraced in his department, the protection of settlers on the frontier, guarding and keeping open lines of travel, and furthering and protecting the work of the construction of railways at that time being built westward through the Department of Dakota toward the Pacific Coast.

The Government having adopted the policy of settling the Indians on reservations, one object of keeping a military force in that region was to be ready for service

---

* It was in reference to the court that the Secretary of War (General Schofield) addressed a letter to General Hancock, dated Washington, D. C., September 19, 1868, in which he says:

"My Dear Sir: I am very sorry, indeed, to hear of your trouble with that old wound, and hope it will not prove so bad as you apprehend. I shall hardly know who to substitute on the court. I would rather postpone the day of meeting a short time than change the detail. Please let me know as soon as you can what the prospects are of your being able to go on, say in a week or two after the time, if not at the time appointed.

"The President has given his consent for the removal of your headquarters to New York."

15

in case of outbreaks among the Indians, which it was apprehended might arise in the process of placing the several tribes in their respective reservations.   No outbreaks occurred, however, these doubtless being prevented by the presence of the troops.   General Hancock accordingly distributed his men to stations where they might be most useful; posts established by him with a view to control the peaceful settlement of the Indians on their reservations and to preserve the general quiet.

In May and June of 1869, he personally visited all these stations, and gave such directions and instructions as were required to insure the erection, before the advent of winter, of the necessary quarters and storehouses for the shelter of the troops and the storage of their provisions during the inclement season.

A new post was established near Pembina, on the Red River of the North, in the vicinity of the point where that river crosses our northern boundary.   Congress appropriated fifty thousand dollars for this purpose.   Two companies were sent to Pembina and a fort was erected. Early in the fall General Hancock made a tour of inspection extending as far as this point, and made a report in which he wrote in high terms of the character and prospective resources and value of the Red River country, recommending that measures should be speedily inaugurated for authoritatively determining the boundary line between us and the British possessions.

During most of the time while in command of the Department of Dakota, General Hancock's headquarters were at St. Paul, Minnesota.   He continued in that command during the year 1871, its duties, though laborious and calling for constant vigilance, being generally barren of incident and furnishing little material for history.   On

November 25, 1872, he was again transferred to the command of the Division of the Atlantic, with headquarters at New York, being in the city itself for several years, but in 1878 transferred to Governor's Island, New York Harbor.

The year 1872 witnessed another Presidential election, when General Grant was unanimously renominated by the Republican convention in Philadelphia, and Horace Greeley by the Liberal Republicans and Democrats at their conventions in Cincinnati and Baltimore. At the election in November, General Grant was reëlected by a popular vote of 3,579,070 against 2,834,079 for Horace Greeley, and 35,008 scattering, the entire electoral vote of 286 being for U. S. Grant.

In the consideration of the merits and availability of candidates for the Democratic nomination precedent to the nominating convention, General Hancock's name was again very generally and warmly considered. Pennsylvania, his native State, was solid in his favor, and there is no doubt that he would have made a good run for the nomination. But the political situation was peculiar, and even the shrewdest politicians in the Democratic party were doubtful and inclined to hedge. The dissatisfaction in the Republican party, which had begun at this time and which continued thereafter to increase, offered inducements for a compromise candidate. The selection of Horace Greeley was the result of the situation; and the ruin, insanity, and death of the eccentric but gifted Republican journalist became the sacrifice demanded by his old-time party followers, for the high crime and misdemeanor of daring to identify himself with a movement in opposition to the mischief-making radicalism which was now rampant.

Some idea of the feeling in favor of Hancock at this time may be derived from the following quotation from an editorial published in the " St. Louis Republican," under date of September 4, 1871.   In commenting upon the names of the Democratic candidates for the Presidency, this article says :

"In the matter of general admirable, popular reputation, it is supposed that Hancock bears off the palm from all competitors.   His name is inseparably and honorably connected with those great achievements of the war in which are bound up the affections of our Union soldiers, upon which their admiration is immovably fixed, and around which will cluster, while they breathe, all the honor and glory of their country. . . . His name is familiar to the hosts of our Union soldiery.   Thousands and hundreds of thousands of those soldiers have known him personally.   Which of the other gentlemen named for the Presidency can be compared with him in this ? . . . . It is also suggested that Hancock is favorably known to soldiers who fought on the side of the rebellion.   There is something peculiar in the fact, yet the fact is undoubted, that honorable and brave men who fight each other, never so desperately, are more ready than others to be friends when the strife has ceased.   Why may not Hancock command the respect and admiration of Southern soldiers ?   In him they behold the chevalier without fear and without reproach—the Union leader of all others the most terrible in the rush of battle, the most generous and magnanimous in victory."

So also a writer in the " Boston Post," January 30, 1872, in discussing the same subject said : " I need not speak of Hancock, the soldier statesman, whose generous and heroic spirit rolled back the tide of despotism, whose orders and letters are among the noblest appeals for the supremacy of civil law to be found in the annals of any country."

But his hour had not yet come. The conservative influence of time would but enhance the brilliancy of his record, and he could afford to wait.

CHAPTER XXXIV.

THE position of Commander of the Division of the
Atlantic, while sufficiently engrossing in the details ac-
companying the control of so vast a territory—practically
covering the entire country east of the Mississippi, excepting Illinois, and including Arkansas and that part of
Louisiana west of the Mississippi—has not, since the war,
afforded material for thrilling narrative. Incidents have
occurred, however, during the period in question, apart
from the official duties entailed by the command, which
are important in their relation to the life of General Hancock, and to these we will now direct the attention of the
reader.

At the close of the year 1875, General Babcock, private secretary to President Grant, fell under suspicion of
complicity with certain frauds on the revenue, and, pending whatever civil action might be taken, and at his own
request, a Military Court of Inquiry was convened in
Chicago on December 9th to investigate and pronounce
upon his guilt or innocence in the premises. Upon this
Court of Inquiry, of which Lieutenant-General Sheridan
was president, were also appointed by President Grant
Generals Hancock and Terry.

COMMANDANT'S RESIDENCE, GOVERNOR'S ISLAND.

The Court assembled on December 9th and adjourned until the following day. In the mean time the grand jury at St. Louis brought in a true bill of indictment against General Babcock. On the reassembling of the Court of Inquiry on the 10th, General Hancock rose, and addressed the Court in the following language:

"A sense of duty to the laws, to the military service, and to the accused, impels me to ask your concurrence in a postponement of this inquiry for the present. We are all bound to believe in the entire innocence of Colonel Babcock, and the presumption can not be repelled without clear evidence. It is due to him to suppose that this Court of Inquiry was asked in good faith for the reasons given. What were those reasons? In the course of a legal trial in St. Louis, Colonel Babcock was alleged to be guilty of a high criminal offense. He asked for a hearing in the same court, but was informed he could not have it because the evidence was closed. Those circumstances led him to demand a Court of Inquiry as the only means of vindication that was left. Since then he has been formally indicted, and he is now certain of getting that full and fair trial before an impartial jury which the laws of the country guarantee to all its citizens. The supposed necessity for convening a military court for the determination of his guilt or innocence no longer exists. It is believed that our action as a military tribunal can not oust the jurisdiction of the court while the indictment is pending. The President has said through the Attorney-General that such was not the intention. Then the trial at St. Louis and this inquiry must go on at the same time. Unless we await the result of the inquiry there, the difficulties are very formidable. The accused must be present at

the trial of the indictment. Shall we proceed and hear
the cause behind his back, or shall we vex him with two
trials at once? The injustice of this is manifest. I presume, from the nature of the case, that the evidence is
very voluminous, consisting of records, papers, and oral
testimony. Can we compel the production of these while
they are wanted for the purposes of the trial at St. Louis?
Certainly not, if the military be, as the Constitution declares, subordinate to the civil authorities. Shall we proceed without evidence, and give an opinion in ignorance
of the facts? That can not be the wish of anybody. I
take it for granted that the trial at St. Louis will be fair
as well as legal, and that the judgment will be according
to the very truth and justice of the cause. It will without question be binding and conclusive upon us, upon the
Government, upon the accused, and upon all the world.
If he should be convicted, no decision of ours could rescue
him out of the hands of the law. If he is acquitted, our
belief in his innocence will be of no consequence. If we
anticipate the trial in the civil court, our judgment,
whether for the accused or against him, will have, and
ought to have, no effect upon the jurors. It can not even
be made known to them, and any attempt to influence
them by it would justly be regarded as an obstruction of
public justice. On the other hand, his conviction there
would be conclusive evidence of his guilt, and his acquittal will relieve him from the necessity of showing anything but the record. I do not propose to postpone in-
definitely, but simply to adjourn from day to day, until
the evidence upon the subject of our inquiry shall receive
that definite and conclusive shape which will be impressed
upon it by a verdict of the jury, or until our action, having been referred to the War Department, with our opin-

ion that our proceedings should be stayed during the proceedings of the court of law, shall have been confirmed. In case of acquittal by the civil court, the functions of this Court will not necessarily have terminated. The accused may be pronounced innocent of any crime against the statute, and yet be guilty of some act which the military law might punish by expulsion from the army. In case of acquittal he may insist upon showing to us that he has done nothing inconsistent with the conduct of an officer and gentleman, as the Article of War runs, but the great and important question is, guilty or not in manner and form, as he stands indicted—and this can be legally answered only by a jury of his country."

Immediately on the conclusion of this address, the Court of Inquiry adjourned, in full accord with its sense and motive.

This occasion and the course of General Hancock in regard to it afford one other illustration of the spirit of subordination to the civil law which has characterized the General throughout his public life. It also affords renewed evidence—if any were needed—of the keen insight into the relations of civil and military authority with which he is preëminently gifted, and of his clear and convincing method of expressing his views on all occasions when perspicuity is a needed virtue.*

This brings us to the year 1876, when a new Presidential election—by the manner of its conduct, by the vast and engrossing interests at stake, and by the extreme point to which party rancor and political excitement were permitted to reach—threatened danger to the con-

* It is due to General Babcock to state that in the trial at St. Louis he was acquitted.

stitutional structure of the Union, and lighted anew the
fires of sectional hatred.

It is no part of this history to recount the incidents
of this exciting period. By a fair half of the population
of the country it was religiously believed that Samuel
J. Tilden had been elected to the high office of President of the United States; by the remaining moiety it
was vigorously claimed that Rutherford B. Hayes had
achieved this triumph. The official count showed a popular majority of a quarter of a million in favor of Mr. Tilden. In the Electoral College the question turned on the
just possession by one candidate or the other of a single
vote. Wise men stumbled when brought to encounter
this new factor in a republican system of government;
good men were appalled at the possible consequences of
a decision either way. Daring not to conclude the government of more than forty millions of free people on
the basis of what evidence was available, those in whose
hands the terrible responsibility rested had recourse to
the old-time refuge of daunted public leaders—a compromise. An "Electoral Commission" was evoked out
of nothing, an extra-constitutional act; and, by the memorable vote of "eight to seven," this anomalous body
declared Rutherford B. Hayes to have received one hundred and eighty-five, and Samuel J. Tilden one hundred
and eighty-four of the electoral votes cast for President of
the United States—and President Hayes entered upon the
occupancy of the office and the performance of its duties.

But, in this republican and free country, no such vast
and organic disturbance in the body politic could by possibility occur without shaking to its crown the substance
of public opinion; without permeating with its terrible
and sardonic questioning every stratum of society. And

it befell that, from the highest to the lowest—man, woman, and child; the millionaire capitalist in the metropolis and the Georgia "cracker"; the ex-slave working his own bit of a cotton-field; the old-fashioned conservative Mississippi planter; the Irish-American and the German-American—with one and all, the question paramount occupied all minds and hearts, and deferred all other questions until its settlement should be effected.

And naturally it befell that the soldier—whether he had worn the gray or the blue—became engrossed with the rest in this new and suddenly awakened tempest of inquiry. But to those officers of the United States Army —men who had swayed its fortunes and the fortunes of the country from Alexandria to Appomattox; those who stood high in rank, and held in charge a fealty to freedom, to the Constitution, and to the Union that only death could loosen; to those great captains in the war who still in peace held watch and ward over the safety and honor of their country—the questions that were rending the fabric of our republicanism in 1876 appealed with stern and unrelenting mastery, and would not be withheld.

And, as a part of the history of those troublous times, General W. T. Sherman addressed in conference Major-General Winfield Scott Hancock, which act brought about a correspondence which we are now permitted to lay before our readers. Prominent in this correspondence will be found the important letter of General Hancock from Carondelet—a letter which lay for four years silent, to speak at last in loud reply to whispered slanders and contemptuous reference, with such force of righteous purpose, and with such dignity of manly power and knowledge, as to send hurtling back among a crowd

of defamers the paper pellets of libel and defamation
changed to fiery missiles of shaming and condemnation.

General Hancock's letter was written at a time while
he was alone, attending to family affairs, at Carondelet,
without an amanuensis, and was copied by the General
himself, the first draft being unpresentable. In the course
of the campaign of 1880 some knowledge of the writing of
this letter was brought to the Republican press, and charges
were at once instigated in that quarter, to the effect that
the communication to General Sherman had been of a
treasonable character, and was calculated, if made public,
to damage the reputation of its writer as a soldier and a
patriot; this, too, in entire disregard of the contingent
insult inflicted upon the noble soldier and gentleman to
whom the letter was written, by the judgment that he
could by any possibility have agreed in a traitorous correspondence with the hero of Gettysburg. With such
blindness in seasons of political excitement are stricken
those to whom politics is a profession and the honor and
progress of their country a pecuniary interest alone.

CHAPTER XXXV.

The Sherman-Hancock Correspondence—Telegram from General Sherman—
General Sherman's Letter of December 4, 1876—Hancock to Sherman ;
Leave of Absence—General Sherman's Letter of December 17, 1876:
A Newspaper Story—General Hancock's Letter from Carondelet—Telegram: Hancock to Sherman—General Sherman's Letter of January 2,
1877 ; Reply to the Carondelet Letter—Hancock to Sherman : Contemplated Uprising—Hancock to Sherman—Hancock to the Editor of the
" World "—Hancock to Sherman : the Electoral Commission—Sherman to Hancock : January 29, 1877.

[THE publishers acknowledge the courtesy of the
General of the Army in furnishing them with the following correspondence upon their solicitation. This
is exclusive of the letter of December 28th from Carondelet, which was given to the public through the enterprise of the editor of the New York "World," who
dispatched a special messenger to General Sherman, in
Dakota, to obtain the necessary permission.]

(COPY OF TELEGRAM.)

"HEADQUARTERS, ARMY OF THE UNITED STATES,
"WASHINGTON, D. C., *December* 4, 1876.

" *To* GENERAL W. S. HANCOCK, *Commanding Division
of the Atlantic, New York City.*

" You can take your leave now—the time is appropriate.

(Signed)   " W. T. SHERMAN, *General.*

" *A true copy.*
"JNO. M. BACON, *Colonel and A. D. C.*"

"HEADQUARTERS, ARMY OF THE UNITED STATES,
"WASHINGTON, D. C., *December* 4, 1876.

" GENERAL W. S. HANCOCK, *New York City.*

" DEAR GENERAL : I have just received your letter of the 3d, and have telegraphed you my consent to your proposed trip. I can not foresee any objections, and hope soon that events will admit of the return to their posts of the companies detached at the South ; but every time I make a move in that direction I am met by insurmountable objections. Three of the companies of the First Artillery from Fort Sill reported at Columbus, Ohio, yesterday, and will be here this evening. Everything is ready for them. The last company, I suppose, was detained at Sill to await the relief on the way. Tell General Fry (Adjutant-General) that, in case of any orders, I will have them sent to you at New York, and he can execute them. The political orders to Ruger at Columbia I preferred should go from the President to him through the Secretary of War. They were not military. I dislike much to have our soldiers used in connection with a legislative body, but orders coming from the President have to be obeyed. They form a bad precedent, but thus far have prevented a collision of arms between inflamed partisans.

" I trust you will find Mrs. Hancock and your St. Louis friends well.

" Truly yours,
(Signed)   " W. T. SHERMAN, *General.*
" *A true copy.*
" JNO. M. BACON, *Colonel and A. D. C.*"

"HEADQUARTERS, MILITARY DIVISION OF THE ATLANTIC,
"NEW YORK, *December 6, 1876.*

"THE ADJUTANT GENERAL, *U. S. Army, Washington,
D. C.*

"SIR: I have the honor to inform you that I leave New York this evening for St. Louis for a short absence by permission of the General of the Army.

"My post-office address, while absent, will be Carondelet P. O., South St. Louis, Mo., and my telegraphic address will be 'care of Commanding Officer, St. Louis Arsenal, Jefferson Barracks, Mo.'

"Very respectfully, your obedient servant,
(Signed)   "WINFIELD S. HANCOCK,
"*Major-General Commanding.*

"*A true copy.*
"JOHN M. BACON, *Colonel and A. D. C.*"

"HEADQUARTERS, ARMY OF THE UNITED STATES.
"WASHINGTON, D. C., *December 17, 1876.*

"GENERAL W. S. HANCOCK, *Jefferson Barracks, Missouri.*

"MY DEAR GENERAL: Lest your peace of mind may be disturbed by the foolish report, bandied in the newspapers, about your being ordered from New York, I will tell you that there is not a word of truth in it.

"Neither the President nor Secretary of War has ever intimated to me such a purpose, and I know I have never said a word or written a syllable to the effect.

"I see in the 'Republican' (of St. Louis) that not only was the order made, but that I destroyed it and tore out the leaves of the record book containing the copy. The whole thing was, and is, an invention by somebody who wanted to create a sensation. The same is true about John Sherman intriguing to be President of the Senate, that he might be President *ad interim.* He has told me that he has never heard the subject broached; that he would not accept the place, as he prefers to be what he is now, Chairman of the Senate Committee on Finance. I hope you find the family in good health and spirits, and I hope you will spend with me a peaceful and happy week of holidays. This letter may be superfluous, but the emphatic repetitions of a wild rumor in the ' St. Louis Republican' suggested to me the propriety of my correcting an impression, if made on you.

"No serious changes in command are being contemplated; and, when they are, you may be sure that I will give you the earliest notice. There are men, on mischief intent, who would gladly sow the seeds of dissension among us of the army.

"Truly your friend,

(Signed) "W. T. SHERMAN.

"*A true copy.*
"JNO. M. BACON, *Colonel and A. D. C.*"

"CARONDELET P. O., ST. LOUIS, MO.,
"*December* 28, 1876.

"*To* GENERAL W. T. SHERMAN, *Commanding Army of the United States, Washington, D. C.*

"MY DEAR GENERAL: Your favor of the 4th instant reached me in New York on the 5th, the day before I left for the West. I intended to reply to it before leaving, but cares incident to departure interfered. Then again, since my arrival here, I have been so occupied with personal affairs of a business nature that I have deferred writing from day to day until this moment, and now I find myself in debt to you another letter in acknowledgment of your favor of the 17th, received a few days since.

"I have concluded to leave here on the 29th (to-morrow) P. M., so that I may be expected in New York on the 31st inst. It has been cold and dreary since my arrival here. I have worked 'like a Turk' (I presume that means hard work) in the country, in making fences, cutting down trees, and repairing buildings, and am at least able to say that St. Louis is the coldest place in the winter, as it is the hottest in the summer, of any that I have encountered in a temperate zone. I have known St. Louis in December to have genial weather throughout the month; this December has been frigid, and the river has been frozen more solid than I have ever known it.

"When I heard the rumor that I was ordered to the Pacific coast, I thought it probably true, considering the past discussion on that subject. The *possibilities* seemed to me to point that way. Had it been true, I should, of course, have presented no complaint nor made resistance of any kind. I would have gone quietly, if not prepared to go promptly. I certainly would have been relieved from the responsibility and anxieties concerning Presidential matters, which may fall to those "near the throne" or in authority within the next few months, as well as from other incidents or matters which I could not control, and the action concerning which I might not approve. I was not exactly prepared to go to the Pacific, however, and I therefore felt relieved when I received your note informing me that there was no truth in the rumors.

"Then I did not wish to appear to be escaping from responsibilities and possible dangers which may cluster around military commanders in the East, especially in the critical period fast approaching. 'All's well that ends well.' The whole matter of the Presidency seems to me to be simple and to admit of a peaceful solution. The machinery for such a contingency as threatens to present itself has been all carefully prepared. It only requires lubrication, owing to disuse. The army should have nothing to do with the selection or inauguration of Presidents. The people elect the President. The Congress declares in a joint session who he is. We of the army have only to obey his mandates, and are protected in so doing only so far as they may be lawful. Our commissions express that. I like Jefferson's way of inauguration; it suits our system. He rode alone on horseback to the Capitol (I fear it was the 'Old Capitol'), tied his horse to a rail fence, entered, and was duly sworn, then rode to the Executive Mansion and took possession. He inaugurated himself simply by taking the oath of office. There is no other legal inauguration in our system. The people or politicians may institute parades in honor of the event, and public officials may add to the pageant by assembling troops and banners, but all that only comes properly after the inauguration—not before; and it is not a part of it. Our system does not provide that one President should inaugurate another. There might be danger in that, and it was studiously left out of the charter. But you are placed in an exceptionally important position in connection with coming events. The capital is in my jurisdiction also, but I am a subordinate, and not on the spot, and, if I were, so also would be my superior in authority, for there is the station of the general-in-chief.

"On the principle that a regularly elected President's term of office expires with the 3d of March (of which I have not the slightest doubt), and which the laws bearing on the subject uniformly recognize, and in consideration of the possibility that the lawfully elected President may not appear until the 5th of March, a great deal of responsibility may necessarily fall upon you. You hold over! You will have power and prestige to support you. The Secretary of War, too, probably holds over; but, if no President appears, he may not be able to exercise functions in the name of a President, for his proper acts are those of a known superior—a lawful President. You act on your own responsibility, and by virtue of a commission only restricted by the law. The Secretary of War is the mouthpiece of a President. You are not. If neither candidate has a constitutional majority of the Electoral College, or the Senate and House on the occasion of the count do not unite in declaring some person legally elected by the people, there is a lawful machinery already provided to meet that contingency and to decide the question peacefully. It has not been recently used, no occasion presenting itself, but our forefathers provided it. It has been exercised, and has been recognized and submitted to as lawful on every hand. That machinery would probably elect Mr. Tilden President, and Mr. Wheeler Vice-President. That would be right enough, for the law provides that, in a failure to elect duly by the people, the House shall immediately elect the President, and the Senate the Vice-President. Some tribunal must decide whether the people have duly elected a President. I presume, of course, that it is in the joint affirmative action of the Senate and House, or why are they present to witness the count if not to see that it is fair and just? If a failure to agree arises between the two bodies, there can be no lawful affirmative decision that the people have elected a President, and the House must then proceed to act, *not* the Senate. The Senate elects Vice-Presidents, not Presidents. Doubtless, in case of a failure by the

House to elect a President by the 4th of March, the President of the Senate (if there be one) would be the legitimate person to exercise Presidential authority for the time being, or until the appearance of a lawful President, or for the time laid down in the Constitution. Such courses would be peaceful, and, I have a firm belief, lawful.

"I have no doubt Governor Hayes would make an excellent President. I have met him and know of him. For a brief period he served under my command; but, as the matter stands, I can't see any likelihood of his being duly declared elected by the people, unless the Senate and House come to be in accord as to that fact, and the House would, of course, not *otherwise* elect him. What the people want is a peaceful determination of this matter, as fair a determination as possible, and a lawful one. No other determination could stand the test. The country, if not plunged into revolution, would become poorer day by day, business would languish, and our bonds would come home to find a depreciated market.

"I was not in favor of the military action in South Carolina recently, and, if General Ruger had telegraphed to me or asked for advice, I would have advised him not, under any circumstances, to allow himself or his troops to determine who were the lawful members of a State Legislature. I could have given him no better advice than to refer him to the special message of the President in the case of Louisiana some time before.

"But, in South Carolina, he had the question settled by a decision of the Supreme Court of the State—the highest tribunal which had acted on the question—so that his line of duty seemed even to be clearer than the action in the Louisiana case. If the Federal court had interfered and overruled the decision of the State court, there might have been a doubt, certainly; but the Federal court only interfered to complicate—not to decide or overrule.

"Anyhow, it is no business of the army to enter upon such questions, and even if it might be so in any event, if the civil authority is supreme, as the Constitution declares it to be, the South Carolina case was one in which the army had a plain duty.

"Had General Ruger asked me for advice, and if I had given it, I should of course have notified you of my action immediately, so that it could have been promptly overruled if it should have been deemed advisable by you or other superior authority. General Ruger did not ask for my advice, and I inferred from that and other facts that he did not desire it, or—being in direct communication with my military superiors at the seat of Government, who were nearer to him in time and distance than I was—he deemed it unnecessary. As General Ruger had the ultimate responsibility of action, and had really the greater danger to confront in the final action in the matter, I did not venture to embarrass him by suggestions. He was a Department Commander, and the lawful head of the military administration within the limits of the Department; besides, I knew that he had been called to Washington for consultation before taking command, and was probably aware of the views of the Administration as to civil affairs in his command. I knew that he was in direct communication with my superiors in authority in reference to the delicate subjects presented for his consideration, or had ideas of his own which he believed to be sufficiently in accord with the views of our common superiors to enable him to act intelligently according to his judgment, and without suggestions from those not on the spot and not so fully acquainted with the facts as himself. He desired, too, to be free to act, as he had the eventual greater responsibility, and so the matter was governed as between him and myself.

"As I have been writing thus freely to you, I may still further unbosom myself by stating that I have not thought it lawful or wise to use Federal troops in such matters as have transpired east of the Mississippi within the last few months, save as far as they may be brought into action under the Constitution, which contemplates meeting armed resistance or invasion of a State more powerful than the State authorities can subdue by the ordinary processes, and then only when requested by the Legislature, or, if it could not be convened in season, by the Governor; and when the President of the United States intervenes in that manner it is a state of war, *not* peace.

"The army is laboring under disadvantages, and has been used unlawfully at times, in the judgment of the people (in mine certainly), and we have lost a great deal of the kindly feeling which the community at large once felt for us. It is time to stop and unload.

"Officers in command of troops often find it difficult to act wisely and safely when superiors in authority have different views of the law from theirs, and when legislation has sanctioned action seemingly in conflict with the fundamental law, and they generally defer to the known judgment of their superiors. Yet the superior officers of the army are so regarded in such great crises, and are held to such responsibility, especially those at or near the head of it, that it is necessary on such momentous occasions to dare to determine for themselves what is lawful and what is not lawful under our system, if the military authorities should be invoked, as might possibly be the case in such exceptional times when there existed such divergent views as to the correct result. The army will suffer from its past action if it has acted wrongfully. Our regular army has little hold upon the affections of the people of to-day, and its superior officers should certainly, as far as lies in their power, legally and with righteous intent, aim to defend the right, which to us is THE LAW, and the institution which they represent. It is a well-meaning institution, and it would be well if it should have an opportunity to be recognized as a bulwark in support of the rights of the people and of THE LAW.   I am truly yours,

"WINFIELD S. HANCOCK.

" *To* GENERAL W. T. SHERMAN,
   " *Commanding Army of the United States, Washington, D. C.*"

(COPY OF TELEGRAM.)

"ST. LOUIS ARSENAL, MO., *December* 29, 1876.

" *To* GENERAL W. T. SHERMAN, *U. S. A., Washington, D. C.*

" I leave this evening for New York.
   (Signed)   " HANCOCK,
                                     " *Major-General.*

   " *A true copy.*
" JNO. M. BACON, *Colonel and A. D. C.*"

" HEADQUARTERS, ARMY OF THE UNITED STATES,
         " WASHINGTON, D. C., *January* 2, 1877.

" GENERAL W. S. HANCOCK, *New York.*

" DEAR GENERAL: I did not receive your most interesting letter of December 28th, from Carondelet, Mo., till yesterday. I am very glad to have your views *in extenso* upon subjects of such vital importance. Our standard opinions are mostly formed on the practice of our predecessors; but a great change was made after the close of the civil war, by the amendments of the Constitution giving to the freed slaves certain civil and political rights, and empowering Congress to make the laws necessary to enforce these rights. This power is new and absolute, and Congress has enacted laws with which we are not yet familiar and accustomed. See pages 348, 349, and 350, Revised Statutes (Section 1989), Edition 1873–'4.

" As a matter of fact, I dislike to have our army used in these civil conflicts, but the President has the lawful right to use the army and navy, and has exercised the right, as he believes, lawfully and rightfully, and our duty has been, and is, to sustain him with zeal and sincerity.

" As to the Presidential election, we are in no manner required to take the least action, but to recognize him as President whom the lawfully appointed officers declare to be such person. I hope and pray that the Congress will agree on some method before the day and hour arrive. But, in case of failure to elect by or before the 4th of March, there will be a vacancy in *both* offices of President and Vice-President, in which event the President of the Senate becomes President *pro tempore*, and a new election will have to be held under the law of 1792. See Title III., chap. I., pages 21, 22, and 23, Revised Statutes.

" It is well we should compare notes and agree before the crisis is on us; but I surely hope we may pass this ordeal safely and peacefully.

" I will be pleased to hear from you at any time.
(Signed)   " W. T. SHERMAN."

" *A true copy.*
" JNO. M. BACON, *Colonel and A. D. C.*"

"HEADQUARTERS, MILITARY DIVISION OF THE ATLANTIC,
"NEW YORK, *January* 2, 1877.

"GENERAL W. T. SHERMAN, *United States Army, Washington, D. C.*

"GENERAL: An anonymous communication to the Secretary of War, dated Louisville, Kentucky, December 16, 1876, reached my headquarters on the 27th of that month, from the office of the Adjutant-General of the Army.

"It represents that, 'in the contemplated uprising of the people to enforce the inauguration of Tilden and Hendricks, the depot at Jeffersonville is to be seized, and is expected to arm and clothe the Indiana army of Democrats.'

"The endorsement on this communication, made at your headquarters, dated December 26, 1876, is as follows:

"'Official copy respectfully referred to Major-General W. S. Hancock, Commanding Division of the Atlantic, who *may* draw a company from General Ruger, Commanding Department of the South, and post it at the Jeffersonville depot, with orders to protect it against any danger.'

"The terms of the endorsement imply an exercise of discretion on my part, which leads me to write you before taking action.

"In my judgment there is no danger of the kind the anonymous communication sets forth, or other kind, at Jeffersonville depot to justify a movement of troops to that place. Such a movement, it seems to me, would involve unnecessary expense, and would create or increase apprehension for which there is no real foundation.

"There are no arms or ammunition at the Jefferson-

16

ville depot, and, if such a force as is referred to could be raised for rebellious purposes, it is not likely that it would begin by seizing a depot of army uniforms; and, therefore, if there are grounds for action of the Government, I see no danger in the delay which will result from this presentation of the subject to you.

"If, however, in your better judgment, a company should be sent there, it shall be promptly done as soon as you notify me to that effect. As I have already said, I do not act at once, because in your instructions you say I '*may*' send a company there, which I construe as leaving it somewhat discretionary with me.

"I returned on the 31st of December, 1876, from St. Louis.

"I am, very truly yours,
(Signed)   "WINFIELD S. HANCOCK,
                    "*Major-General Commanding.*
     "*A true copy.*
"JNO. M. BACON, *Colonel and A. D. C.*"

                    "NEW YORK, *January 9*, 1877.
"GENERAL W. T. SHERMAN, *Commanding U. S. Army,*
     Washington, D. C.

"MY DEAR GENERAL: I have been intending to write to you in acknowledgment of your two recent notes, but I have been so much engaged in hunting a place for the winter and 'gathering' up my affairs of business as well as personal matters, owing to my recent absence, that I have deferred doing so.

"Now I write to inclose you a copy of a letter I addressed yesterday to the editor of the 'World,' in reference to an article (special dispatch) which appeared in that paper on Sunday, the 7th. The 'World' corrects

the matter in its issue of this morning. I would have
preferred the publication of my letter, but, as I gave the
editor latitude as to the manner of correction, I can not
complain, I suppose.

"I have written to no one on the subject of my order
to go to the Pacific—reported by the newspapers—save
yourself. I have said nothing to any one differing in
letter or spirit from what I wrote to you; and I have not
seen Buford for years, or heard of him, nor do I know of
any person who has, in that time, met or communicated
with him.

"I inclose you a copy of the 'World's' publication.

"I am, very truly yours,

(Signed)   "WINFIELD S. HANCOCK,

"*Major-General.*

"*A true copy.*
"JNO. M. BACON, *Colonel and A. D. C.*"

"INCLOSURE."

"NEW YORK, *January* 8, 1877.

"MY DEAR SIR: I inclose a slip cut from the 'World'
of yesterday (a special dispatch from Washington)
headed:

"A RESCINDED ORDER.

"Did General Hancock refuse to be transferred to
the Pacific coast?

"As an authority is given for the communication, it
seems that I should publicly notice the same, and it
would gratify me if you would, in the manner you may
deem best, make such correction as would be most likely
to remove any misapprehension on the subject.

"I have not received any orders transferring me from
this station, nor any intimation of the existence or con-
templation of such orders. Hence, I did not refuse to be

transferred to the Pacific coast. I have not tendered my resignation. All of my information in the matter has been derived from the newspapers of the day. I had no communication whatever relating to the subject with the authorities until after the rumor of my removal was published from Washington as groundless. Then General Sherman wrote me a note to the same effect.

"I am in no wise responsible for any statement contained in the dispatch in question, or for any misconception which has arisen concerning this subject from first to last.

"I am, very truly yours,

(Signed)   "WINFIELD S. HANCOCK."

" To Mr. WILLIAM H. HURLBURT, *Editor New York 'World,' No. 32 Waverly Place, New York.*

"*A true copy.*

(Signed)   "JOHN S. WHARTON.

"*A true copy.*

"JNO. M. BACON, *Colonel and A. D. C.*"

"NEW YORK, *January* 19, 1877.

"GENERAL W. T. SHERMAN, *United States Army, Washington, D. C.*

"MY DEAR GENERAL : I have been quite busy since my arrival, and have not felt like writing much, so that I have not yet written to you as I intended, in reply to your favor acknowledging receipt of my letter from Carondelet. I wished to notice simply your reference to the Revised Statutes, and one or two other points, in a brief way. I will do so yet, but not to day, as I am house-hunting, or apartment or hotel hunting rather. It is too late in the season to accomplish much here in that way—save to pay out money and get but little satisfaction in return.

"The proposition for the joint committee insures a peaceful solution of the Presidential question if it becomes a law, and, in my opinion, gives to General Hayes chances he did not have before. I have considered that Mr. Tilden's chances were impregnable. . . . Not so Mr. Hendricks's. Now it seems to me that Governor Hayes has something more than an equal chance, but the definite results can not be foreshadowed. Fortunately, trouble *need* not be provided against by the use of the army, should the bill become a law.

"If the bill passes, and General Grant vetoes it, Mr. Tilden's chances will be stronger than before—certainly if he and his friends supported the measure. Public opinion will strengthen his position.

"The danger in the compromise question or joint committee plan is, that the defeated candidate might appeal to the Supreme Court on grounds of illegal (unconstitutional) decisions.

"I am, very truly yours,

(Signed) "WINFIELD S. HANCOCK.

"P. S. Somebody, possibly Fry, has been writing on the subject of military discipline, etc., in the 'Army and Navy Journal' of this week. It is worth reading.

"*A true copy.*
"JNO. M. BACON, *Colonel and A. D. C.*"

"HEADQUARTERS, ARMY OF THE UNITED STATES,
"WASHINGTON, D. C., *January* 29, 1877.

"GENERAL W. S. HANCOCK, *Commanding Military Division of the Atlantic.*

"GENERAL: The passage of the bill for counting the electoral vote, approved by the President, ends, in my judgment, all possible danger of confusion or disorder in connection with the Presidential imbroglio. I feel certain that the dual governments in South Carolina and Louisiana will be decided by the same means which determines who is to be the next President of the United States.   Therefore, with the consent and approval of the Secretary of War, now absent, I want to return the troops, temporarily detached, back as soon as possible to the posts occupied before the election, with this exception, that twelve companies (now thirteen), or the equivalent of a regiment, remain here in Washington for a time.

" The Artillery School should be resumed, and this will take back to Fort Monroe companies ' G ' of the First, ' A ' of the Third, ' I ' of the Fourth, and ' C ' of the Fifth Artillery.

" These should be replaced by three companies now temporarily serving in the Department of the South, say, Companies ' D ' and ' L ' Second Artillery, now at Columbia, S. C., and Company ' L,' First Artillery.   Company ' M,' Third Artillery, now at Fort McHenry, should return to its post at Fort Wadsworth, and the remaining companies First Artillery in South Carolina, viz. : ' B,' ' D,' ' H,' ' I,' and ' M,' would return to their posts.

" Indiana is in your command, and Company ' G,' Third Artillery, can remain at the arsenal at Indianapolis for a time.

" The movement should not begin till I give you notice and orders, as the Potomac is still frozen, and the school companies can not economically move till a steamboat can take them from the Arsenal here to Fort Monroe.

" Please have General Fry to make the draft of an order to complete these movements—send it to me, I will approve, and then indicate the time to begin—say in about ten days.

" Yours truly,

(Signed)   " W. T. SHERMAN,

" General.

" *A true copy.*
" JNO. M. BACON, *Colonel and A. D. C.*"

CHAPTER XXXVI.

THE year 1877 opened with the conclusion of the
Electoral trouble by the seating of President Hayes, and
the American people began to "breathe freely"; a process in which they certainly had not indulged since the
preceding November.

The financial and economical condition of the country
during the period which had elapsed since the "panic"
of 1873, had been very unsatisfactory. There had been
a sharp contraction of values and prices; our bonds, returned from abroad, had drained the country in enormous
sums; capital had long been alarmed to the extent of refusing investment in new enterprises, or even sustaining
those which were established; the list of failures had
reached nine thousand in a single year (1876), being three
times the number of 1871, and an increase in regular pro-
gression; two thirds of the furnaces in the country were
out of blast, and a large proportion of the great manufac-
tories were closed; strikes were frequent, and it was alleged by the "New York Herald" that four millions of
men were out of employment.

But, with the election and peaceful inauguration of President Hayes—by virtue of the Electoral Commission—it was claimed by the Republican press, and believed by large numbers of the business men of the country, that a revival of trade was to take place, capital would be invested, labor be in demand, and values speedily regain their former standard.

During six months these rose-colored predictions found faithful believers. Then, as suddenly as though it were a convulsion of nature, came the shock and the collapse.

On July 14, 1877, the strike occurred of the train-hands on the Baltimore and Ohio Railroad, and, with a rush like wildfire, the dangerous epidemic sped along the iron rails, until, in less than a week, perhaps, one hundred thousand railroad men and forty thousand miners were "on strike," and as many as six thousand miles of railway, covering most of the trunk lines, were in the hands of the strikers, who were now backed and sustained by vast masses of rioters, who crawled out of the slums of the great cities, and left their "tramp" along the country roads, to engage in general spoliation, incendiarism, and outrage. The wheels of progress were clogged, the great mechanism for the transportation of forty-five millions of active, industrious people was idle, the existence of social order and the supremacy of the law were threatened.

Here was a commentary upon the progress of the country under the management and control of that party which had for nearly seventeen years held the reins of power.

At such a juncture it became necessary to call upon whatever drilled and disciplined forces existed; and, while the militia of the different States, where riotous proceedings interrupted the peaceful progress of events, were at once armed and summoned to the field, the United States Army, now scattered to all parts of the Union, was hastily brought together in such proportion as was practicable, and called to defend peaceful citizens, to protect public and private property, and to sustain Law and Order.

A large number of the regulars were at this time engaged, with General Howard and Colonel Miles, fighting the Nez Percés Indians, and in other disturbed parts of the Indian country. As the principal weight of the riotous demonstrations was felt east of the Mississippi, the duty of employing the United States forces for their suppression fell to General Hancock, being within his command of the Division of the Atlantic. Making his headquarters at Philadelphia, General Hancock drew from all possible quarters with the greatest celerity, and dispatched to threatened points, or employed for the protection of railroad and other property actually attacked, all the soldiers, sailors, and marines possible to be obtained and transported in time to be of service. Along the Baltimore and Ohio line, in Maryland and West Virginia, single trains were run under the protection of the Federal forces. In the city of Baltimore the soldiers were stoned by the rioters; but it is a fact that no serious resistance was offered to the regular army, the insubordinate classes seeming to stand in awe of the Federal forces, though so few in number, while to the State militia they displayed positive hatred, and in many instances successfully resisted. While the militia lost heavily in killed and badly injured during the continuance of the riots, the regular army accomplished a most excellent purpose—often by their mere presence—and without losing a man in General Hancock's entire command, or the destruction of any life.

The railroad riots continued until the end of July; the losses, chiefly in Pittsburgh Pa., but also in Chicago, Cincinnati, Buffalo, Albany, and at other points, have never been fully estimated. In Pittsburgh alone, besides much other property, the loss by the railroads was enormous. Two thousand freight cars with their contents were destroyed, and the direct loss of railroad property was estimated to be between $8,000,000 and $10,000,000.

No active military operations occurred in General Hancock's command, after 1877, of sufficient importance to need chronicling here.

And, reaching the year 1880, we enter upon the last phase in General Hancock's life to be recorded here, and which resulted in his nomination by the Democratic convention as the candidate of that party for the office of President of the United States.

The National Republican convention had met at Chicago, June 2d, and, after an exciting and protracted session, had nominated James A. Garfield, of Ohio, for President and Chester A. Arthur, of New York, for Vice-President.

The National Democratic convention met at Cincinnati on June 22d, and organized with Judge Hoadley, of Cincinnati, as temporary chairman. Among the prominent candidates for the Presidential nomination was Samuel J. Tilden, with Hancock, Bayard, Payne, Thurman, Hendricks, Jewett, Field, Morrison, and a number of other prominent Democrats, the list of gentlemen favorably mentioned being large.

A permanent organization of the convention was effected on the 23d, with Hon. John W. Stevenson, of Kentucky, as permanent chairman, and the following named gentlemen as vice-presidents and secretaries:

STATES.	Vice-Presidents.	Secretaries.
Alabama	C. C. Langdon.	J. S. Ferguson.
Arkansas.............	C. A. Gault.	J. P. Coffin.
California	W. C. Hendricks......	J. B. Metcalf.
Colorado.............	Alva Adams........	John Stone.
Connecticut..........	Curtis Bacon........	Samuel Simpson.
Delaware.............	James Williams......	A. P. Robinson.
Florida..............	William Judge.......	J. B. Marshall.
Georgia	J. R. Alexander......	Mark A. Hardin.
Illinois...............	H. M. Vanderen......	W. A. Day.
Indiana	J. R. Slack	Rufus Magee.
Iowa.................	S. B. Evans..........	J. J. Snouffer.
Kansas..............	W. V. Bennett.......	J. B. Chapman.
Kentucky............	Henry Burnett	T. G. Stuart.
Louisiana............	J. D. Jeffries........	M. McNamara.
Maine............ ...	Darius Alden........	J. R. Redman.
Maryland.....	Philip F. Thomas.....	M. A. Thomas.
Massachusetts..........	Jonas H. French	J. M. Thayer.
Michigan..............	C. H. Richmond......	A. J. Shakespeare.
Minnesota............	L. L. Baxter.........	L. A. Evans.
Mississippi.......... ...	W. S. Featherson.....	R. C. Patty.
Missouri..............	B. F. Dillon..........	N. C. Dryden.
Nebraska.............	R. S. Maloney.......	James North.
Nevada..............	Not named..........	Not named.
New Hampshire........	Frank Jones.........	Charles A. Busiel.
New Jersey...........	H. B. Smith.........	J. S. Coleman.
New York............	Not named...........	Not named.
North Carolina........	W. T. Dortch........	R. M. Furman.
Ohio.................	J. L. McSweeny......	C. T. Lewis.
Oregon...............	J. W. Winson........	A. Noltner.
Pennsylvania...........	D. E. Efmentraut.....	Not named.
Rhode Island..........	Thomas W. Segar.....	John Waters.
South Carolina.........	M. C. Butler.........	J. R. Abney.
Tennessee......	J. W. Childress.......	C. L. Ridley.
Texas.............	Joel W. Robinson	B. P. Paddock.
Vermont.............	N. P. Bowman	H. W. McGettrick.
Virginia.............	J. W. Daniel.........	R. W. Hunter.
West Virginia.........	C. P. Snyder.........	H. C. Simms.
Wisconsin	J. C. Gregory	J. M. Smith.

A letter from Mr. Tilden was read to the convention, in which he pointedly declined to permit the use of his name as a candidate for the nomination. Balloting began on this day (Wednesday, June 23d), when, on the first ballot, General Hancock led with 171 votes, Bayard being next with 153½, and Payne, Thurman, Field, Morrison, and Hendricks following in this order.

On the second ballot, which was taken on Thursday (24th), General Hancock received 705 votes, when his nomination was declared unanimous. The convention then proceeded to ballot for Vice-President, when Hon. William H. English, of Indiana, was unanimously nominated.

The platform of the Democratic party as announced at this convention is as follows:

PLATFORM.

The Democrats of the United States, in convention assembled, declare:

1. We pledge ourselves anew to the constitutional doctrines and traditions of the Democratic party as illustrated by the teachings and example of a long line of Democratic statesmen and patriots, and embodied in the platform of the last National convention of the party.

2. Opposition to centralization and to that dangerous spirit of encroachment which tends to consolidate the powers of all the departments in one, and thus to create, whatever be the form of government, a real despotism; no sumptuary laws; separation of Church and State for the good of each; common schools fostered and protected.

3. Home rule; honest money, consisting of gold and silver, and paper convertible into coin on demand; the strict maintenance of the public faith, State and National, and a tariff for revenue only.

4. The subordination of the military to the civil power, and a genuine and thorough reform of the Civil Service.

5. The right to a free ballot is a right preservative of all rights, and must and shall be maintained in every part of the United States.

6. The existing administration is the representative of conspiracy only; and its claim of right to surround the ballot boxes with troops and deputy marshals, to intimidate and obstruct the election, and the unprecedented use of the veto to maintain its corrupt and despotic powers, insult the people and imperil their institutions.

7. We execrate the course of this administration in making places in the Civil Service a reward for political crime, and demand a reform by statute which shall make it forever impossible for a defeated candidate to bribe his way to the seat of a usurper by billeting villains upon the people.

8. The great fraud of 1876-'77, by which, upon a false count of the electoral votes of two States, the candidate defeated at the polls was declared to be President, and, for the first time in American history, the will of the people was set aside under a threat of military violence, struck a deadly blow at our system of representative government. The Democratic party, to preserve the country from the horrors of a civil war, submitted for the time, in firm and patriotic faith that the people would punish this crime in 1880. This 'issue precedes and dwarfs every other. It imposes a more sacred duty upon the people of the Union than ever addressed the consciences of a nation of freemen.

9. The resolution of Samuel J. Tilden not again to be a candidate for the exalted place to which he was elected by a majority of his countrymen, and from which he was excluded by the leaders of the Republican party, is received by the Democrats of the United States with

deep sensibility, and they declare their confidence in his wisdom, patriotism, and integrity unshaken by the assaults of the common enemy; and they further assure him that he is followed into the retirement he has chosen for himself by the sympathy and respect of his fellow citizens, who regard him as one who, by elevating the standard of public morality and adorning and purifying the public service, merits the lasting gratitude of his country and his party.

10. Free ships and a living chance for American commerce on the seas, and on the land no discrimination in favor of transportation lines, corporations, or monopolies.

11. Amendment of the Burlingame treaty; no more Chinese immigration, except for travel, education, and foreign commerce, and that even carefully guarded.

12. Public money and public credit for public purposes solely, and public land for actual settlers.

13. The Democratic party is the friend of labor and the laboring man, and pledges itself to protect him alike against the cormorants and the Commune.

14. We congratulate the country upon the honesty and thrift of a Democratic Congress which has reduced the public expenditures $40,000,000 a year; upon the continuation of prosperity at home and the national honor abroad; and, above all, upon the promise of such a change in the administration of the Government as shall insure us genuine and lasting reform in every department of the public service.

The honor of naming General Hancock before the convention fell to that distinguished orator, gentleman, and scholar Hon. Daniel Dougherty, of Pennsylvania, who addressed the convention in the following language:

"MR. CHAIRMAN: I propose to present to the thoughtful consideration of the convention the name of one who, on the field of battle, was styled 'The Superb,' yet won a still nobler renown as a military governor, whose first act, when in command of Louisiana and Texas was to salute the Constitution by proclaiming that ' the military rule shall ever be subservient to the civil power.' The plighted word of a soldier was proved by the acts of a statesman.

" I nominate one whose name will suppress all faction ; which will be alike acceptable to the North and to the South. A name that will thrill the Republic. A name, if nominated, of a man who will crush the last embers of sectional strife, and whose name will be the dawning of that day so long looked for, the day of perpetual brotherhood among the people of America.

" With him as our champion, we can fling away our shields and wage an aggressive war. With him, we can appeal to the supreme majesty of the American people against the corruptions of the Republican party and their untold violations of constitutional liberty. With him as our standard-bearer, the bloody banner of Republicanism will fall palsied to the ground. O my Countrymen! In this supreme hour, when the destinies of the Republic, when the imperiled liberties of the people are in your hands, pause, reflect, take heed, make no mistake! I say I nominate one whose nomination would carry every State of the South. I nominate one who will carry Pennsylvania, carry Indiana, carry Connecticut, carry New Jersey, carry New York. I propose the name—[a voice —' Carry Ohio! ']—Aye, carry Ohio!—I propose the name of the soldier statesman, whose record is as stainless as his sword—Winfield Scott Hancock.

"One word more: if elected, *he will take his seat!*"

On July 13, 1880, General Hancock was formally notified, at Governor's Island, of his nomination by the Democratic party, the following being the announcement and response:

"NEW YORK, *July* 13, 1880.

"SIR: The National Convention of the Democratic party, which assembled at Cincinnati on the 22d of last month, unanimously nominated you as their candidate for the office of President of the United States. We have been directed to inform you of your nomination for this exalted trust, and to ask its acceptance.

"In accordance with the uniform custom of the Democratic party, the Convention have announced their views upon the important issues which are before the country, in a series of resolutions to which we invite your attention. These resolutions embody the general principles upon which the Democratic party demand the government shall be conducted, and they also emphatically condemn the maladministration of the Government by the party in power, its crimes against the Constitution, and especially against the right of the people to choose and install their President, which have wrought so much injury and dishonor to our country.

"That which chiefly inspired your nomination was the fact that you had conspicuously recognized and exemplified the yearning of the American people for reconciliation and brotherhood under the shield of the Constitution, with all its jealous care and guarantees for the rights of persons and of States.

"Your nomination was not made alone because in the midst of arms you illustrated the highest qualities of the soldier, but because, when the war had ended, and when in recognition of your courage and fidelity you were placed in command of a part of the Union undergoing the process of restoration, and while you were thus clothed with absolute power, you used it not to subvert but to sustain the civil laws, and the rights they were established to protect.

"Your fidelity to these principles, manifested in the important trusts heretofore confided to your care, gives proof that they will control your administration of the National Government, and assures the country that our indissoluble Union of indestructible States, and the Constitution, with its wise distributions of power and regard for the boundaries of State and Federal authority, will not suffer in your hands; that you will maintain the subordination of the military to the civil power, and will accomplish the purification of the public service, and especially that the Government which we love will be free from the reproach or stain of sectional agitation or malice in any shape or form.

"Rejoicing in common with the masses of the American people at this bright promise for the future of our country, we wish also to express to you personally the assurance of the general esteem and confidence which have summoned you to this high duty, and will aid you in its performance.

"Your Fellow Citizens,
"John W. Stevenson,
"*President of the Convention,*
"Nicholas M. Bell,
"*Secretary,*
"*And other Members of the Committee.*"
"*To* General Winfield Scott Hancock."

To which General Hancock replied as follows:

"Mr. Chairman and Gentlemen of the Committee: I appreciate the honor conferred upon me by the "National Democratic Convention" lately assembled in Cincinnati. I thank you for your courtesy in making that honor known to me.

"As soon as the importance of the matter permits, I will prepare and send to you a formal acceptance of my nomination to the office of President of the United States.

"Winfield S. Hancock.

On July 29th he accepted the nomination by letter, as follows:

"Governor's Island, New York City, July 29, 1880.

"Gentlemen: I have the honor to acknowledge the receipt of your letter of July 13, 1880, apprising me formally of my nomination to the office of President of the United States by the "National Democratic Convention" lately assembled in Cincinnati. I accept the nomination with grateful appreciation of the confidence reposed in me.

"The principles enunciated by the Convention are those I have cherished in the past and shall endeavor to maintain in the future.

"The thirteenth, fourteenth, and fifteenth amendments to the Constitution of the United States, embodying the results of the war for the Union, are inviolable. If called to the Presidency, I should deem it my duty to resist with all of my power any attempt to impair or evade the full force and effect of the Constitution, which, in every article, section, and amendment is the supreme law of the land. The Constitution forms the basis of the marine, extend our commerce with foreign nations, assist our merchants, manufacturers, and producers to develop our vast natural resources, and increase the prosperity and happiness of our people.

"If elected, I shall, with the Divine favor, labor with what ability I possess to discharge my duties with fidelity according to my convictions, and shall take care to protect and defend the Union, and to see that the laws be faithfully and equally executed in all parts of the country alike. I will assume the responsibility, fully sensible of the fact that to administer rightly the functions of government is to discharge the most sacred duty that can devolve upon an American citizen.

"I am, very respectfully, yours,

"WINFIELD S. HANCOCK."

"*To the* Hon. John W. Stevenson, *President of the Convention;* Hon. John P. Stockton, *Chairman, and others of the Committee of the National Democratic Convention.*"

GENERAL HANCOCK AND FAMILY.

CHAPTER XXXVII.

In concluding the present account of the life of General Hancock, we find ourselves confronted with a mass of unused material, very much of which might properly find place here in further illustration. Exigencies, inseparable from the character of the work, have prevented the insertion of writings in the nature of additional criticism and analysis of his character and his acts, on the part of men calculated by circumstances of acquaintance, or other position, to be well informed, and, by their unquestioned capacity, to be wise and just in judgment. It is with regret that we have been compelled to exclude so much of such material, and we can not faithfully complete our task without employing some of it. That which follows is accordingly inserted, each part by reason of its own merit or value, and without regard to the general coherence of the book.

A correspondent of the "Lancaster Intelligencer" gives the following anecdote, as told him by Mr. James McDougal, a prominent Republican of Baltimore:

"When Mr. Lincoln issued his Emancipation Proclamation—I believe that was the occasion—a deputation of
citizens from Baltimore went on to Washington to congratulate him.   Mr. McDougal was one of the number.

"'Take seats, boys, take seats!' exclaimed Mr. Lincoln, as he rang the bell for chairs to be brought in.

"The visitors sat down, and spent nearly an hour in
conversation.   Presently the subject of generals came up,
and various opinions were expressed as to who was the
ablest officer on our side.   When a great many opinions
had been given, Mr. Lincoln said:

"'Gentlemen, in my judgment, you have not struck
the right man yet.'

"And of course all were anxious to hear him name
the man, and asked him to do so.   He said:

"'It is General Hancock.'

"The countenances of his visitors expressed their
surprise, and one of them ventured to say that he feared
Hancock was too rash.

"'Yes,' said Mr. Lincoln, 'so some of the older generals have said to me, and I have said to them that I have
watched General Hancock's conduct very carefully, and
I have found that when he goes into action he achieves his
purpose, and comes out with a smaller list of casualties
than any of them.   Bold he is, but not rash.   Why, gentlemen, do you know what his record was at West Point?'

"And Mr. Lincoln went to his book-shelf, and, taking
down an 'Army Register,' showed the position in which
Hancock had graduated, and that, furthermore, in a class
that was one of the most distinguished that had ever
graduated at the Military Academy.   Continuing to speak
of him in the highest terms, he further said:

"'I tell you, gentlemen, that, if his life and strength

are spared, I believe that General Hancock is destined to be one of the most distinguished men of the age. Why, when I go down in the morning to open my mail—and I arise at four o'clock—I declare that I do it in fear and trembling, lest I may hear that Hancock has been killed or wounded.' "

It was a fact well known to many who saw much of the President, that on occasions of great battles, like the Wilderness, Gettysburg, etc., when Mr. Lincoln was obtaining, of course, dispatches that no one else received, he was in the habit of saying, frequently, when he knew the Second Corps had gone into action, "I am afraid Hancock is going to be killed to-day."

Policeman Albert Bradley, of New Haven, Connecticut (according to the New Haven "Union"), who was formerly a member of the Twenty-seventh Regiment, Connecticut Volunteers, tells a characteristic story of Hancock. "It was at the battle of Chancellorville. The rebels attacked a battery on the left of our line, and rained such a storm of shot and shell upon it that many of the gunners were killed and the rest were driven away. General Hancock rode up among the infantry and called for volunteers to man the guns. A sufficient number of men at once volunteered. General Hancock rode at their head through the terrible fire. He was a picture of manly strength and beauty—truly a 'superb' man. It was impossible that horse and rider should escape, and the former went down. The gallant leader was deeply affected. He looked for a moment to see if the animal was really fatally hurt, and then he stooped quickly and passionately caressed the faithful charger. Brushing his hands across his eyes, he said: 'To the guns, men!' and, on foot, he remained at the head of his men until every

17

gun was once more righted and pouring its death-dealing missiles into the enemy. I shall never forget the sight, and ever since have cherished a tender regard for General Hancock. That incident made a deep impression on his men, and, although I am a Republican, I know that nearly all of the boys who fought under him will vote for General Hancock."

So much has the idea that a soldier must necessarily be ignorant of the principles of civil law and the administration of civil government been employed as a challenge of General Hancock's competency in this direction, that even his incapacity to write his own letters and orders has been charged upon him. Accordingly his inimitable " Order No. 40 " was claimed to have been the work of Hon. J. S. Black, until the statement was distinctly denied by that gentleman ; and his celebrated " Pease " letter was equally alleged to have originated at the hands of some one other than himself. To stifle for ever this latter fatuous and baseless assertion, we present here very competent evidence with regard to this marvelous specimen of argumentative writing : it is from General James B. Steadman, and is given in his own words: "It was in February, I think, 1868," said General Steadman, " at any rate before the delegates in Louisiana were elected to the National Convention, because it was on account of the sentiments expressed that General Hancock was made the candidate, for President, of the Louisiana and Texas delegations. I was daily at his headquarters in New Orleans, and saw him at work upon the letter. It was his own conception, and his own composition, every word of it, and he talked about it considerably. He took the ground himself, without the suggestion of a human being, as I believe, that it was the duty of the military to aid and support and uphold the civil authority. The strength of his utterances impressed me greatly. I had never heard any man talk more clearly on the subject, or with a clearer conception of what he held was military duty. He was at work on the letter three particular days. In going in and out during the time, I saw the manuscript, and he read paragraphs of the letter to me—perhaps, in all, the greater portion of it. I could almost go on the witness stand and swear, to my knowledge, that Winfield Scott Hancock wrote the letter."

· · · · · · · ·

The two quotations following explain themselves:

General Sherman said of him to a reporter: "If you will sit down and write the best thing that can be put in language about General Hancock as an officer and a gentleman, I will sign it without hesitation."

General Sheridan said of him:

"I am not in politics, but General Hancock is a good and great man. The Democrats have not made any mistake this time. They have nominated an excellent and strong ticket."

· · · · · · · ·

At a public meeting held at Tammany Hall, New York, March 8, 1864, the object being the encouraging of enlistments to fill up the Second Corps, General Hancock spoke as follows:

"I am highly honored by the invitation to meet so many of the citizens of New York on this occasion, in this ancient temple of the Democracy. I am delighted to accompany on the war-path that element of the politi-

cal parties of the country which has heretofore been so
successful in shaping its destinies. With the assistance
of the powers beyond, there should be no such word as
failure in any operation, not even that of putting down
by force of arms the existing gigantic Rebellion against
the Constitutional rule of the Government. We have
come here to-night, not to talk of peace—for, in the
opinion of practical men, that time is past. We find
a rebellion on our hands of proportions not equaled in
modern times. We have not met here to discuss the
manner of putting it down. That men sensitive of honor
have decided can only be done by blows. We have
been engaged in that operation for a considerable time,
and are determined to persevere in it until the desired
result is obtained. We know, also, that our integrity
and honor are at stake in carrying it through to a successful issue. We are here to night for war, and, when war
has performed its part, we then will leave it to those to
discuss the terms of peace whom the Constitution of the
country has invested with that power, and our terms of
peace are the integrity of and obedience to the civil laws
of the land. Our armies have been prosperous, as can
be readily seen by looking at the map of the country occupied by the contending forces; but the Rebellion is
gaining heart by the distractions among our people,
caused by unpatriotic factions, and by the sympathies of
the disloyal among us, and is determined to make one
grand effort to force us back. It will probably be the
last. To make it sure that the enemy shall not resist our
triumphant march, it is necessary for us to give to the
Government a sufficient force to make such a result impossible. With our great preponderance of population,
it is easy for us to do so. With a great force on our

side, this war will be short. Let us all, therefore, take a part, and the honor may be equally divided. No man can afford to be unpatriotic in time of war. That has been proven, and there are numbers of persons living who are evidences of the fact. Let every man, therefore, who values his honor and that of his children, enter the service of his country, if he is in circumstances to permit him to do so; and, if not, let him, if possible, keep a representative in the field. For the mass of men, inducements to enter the service are now so great that no one need claim he should be exempt because they are not greater. Every one whose circumstances permitted him to shoulder a musket in this war, and has failed to do so, and those who have not done their duty at home in assisting to put men in the field, will regret their want of action when peace again smiles over the country. Too late then for them to repair their error. Even their children will despise them, and woman, too, who judges man by his deeds, will smile upon only those who, in this war, have acted with manliness and patriotism. I have command of the Second Corps, composed of fifty regiments of veteran troops. They have trod the paths of glory so well that no man need be afraid of going astray who may join them. Nineteen of these regiments are from your State, and thirteen from your city. Men entering either of those organizations need not fear but on the march, and in camp, and in time of battle they will feel confidence in themselves from the fact of being surrounded by veterans so ready to share with them all the danger, and who will equally divide the honor, claiming no advantage on account of their greater experience. No one need fear that he will not make a good soldier. The man on his right and on his left will give him confidence.

They have trod the paths of glory before. We have room for all nationalities. We have the Irish Brigade. We have the German legions, and many others known to you by some means. We had a Tammany regiment also. Any man can find in the New York City regiments of the Second Corps companions who sympathize with him. There are places for all. Let them come. I will also say to the representatives of the sturdy class which form the backbone of our army, that no men are more deeply interested in this war than themselves. If the Government is preserved, they will preserve their liberties, and the result to them may be a sad experience if the Government should fail in putting down the Rebellion for the want of strong arms. Come, then, and join the force in the field. Come now, for you are wanted. The veterans, by reënlisting, have set an example well worth following. Their acts show their confidence in the future."

The following occurrence took place on the occasion of a serenade, which was tendered to General Hancock at Washington, on September 24, 1867, just before he was ordered off to New Orleans, to take command of the Fifth Military District.

An immense audience was assembled, and General Hancock was introduced by Hon. Amasa Cobb, of Wisconsin, then a Republican member of Congress, and now a Republican Judge of the Supreme Court of Nebraska. General Cobb said:

"To me has been intrusted the pleasure and duty of appearing before you in the capacity of an old friend and comrade of the distinguished General now before you, to introduce him to you on this occasion. Six years ago I had the honor to be in command of a volunteer regiment in the Army of the Potomac, and, with three other regiments, had the good fortune to be placed under the command of the then newly appointed Brigadier-General Hancock. During the long and tedious winter of 1861 and 1862, we did duty in front of this capital, devoting the days to discipline and the nights to watching and picket. We were volunteers. The General was a Regular army officer. All of you who passed through similar experience will bear me witness that volunteers felt the rigors of discipline when placed under such disciplinarians as that army was commanded by; and its discipline and after efficiency were owing chiefly, if not wholly, to this fact. The winter passed away, and the army finally moved, and in the course of the war they were brought in front of the enemy. General Hancock's first brigade succeeded in turning the enemy's left at Williamsburg, and afterward he prevented the victorious enemy from driving the lines of McClellan from the Chickahominy, and, later on, it came up to save the day at Antietam; and now I esteem it a great honor bestowed upon me and my old regiment to have the opportunity of standing here by that great General's side, bearing testimony to his kindness of heart, his gallantry as a soldier, and his trueness as a man."

The speaker here turned to General Hancock, and said :

"Allow me to say that to your new field of duty the hearts of our old brigade go with you, knowing that, wherever you may go, the country will have a brave and efficient soldier, and that flag a gallant defender."

General Hancock was received with much applause, and replied as follows :

" CITIZENS OF WASHINGTON : I thank you for this testimony of your confidence in my ability to perform my duty in a new and different sphere. Educated as a soldier in the military school of our country, and on the field of the Mexican War and the American Rebellion, I need not assure you that my course as a district commander will be characterized by the same strict soldierly obedience to the law there taught me as a soldier—I know no other guide or higher duty. Misrepresentation and misconstruction, arising from the passions of the hour, and spread by those who do not know that devotion to duty has governed my actions in every trying hour, may meet me, but I fear them not. My highest desire will be to perform the duties of my new sphere, not in the interest of parties or partisans, but for the benefit of my country, the honor of my profession, and I trust, also, for the welfare of the people committed to my care. I ask, then, citizens, that time may be permitted to develop my actions. Judge me by the deeds I may perform, and, conscious of my devotion to duty and my country, I shall be satisfied with your verdict ; and, if a generous country shall approve my actions in the future as it has in the past, my highest ambition will have been achieved. As a soldier, I am to administer duties rather than discuss them. If I can administer them to the satisfaction of the country, I shall indeed be happy in the consciousness of a duty performed. I am about to leave your city, the capital of our country, bearing the proud name of Washington. As an American citizen, the rapid development and increase of its wealth, beauty, and prosperity, is a matter in which I am deeply interested. But far beyond this, citizens of Washington, I rejoice with you that in the trying hour of the rebellion the capital of the nation contributed as fully as any State in the Union to the brave volunteer army, which has demonstrated to the world the strength and invincibility of a republican form of government. I shall carry with me the recollections of this occasion, and, when I return, may I not hope that none who are here will regret their participation in the honor you have done me to-night?"

The following eloquent and poetic tribute to General Hancock is quoted from a lecture on "The Solid South," which was delivered by James Elbert Powell, of Kansas City:

"I can not close this allusion to the era of Reconstruction in the South, ladies and gentlemen, without offering a tribute to that man, who, tried by the true test of greatness, has proven himself to be a peer—whose young sword flashed like a meteor over the bloody fields of Mexico, and flung its gleams across the deepening twilight of Spottsylvania and Gettysburg—whose splendid energies and Spartan prowess have ever dedicated it to the cause of individual justice and national honor—whose gallantry is emblazoned upon the brightest pages of American history—whose glory as a warrior is eclipsed by the grandeur of the civilian—who was no less a hero beneath the olive branch of peace than when leading the charge under the red banner of war—who never feared to draw his sword at the call of his country, or to lay it, sheathed, upon the shrine of constitutional government, when the dust of conflict had drifted away—who crystallized his views and molded his measures with that royal compassion which yielded to a conquered and impoverished foe the inviolable inheritance of civil liberty—who is one of the grandest men in the land, recognized by

18

the brilliancy of his individual luster, and not reflecting
the borrowed rays of other luminaries—to that defender
of the Union, that champion of the Constitution, that
sovereign of soldiers, that pioneer of peace, that prince
of patriots, General Winfield Scott Hancock, the exponent of great virtue, of tried courage, of lofty wisdom, of
broad intelligence, of earnest patriotism, of noble aspira-
tion, and of true manhood.

" He is a soldier, not alone of manners or of rank, but
of merit and of mind—he is a soldier who distinguished
himself in the defense of liberty, and the vanquishment
of despotism—he is a soldier who lifted himself above
the ignorance and prejudice of the day, and planted the
royal banner of pardon and love upon the battlements of
sectionalism and strife—he is a soldier, not by the power
of fear, but by the force of splendid superiority; he is a
soldier upon whose bosom radiates the star of honor, and
to whose memory will be issued the highest patent of
nobility.

" When, at the foot of Bunker Hill, in the shadow of
that royal shaft which stands a monumental emblem of
heroic valor, whose remembrance is consecrated in the
hearts of fifty millions of patriots, beneath the rays of
the stars and the light of the centuries, the goddess of
historic unity and liberty, the guardian of our national
faith, shall call the roll of the grand army of heroes, there
will be no more gallant, no more glorious, response than
that which swells from the heart and the record of Winfield S. Hancock.

" He believed that, when the Southern chieftain surrendered his sword to the Northern conqueror beneath
the historic tree at Appomattox, the Southern sun went
down, and with its setting were buried the passion and

pain of war—that the blue and gray would clasp hands for ever, and the Northern sigh meet the Southern sorrow above the same graves, garlanded with the same flowers, gathered by the same hands, consecrated by the same regrets, and bedewed with the same tears.

"He has recently been nominated by a great political body for the highest office in the gift of the American people, and, though I come to-night as the advocate of no faction—the champion of no party—as a lover of my country, I must say that, if the star which now rises above General Hancock's destiny casts its meridian beams upon him in the White House, they will fall upon an executive from whose hands the scepter of justice will not drop in helpless impotence, but one who will continue to battle for Union and liberty while truth, courage, and fidelity to principle shall find a home in the hearts and hopes of men. He will not be a politician for the sake of party, as he has not been a soldier for the sake of glory, but he will be a man for the sake of manhood, and a patriot for the sake of his country. He is a man the corner-stone of whose character is integrity. He is a man whose virtues are not negative or obstructive, but positive and aggressive. He is a man with a strong mind, a pure heart, and a ready hand. He is a man who will set his face against any system of political looseness, and link honor and valor to sympathy with the people. He is a man whose favor no spoils of office can buy, whose voice no mocking flattery can silence; he is a man upon whose escutcheon rests no stain or semblance of dishonor; he is a man who will bind together the fragments of our dismembered Union ; he is a man who will heal the wounds of sectional hate, and kindle the warmth of fraternal affection ; he is a man who will rise above the level of partisan zeal, above the reach of personal venality, above the influence or suspicion of corruption, above the scope of moral cowardice—a man who will bring courage, bring peace to our unhappy country, where now

> " 'Freedom weeps,
> Wrong rules the land,
> And waiting justice sleeps.' "

And, after this thrilling and soul-stirring composition, we can not do better than to present the following original poem, written by Colonel A. J. H. Duganne, of Belmont, Fordham, New York City, for the columns of the New York "Era," and first published in that journal July 17, 1880.

HANCOCK!

By Colonel A. J. H. Duganne.

In the days when MANHOOD rose,
Answering unto FREEDOM's throes;
And the womb of Freedom yielded
UNION, with her Stars enshielded;
In the days when MEN were MEN—
Sword with sword, and pen with pen—
And in line, their lives to mix,
And their SOULS, as SEALS, to fix,
Stood the Immortal FIFTY-SIX—
Then, to witness Freedom's claim,
MANHOOD wrote that deathless name—
            "HANCOCK!"

Never an army's clarion blast
Rang through all our human Past,
Like those words of DECLARATION,
Christening FREEDOM's new-born NATION!
Voiceful unto all the lands—
"Rise! and break your servile bands!"

While the BELL, with brazen call,
Swung o'er Independence Hall—
Answering—" LIBERTY FOR ALL! "
And beneath VIRGINIA's light,
MASSACHUSETTS rose, to write—
                    " HANCOCK! "

FIRST of all the immortal roll,
Signed he FREEDOM's lifted scroll;
When to SIGN was danger facing—
When to LEAD, was doom embracing—
First of all his compeers known,
Signed he Freedom's scroll—alone!
And his NAME, for North and South—
Flame-like, over prairie drouth,
Fiery tongued, from mouth to mouth—
MOULTRIE wrote, with glowing guns,
Answering, unto LEXINGTON's—
                    " HANCOCK! '

In the Days when MANHOOD rose—
Quivering with our UNION's throes;
And the coils, for ages woven
Round her laboring heart, were cloven;
When from FREEDOM's loins, in war,
Slavery's poisonous robe we tore—
NESSUS' shirt—from HERCULES—
Smiting off, on blood-red leas,
Bands that bowed us to our knees—
In those Days when MEN were MEN,
MANHOOD wrote that name again—
                    " HANCOCK! "

Tell me, ye whose soldier-clay,
Mingling, molders—BLUE with GRAY;
Tell me, SOULS OF MEN! whose marches
Still advance, where Heaven o'erarches!
What was LOST, when MANLY strife
Gained a MANLY NATION's life?

What was LOST, when Southern BARS
Backward fought, from Union STARS—
Gilding starry light with scars?
When, o'er GETTYSBURG, in flame
On the "Round Top" rose that Name—
"HANCOCK!"

What was LOST—when ALL IS OURS?
Manlier men, with manlier powers?
Memories under May-flowers lying;
Sweetening dust with DEEDS undying!
UNION, mingling mutual marts;
MANHOOD, mingling kindred hearts!—
Steadier march our ranks pursue;
LOCK-STEP, now—for GRAY and BLUE!
And in line that SOLDIERS knew,
When, "the Wilderness" they trod,
FORWARD, following—under GOD—
"HANCOCK!"

The following quotation, from a letter written to the "Presbyterian," in September, 1878, by Dr. Junkin, is the latest testimonial of that distinguished divine and good man to the personal character of General Hancock:

"General Hancock, whose guest I am, and at whose desk these lines are penned, is, as you know, a Pennsylvanian of the Pennsylvanians. Born near to your city (at Montgomery Square), he still has a warm love for Pennsylvanians. His fame needs no impulse from my pen. But I know the readers of the "Presbyterian" will be happy to be told that, unlike some other distinguished men, his social character and private morals are as pure as his military career has been brilliant and his civil record magnanimous."

THE END.

NEW BOOKS.

MEMORIES OF MY EXILE. By Louis Kossuth. Translated from the original Hungarian by Ferencz Jausz. One vol., crown 8vo. Cloth. Price, $2.00.

"A most piquant and instructive contribution to contemporary history."—*New York Sun.*

"These 'Memories' disclose a curious episode in the inner life of English domestic politics."—*The Nation.*

THE HISTORICAL POETRY OF THE ANCIENT HEBREWS. Translated and critically examined by Michael Heilprin. Vol. II. Crown 8vo. Cloth. Price, $2.00.

"The notion has somehow got abroad that the scientific study of the Bible is inconsistent with the most tender reverence for its contents, or with their persistent fascination. But the reverence of Mr. Heilprin for the subject-matter of his criticism could hardly be surpassed; and, that it has not lost its power to interest and charm, his book itself is ample evidence, which will be reënforced by the experience of every intelligent reader of its too brief contents."—*New York Nation*, July 24, 1879.

HEALTH. By W. H. Corfield, Professor of Hygiene and Public Health at University College, London. 12mo. Cloth. Price, $1.25.

FRENCH MEN OF LETTERS. Personal and Anecdotical Sketches of Victor Hugo; Alfred de Musset; Théophile Gautier; Henri Murger; Sainte-Beuve; Gérard de Nerval; Alexandre Dumas, fils; Émile Augier; Octave Feuillet; Victorien Sardou; Alphonse Daudet; and Émile Zola. By Maurice Maunis. Appletons' "New Handy-Volume Series." Paper, 35 cents; cloth, 60 cents.

A THOUSAND FLASHES OF FRENCH WIT, WISDOM, AND WICKEDNESS. Collected and translated by J. de Finod. One vol., 16mo. Cloth. Price, $1.00.

This work consists of a collection of wise and brilliant sayings from French writers, making a rich and piquant book of fresh quotations.

"The book is a charming one to take up for an idle moment during the warm weather, and is just the thing to read on the hotel piazza to a mixed company of ladies and gentlemen. Some of its sayings about the first mentioned would no doubt occasion lively discussion, but that is just what is needed to dispel the often wellnigh intolerable languor of a summer afternoon."—*Boston Courier.*

SCIENTIFIC BILLIARDS. Garnier's Practice Shots, with Hints to Amateurs. With 106 Diagrams in Colors. By Albert Garnier. Oblong 12mo. Price, $3.50.

For sale by all booksellers; or any work sent post-paid to any address in the United States, on receipt of price.

D. APPLETON & CO., Publishers,

1, 3, & 5 Bond Street, New York.

D. APPLETON & CO.'S

RECENT PUBLICATIONS.

I.

FIFTH AND LAST VOLUME OF THE LIFE OF THE PRINCE CONSORT.

The Life of His Royal Highness the Prince Consort.

By Sir THEODORE MARTIN. Fifth and concluding volume. One vol., 12mo. Cloth. Price, $2.00. Vols. I, II, III, and IV, at same price per volume.

"The literature of England is richer by a book which will be read with profit by succeeding generations of her sons and daughters."—*Blackwood.*

"Sir Theodore Martin has completed his work, and completed it in a manner which has fairly entitled him to the honor conferred upon him on its conclusion. It is well done from beginning to end."—*Spectator.*

II.

The Life and Writings of Henry Thomas Buckle.

By ALFRED HENRY HUTH. 12mo. Cloth. Price, $2.00.

"To all admirers of Buckle Mr. Huth has rendered a welcome service by the publication of these volumes, while to those who have been prejudiced against him, either by his own bold writings or by the unjust treatment he has received at the hands of many critics, and even some would-be panegyrists, they should be of yet greater service."—*London Athenæum.*

III.

Science Primers: Introductory.

By Professor HUXLEY, F.R.S. 18mo. Flexible cloth. Price, 45 cents.

IV.

The Fundamental Concepts

OF MODERN PHILOSOPHIC THOUGHT, CRITICALLY AND HISTORICALLY CONSIDERED. By RUDOLPH EUCKEN, Ph.D., Professor in Jena. With an Introduction by NOAH PORTER, President of Yale College. One vol., 12mo, 304 pages. Cloth. Price, $1.75.

President Porter declares of this work that "there are few books within his knowledge which are better fitted to aid the student who wishes to acquaint himself with the course of modern speculation and scientific thinking, and to form an intelligent estimate of most of the current theories."

v.

The Household Dickens.

The Household Edition of Charles Dickens's Works, now complete, and put up in ten-volume sets in box. In cloth, gilt side and back, price, $30.00.

This edition of the WORKS OF CHARLES DICKENS, known as "Chapman & Hall's Household Edition," *in size of page, type, and general style, excels every other in the market. It contains all the writings of Dickens acknowledged by him, includes "THE LIFE OF DICKENS" by JOHN FORSTER, and is superbly illustrated with 900 engravings.*

VI.

A Short Life of Charles Dickens.

With Selections from his Letters. By CHARLES H. JONES, author of "Macaulay: his Life, his Writings." "Handy-Volume Series." Paper, 35 cents; cloth, 60 cents.

The work is an attempt to give, in a compact form, such an account of the life of Dickens as will meet the requirements of the general reader. Liberal extracts are made from the letters of Dickens, in order that, so far as possible, he may depict himself and tell his own story.

VII.

Memoirs of Madame de Remusat.

1802–1808. Edited by her Grandson, PAUL DE RÉMUSAT, Senator. In three vols., paper covers, 8vo. Price, $1.50. Also, in one vol., cloth, 12mo. Price, $2.00.

"Notwithstanding the enormous library of works relating to Napoleon, we know of none which cover precisely the ground of these Memoirs. Madame de Rémusat was not only lady-in-waiting to Josephine during the eventful years 1802–1808, but was her intimate friend and trusted confidant. Thus we get a view of the daily life of Bonaparte and his wife and the terms on which they lived not elsewhere to be found."—*New York Mail.*

VIII.

Memoirs of Napoleon.

His Court and Family. By the Duchess D'ABRANTES. In two vols., 12mo, cloth. Price, $3.00.

The interest excited in the first Napoleon and his Court by the "Memoirs of Madame de Rémusat" has induced the publishers to issue the famous "Memoirs of the Duchess d'Abrantes," which have hitherto appeared in a costly octavo edition, in a much cheaper form, and in style to correspond with the 12mo edition of De Rémusat. This work will be likely now to be read with awakened interest, especially as it presents a much more favorable portrait of the great Corsican than that limned by Madame de Rémusat.

IX.

Recollections and Opinions of an Old Pioneer.

By Peter H. Burnett, the First Governor of the State of California. 1 vol., 12mo, 468 pages, cloth. Price, $1.75.

Mr. Burnett's life has been full of varied experience, and the record takes the reader back prior to the discovery of gold in California, and leads him through many adventures and incidents to the time of the beginning of the late war. The volume is replete with interest.

X.

Elihu Burritt:

A Memorial Volume, containing a Sketch of his Life and Labors, with Selections from his Writings and Lectures, and Extracts from his Private Journals in Europe and America. Edited by Charles Northend, A. M. 12mo, cloth. Price, $1.75.

XI.

The Life of David Glasgow Farragut,

First Admiral of the United States Navy, embodying his Journal and Letters. By his Son, Loyall Farragut. With Portraits, Maps, and Illustrations. 8vo. Cloth. Price, $4.00.

" The book is a stirring one, of course ; the story of Farragut's life is a tale of adventure of the most ravishing sort, so that, aside from the value of this work as an authentic biography of the greatest of American naval commanders, the book is one of surpassing interest, considered merely as a narrative of difficult and dangerous enterprises and heroic achievements."—*New York Evening Post.*

" Two of the most brilliant and important naval exploits of the war were achieved by Farragut, and no name in the service rivaled his either in the estimation of his countrymen or in the opinion of foreign observers."—*Saturday Review.*

XII.

Erasmus Darwin.

By Ernst Krause. Translated from the German by W. S. Dallas. With a Preliminary Notice by Charles Darwin. With Portrait and Woodcuts. One vol., 12mo. Cloth. Price, $1.25.

XIII.

NEW ILLUSTRATED COOPER.

The Novels of J. Fenimore Cooper.

With 64 Engravings on Steel, from Drawings by F. O. C. Darley. Complete in 16 volumes. Price for the complete set, $20.00.

*** This edition of the Novels of Cooper is the cheapest ever offered to the public. It contains the entire series of novels, two being bound in each volume; and the series of steel plates, from drawings by F. O. C. Darley, originally engraved for the finer editions, at a great cost, which are conceded to be the best work on steel ever produced in America.

XIV.

Rodman the Keeper:

Southern Sketches. By CONSTANCE FENIMORE WOOLSON. One vol., 12mo. Cloth. Price, $1.25.

"The reader of these sketches can not fail to discover for himself their intensely poetic quality—can not fail to recognize the poet's hand in every touch. Tropical vegetation is not richer or more spontaneous than the author's fancy is. She has spoken face to face with the spirit of the South, and has learned its sad secret. She knows its nameless joy, and its undefinable melancholy. She has felt the opulence of the sunlight there, she has breathed the drowsy breath of the stiflingly fragrant flowers. The characters sketched are strongly dramatic conceptions, and the portraiture is very fine and distinct. Each of the sketches has that breath of life in it which belongs alone to what is called human interest. The pathos of the stories is wonderful, but it is wholesome, natural pathos, not the pathos manufactured by the literary emotion-monger. Miss Woolson's art is superb, and she is lovingly faithful to it."—*New York Evening Post.*

XV.

The Return of the Princess.

From the French of JACQUES VINCENT. "New Handy-Volume Series." Paper, 25 cents.

XVI.

Sebastian Strome.

A Novel. By JULIAN HAWTHORNE. 8vo. Paper cover. Price, 75 cents.

"May be pronounced the most powerful novel Mr. Hawthorne has ever written."—*London Athenæum.*
"There is a force and power of genius in the book which it is impossible to ignore."—*London Spectator.*

XVII.

The Seamy Side.

A Novel. By WALTER BESANT and JAMES RICE. 8vo. Paper cover. Price, 50 cents.

"'The Seamy Side' is the title of a new novel, by Walter Besant and James Rice, the authors of 'The Golden Butterfly,' 'By Celia's Arbor,' and half a dozen other stories. There are several strong characters in it. 'Anthony Hamblin,' a great self-sacrificing London merchant, his relative 'Alison,' his brother 'Stephen,' and a 'Miss Nethersole,' are boldly outlined, and touched in places with great spirit and life. Like 'The Golden Butterfly,' the best feature of the book is the vein of enjoyable humor which runs through it."—*Hartford Daily Times.*

XVIII.

Manch.

A Novel. By MARY E. BRYAN, Editor of the "Sunny South." One vol., 12mo. Cloth. Price, $1.50.

"We have in 'Manch' a lurid, melodramatic story, which has an artistic right and reason to be lurid and melodramatic. Its 'sensationalism,' although somewhat exaggerated, is proper to it, aiding instead of hindering its artistic purpose, precisely as scenes of fighting, which would be out of place in a story of peaceful life, aid the artistic purpose of a military novel. Moreover, this strongly sensational story is told with great vigor and skill; its dramatic incidents are presented dramatically; the characters of its personages are cleverly discriminated; in a word, the workmanship of the piece is in the main so good as to justify us in saying that the author has positive gifts as a novelist."—*New York Evening Post.*

"I regard it as one of the most interesting and thrilling stories I ever read."—Alexander H. Stephens.

XIX.

Di Cary.

A Novel of Virginia Life since the War. By M. Jacqueline Thornton. 8vo. Paper cover. Price, 75 cents.

"It is one of the best Southern novels that has yet come under our observation."—*Philadelphia Press.*

XX.

A Gentle Belle.

A Novel. By Christian Reid, author of "Valerie Aylmer," "Morton House," etc. 8vo. Paper cover. Price, 75 cents.

"'A Gentle Belle' has a strong dramatic interest, and freshness and originality of plot. Like its author's previous essays in fiction, it is well written, and is attractive in style and character. The interest never flags, and the moral is sweet and wholesome. Taken for all in all, the work is the most artistic in design and execution that its writer has produced."—*Boston Gazette.*

XXI.

The Life and Words of Christ.

By Cunningham Geikie, D. D. A new and cheap edition, printed from the same stereotype plates as the fine illustrated edition. Complete in one vol., 8vo, 1,258 pages. Cloth. Price, $1.50.

This is the only cheap edition of Geikie's Life of Christ that contains the copious notes of the author, the marginal references, and an index. In its present form it is a marvel of cheapness.

"A work of the highest rank, breathing the spirit of true faith in Christ."—*Dr. Delitzsch, the Commentator.*

"A most valuable addition to sacred literature."—*A. N. Littlejohn, D. D., Bishop of Long Island.*

"I have never seen any life of our Lord which approached so near my ideal of such a work."—*Austin Phelps, D. D., author of "The Still Hour," etc.*

"A great and noble work, rich in information, eloquent and scholarly in style, earnestly devout in feeling."—*London Literary World.*

XXII.

The Longer Epistles of Paul.

Viz.: Romans, I Corinthians, II Corinthians. By the Rev. Henry Cowles, D. D. One vol., 12mo. Cloth. Price, $2.00.

www.ingramcontent.com/pod-product-compliance
Lightning Source LLC
Chambersburg PA
CBHW020859130726
47900CB00014B/1108